Classics

$\frac{3}{21}$

THE MYSTERIOUS ISLAND

Jules Verne

AUTHOR OF
"THE TOUR OF THE WORLD IN EIGHTY DAYS,"
"A JOURNEY TO THE CENTRE OF THE EARTH,"
"TWENTY THOUSAND LEAGUES UNDER THE SEA,"
ETC.,ETC.

THE MYSTERIOUS ISLAND

BIBLIOBAZAAR

THE MYSTERIOUS ISLAND

CONTENTS

PART I SHIPWRECKED IN THE AIR

PART II THE ABANDONED

PART III THE SECRET OF THE ISLAND

PART I

SHIPWRECKED IN THE AIR

CHAPTER I.

THE HURRICANE OF 1865—CRIES IN THE AIR—
A BALLOON CAUGHT BY A WATERSPOUT—ONLY THE
SEA IN SIGHT—FIVE PASSENGERS—WHAT TOOK
PLACE IN THE BASKET—LAND AHEAD!—THE END.

"Are we going up again?"

"No. On the contrary; we are going down!"

"Worse than that, Mr. Smith, we are falling!"

"For God's sake throw over all the ballast!"

"The last sack is empty!"

"And the balloon rises again?"

"No!"

"I hear the splashing waves!"

"The sea is under us!"

"It is not five hundred feet off!"

Then a strong, clear voice shouted:—

"Overboard with all we have, and God help us!"

Such were the words which rang through the air above the vast wilderness of the Pacific, towards 4 o'clock in the afternoon of the 23d of March, 1865:—

Doubtless, no one has forgotten that terrible northeast gale which vented its fury during the equinox of that year. It was a hurricane lasting without intermission from the 18th to the 26th of March. Covering a space of 1,800 miles, drawn obliquely to the equator, between the 35° of north latitude and 40° south, it occasioned immense destruction both in America and Europe and Asia. Cities in ruins, forests uprooted, shores devastated by the mountains of water hurled upon them, hundreds of shipwrecks, large tracts of territory desolated by the waterspouts which destroyed everything in their path, thousands of persons crushed to the earth or engulfed in the sea; such were the witnesses to its fury left behind by this terrible hurricane. It surpassed in disaster those storms which ravaged Havana and Guadeloupe in 1810 and 1825.

While these catastrophes were taking place upon the land and the sea, a scene not less thrilling was enacting in the disordered heavens.

A balloon, caught in the whirl of a column of air, borne like a ball on the summit of a waterspout, spinning around as in some aerial whirlpool, rushed through space with a velocity of ninety miles an hour. Below the balloon, dimly visible through the dense vapor, mingled with spray, which spread over the ocean, swung a basket containing five persons.

From whence came this aerial traveller, the sport of the awful tempest? Evidently it could not have been launched during the storm, and the storm had been raging five days, its symptoms manifesting themselves on the 18th. It must, therefore, have come from a great distance, as it could not have traversed less than 2,000 miles in twenty-four hours. The passengers, indeed, had been unable to determine the course traversed, as they had nothing with which to calculate their position; and it was a necessary effect, that, though borne along in the midst of this tempest; they were unconscious of its violence. They were whirled and spun about and carried up and down without any sense of motion. Their vision could not penetrate the thick fog massed together under the balloon. Around them everything was obscure. The clouds were so dense that they could not tell the day from the night. No reflection of light, no sound from the habitations of men, no roaring of the ocean had penetrated that profound obscurity in which they were suspended during their passage through the upper air. Only on their rapid descent had they become conscious of the danger threatening them by the waves.

Meanwhile the balloon, disencumbered of the heavy articles, such as munitions, arms, and provisions, had risen to a height of 4,500 feet, and the passengers having discovered that the sea was beneath them, and realizing that the dangers above were less formidable than those below, did not hesitate to throw overboard everything, no matter how necessary, at the same time endeavoring to lose none of that fluid, the soul of the apparatus, which sustained them above the abyss.

The night passed in the midst of dangers that would have proved fatal to souls less courageous; and with the coming of day the hurricane showed signs of abatement. At dawn, the emptied clouds rose high into the heavens; and, in a few hours more, the whirlwind had spent its force. The wind, from a hurricane, had subsided into what sailors would call a "three reef breeze."

Toward eleven o'clock, the lower strata of the air had lightened visibly. The atmosphere exhaled that humidity which is noticeable after the passage of great meteors. It did not seem as if the storm had moved westward, but rather as if it was ended. Perhaps it had flowed off in electric sheets after the whirlwind had spent itself, as is the case with the typhoon in the Indian Ocean.

Now, however, it became evident that the balloon was again sinking slowly but surely. It seemed also as if it was gradually collapsing, and that its envelope was lengthening and passing from a spherical into an oval form. It held 50,000 cubic feet of gas, and therefore, whether soaring to a great height or moving along horizontally, it was able to maintain itself for a long time in the air. In this emergency the voyagers threw overboard the remaining articles which weighed down the balloon, the few provisions they had kept, and everything they had in their pockets, while one of the party hoisted himself into the ring to which was fastened the cords of the net, and endeavored to closely tie the lower end of the balloon. But it was evident that the gas was escaping, and that the voyagers could no longer keep the balloon afloat.

They were lost!

There was no land, not even an island, visible beneath them. The wide expanse of ocean offered no point of rest, nothing upon which they could cast anchor. It was a vast sea on which the waves were surging with incomparable violence. It was the limitless ocean, limitless even to them from their commanding height. It was a liquid plain, lashed and beaten by the hurricane, until it seemed like a circuit of tossing billows, covered with a net-work of foam. Not even a ship was in sight.

In order, therefore, to save themselves from being swallowed up by the waves it was necessary to arrest this downward movement, let it cost what it might. And it was evidently to the accomplishment of this that the party were directing their efforts. But in spite of all they could do the balloon continued to descend, though at the same time moving rapidly along with the wind toward the southwest.

It was a terrible situation, this, of these unfortunate men. No longer masters of the balloon, their efforts availed them nothing. The envelope collapsed more and more, and the gas continued to escape. Faster and faster they fell, until at 1 o'clock they were not more than 600 feet above the sea. The gas poured out of a rent in the silk. By lightening the basket of everything the party had been able to continue their suspension in the air for several hours, but now the inevitable catastrophe could only be delayed, and unless some land appeared before nightfall, voyagers, balloon, and basket must disappear beneath the waves.

It was evident that these men were strong and able to face death. Not a murmur escaped their lips. They were determined to struggle to the last second to retard their fall, and they tried their last expedient. The basket, constructed of willow osiers, could not float, and they had no means of supporting it on the surface of the water. It was 2 o'clock, and the balloon was only 400 feet above the waves.

Then a voice was heard—the voice of a man whose heart knew no fear—responded to by others not less strong:—

"Everything is thrown out?"

"No, we yet have 10,000 francs in gold."

A heavy bag fell into the sea.

"Does the balloon rise?"

"A little, but it will soon fall again."

"Is there nothing else we can gut rid of?"

"Not a thing."

"Yes there is; there's the basket!"

"Catch hold of the net then, and let it go."

The cords which attached the basket to the hoop were cut, and the balloon, as the former fell into the sea, rose again 2,000 feet. This was, indeed, the last means of lightening the apparatus. The five passengers had clambered into the net around the hoop, and, clinging to its meshes, looked into the abyss below.

Every one knows the statical sensibility of a balloon. It is only necessary to relieve it of the lightest object in order to have it rise. The apparatus floating in air acts like a mathematical balance. One can readily understand, then, that when disencumbered of every weight relatively great, its upward movement will be sudden and considerable. It was thus in the present instance. But after remaining poised for a moment at its height, the balloon began to descend. It was impossible to repair the rent, through which the gas was rushing, and the men having done everything they could do, must look to God for succor.

At 4 o'clock, when the balloon was only 500 feet above the sea, the loud barking of a dog, holding itself crouched beside its master in the meshes of the net, was heard.

"Top has seen something!" cried one, and immediately afterwards another shouted:—

"Land! Land!"

The balloon, which the wind had continued to carry towards the southwest, had since dawn passed over a distance of several hundred miles, and a high land began to be distinguishable in that direction. But it was still thirty miles to leeward, and even supposing they did not drift, it would take a full hour to reach it. An hour! Before that time could pass, would not the balloon be emptied of what gas remained? This was the momentous question.

The party distinctly saw that solid point which they must reach at all hazards. They did not know whether it was an island or a continent, as they were uninformed as to what part of the world the tempest had hurried them. But they knew that this land, whether inhabited or desert, must be reached.

At 4 o'clock it was plain that the balloon could not sustain itself much longer. It grazed the surface of the sea, and the crests of the higher waves several times lapped the base of the net, making it heavier; and, like a bird with a shot in its wing, could only half sustain itself.

A half hour later, and the land was scarcely a mile distant. But the balloon, exhausted, flabby, hanging in wrinkles, with only a little gas remaining in its upper portion, unable to sustain the weight of those clinging to the net, was plunging them in the sea, which lashed them with its furious billows. Occasionally the envelope of the balloon would belly out, and the wind taking it would carry it along like a ship. Perhaps by this means it would reach the shore. But when only two cables' length away four voices joined in a terrible cry. The balloon, though seemingly unable to rise again, after having been struck by a tremendous wave, made a bound into the air, as if it had been suddenly lightened of some of its weight. It rose 1,500 feet, and encountering a sort of eddy in the air, instead of being carried directly to land, it was drawn along in a direction nearly parallel thereto. In a minute or two, however, it reapproached the shore in an oblique direction, and fell upon the sand above the reach of the breakers. The passengers, assisting each other, hastened to disengage themselves from the meshes of the net; and the balloon, relieved of their weight, was caught up by the wind, and, like a wounded bird recovering for an instant, disappeared into space.

The basket had contained five passengers and a dog, and but four had been thrown upon the shore. The fifth one, then, had been washed off by the great wave which had struck the net, and it was owing to this accident that the lightened balloon had been able to rise for the last time before falling upon the land. Scarcely had the four castaways felt the ground beneath their feet than all thinking of the one who was lost, cried:—"Perhaps he is trying to swim ashore. Save him! Let us save him!"

CHAPTER II.

AN EPISODE OF THE REBELLION-THE ENGINEER
CYRUS SMITH—GIDEON SPILETT—THE NEGRO NEB—
THE SAILOR PENCROFF—THE YOUTH, HERBERT—
AN UNEXPECTED PROPOSAL—RENDEZVOUS AT
10 O'CLOCK P.M.—DEPARTURE IN THE STORM.

They were neither professional aeronauts nor amateurs in aerial navigation whom the storm had thrown upon this coast. They were prisoners of war whose audacity had suggested this extraordinary manner of escape. A hundred times they would have perished, a hundred times their torn balloon would have precipitated them into the abyss, had not Providence preserved them for a strange destiny, and on the 20th of March, after having flown from Richmond, besieged by the troops of General Ulysses Grant, they found themselves 7,000 miles from the Virginia capital, the principal stronghold of the Secessionists during that terrible war. Their aerial voyage had lasted five days.

Let us see by what curious circumstances this escape of prisoners was effected,—an escape which resulted in the catastrophe which we have seen.

This same year, in the month of February, 1865, in one of those surprises by which General Grant, though in vain, endeavored to take Richmond, many of his officers were captured by the enemy and confined within the city. One of the most distinguished of those taken was a Federal staff officer named Cyrus Smith.

Cyrus Smith was a native of Massachusetts, an engineer by profession, and a scientist of the first order, to whom the Government had given, during the war, the direction of the railways, which played such a great strategic part during the war.

A true Yankee, thin, bony, lean, about forty-five years old, with streaks of grey appearing in his close cut hair and heavy moustache. He had one of those fine classical heads that seem as if made to be copied upon medals; bright eyes, a serious mouth, and the air of a practiced officer. He was one of these engineers who began of his own wish with the pick and shovel, as there are generals who have preferred to rise from the ranks. Thus, while possessing inventive genius, he had acquired manual dexterity, and his muscles showed remarkable firmness. He was as much a man of action as of study; he moved without effort, under the influence of a strong vitality and his sanguine temperament defied all misfortune. Highly educated, practical, "clear-headed," his temperament was superb, and always retaining his presence of mind he combined in the highest degree the three conditions whose union regulates the energy of man: activity of body, strength of will, and determination. His motto might have been that of William of Orange in the XVIIth century—"I can undertake without hope, and persevere through failure."

Cyrus Smith was also the personification of courage. He bad been in every battle of the war. After having begun under General Grant, with the Illinois volunteers, he had fought at Paducah, at Belmont, at Pittsburg Landing, at the siege of Corinth, at Port Gibson, at the Black River, at Chattanooga, at the Wilderness, upon the Potomac, everywhere with bravery, a soldier worthy of the General who said "I never counted my dead." And a hundred times Cyrus Smith would have been among the number of those whom the terrible Grant did not count; but in these combats, though he never spared himself, fortune always favored him, until the time he was wounded and taken prisoner at the siege of Richmond.

At the same time with Cyrus Smith another important personage fell into the power of the Southerners. This was no other than the honorable Gideon Spilett, reporter to the New York Herald, who had been detailed to follow the fortunes of the war with the armies of the North.

Gideon Spilett was of the race of astonishing chroniclers, English or American, such as Stanley and the like, who shrink from nothing in their endeavor to obtain exact information and to transmit it to their journal in the quickest manner. The journals of the United States, such as the New York *Herald*, are true powers, and their delegates are persons of importance. Gideon Spilett belonged in the first rank of these representatives.

A man of great merit; energetic, prompt, and ready; full of ideas, having been all over the world; soldier and artist; vehement in council; resolute in action; thinking nothing of pain, fatigue, or danger when seeking information, first for himself and afterwards for his journal; a master of recondite information of the unpublished, the unknown, the impossible. He was one of those cool observers who write amid the cannon balls, "reporting" under the bullets, and to whom all perils are welcome.

He also had been in all the battles, in the front rank, revolver in one hand and notebook in the other, his pencil never trembling in the midst of a cannonade. He did not tire the wires by incessant telegraphing, like those who speak when they have nothing to say, but each of his messages was short, condensed, clear, and to the purpose. For the rest, he did not lack humor. It was he who, after the affair of Black river, wishing at any price to keep his place at the telegraph wicket in order to announce the result, kept telegraphing for two hours the first chapters of the Bible. It cost the New York *Herald* $2,000, but the New York *Herald* had the first news.

Gideon Spilett was tall. He was forty years old or more. Sandy-colored whiskers encircled his face. His eye was clear, lively, and quick moving. It was the eye of a man who was accustomed to take in everything at a glance. Strongly built, he was tempered by all climates as a bar of steel is tempered by cold water. For ten years Gideon Spilett had been connected with the New York *Herald*, which he had enriched with his notes and his drawings, as he wielded the pencil as well as the pen. When captured he was about making a description and a sketch of the battle. The last words written in his note-book were these:—"A Southerner is aiming at me and—." And Gideon Spilett was missed; so, following his invariable custom, he escaped unscratched.

Cyrus Smith and Gideon Spilett, who knew each other only by reputation, were both taken to Richmond. The engineer recovered rapidly from his wound, and it was during his convalescence he met the reporter. The two soon learned to appreciate each-other. Soon their one aim was to rejoin the army of Grant and fight again in the ranks for the preservation of the Union.

The two Americans had decided to avail themselves of any chance; but although free to go and come within the city, Richmond was so closely guarded that an escape might be deemed impossible.

During this time Cyrus Smith was rejoined by a devoted servant. This man was a negro, born upon the engineer's estate, of slave parents, whom Smith, an abolitionist by conviction, had long since freed. The negro, though free, had no desire to leave his master, for whom he would have given his life. He was a man of thirty years, vigorous, agile, adroit, intelligent, quick, and self-possessed, sometimes ingenuous always smiling, ready and honest. He was named Nebuchadnezzar, but he answered to the nickname of Neb.

When Neb learned that his master had been taken prisoner he left Massachusetts without waiting a moment, arrived before Richmond, and, by a ruse, after having risked his life twenty times, he was able to get within the besieged city. The pleasure of Cyrus Smith on seeing again his servant, and the joy of Neb in finding his master, cannot be expressed. But while he had been able to get into Richmond it was much more difficult to get out, as the watch kept upon the Federal prisoners was very strict. It would require an extraordinary opportunity in order to attempt an escape with any chance of success; and that occasion not only did not present itself, but it was difficult to make. Meanwhile, Grant continued his energetic operations. The victory of Petersburg had been vigorously contested. His forces, reunited to those of Butler, had not as yet obtained any result before Richmond, and nothing indicated an early release to the prisoners. The reporter, whose tiresome captivity gave him no item worthy of note, grew impatient. He had but one idea; to get out of Richmond at any risk. Many times, indeed, he tried the experiment, and was stopped by obstacles insurmountable.

Meanwhile, the siege continued, and as the prisoners were anxious to escape in order to join the army of Grant, so there were certain of the besieged no less desirous to be free to join the army of the Secessionists; and among these was a certain Jonathan Forster, who was a violent Southerner. In truth, the Confederates were no more able to get out of the city than the Federal prisoners, as the army of Grant invested it around. The Mayor of Richmond had not for some time been able to communicate with General Lee, and it was of the highest importance to make the latter aware of the situation of the city, in order to hasten the march of the rescuing army. This Jonathan Forster had conceived the idea of passing over the lines of the besiegers in a balloon, and arriving by this means in the Confederate camp.

The Mayor authorized the undertaking, a balloon was made and placed at the disposal of Forster and five of his companions. They were provided with arms as they might have to defend themselves in descending, and food in case their aerial voyage should be prolonged. The departure of the balloon had been fixed for the 18th of March. It was to start in the night, and with a moderate breeze from the northeast, the party expected to arrive at the quarters of General Lee in a few hours. But the wind from the northeast was not a mere breeze.

On the morning of the 18th there was every symptom of a storm, and soon the tempest broke forth, making it necessary for Forster to defer his departure, as it was impossible to risk the balloon and those whom it would carry, to the fury of the elements.

The balloon, inflated in the great square of Richmond, was all ready, waiting for the first lull in the storm; and throughout the city there was great vexation at the settled bad weather. The night of the 19th and 20th passed, but in the morning the storm was only developed in intensity, and departure was impossible.

On this day Cyrus Smith was accosted in one of the streets of Richmond by a man whom he did not know. It was a sailor named Pencroff, aged from thirty-five to forty years, strongly built, much sunburnt, his eyes bright and glittering, but with a good countenance.

This Pencroff was a Yankee who had sailed every sea, and who had experienced every kind of extraordinary adventure that a two-legged being without wings could encounter. It is needless to say that he was of an adventurous nature, ready to dare anything and to be astonished at nothing. Pencroff, in the early part of this year, had come to Richmond on business, having with him Herbert Brown, of New Jersey, a lad fifteen years old, the son of Pencroff's captain, and an orphan whom he loved as his own child. Not having left the city at the beginning of the siege, he found himself, to his great displeasure, blocked. He also had but one idea: to get out. He knew the reputation of the engineer, and he knew with what impatience that determined man chaffed at his restraint. He did not therefore hesitate to address him without ceremony.

"Mr. Smith, have you had enough of Richmond?"

The engineer looked fixedly at the man who spoke thus, and who added in a low voice:—

"Mr. Smith, do you want to escape?"

"How?" answered the engineer, quickly, and it was evidently an inconsiderate reply, for he had not yet examined the man who spoke.

"Mr. Smith, do you want to escape?"

""Who are you?" he demanded, in a cold voice.

Pencroff made himself known.

"Sufficient," replied Smith. "And by what means do you propose to escape?"

"By this idle balloon which is doing nothing, and seems to me all ready to take us!"—

The sailor had no need to finish his sentence. The engineer had understood all in a word. He seized Pencroff by the arm and hurried him to his house. There the sailor explained his project, which, in truth, was simple enough:—They risked only their lives in carrying it out. The storm was at its height, it is true; but a skilful and daring engineer like Smith would know well how to manage a balloon. He, himself, would not have hesitated to have started, had he known how—with Herbert, of course. He had seen many storms and he thought nothing of them.

Cyrus Smith listened to the sailor without saying a word, but with glistening eyes. This was the opportunity, and he was not the man to let it escape him. The project was very dangerous, but it could be accomplished. During the night, in spite of the guards, they might reach the balloon, creep into the basket, and then cut the lines which held it! Certainly they risked being shot, but on the other hand they might succeed, and but for this tempest—but without this tempest the balloon would have been gone and the long-sought opportunity would not have been present.

"I am not alone," said Smith at length.

"How many would you want to take?" demanded the sailor.

"Two; my friend Spilett, and my man Neb."

"That would be three," replied Pencroff; "and, with Herbert and myself, five. Well, the balloon can carry six?"

"Very well. We will go!" said the engineer.

This "we" pledged the reporter, who was not a man to retreat, and who, when the project was told him, approved of it heartily. What astonished him was, that so simple a plan had not already occurred to himself. As to Neb, he followed his master wherever his master wanted to go.

"To-night, then," said Pencroff.

"To-night, at ten o'clock," replied Smith; "and pray heaven that this storm does not abate before we get off."

Pencroff took leave of the engineer, and returned to his lodging, where he found young Herbert Brown. This brave boy knew the plans of the sailor, and he was not without a certain anxiety as to the result of the proposal to the engineer. We see, therefore, five persons determined to throw themselves into the vortex of the storm.

The storm did not abate. And neither Jonathan Forster nor his companion dreamed of confronting it in that frail basket. The journey would be terrible. The engineer feared but one thing; that the balloon, held to the ground and beaten down under the wind, would be torn into a thousand pieces. During many hours he wandered about the nearly deserted square, watching the apparatus. Pencroff, his hands in his pockets, yawning like a man who is unable to kill time, did the same; but in reality he also feared that the balloon would be torn to pieces, or break from its moorings and be carried off.

Evening arrived and the night closed in dark and threatening. Thick masses of fog passed like clouds low down over the earth. Rain mingled with snow fell. The weather was cold. A sort of mist enveloped Richmond. It seemed as if in the face of this terrible tempest a truce had been agreed upon between the besiegers and besieged, and the cannon were silent before the heavy detonations of the storm. The streets of the city were deserted; it had not even seemed necessary, in such weather, to guard the square in which swung the balloon. Everything favored the departure of the prisoners; but this voyage, in the midst of the excited elements!—

"Bad weather," said Pencroff, holding his hat, which the wind was trying to take off, firmly to his head, "but pshaw, it can't last, all the same."

At half-past 9, Cyrus Smith and his companions glided by different routes to the square, which the gas lights, extinguished by the wind, left in profound darkness. They could not see even the huge balloon, as it lay pressed over against the ground. Beside the bags of ballast which held the cords of the net, the basket was held down by a strong cable passed through a ring fastened in the pavement, and the ends brought back on board.

The five prisoners came together at the basket. They had not been discovered, and such was the darkness that they could not see each other. Without saying a word, four of them took their places in the basket, while Pencroff, under the direction of the engineer, unfastened successively the bundles of ballast. It took but a few moments, and then the sailor joined his companions. The only thing that then held the balloon was the loop of the cable, and Cyrus Smith had but to give the word for them to let it slip. At that moment, a dog leaped with a bound into the basket. It was Top, the dog of the engineer, who, having broken his chain, had followed his master. Cyrus Smith, fearing to add to the weight, wanted to send the poor brute back, but Pencroff said, "Pshaw, it is but one more!" and at the same time threw overboard two bags of sand. Then, slipping the cable, the balloon, shooting off in an oblique direction, disappeared, after having dashed its basket against two chimneys, which it demolished in its rush.

Then the storm burst upon them with frightful violence. The engineer did not dare to descend during the night, and when day dawned all sight of the earth was hidden by the mists. It was not until five days later that the breaking of the clouds enabled them to see the vast sea extending below them, lashed by the wind into a terrific fury.

We have seen how, of these five men, who started on the 20th of March, four were thrown, four days later, on a desert coast, more than

6,000 miles from this country. And the one who was missing, the one to whose rescue the four survivors had hurried was their leader, Cyrus Smith.

[The 5th of April, Richmond fell into the hands of Grant, the Rebellion was repressed, Lee retreated into the West (*sic*) and the cause of the Union triumphed.]

CHAPTER III.

FIVE O'CLOCK IN THE AFTERNOON—THE LOST
ONE—THE DESPAIR OF NEB—SEARCH TO THE
NORTHWARD—THE ISLAND—A NIGHT OF
ANGUISH—THE FOG OF THE MORNING—NEB
SWIMMING—SIGHT OF THE LAND—FORDING
THE CHANNEL.

The engineer, on the giving way of the net, had been swept away by a wave. His dog had disappeared at the same time. The faithful animal had of its own accord sprung to the rescue of its master.

"Forward!" cried the reporter, and all four, forgetting weakness and fatigue, began their search. Poor Neb wept with grief and despair at the thought of having lost all that he loved in the world.

Not more than two minutes had passed between the moment that Smith had disappeared, and the instant of his companions landing. They were, therefore, hopeful of being in time to rescue him.

"Hunt, hunt for him," cried Neb.

"Yes, Neb, and we will find him," replied Spilett.

"Alive?"

"Alive!"

"Can he swim?" demanded Pencroff.

"Oh, yes," responded Neb. "And, besides, Top is with him—"

The sailor, looking at the roaring sea, shook his head.

It was at a point northward from this shore, and about half a mile from the place where the castaways had landed, that the engineer had disappeared, and if he had come ashore at the nearest point it was at least that distance from where they now were.

It was nearly 6 o'clock. The fog had risen and made the night very dark. The castaways followed northward along the shore of that land upon which chance had thrown them. A land unknown, whose geographical situation they could not guess. They walked upon a sandy soil, mixed with stones, seemingly destitute of any kind of vegetation. The ground, very uneven, seemed in certain places to be riddled with small holes, making the march very painful. From these holes, great, heavy-flying birds rushed forth, and were lost in the darkness. Others, more active, rose in flocks, and fled away like the clouds. The sailor thought he recognized gulls and sea-mews, whose sharp cries were audible above the raging of the sea.

From time to time the castaways would stop and call, listening for an answering voice from the ocean. They thought, too, that if they were near the place where the engineer had been, washed ashore, and he had been unable to make any response, that, at least, the barking of the dog Top would have been heard. But no sound was distinguishable above the roaring of the waves and the thud of the surf. Then the little party would resume their march, searching all the windings of the shore.

After a walk of twenty minutes the four castaways were suddenly stopped by a foaming line of breakers. They found themselves upon the extremity of a sharp point upon which the sea broke with fury.

"This is a promontory," said the sailor, "and it will be necessary to turn back, keeping to the right in order to gain the main land."

"But if he is there!" cried Neb, pointing towards the ocean, whose enormous waves showed white through the gloom.

"Well, let us call again."

And all together, uniting their voices, uttered a vigorous cry, but without response. They waited for a lull, and tried once more. And again there was no answer.

Then the castaways turned back, following the opposite side of the promontory over ground equally sandy and rocky. However, Pencroff observed that the shore was bolder, that the land rose somewhat, and he thought that it might gradually slope up to the high hill which was dimly visible through the darkness. The birds were less numerous on this shore. The sea also seemed less surging and tempestuous, and it was noticeable that the agitation of the waves was subsiding. They hardly heard the sound of the surf, and doubtless, this side of the promontory formed a semi-circular bay, protected by its sharp point from the long roll of the sea.

But by following this direction they were walking towards the south, which was going away from that place where Smith would have landed. After a tramp of a mile and a half, the shore presented no other curve which would permit of a return towards the north. It was evident that this promontory, the point of which they had turned, must be joined to the mainland. The castaways, although much fatigued, pushed on courageously, hoping each moment to find a sudden turn which would take them in the desired direction. What, then, was their disappointment when, after having walked nearly two miles, they found themselves again arrested by the sea, upon a high promontory of slippery rocks.

"We are on an island," exclaimed Pencroff; "and we have measured it from end to end!"

The words of the sailor were true. The castaways had been thrown, not upon a continent, but upon an island not more than two miles long, and of inconsiderable breadth.

This desert isle, covered with stones, without vegetation, desolate refuge of sea-birds, did it belong to a more important archipelago? They could not tell. The party in the balloon, when from their basket they saw the land through the clouds, had not been able to determine its size. But Pencroff, with the eyes of a sailor accustomed to piercing the gloom, thought, at the moment, that he could distinguish in the west confused masses, resembling a high coast. But at this time they were unable, on account of the obscurity, to determine to what system, whether simple or complex, their isle belonged. They were unable to get off, as the sea surrounded them, and it was necessary to wait until the next day to search for the engineer; who, alas! had made no cry to signal his presence.

"The silence of Cyrus proves nothing," said the reporter. "He may have fainted, or be wounded, and unable to reply, but we will not despair."

The reporter then suggested the idea of lighting a fire upon the point of the island, which would serve as a signal for the engineer. But they searched in vain for wood or dry branches. Sand and stones were all they found.

One can understand the grief of Neb and his companions, who were strongly attached to their brave comrade. It was too evident that they could not help him now, and that they must wait till day. The engineer had escaped, and was already safe upon the land, or he was lost forever. The hours were long and dreadful, the cold was intense, and the castaways suffered keenly, but they did not realize it. They did not think of sleep. Thinking only of their chief, hoping, wishing to hope, they moved back and forth upon that arid island, constantly returning to the northern end, where they would be closest to the place of the catastrophe. They listened, they shouted, they tried to catch some call, and, as a lull would come, or the roar of the surf fall with the waves, their hallooes must have sounded far into the distance.

Once the cry of Neb was answered by an echo; and Herbert made Pencroff notice it, saying:—"That proves that there is land not far to the west."

The sailor nodded; he knew his eyes could not deceive him. He thought he had seen land, and it must be there. But this distant echo was the only answer to the cries of Neb, and the silence about the island remained unbroken. Meanwhile the sky was clearing slowly. Towards midnight, some stars shone out, and, had the engineer been there with his companions, he would have noticed that these stars did not belong to the northern hemisphere. The pole star was not visible in this new horizon, the constellations in the zenith were not such as they had been accustomed to see from North America, and the Southern Cross shone resplendent in the heavens.

The night passed; and towards 5 o'clock in the morning the middle heavens began to brighten, though the horizon remained obscure; until with the first rays of day, a fog rose from the sea, so dense that the eye could scarcely penetrate twenty paces into its depths, and separated into great, heavy-moving masses. This was unfortunate, as the castaways were unable to distinguish anything about them. While the gaze of Neb and the reporter was directed towards the sea, the sailor and Herbert searched for the land in the west; but they could see nothing.

"Never mind," said Pencroff, "if I do not see the land. I feel that it is there,—just as sure as that we are not in Richmond."

But the fog, which was nothing more than a morning mist, soon rose. A clear sun warmed the upper air, its heat penetrating to the surface of the island. At half-past 6, three quarters of an hour after sunrise, the mist was nearly gone. Though still thick overhead, it dissolved, below, and soon all the island appeared, as from a cloud. Then the sea appeared, limitless towards the east, but bounded on the west by a high and abrupt coast.

Yes, the land was there! There, safety was at least provisionally assured. The island and the main land were separated by a channel half a mile wide, through which rushed a strong current. Into this current one of the party, without saying a word or consulting with his companions, precipitated himself. It was Neb. He was anxious to be upon that coast and to be pushing forward towards the north. No one could keep him back. Pencroff called to him in vain. The reporter prepared to follow, but the sailor ran to him, exclaiming:—

"Are you determined to cross this channel?"

"I am," replied Spilett.

"Well, then, listen to me a moment. Neb can rescue his master alone. If we throw ourselves into the channel we are in danger of being carried out to sea by this strong current. Now, if I am not mistaken it is caused by the ebb. You see the tide is going out. Have patience until low water and then we may ford it."

"You are right," answered the reporter; "we will keep together as much as possible."

Meantime, Neb was swimming vigorously in a diagonal direction, against the current; his black shoulders were seen rising with each stroke. He was drawn backward with swiftness, but he was gaining towards the other shore. It took him more than half an hour to cross the half mile which separated the isle from the mainland, and when he reached the other side it was at a place a long distance from the point opposite to that which he had left.

Neb, having landed at the base of a high rocky wall, clambered quickly up its side, and, running, disappeared behind a point projecting into the sea, about the same height as the northern end of the island.

Neb's companions had watched with anxiety his daring attempt, and, when he was out of sight, they fixed their eyes upon that land from which they were going to demand refuge. They ate some of the shellfish which they found upon the sands; it was a poor meal, but then it was better than nothing.

The opposite coast formed an immense bay, terminated to the south by a sharp point bare of all vegetation, and having a most forbidding aspect. This point at its junction with the shore was abutted by high granite rocks. Towards the north, on the contrary, the bay widened, with a shore more rounded, extending from the southwest to the northeast, and ending in a narrow cape. Between these two points, the distance must have been about eight miles. A half mile from the shore the island, like an enormous whale, lay upon the sea. Its width could not have been greater than a quarter of a mile.

Before the Island, the shore began with a sandy beach strewn with black rocks, at this moment beginning to appear above the receding tide. Beyond this rose, like a curtain, a perpendicular granite wall, at least 300 feet high and terminated by a ragged edge. This extended for about three miles, ending abruptly on the right in a smooth face, as if cut by the hand of man. To the left on the contrary, above the promontory, this kind of irregular cliff, composed of heaped-up rocks and glistening in the light, sank and gradually mingled with the rocks of the southern point.

Upon the upper level of the coast not a tree was visible. It was a table-land, as barren though not as extensive as that around Cape Town, or at the Cape of Good Hope. At least so it appeared from the islet. To the right, however, and back of the smooth face of rock, some verdure appeared. The confused massing of large trees was easily distinguishable extending far as the eye could reach. This verdure gladdened the sight tired by the rough face of granite. Finally, back of and above the plateau, distant towards the northwest about seven miles, shone a white summit, reflecting the sun's rays. It was the snowy cap of some lofty mountain.

It was not possible at present to say whether this land was an island or part of a continent; but the sight of the broken rocks heaped together on the left would have proved to a geologist their volcanic origin, as they were incontestably the result of igneous action.

Gideon Spilett, Pencroff, and Herbert looked earnestly upon this land where they were to live, perhaps for long years; upon which, if out of the track of ships, they might have to die.

"Well," demanded Herbert, "what do you think of it, Pencroff?"

"Well," replied the sailor, "there's good and bad in it, as with everything else. But we shall soon see; for look; what I told you. In three hours we can cross, and once over there, we will see what we can do towards finding Mr. Smith."

Pencroff was not wrong in his predictions. Three hours later, at low tide, the greater part of the sandy bed of the channel was bare. A narrow strip of water, easily crossed, was all that separated the island from the shore. And at 10 o'clock, Spilett and his two companions, stripped of their clothing, which they carried in packages on their heads, waded through the water, which was nowhere more than five feet deep. Herbert, where the water was too deep, swam like a fish, acquitting himself well; and all arrived without difficulty at the other shore. There, having dried themselves in the sun, they put on their clothes, which had not touched the water, and took counsel together.

CHAPTER IV.

THE LITHODOMES—THE MOUTH OF THE RIVER—
THE "CHIMNEYS"—CONTINUATION OF THE
SEARCH—THE FOREST OF EVERGREENS—GETTING
FIREWOOD—WAITING FOR THE TIDE—ON TOP OF
THE CLIFF—THE TIMBER-FLOAT—THE RETURN TO
THE COAST.

Presently the reporter told the sailor to wait just where he was until he should come back, and without losing a moment, he walked back along the coast in the direction which Neb had taken some hours before, and disappeared quickly around a turn in the shore.

Herbert wished to go with him.

"Stay, my boy," said the sailor. "We must pitch our camp for the night, and try to find something to eat more satisfying than shellfish. Our friends will need food when they come back."

"I am ready, Pencroff," said Herbert.

"Good," said the sailor. "Let us set to work methodically. We are tired, cold, and hungry: we need shelter, fire, and food. There is plenty of wood in the forest, and we can get eggs from the nests; but we must find a house."

"Well," said Herbert, "I will look for a cave in these rocks, and I shall certainly find some hole in which we can stow ourselves."

"Right," said Pencroff; "let us start at once."

They walked along the base of the rocky wall, on the strand left bare by the receding waves. But instead of going northwards, they turned to the south. Pencroff had noticed, some hundreds of feet below the place where they had been thrown ashore, a narrow inlet in the coast, which he thought might be the mouth of a river or of a brook. Now it was important to pitch the camp in the neighborhood of fresh water; in that part of the island, too, Smith might be found.

The rock rose 300 feet, smooth and massive. It was a sturdy wall of the hardest granite, never corroded by the waves, and even at its base there was no cleft which might serve as a temporary abode. About the summit hovered a host of aquatic birds, mainly of the web-footed tribe, with long, narrow, pointed beaks. Swift and noisy, they cared little for the unaccustomed presence of man. A shot into the midst of the flock would have brought down a dozen; but neither Pencroff nor Herbert had a gun. Besides, gulls and sea-mews are barely eatable, and their eggs have a very disagreeable flavor.

Meanwhile Herbert, who was now to the left, soon noticed some rocks thickly strewn with sea weed, which would evidently be submerged again in a few hours. On them lay hosts of bivalves, not to be disdained by hungry men. Herbert called to Pencroff, who came running to him.

"Ah, they are mussels," said the sailor. "Now we can spare the eggs."

"They are not mussels," said Herbert, examining the mollusks carefully, "they are lithodomes."

"Can we eat them?" said Pencroff.

"Certainly."

"Then let us eat some lithodomes."

The sailor could rely on Herbert, who was versed in Natural History and very fond of it. He owed his acquaintance with this study in great part to his father, who had entered him in the classes of the best professors in Boston, where the child's industry and intelligence had endeared him to all.

These lithodomes were oblong shell-fish, adhering in clusters to the rocks. They belonged to that species of boring mollusk which can perforate a hole in the hardest stone, and whose shell has the peculiarity of being rounded at both ends.

Pencroff and Herbert made a good meal of these lithodomes. which lay gaping in the sun. They tasted like oysters, with a peppery flavor which left no desire for condiments of any kind.

Their hunger was allayed for the moment, but their thirst was increased by the spicy flavor of the mollusks. The thing now was to find fresh water, which was not likely to fail them in a region so undulating. Pencroff and Herbert, after having taken the precaution to fill their pockets and handkerchiefs with lithodomes, regained the foot of the hill.

Two hundred feet further on they reached the inlet, through which, as Pencroff had surmised, a little river was flowing with full current Here the rocky wall seemed to have been torn asunder by some volcanic convulsion. At its base lay a little creek, running at an acute angle. The water in this place was 100 feet across, while the banks on either side were scarcely 20 feet broad. The river buried itself at once between the two walls of granite, which began to decline as one went up stream.

"Here is water," said Pencroff, "and over there is wood. Well, Herbert, now we only want the house."

The river water was clear. The sailor knew that as the tide was now low there would be no influx from the sea, and the water would be fresh. When this important point had been settled, Herbert looked for some cave which might give them shelter, but it was in vain. Everywhere the wall was smooth, flat, and perpendicular.

However, over at the mouth of the watercourse, and above high-water mark, the detritus had formed, not a grotto, but a pile of enormous rocks, such as are often met with in granitic countries, and which are called *Chimneys*.

Pencroff and Herbert went down between the rocks, into those sandy corridors, lighted only by the huge cracks between the masses of granite, some of which only kept their equilibrium by a miracle. But with the light the wind came in, and with the wind the piercing cold of the outer air. Still, the sailor thought that by stopping up some of these openings with a mixture of stones and sand, the Chimneys might be rendered habitable. Their plan resembled the typographical sign, &, and by cutting off the upper curve of the sign, through which the south and the west wind rushed in, they could succeed without doubt in utilizing its lower portion.

"This is just what we want," said Pencroff, and if we ever see Mr. Smith again, he will know how to take advantage of this labyrinth."

"We shall see him again, Pencroff," said Herbert, "and when he comes back he must find here a home that is tolerably comfortable. We can make this so if we can build a fireplace in the left corridor with an opening for the smoke."

"That we can do, my boy," answered the sailor, "and these Chimneys will just serve our purpose. But first we must get together some firing. Wood will be useful, too, in blocking up these great holes through which the wind whistles so shrilly."

Herbert and Pencroff left the Chimneys, and turning the angle, walked up the left bank of the river, whose current was strong enough to bring down a quantity of dead wood. The return tide, which had already begun, would certainly carry it in the ebb to a great distance. "Why not utilize this flux and reflux," thought the sailor, "in the carriage of heavy timber?"

After a quarter of an hour's walk, the two reached the elbow which the river made in turning to the left. From this point onward it flowed through a forest of magnificent trees, which had preserved their verdure in spite of the season; for they belonged to that great cone-bearing family indigenous everywhere, from the poles to the tropics. Especially conspicuous were the "deodara," so numerous in the Himalayas, with their pungent perfume. Among them were clusters of pines, with tall trunks and spreading parasols of green. The ground was strewn with fallen branches, so dry as to crackle under their feet.

"Good," said the sailor, "I may not know the name of these trees, but I know they belong to the genus firewood, and that's the main thing for us."

It was an easy matter to gather the firewood. They did not need even to strip the trees; plenty of dead branches lay at their feet. This dry wood would burn rapidly, and they would need a large supply. How could two men carry such a load to the Chimneys? Herbert asked the question.

"My boy," said the sailor, "there's a way to do everything. If we had a car or a boat it would be too easy."

"We have the river," suggested Herbert.

"Exactly," said Pencroff. "The river shall be our road and our carrier, too. Timber-floats were not invented for nothing."

"But our carrier is going in the wrong direction," said Herbert, "since the tide is coming up from the sea."

"We have only to wait for the turn of tide," answered the sailor. "Let us get our float ready."

They walked towards the river, each carrying a heavy load of wood tied up in fagots. On the bank, too, lay quantities of dead boughs, among grass which the foot of man had probably never pressed before. Pencroff began to get ready his float.

In an eddy caused by an angle of the shore, which broke the flow of the current, they set afloat the larger pieces of wood, bound together by liana stems so as to form a sort of raft. On this raft they piled the rest of the wood, which would have been a load for twenty men. In an hour their work was finished, and the float was moored to the bank to wait for the turn of the tide. Pencroff and Herbert resolved to spend the mean time in gaining a more extended view of the country from the higher plateau. Two hundred feet behind the angle of the river, the wall terminating in irregular masses of rocks, sloped away gently to the edge of the forest.

The two easily climbed this natural staircase, soon attained the summit, and posted themselves at the angle overlooking the mouth of the river.

Their first look was at that ocean over which they had been so frightfully swept. They beheld with emotion the northern part of the coast, the scene of the catastrophe, and of Smith's disappearance. They hoped to see on the surface some wreck of the balloon to which a man might cling. But the sea was a watery desert. The coast, too, was desolate. Neither Neb nor the reporter could be seen.

"Something tells me," said Herbert, "that a person so energetic as Mr. Smith would not let himself be drowned like an ordinary man. He must have got to shore; don't you think so, Pencroff?"

The sailor shook his head sadly. He never thought to see Smith again; but he left Herbert a hope.

"No doubt," said he, "our engineer could save himself where any one else would perish."

Meanwhile he took a careful observation of the coast. Beneath his eyes stretched out the sandy beach, bounded, upon the right of the river-mouth, by lines of breakers. The rocks which still were visible above the water were like groups of amphibious monsters lying in the surf. Beyond them the sea sparkled in the rays of the sun. A narrow point terminated the southern horizon, and it was impossible to tell whether the land stretched further in that direction, or whether it trended southeast and southwest, so as to make an elongated peninsula. At the northern end of the bay, the outline of the coast was continued to a great distance. There the shore was low and flat, without rocks, but covered by great sandbanks, left by the receding tide.

When Pencroff and Herbert walked back towards the west, their looks fell on the snowcapped mountain, which rose six or seven miles away. Masses of tree-trunks, with patches of evergreens, extended from its first declivities to within two miles of the coast. Then from the edge of this forest to the coast stretched a plateau strewn at random with clumps of trees. On the left shore through the glades the waters of the little river, which seemed to have returned in its sinuous course to the mountains which gave it birth.

"Are we upon an island?" muttered the sailor.

"It is big enough, at all events," said the boy.

"An island's an island, no matter how big," said Pencroff.

But this important question could not yet be decided. The country itself, isle or continent, seemed fertile, picturesque, and diversified in its products. For that they must be grateful. They returned along the southern ridge of the granite plateau, outlined by a fringe of fantastic rocks, in whose cavities lived hundreds of birds. A whole flock of them soared aloft as Herbert jumped over the rocks.

"Ah!" cried he, "these are neither gulls nor sea-mews."

"What are they?" said Pencroff. "They look for all the world like pigeons."

"So they are," said Herbert, "but they are wild pigeons, or rock pigeons." I know them by the two black bands on the wing, the white rump, and the ash-blue feathers. The rock pigeon is good to eat, and its eggs ought to be delicious; and if they have left a few in their nests—"

"We will let them hatch in an omelet," said Pencroff, gaily.

"But what will you make your omelet in?" asked Herbert; "in your hat?"

"I am not quite conjurer enough for that," said the sailor. "We must fall back on eggs in the shell, and I will undertake to despatch the hardest."

Pencroff and the boy examined carefully the cavities of the granite, and succeeded in discovering eggs in some of them. Some dozens were collected in the sailor's handkerchief, and, high tide approaching, the two went down again to the water-course.

It was 1 o'clock when they arrived at the elbow of the river, and the tide was already on the turn. Pencroff had no intention of letting his timber float at random, nor did he wish to get on and steer it. But a sailor is never troubled in a matter of ropes or cordage, and Pencroff quickly twisted from the dry lianas a rope several fathoms long. This was fastened behind the raft, and the sailor held it in his hand, while Herbert kept the float in the current by pushing it off from the shore with a long pole.

This expedient proved an entire success. The enormous load of wood kept well in the current. The banks were sheer, and there was no fear lest the float should ground; before 2 o'clock they reached the mouth of the stream, a few feet from the Chimneys.

CHAPTER V.

ARRANGING THE CHIMNEYS—THE IMPORTANT
QUESTION OF FIRE—THE MATCH BOX—SEARCH
OVER THE SHORE—RETURN OF THE REPORTER AND
NEB—ONE MATCH—THE CRACKLING FIRE—
THE FISH SUPPER—THE FIRST NIGHT ON LAND.

The first care of Pencroff, after the raft had been unloaded, was to make the Chimneys habitable, by stopping up those passages traversed by the draughts of air. Sand, stones, twisted branches, and mud, hermetically sealed the galleries of the & open to the southerly winds, and shut out its upper curve. One narrow, winding passage, opening on the side; was arranged to carry out the smoke and to quicken the draught of the fire. The Chimneys were thus divided into three or four chambers, if these dark dens, which would hardly have contained a beast, might be so called. But they were dry, and one could stand up in them, or at least in the principal one, which was in the centre. The floor was covered with sand, and, everything considered, they could establish themselves in this place while waiting for one better.

While working, Herbert and Pencroff chatted together.

"Perhaps," said the boy, "our companions will have found a better place than ours."

"It is possible." answered the sailor, "but, until we know, don't let us stop. Better have two strings to one's bow than none at all!"

"Oh," repeated Herbert, "if they can only find Mr. Smith, and bring him back with them, how thankful we will be!"

"Yes," murmured Pencroff. "He was a good man."

"Was!" said Herbert. "Do you think we shall not see him again?"

"Heaven forbid!" replied the sailor.

The work of division was rapidly accomplished, and Pencroff declared himself satisfied. "Now," said he, "our friends may return, and they will find a good enough shelter."

Nothing remained but to fix the fireplace and to prepare the meal, which, in truth, was a task easy and simple enough. Large flat stones were placed at the mouth of the first gallery to the left, where the smoke passage had been made; and this chimney was made so narrow that but little heat would escape up the flue, and the cavern would be comfortably warmed. The stock of wood was piled up in one of the chambers, and the sailor placed some logs and broken branches upon the stones. He was occupied in arranging them when Herbert asked him if he had some matches.

"Certainly," replied Pencroff, "and moreover, fortunately; for without matches or tinder we would indeed be in trouble."

"Could not we always make fire as the savages do," replied Herbert, "by rubbing two bits of dry wood together?"

"Just try it, my boy, some time, and see if you do anything more than put your arms out of joint."

"Nevertheless, it is often done in the islands of the Pacific."

"I don't say that it is not," replied Pencroff, "but the savages must have a way of their own, or use a certain kind of wood, as more than once I have wanted to get fire in that way and have never yet been able to. For my part, I prefer matches; and, by the way, where are mine?"

Pencroff, who was an habitual smoker, felt in his vest for the box, which he was never without, but, not finding it, he searched the pockets of his trowsers, and to his profound amazement, it was not there.

"This is an awkward business," said he, looking at Herbert. "My box must have fallen from my pocket, and I can't find it. But you, Herbert, have you nothing: no steel, not anything, with which we can make fire?"

"Not a thing, Pencroff."

The sailor, followed by the boy, walked out, rubbing his forehead.

On the sand, among the rocks, by the bank of the river, both of them searched with the utmost care, but without result. The box was of copper, and had it been there, they must have seen it.

"Pencroff," asked Herbert, "did not you throw it out of the basket?"

"I took good care not to," said the sailor. "But when one has been knocked around as we have been, so small a thing could easily have been lost; even my pipe is gone. The confounded box; where can it be?"

"Well, the tide is out; let us run to the place where we landed," said Herbert.

It was little likely that they would find this box, which the sea would have rolled among the pebbles at high water; nevertheless, it would do no harm to search. They, therefore, went quickly to the place where they had first landed, some 200 paces from the Chimneys. There, among the pebbles, in the hollows of the rocks, they made minute search, but in vain. If the box had fallen here it must have been carried out by the waves. As the tide went down, the sailor peered into every crevice, but without Success. It was a serious loss, and, for the time, irreparable. Pencroff did not conceal his chagrin. He frowned, but did not speak, and Herbert tried to console him by saying, that, most probably, the matches would have been so wetted as to be useless.

"No, my boy," answered the sailor. "They were in a tightly closing metal box. But now, what are we to do?"

"We will certainly find means of procuring fire," said Herbert. "Mr. Smith or Mr. Spilett will not be as helpless as we are."

"Yes, but in the meantime we are without it," said Pencroff, "and our companions will find but a very sorry meal on their return."

"But," said Herbert, hopefully, "it is not possible that they will have neither tinder nor matches."

"I doubt it," answered the sailor, shaking his head. "In the first place, neither Neb nor Mr. Smith smoke, and then I'm afraid Mr. Spilett has more likely kept his notebook than his match-box."

Herbert did not answer. This loss was evidently serious. Nevertheless, the lad thought surely they could make a fire in some way or other, but Pencroff, more experienced, although a man not easily discouraged, knew differently. At any rate there was but one thing to do:—to wait until the return of Neb and the reporter. It was necessary to give up the repast of cooked eggs which they had wished to prepare, and a diet of raw flesh did not seem to be, either for themselves or for the others, an agreeable prospect.

Before returning to the Chimneys, the companions, in case they failed of a fire, gathered a fresh lot of lithodomes, and then silently took the road to their dwelling. Pencroff, his eyes fixed upon the ground, still searched in every direction for the lost box. They followed again up the left bank of the river, from its mouth to the angle where the raft had been built. They returned to the upper plateau, and went in every direction, searching in the tall grass on the edge of the forest, but in vain. It was 5 o'clock when they returned again to the Chimneys, and it is needless to say that the passages were searched in their darkest recesses before all hope was given up.

Towards 6 o'clock, just as the sun was disappearing behind the high land in the west, Herbert, who was walking back and forth upon the shore, announced the return of Neb and of Gideon Spilett. They came back alone, and the lad felt his heart sink. The sailor had not, then, been wrong in his presentiments; they had been unable to find the engineer.

The reporter, when he came up, seated himself upon a rock, without speaking. Fainting from fatigue, half dead with hunger, he was unable to utter a word. As to Neb, his reddened eyes showed how he had been weeping, and the fresh tears which he was unable to restrain, indicated, but too clearly, that he had lost all hope.

The reporter at length gave the history of their search. Neb and he had followed the coast for more than eight miles, and, consequently, far beyond the point where the balloon had made the plunge which was followed by the disappearance of the engineer and Top. The shore was deserted. Not a recently turned stone, not a trace upon the sand, not a footprint, was upon all that part of the shore. It was evident that nobody inhabited that portion of the island. The sea was as deserted as the land; and it was there, at some hundreds of feet from shore, that the engineer had found his grave.

At that moment Neb raised his head, and in a voice which showed how he still struggled against despair, exclaimed:—

"No, he is not dead. It is impossible. It might happen to you or me, but never to him. He is a man who can get out of anything!"

Then his strength failing him, he murmured, "But I am used up."

Herbert ran to him and cried:—

"Neb, we will find him; God will give him back to us; but you, you must be famishing; do eat something."

And while speaking the lad offered the poor negro a handful of shell-fish—a meagre and insufficient nourishment enough.

But Neb, though he had eaten nothing for hours, refused them. Poor fellow! deprived of his master, he wished no longer to live.

As to Gideon Spilett, he devoured the mollusks, and then laid down upon the sand at the foot of a rock. He was exhausted, but calm. Herbert, approaching him, took his hand.

"Mr. Spilett," said he, "we have discovered a shelter where you will be more comfortable. The night is coming on; so come and rest there. To-morrow we will see—"

The reporter rose, and, guided by the lad, proceeded towards the Chimneys. As he did so, Pencroff came up to him, and in an off-hand way asked him if, by chance, he had a match with him. The reporter stopped, felt in his pockets, and finding none, said:—

"I had some, but I must have thrown them all away."

Then the sailor called Neb and asked him the same question, receiving a like answer.

"Curse it!" cried the sailor, unable to restrain the word.

The reporter heard it, and going to him said:—"Have you no matches?"

"Not one; and, of course, no fire."

"Ah," cried Neb, "if he was here, my master, he could soon make one."

The four castaways stood still and looked anxiously at each other. Herbert was the first to break the silence, by saying:—

"Mr. Spilett, you are a smoker, you always have matches about you; perhaps you have not searched thoroughly. Look again; a single match will be enough."

The reporter rummaged the pockets of his trowsers, his vest, and coat, and to the great joy of Pencroff, as well as to his own surprise, felt a little sliver of wood caught in the lining of his vest. He could feel it from the outside, but his fingers were unable to disengage it. If this should prove a match, and only one, it was extremely necessary not to rub off the phosphorus.

"Let me try," said the lad. And very adroitly, without breaking it, he drew out this little bit of wood, this precious trifle, which to these poor men was of such great importance. It was uninjured.

"One match!" cried Pencroff." "Why, it is as good as if we had a whole ship-load!"

He took it, and, followed by his companions, regained the Chimneys. This tiny bit of wood, which in civilised lands is wasted with indifference, as valueless, it was necessary here to use with the utmost care. The sailor, having assured himself that it was dry, said:—

"We must have some paper."

"Here is some," answered Spilett, who, after a little hesitation, had torn a leaf from his note-book.

Pencroff took the bit of paper and knelt down before the fire-place, where some handfuls of grass, leaves, and dry moss had been placed under the faggots in such a way that the air could freely circulate and make the dry wood readily ignite. Then Pencroff shaping the paper into a cone, as pipe-smokers do in the wind, placed it among the moss. Taking, then, a slightly rough stone and wiping it carefully, with beating heart and suspended breath, he gave the match a little rub. The first stroke produced no effect, as Pencroff fearing to break off the phosphorus had not rubbed hard enough.

"Ho, I won't be able to do it," said he; "my hand shakes—the match will miss—I can't do it—I don't want to try!" And, rising, he besought Herbert to undertake it.

Certainly, the boy had never in his life been so affected. His heart beat furiously. Prometheus, about to steal the fire from heaven, could not have been more excited.

Nevertheless he did not hesitate, but rubbed the stone with a quick stroke. A little sputtering was heard, and a light blue flame sprung out and produced a pungent smoke. Herbert gently turned the match, so as to feed the flame, and then slid it under the paper cone. In a few seconds the paper took fire, and then the moss kindled. An instant later, the dry wood crackled, and a joyous blaze, fanned by the breath of the sailor, shone out from the darkness.

"At length," cried Pencroff, rising, "I never was so excited in my life!"

It was evident that the fire did well in the fireplace of flat stones. The smoke readily ascended through its passage; the chimney drew, and an agreeable warmth quickly made itself felt. As to the fire, it would be necessary to take care that it should not go out, and always to keep some embers among the cinders. But it was only a matter of care and attention as the wood was plenty, and the supply could always be renewed in good time.

Pencroff began at once to utilize the fire by preparing something more nourishing than a dish of lithodomes. Two dozen eggs were brought by

Herbert, and the reporter, seated in a corner, watched these proceedings without speaking. A triple thought held possession of his mind. Did Cyrus still live? If alive, where was he? If he had survived his plunge, why was it he had found no means of making his existence known? As to Neb, he roamed the sand like one distracted.

Pencroff, who knew fifty-two ways of cooking eggs, had no choice at this time. He contented himself with placing them in the hot cinders and letting them cook slowly. In a few minutes the operation was finished, and the sailor invited the reporter to take part in the supper. This was the first meal of the castaways upon this unknown coast. The hard eggs were excellent, and as the egg contains all the elements necessary for man's nourishment, these poor men found them sufficient, and felt their strength reviving.

Unfortunately, one was absent from this repast. If the five prisoners who had escaped from Richmond had all been there, under those piled-up rocks, before that bright and crackling fire upon that dry sand, their happiness would have been complete. But the most ingenious, as well as the most learned—he who was undoubtedly their chief, Cyrus Smith—alas! was missing, and his body had not even obtained burial.

Thus passed the 25th of March. The night was come. Outside they heard the whistling of the wind, the monotonous thud of the surf, and the grinding of the pebbles on the beach.

The reporter had retired to a dark corner, after having briefly noted the events of the day—the first sight of this new land, the loss of the engineer, the exploration of the shore, the incidents of the matches, etc.; and, overcome by fatigue, he was enabled to find some rest in sleep.

Herbert fell asleep at once. The sailor, dozing, with one eye open, passed the night by the fire, on which he kept heaping fuel.

One only of the castaways did not rest in the Chimneys. It was the inconsolable, the despairing Neb, who, during the whole night, and in spite of his companions' efforts to make him take some rest, wandered upon the sands calling his master.

CHAPTER VI.

THE CASTAWAYS' INVENTORY—NO EFFECTS—THE
CHARRED LINEN—AN EXPEDITION INTO THE FOREST—
THE FLORA OF THE WOODS—THE FLIGHT OF THE
JACAMAR—TRACKS OF WILD BEASTS—THE COUROUCOUS—
THE HEATH-COCK—LINE-FISHING EXTRAORDINARY.

The inventory of the castaways can be promptly taken. Thrown upon
a desert coast, they had nothing but the clothes they wore in the balloon.
We must add Spilett's watch and note-book, which he had kept by some
inadvertence; but there were no firearms and no tools, not even a pocket
knife. Every thing had been thrown overboard to lighten the balloon.
Every necessary of life was wanting!

Yet if Cyrus Smith had been with them, his practical science and
inventive genius would have saved them from despair. But, alas! they
could hope to see him no more. The castaways could rely on Providence
only, and on their own right hands.

And, first, should they settle down on this strip of coast without an
effort to discover whether it was island or continent, inhabited or desert?
It was an urgent question, for all their measures would depend upon its
solution. However, it seemed to Pencroff better to wait a few days before
undertaking an exploration. They must try to procure more satisfying food
than eggs and shellfish, and repair their strength, exhausted by fatigue and
by the inclemency of the weather. The Chimneys would serve as a house
for a while. Their fire was lit, and it would be easy to keep alive some
embers. For the time being there were plenty of eggs and shell-fish. They
might even be able to kill, with a stick or a stone, some of the numerous

pigeons which fluttered among the rocks. They might find fruit-trees in the neighboring forest, and they had plenty of fresh water. It was decided then to wait a few days at the Chimneys, and to prepare for an expedition either along the coast or into the interior of the country.

This plan was especially agreeable to Neb, who was in no hurry to abandon that part of the coast which had been the scene of the catastrophe. He could not and would not believe that Smith was dead. Until the waves should have thrown up the engineer's body—until Neb should have seen with his eyes and handled with his hands his master's corpse, he believed him alive. It was an illusion which the sailor had not the heart to destroy; and there was no use in talking to Neb. He was like the dog who would not leave his master's tomb, and his grief was such that he would probably soon follow him.

Upon the morning of the 26th of March, at daybreak, Neb started along the coast northward to the spot where the sea had doubtless closed over the unfortunate engineer.

For breakfast that morning they had only eggs and lithodomes, seasoned with salt which Herbert had found in the cavities of the rocks. When the meal was over they divided forces. The reporter stayed behind to keep up the fire, and in the very improbable case of Neb's needing him to go to his assistance. Herbert and Pencroff went into the forest.

"We will go hunting, Herbert, "said the sailor. "We shall find ammunition on our way, and we will cut our guns in the forest."

But, before starting, Herbert suggested that as they had no tinder they must replace it by burnt linen. They were sorry to sacrifice a piece of handkerchief, but the need was urgent, and a piece of Pencroff's large check handkerchief was soon converted into a charred rag, and put away in the central chamber in a little cavity of the rock, sheltered from wind and dampness.

By this time it was 9 o'clock. The weather was threatening and the breeze blew from the southeast. Herbert and Pencroff, as they left the

Chimneys, cast a glance at the smoke which curled upwards from amid the rocks; then they walked up the left bank of the river.

When they reached the forest, Pencroff broke from the first tree two thick branches which he made into cudgels, and whose points Herbert blunted against a rock. What would he not have given for a knife? Then the hunters walked on in the high grass along the bank of the river, which, after its turn to the southwest, gradually narrowed, running between high banks and over-arched by interlacing trees. Pencroff, not to lose his way, determined to follow the course of the stream, which would bring him back to his point of departure. But the bank offered many obstacles. Here, trees whose flexible branches bent over to the brink of the current; there, thorns and lianas which they had to break with their sticks. Herbert often glided between the broken stumps with the agility of a young cat and disappeared in the copse, but Pencroff called him back at once, begging him not to wander away.

Meanwhile, the sailor carefully observed the character and peculiarities of the region. On this left bank the surface was flat, rising insensibly towards the interior. Sometimes it was moist and swampy, indicating the existence of a subterranean network of little streams emptying themselves into the river. Sometimes, too, a brook ran across the copse, which they crossed without trouble. The opposite bank was more undulating, and the valley, through whose bottom flowed the river, was more clearly defined. The hill, covered with trees rising in terraces, intercepted the vision. Along this right bank they could hardly have walked, for the descent was steep, and the trees which bent over the water were only sustained by their roots. It is needless to say that both forest and shore seemed a virgin wilderness. They saw fresh traces of animals whose species was unknown to them. Some seemed to them the tracks of dangerous wild beasts, but nowhere was there the mark of an axe on a tree-trunk, or the ashes of a fire, or the imprint of a foot. They should no doubt have been glad that it was so, for on this land in the mid-Pacific, the presence of man was a thing more to be dreaded than desired.

They hardly spoke, so great were the difficulties of the route; after an hour's walk they had but just compassed a mile. Hitherto their hunting bad been fruitless. Birds were singing and flying to and fro under the trees; but they showed an instinctive fear of their enemy man. Herbert descried among them, in a swampy part of the forest, a bird with narrow and elongated beak, in shape something like a kingfisher, from which it was distinguished by its harsh and lustrous plumage.

"That must be a jacamar," said Herbert, trying to get within range of the bird.

"It would be a good chance to taste jacamar," answered the sailor, "if that fellow would only let himself be roasted."

In a moment a stone, adroitly aimed by the boy, struck the bird on the wing; but the jacamar took to his legs and disappeared in a minute.

"What a muff I am," said Herbert. 'Not at all," said the sailor. "It was a good shot, a great many would have missed the bird. Don't be discouraged, we'll catch him again some day."

The wood opened as the hunters went on, and the trees grew to a vast height, but none had edible fruits. Pencroff sought in vain for some of those precious palm trees, which lend themselves so wonderfully to the needs of mankind, and which grow from 40° north latitude to 35° south. But this forest was composed only of conifers, such as the deodars, already recognized by Herbert; the Douglas pines, which grow on the northeast coast of America; and magnificent fir trees, 150 feet high. Among their branches was fluttering a flock of birds, with small bodies and long, glittering tails. Herbert picked up some of the feathers, which lay scattered on the ground, and looked at them carefully.

"These are 'couroucous,'" said he.

"I would rather have a guinea-hen, or a heath-cock," said Pencroff, "but still, if they are good to eat"—

"They are good to eat," said Herbert; "their meat is delicious. Besides, I think we can easily get at them with our sticks."

Slipping through the grass, they reached the foot of a tree whose lower branches were covered with the little birds, who were snapping at the flying insects. Their feathered claws clutched tight the twigs on which they were sitting. Then the hunters rose to their feet, and using their sticks like a scythe, they mowed down whole rows of the couroucous, of whom 105 were knocked over before the stupid birds thought of escape.

"Good," said Pencroff, "this is just the sort of game for hunters like us. We could catch them in our hands."

They skewered the couroucous on a switch like field-larks, and continued to explore. The object of the expedition was, of course, to bring back as much game as possible to the Chimneys. So far it had not been altogether attained. They looked about everywhere, and were enraged to see animals escaping through the high grass. If they had only had Top! But Top, most likely, had perished with his master.

About 3 o'clock they entered a wood full of juniper trees, at whose aromatic berries flocks of birds were pecking. Suddenly they heard a sound like the blast of a trumpet. It was the note of those gallinaceæ, called "tetras" in the United States. Soon they saw several pairs of them, with brownish-yellow plumage and brown tails. Pencroff determined to capture one of these birds, for they were as big as hens, and their meat as delicious as a pullet. But they would not let him come near them. At last, after several unsuccessful attempts, he said,

"Well, since we can't kill them on the wing, we must take them with a line."

"Like a carp," cried the wondering Herbert.

"Like a carp," answered the sailor, gravely.

Pencroff had found in the grass half-a-dozen tetras nests, with two or three eggs in each.

He was very careful not to touch these nests, whose owners would certainly return to them. Around these he purposed to draw his lines, not as a snare, but with hook and bait. He took Herbert to some distance from the nests, and there made ready his singular apparatus with the care of a true disciple of Isaac Walton. Herbert watched the work with a natural interest, but without much faith in its success. The lines were made of small lianas tied together, from fifteen to twenty feet long, and stout thorns with bent points, broken from a thicket of dwarf acacias, and fastened to the ends of the lianas, served as hooks, and the great red worms which crawled at their feet made excellent bait. This done, Pencroff, walking stealthily through the grass, placed one end of his hook-and-line close to the nests of the tetras. Then he stole back, took the other end in his hand, and hid himself with Herbert behind a large tree. Herbert, it must be said, was not sanguine of success.

A good half hour passed, but as the sailor had foreseen, several pairs of tetras returned to their nests. They hopped about, pecking the ground, and little suspecting the presence of the hunters, who had taken care to station themselves to leeward of the gallinaceæ. Herbert held his breath with excitement, while Pencroff, with dilated eyes, open month, and lips parted as if to taste a morsel of tetras, scarcely breathed. Meanwhile the gallinaceæ walked heedlessly among the hooks. Pencroff then gave little jerks, which moved the bait up and down as if the worms were still alive. How much more intense was his excitement than the fisherman's who cannot see the approach of his prey!

The jerks soon aroused the attention of the gallinaceæ, who began to peck at the bait. Three of the greediest swallowed hook and bait together. Suddenly, with a quick jerk, Pencroff pulled in his line, and the flapping of wings showed that the birds were taken.

"Hurrah!" cried he, springing upon the game, of which he was master in a moment. Herbert clapped his hands. It was the first time he had seen birds taken with a line; but the modest sailor said it was not his first attempt, and, moreover, that the merit of the invention was not his.

"And at any rate," said he, "in our present situation we must hope for many such contrivances."

The tetras were tied together by the feet, and Pencroff, happy that they were not returning empty handed, and perceiving that the day was ending, thought it best to return home.

Their route was indicated by the river, and following it downward, by 6 o'clock, tired out by their excursion, Herbert and Pencroff re-entered the Chimneys.

CHAPTER VII.

NEB HAS NOT YET RETURNED—THE REFLECTIONS
OF THE REPORTER—THE SUPPER—PROSPECT OF A
BAD NIGHT—THE STORM IS FRIGHTFUL—THEY GO
OUT INTO THE NIGHT—STRUGGLE WITH THE RAIN
AND WIND.

Gideon Spilett stood motionless upon the shore, his arms crossed, gazing on the sea, whose horizon was darkened towards the east by a huge black cloud mounting rapidly into the zenith. The wind, already strong, was freshening, the heavens had an angry look, and the first symptoms of a heavy blow were manifesting themselves.

Herbert went into the Chimneys, and Pencroff walked towards the reporter, who was too absorbed to notice his approach.

"We will have a bad night, Mr. Spilett," said the sailor. "Wind and rain enough for Mother Cary's chickens."

The reporter turning, and perceiving Pencroff, asked this question:—

"How far off from the shore do you think was the basket when it was struck by the sea that carried away our companion?"

The sailor had not expected this question. He reflected an instant before answering:—

"Two cables' lengths or more."

"How much is a cable's length?" demanded Spilett.

"About 120 fathoms, or 600 feet."

"Then," said the reporter, "Cyrus Smith would have disappeared not more than 1,200 feet from the shore?"

"Not more than that."

"And his dog, too?"

"Yes."

"What astonishes me," said the reporter, "admitting that our companion and Top have perished, is the fact that neither the body of the dog nor of his master has been cast upon the shore."

"That is not astonishing with so heavy a sea," replied the sailor. "Moreover, it is quite possible that there are currents which have carried them farther up the coast."

"Then it is really your opinion that our companion has been drowned?" asked, once more, the reporter.

"That is my opinion."

"And my opinion, Pencroff," said Spilett, "with all respect for your experience, is, that in this absolute disappearance of both Cyrus and Top, living or dead, there is something inexplicable and incredible."

"I wish I could think as you do, sir," responded Pencroff, "but, unhappily, I cannot."

After thus speaking the sailor returned to the Chimneys. A good fire was burning in the fireplace. Herbert had just thrown on a fresh armful of wood, and its flames lit up the dark recesses of the corridor.

Pencroff began at once to busy himself about dinner. It seemed expedient to provide something substantial, as all stood in need of nourishment, so two tetras were quickly plucked, spitted upon a stick, and placed to roast before at blazing fire. The couroucous were reserved for the next day.

At 7 o'clock Neb was still absent, and Pencroff began to be alarmed about him. He feared that he might have met with some accident in this unknown land, or that the poor fellow had been drawn by despair to some rash act. Herbert, on the contrary, argued that Neb's absence was owing to some fresh discovery which had induced him to prolong his researches. And anything new must be to Cyrus Smith's advantage. Why had not Neb come back, if some hope was not detaining him? Perhaps he had found some sign or footprint which had put him upon the track. Perhaps, at this moment he was following the trail. Perhaps, already, he was beside his master.

Thus the lad spoke and reasoned, unchecked by his companions. The reporter nodded approval, but Pencroff thought it more probable that Neb, in his search, had pushed on so far that he had not been able to return.

Meantime, Herbert, excited by vague presentiments, manifested a desire to go to meet Neb. But Pencroff showed him that it would be useless in the darkness and storm to attempt to find traces of the negro, and, that the better course was, to wait. If, by morning, Neb had not returned, Pencroff would not hesitate joining the lad in a search for him.

Gideon Spilett concurred with the sailor in his opinion that they had better remain together, and Herbert, though tearfully, gave up the project. The reporter could not help embracing the generous lad.

The storm began. A furious gust of wind passed over the coast from the southeast. They beard the sea, which was out, roaring upon the reef. The whirlwind drove the rain in clouds along the shore. The sand, stirred up by the wind, mingled with the rain, and the air was filled with mineral as well as aqueous dust. Between the mouth of the river and the cliff's face, the wind whirled about as in a maelstrom, and, finding no other outlet than the narrow valley through which ran the stream, it rushed through this with irresistible violence.

Often, too, the smoke from the chimney, driven back down its narrow vent, filled the corridors, and rendered them uninhabitable. Therefore, when the tetras were cooked Pencroff let the fire smoulder, only preserving some clear embers among the ashes.

At 8 o'clock Neb had not returned; but they could not help admitting that now the tempest alone was sufficient to account for his non-appearance, and that, probably, he had sought refuge in some cavern, waiting the end of the storm, or, at least, daybreak. As to going to meet him under present circumstances, that was simply impossible.

The birds were all they had for supper, but the party found them excellent eating. Pencroff and Herbert, their appetite sharpened by their long walk, devoured them. Then each one retired to his corner, and Herbert, lying beside the sailor, extended before the fireplace, was soon asleep.

Outside, as the night advanced, the storm developed formidable proportions. It was a hurricane equal to that which had carried the prisoners from Richmond. Such tempests, pregnant with catastrophes, spreading terror over a vast area, their fury withstood by no obstacle, are frequent during the equinox. We can understand how a coast facing the east, and exposed to the full fury of the storm, was attacked with a violence perfectly indescribable.

Happily the heap of rocks forming the Chimneys was composed of solid, enormous blocks of granite, though some of them, imperfectly balanced, seemed to tremble upon their foundations. Pencroff, placing his hand against the walls, could feel their rapid vibrations; but he said to himself, with reason, that there was no real danger, and that the improvised retreat would not tumble about their ears. Nevertheless, he heard the sound of rocks, torn from the top of the plateau by the gusts, crashing upon the shore. And some, falling perpendicularly, struck the Chimneys and flew off into fragments. Twice the sailor rose, and went to the opening of the corridor, to look abroad. But there was no danger from these inconsiderable showers of stones, and he returned to his place before the fire, where the embers glowed among the ashes.

In spite of the fury and fracas of the tempest Herbert slept profoundly, and, at length, sleep took possession of Pencroff, whose sailor life had accustomed him to such demonstrations. Gideon Spilett, who was kept awake by anxiety, reproached himself for not having accompanied Neb. We have seen that he had not given up all hope, and the presentiments which had disturbed Herbert had affected him also. His thoughts were fixed upon Neb; why had not the negro returned? He tossed about on his sandy couch, unheeding the warfare of the elements. Then, overcome by fatigue, he would close his eyes for an instant, only to be awakened by some sudden thought.

Meantime the night advanced; and it was about 2 o'clock when Pencroff was suddenly aroused from a deep sleep by finding himself vigorously shaken.

"What's the matter?" he cried, rousing and collecting himself with the quickness peculiar to sailors.

The reporter was bending over him and saying:—

"Listen, Pencroff, listen!"

The sailor listened, but could hear no sounds other than those caused by the gusts.

"It is the wind," he said.

"No," answered Spilett, listening again, "I think I heard—"

"What?"

"The barking of a dog!"

"A dog!" cried Pencroff, springing to his feet.

"Yes—the barking—"

"Impossible!" answered the sailor. "How, in the roarings of the tempest—"

"Wait—listen," said the reporter.

Pencroff listened most attentively, and at length, during a lull, he thought he caught the sound of distant barking.

"Is it?" asked the reporter, squeezing the sailor's hand.

"Yes—yes!" said Pencroff.

"It is Top! It is Top!" cried Herbert, who had just wakened, and the three rushed to the entrance of the Chimneys.

They had great difficulty in getting out, as the wind drove against them with fury, but at last they succeeded, and then they were obliged to steady themselves against the rocks. They were unable to speak, but they looked about them. The darkness was absolute. Sea, sky, and earth, were one intense blackness. It seemed as if there was not one particle of light diffused in the atmosphere.

For some moments the reporter and his two companions stood in this place, beset by the gusts, drenched by the rain, blinded by the sand. Then again, in the hush of the storm, they heard, far away, the barking of a dog. This must be Top. But was he alone or accompanied? Probably alone, for if Neb had been with him, the negro would have hastened, at once, to the Chimneys.

The sailor pressed the reporter's hand in a manner signifying that he was to remain without, and then returning to the corridor, emerged a moment later with a lighted fagot, which he threw into the darkness, at the same time whistling shrilly. At this signal, which seemed to have been looked for, the answering barks came nearer, and soon a dog bounded into the corridor, followed by the three companions. An armful of wood was thrown upon the coals, brightly lighting up the passage.

"It is Top!" cried Herbert.

It was indeed Top, a magnificent Anglo-Norman, uniting in the cross of the two breeds those qualities—swiftness of foot and keenness of scent—indispensable in coursing dogs. But he was alone! Neither his master nor Neb accompanied him.

It seemed inexplicable how, through the darkness and storm, the dog's instinct had directed him to the Chimneys, a place he was unacquainted with. But still more unaccountable was the fact that he was neither fatigued nor exhausted nor soiled with mud or sand. Herbert had drawn him towards him, patting his head; and the dog rubbed his neck against the lad's hands.

"If the dog is found, the master will be found also," said the reporter.

"God grant it!" responded Herbert. "Come, let us set out. Top will guide us!"

Pencroff made no objection. He saw that the dog's cunning had disproved his conjectures.

"Let us set out at once," he said; and covering the fire so that it could be relighted on their return, and preceded by the dog, who seemed to invite their departure, the sailor, having gathered up the remnants of the supper, followed by the reporter and Herbert, rushed into the darkness.

The tempest, then in all its violence, was, perhaps, at its maximum intensity. The new moon had not sufficient light to pierce the clouds. It was difficult to follow a straight course. The better way, therefore, was to trust to the instinct of Top; which was done. The reporter and the lad walked behind the dog, and the sailor followed after. To speak was impossible. The rain, dispersed by the wind, was not heavy, but the strength of the storm was terrible.

Fortunately, as it came from the southeast, the wind was at the back of the party, and the sand, hurled from behind, did not prevent their march. Indeed, they were often blown along so rapidly as nearly to be overthrown. But they were sustained by a great hope. This time, at least, they were not wandering at random. They felt, no doubt, that Neb had found his master and had sent the faithful dog to them. But was the engineer living, or had Neb summoned his companions only to render the last services to the dead?

After having passed the smooth face of rock, which they carefully avoided, the party stopped to take breath. The angle of the cliff sheltered them from the wind, and they could breathe freely after this tramp, or rather race, of a quarter of an hour. They were now able to hear themselves speak, and the lad having pronounced the name of Smith, the dog seemed to say by his glad barking that his master was safe.

"Saved! He is saved! Isn't he, Top?" repeated the boy. And the dog barked his answer.

It was half-past 2 when the march was resumed. The sea began to rise, and this, which was a spring tide backed up by the wind, threatened to be very high. The tremendous breakers thundered against the reef, assailing it so violently as probably to pass completely over the islet, which was invisible. The coast was no longer sheltered by this long breakwater, but was exposed to the full fury of the open sea.

After the party were clear of the precipice the storm attacked them again with fury. Crouching, with backs still to the wind, they followed Top, who never hesitated in his course. Mounting towards the north, they had upon their right the endless line of breakers deafening them with its thunders, and upon their left a region buried in darkness. One thing was certain, that they were upon an open plain, as the wind rushed over them without rebounding as it had done from the granite cliffs.

By 4 o'clock they estimated the distance travelled as eight miles. The clouds had risen a little, and the wind was drier and colder. Insufficiently clad, the three companions suffered cruelly, but no murmur passed their lips. They were determined to follow Top wherever he wished to lead them.

Towards 5 o'clock the day began to break. At first, overhead, where some grey shadowings bordered the clouds, and presently, under a dark band a bright streak of light sharply defined the sea horizon. The crests of the billows shone with a yellow light and the foam revealed its whiteness. At the same time, on the left, the hilly parts of the shore were confusedly defined in grey outlines upon the blackness of the night. At 6 o'clock it was daylight. The clouds sped rapidly overhead. The sailor and his companions were some six miles from the Chimneys, following a very flat shore, bordered in the offing by a reef of rocks whose surface only was visible above the high tide. On the left the country sloped up into downs bristling with thistles, giving a forbidding aspect to the vast sandy region. The shore was low, and offered no other resistance to the ocean than an irregular chain of hillocks. Here and there was a tree, leaning its trunks and branches towards the west. Far behind, to the southwest, extended the borders of the forest.

At this moment Top gave unequivocal signs of excitement. He ran ahead, returned, and seemed to try to hurry them on. The dog had left the coast, and guided by his wonderful instinct, without any hesitation had gone among the downs. They followed him through a region absolutely devoid of life.

The border of the downs, itself large, was composed of hills and hillocks, unevenly scattered here and there. It was like a little Switzerland of sand, and nothing but a dog's astonishing instinct could find the way.

Five minutes after leaving the shore the reporter and his companions reached a sort of hollow, formed in the back of a high down, before which Top stopped with a loud bark. The three entered the cave.

Neb was there, kneeling beside a body extended upon a bed of grass—

It was the body of Cyrus Smith.

CHAPTER VIII.

IS CYPRUS SMITH ALIVE?—NEB'S STORY—
FOOTPRINTS—AN INSOLUBLE QUESTION—THE FIRST
WORDS OF SMITH—COMPARING THE FOOTPRINTS—
RETURN TO THE CHIMNEYS—PENCROFF DEJECTED.

Neb did not move. The sailor uttered one word.

"Living!" he cried.

The negro did not answer. Spilett and Pencroff turned pale. Herbert, clasping his hands, stood motionless. But it was evident that the poor negro, overcome by grief, had neither seen his companions nor heard the voice of the sailor.

The reporter knelt down beside the motionless body, and, having opened the clothing, pressed his ear to the chest of the engineer. A minute, which seemed an age, passed, daring which he tried to detect some movement of the heart.

Neb raised up a little, and looked on as if in a trance. Overcome by exhaustion, prostrated by grief, the poor fellow was hardly recognizable. He believed his master dead.

Gideon Spilett, after a long and attentive examination, rose up.

"He lives!" he said.

Pencroff, in his turn, knelt down beside Cyrus Smith; he also detected some heartbeats, and a slight breath issuing from the lips of the engineer. Herbert, at a word from the reporter, hurried in search of water. A hundred paces off he found a clear brook swollen by the late rains and filtered by the sand. But there was nothing, not even a shell, in which to carry the water; so the lad had to content himself with soaking his handkerchief in the stream, and hastened back with it to the cave.

Happily the handkerchief held sufficient for Spilett's purpose, which was simply to moisten the lips of the engineer. The drops of fresh water produced an instantaneous effect. A sigh escaped from the breast of Smith, and it seemed as if he attempted to speak.

"We shall save him," said the reporter. Neb took heart at these words. He removed the clothing from his master to see if his body was anywhere wounded. But neither on his head nor body nor limbs was there a bruise or even a scratch, an astonishing circumstance, since he must have been tossed about among the rocks; even his hands were uninjured, and it was difficult to explain how the engineer should exhibit no mark of the efforts which he must have made in getting over the reef.

But the explanation of this circumstance would come later, when Cyrus Smith could speak. At present, it was necessary to restore his consciousness, and it was probable that this result could be accomplished by friction. For this purpose they mode use of the sailor's pea-jacket. The engineer, warmed by this rude rubbing, moved his arms slightly, and his breathing began to be more regular. He was dying from exhaustion, and, doubtless, had not the reporter and his companions arrived, it would have been all over with Cyrus Smith.

"You thought he was dead?" asked the sailor.

"Yes, I thought so," answered Neb. "And if Top had not found you and brought you back, I would have buried my master and died beside him."

The engineer had had a narrow escape!

Then Neb told them what had happened. The day before, after having left the Chimneys at day-break, he had followed along the coast in a direction due north, until he reached that part of the beach which he had already visited. There, though, as he said, without hope of success, he searched the shore, the rocks, the sand for any marks that could guide him, examining most carefully that part which was above high-water mark, as below that point the ebb and flow of the tide would have effaced all traces. He did not hope to find his master living. It was the discovery of the body which he sought, that he might bury it with his own hands. He searched a long time, without success. It seemed as if nothing human had ever been upon that desolate shore. Of the millions of shell-fish lying out of reach of the tide, not a shell was broken. There was no sign of a landing having ever been made there. The negro then decided to continue some miles further up the coast. It was possible that the currents had carried the body to some distant point. For Neb knew that a corpse, floating a little distance from a low shore, was almost certain, sooner or later, to be thrown upon the strand, and he was desirous to look upon his master one last time.

"I followed the shore two miles further, looking at it at low and high water, hardly hoping to find anything, when yesterday evening, about 5 o'clock, I discovered footprints upon the sand."

"Footprints," cried Pencroff.

"Yes, sir," replied Neb.

"And did they begin at the water?" demanded the reporter.

"No," answered the negro, "above high-water mark; below that the tide had washed out the others."

"Go on, Neb," said Spilett.

"The sight of these footprints made me wild with joy. They wore very plain, and went towards the downs. I followed them for a quarter of an hour, running so as not to tread on them. Five minutes later, as it was growing dark, I heard a dog bark. It was Top. And he brought me here, to my master."

Neb finished his recital by telling of his grief at the discovery of the inanimate body. Ha had tried to discover some signs of life still remaining in it. But all his efforts were in vain. There was nothing, therefore, to do but to perform the last offices to him whom he had loved so well. Then he thought of his companions. They, too, would wish to look once more upon their comrade. Top was there. Could he not rely upon the sagacity of that faithful animal? So having pronounced several times the name of the reporter, who, of all the engineer's companions, was best known by Top, and having at the same time motioned towards the south, the dog bounded off in the direction indicated.

We have seen how, guided by an almost supernatural instinct, the dog had arrived at the Chimneys.

Neb's companions listened to his story with the greatest attention. How the engineer had been able to reach this cave in the midst of the downs, more than a mile from the beach, was as inexplicable as was his escape from the waves and rocks without a scratch.

"So you, Neb," said the reporter, "did not bring your master to this place?"

"No, it was not I," answered Neb.

"He certainly could not have come alone," said Pencroff.

"But he must have done it, though it does not seem credible," said the reporter.

They must wait for the solution of the mystery until the engineer could speak. Fortunately the rubbing had re-established the circulation of the blood, and life was returning. Smith moved his arm again, then his head, and a second time some incoherent words escaped his lips.

Neb, leaning over him, spoke, but the engineer seemed not to hear, and his eyes remained closed. Life was revealing itself by movement, but consciousness had not yet returned. Pencroff had, unfortunately, forgotten to bring the burnt linen, which could have been ignited with a couple of flints, and without it they had no means of making a fire. The pockets of the engineer were empty of everything but his watch. It was therefore the unanimous opinion that Cyrus Smith must be carried to the Chimneys as soon as possible.

Meantime the attention lavished on the engineer restored him to consciousness sooner than could have been hoped. The moistening of his lips had revived him, and Pencroff conceived the idea of mixing some of the juice of the tetras with water. Herbert ran to the shore and brought back two large shells; and the sailor made a mixture which they introduced between the lips of the engineer, who swallowed it with avidity. His eyes opened. Neb and the reporter were leaning over him.

"My master! my master!" cried Neb.

The engineer heard him. He recognized Neb and his companions, and his hand gently pressed theirs.

Again he spoke some words—doubtless the same which he had before uttered, and which indicated that some thoughts were troubling him. This time the words were understood.

"Island or continent?" he murmured.

"What the devil do we care," cried Pencroff, unable to restrain the exclamation, "now that you are alive, sir. Island or continent? "We will find that out later."

The engineer made a motion in the affirmative, and then seemed to sleep.

Taking care not to disturb him, the reporter set to work to provide the most comfortable means of moving him.

Neb, Herbert, and Pencroff left the cave and went towards a high down on which were some gnarled trees. On the way the sailor kept repeating:—

"Island or continent! To think of that, at his last gasp! What a man!"

Having reached the top of the down, Pencroff and his companions tore off the main branches from a tree, a sort of sea pine, sickly and stunted. And with these branches they constructed a litter, which they covered with leaves and grass.

This work occupied some little time, and it was 10 o'clock when the three returned to Smith and Spilett.

The engineer had just wakened from the sleep, or rather stupor, in which they had found him. The color had come back to his lips, which had been as pale as death. He raised himself slightly, and looked about, as if questioning where he was.

"Can you listen to me without being tired, Cyrus?" asked the reporter.

"Yes," responded the engineer.

"I think," said the sailor, "that Mr. Smith can listen better after having taken some more of this tetra jelly,—it is really tetra, sir," he continued, as he gave him some of the mixture, to which he had this time added some of the meat of the bird.

Cyrus Smith swallowed these bits of tetra, and the remainder was eaten by his companions, who were suffering from hunger, and who found the repast light enough.

"Well," said the sailor, "there are victuals waiting for us at the Chimneys, for you must know, Mr. Smith, that to the south of here we have a house with rooms and beds and fire-place, and in the pantry dozens of birds which our Herbert calls couroucous. Your litter is ready, and whenever you feel strong enough we will carry you to our house."

"Thanks, my friend," replied the engineer, "in an hour or two we will go. And now, Spilett, continue."

The reporter related everything that had happened. Recounting the events unknown to Smith; the last plunge of the balloon, the landing upon this unknown shore, its deserted appearance, the discovery of the Chimneys, the search for the engineer, the devotion of Neb, and what they owed to Top's intelligence, etc.

"But," asked Smith, in a feeble voice, "you did not pick me up on the beach?"

"No," replied the reporter.

"And it was not you who brought me to this hollow?"

"No."

"How far is this place from the reef?"

"At least half a mile," replied Pencroff, "and if you are astonished, we are equally surprised to find you here."

"It is indeed singular," said the engineer, who was gradually reviving and taking interest in these details.

"But," asked the sailor, "cannot you remember anything that happened after you were washed away by that heavy sea?"

Cyrus Smith tried to think, but he remembered little. The wave had swept him from the net of the balloon, and at first he had sunk several fathoms. Coming up to the surface, he was conscious, in the half-light, of something struggling beside him. It was Top, who had sprung to his rescue. Looking up, he could see nothing of the balloon, which, lightened by his and the dog's weight, had sped away like an arrow. He found himself in the midst of the tumultuous sea, more than half a mile from shore. He swum vigorously against the waves, and Top sustained him by his garments; but a strong current seized him, carrying him to the north, and, after struggling for half an hour, he sank, dragging the dog with him into the abyss. From that moment to the instant of his finding himself in the arms of his friends, he remembered nothing.

"Nevertheless," said Pencroff, "you must have been cast upon the shore, and had strength enough to walk to this place, since Neb found your tracks."

"Yes, that must be so," answered the engineer, reflectively. "And you have not seen any traces of inhabitants upon the shore?"

"Not a sign," answered the reporter. "Moreover, if by chance some one had rescued you from the waves, why should he then have abandoned you?"

"You are right, my dear Spilett. Tell me, Neb," inquired the engineer, turning towards his servant, "it was not you—you could not have been in a trance—during which—. No, that's absurd. Do any of the footprints still remain?"

"Yes, master," replied Neb; "there are some at the entrance, back of this mound, in a place sheltered from the wind and rain, but the others have been obliterated by the storm."

"Pencroff," said Cyrus, "will you take my shoes and see if they fit those footprints exactly?"

The sailor did as he had been asked. He and Herbert, guided by Neb, went to where the marks were, and in their absence Smith said to the reporter:—

"That is a thing passing belief."

"Inexplicable, indeed," answered the other.

"But do not dwell upon it at present, my dear Spilett, we will talk of it hereafter."

At this moment the others returned. All doubt was set at rest. The shoes of the engineer fitted the tracks exactly. Therefore it must have been Smith himself who had walked over the sand.

"So," he said, "I was the one in a trance, and not Neb! I must have walked like a somnambulist, without consciousness, and Top's instinct brought me here after he rescued me from the waves. Here, Top. Come here, dog."

The splendid animal sprang, barking, to his master, and caresses were lavished upon him. It was agreed that there was no other way to account for the rescue than by giving Top the credit of it.

Towards noon, Pencroff having asked Smith if he felt strong enough to be carried, the latter, for answer, by an effort which showed his strength of will, rose to his feet. But if he had not leaned upon the sailor he would have fallen.

"Capital," said Pencroff. "Summon the engineer's carriage!"

The litter was brought. The cross-branches had been covered with moss and grass; and when Smith was laid upon it they walked towards the coast, Neb and the sailor carrying him.

Eight miles had to be travelled, and as they could move but slowly, and would probably have to make frequent rests, it would take six hours or more to reach the Chimneys. The wind was still strong, but, fortunately, it had ceased raining. From his couch, the engineer, leaning upon his arm, observed the coast, especially the part opposite the sea. He examined it without comment, but undoubtedly the aspect of the country, its contour, its forests and diverse products were noted in his mind. But after two hours, fatigue overcame him, and he slept upon the litter.

At half-past 5 the little party reached the precipice, and soon after, were before the Chimneys. Stopping here, the litter was placed upon the sand without disturbing the slumber of the engineer.

Pencroff saw, to his surprise, that the terrible storm of the day before had altered the aspect of the place. Rocks had been displaced. Great fragments were strewn over the sand, and a thick carpet of several kinds of seaweed covered all the shore. It was plain that the sea sweeping over the isle had reached to the base of the enormous granite curtain.

Before the entrance to the Chimneys the ground had been violently torn up by the action of the waves. Pencroff, seized with a sudden fear, rushed into the corridor. Returning, a moment after, he stood motionless looking at his comrades.

The fire bad been extinguished; the drowned cinders were nothing but mud. The charred linen, which was to serve them for tinder, had gone. The sea had penetrated every recess of the corridor, and everything was overthrown, everything was destroyed within the Chimneys.

CHAPTER IX.

CYRUS IS HERE-PENCROFF'S ATTEMPTS—RUBBING
WOOD—ISLAND OR CONTINENT—THE PLANS OF
THE ENGINEER—WHEREABOUTS IN THE PACIFIC—
IN THE DEPTHS OF THE FOREST—THE PISTACHIO
PINE—A PIG CHASE—A SMOKE OF GOOD OMEN.

In a few words the others were informed of what had happened. This accident, which portended serious results—at least Pencroff foresaw such—affected each one differently. Neb, overjoyed in having recovered his master, did not listen or did not wish to think of what Pencroff said. Herbert shared in a measure the apprehensions of the sailor. As to the reporter, he simply answered:—

"Upon my word, Pencroff, I don't think it matters much!"

"But I tell you again; we have no fire!"

"Pshaw!"

"Nor any means of lighting one!"

"Absurd!"

"But, Mr. Spilett—"

"Is not Cyrus here?" asked the reporter; "Isn't he alive? He will know well enough how to make fire!"

"And with what?"

"With nothing!"

What could Pencroff answer? He had nothing to say, as, in his heart, he shared his companion's confidence in Cyrus Smith's ability. To them the engineer was a microcosm, a compound of all science and all knowledge. They were better off on a desert island with Cyrus than without him in the busiest city of the Union. With him they could want for nothing; with him they would have no fear. If they had been told that a volcanic eruption would overwhelm the land, sinking it into the depths of the Pacific, the imperturbable answer of these brave men would have been, "Have we not Cyrus!"

Meantime, the engineer had sunk into a lethargy, the result of the journey, and his help could not be asked for just then. The supper, therefore, would be very meagre. All the tetras had been eaten, there was no way to cook other birds, and, finally, the couroucous which had been reserved had disappeared. Something, therefore, must be done.

First of all, Cyrus Smith was carried into the main corridor. There they were able to make for him a couch of seaweeds, and, doubtless, the deep sleep in which he was plunged, would strengthen him more than an abundant nourishment.

With night the temperature, which the northwest wind had raised, again became very cold, and, as the sea had washed away the partitions which Pencroff had constructed, draughts of air made the place scarcely habitable. The engineer would therefore have been in a bad plight if his companions had not covered him with clothing which they took from themselves.

The supper this evening consisted of the inevitable lithodomes, an ample supply of which Herbert and Neb had gathered from the beach. To these the lad had added a quantity of edible seaweed which clung to the high rocks and were only washed by the highest tides. These seaweeds, belonging to the family of Fucaceæ, were a species of Sargassum, which, when dry, furnish a gelatinous substance full of nutritive matter, much used by the natives of the Asiatic coast. After having eaten a quantity of lithodomes the reporter and his companions sucked some of the seaweed, which they agreed was excellent.

"Nevertheless," said the sailor, "it is time for Mr. Smith to help us."

Meantime the cold became intense, and, unfortunately, they had no means of protecting themselves. The sailor, much worried, tried every possible means of procuring a fire. He had found some dry moss, and by striking two stones together he obtained sparks; but the moss was not sufficiently inflammable to catch fire, nor had the sparks the strength of those struck by a steel. The operation amounted to nothing. Then Pencroff, although he had no confidence in the result, tried rubbing two pieces of dry wood together, after the manner of the savages. It is true that the motion of the man, if it could have been turned into heat, according to the new theory, would have heated the boiler of a steamer. But it resulted in nothing except putting him in a glow, and making the wood hot. After half an hour's work Pencroff was in a perspiration, and he threw away the wood in disgust.

"When you can make me believe that savages make fire after that fashion," said he, "it will he hot in winter! I might as well try to light my arms by rubbing them together."

But the sailor was wrong to deny the feasibility of this method. The savages frequently do light wood in this way. But it requires particular kinds of wood, and, moreover, the "knack," and Pencroff had not this "knack."

Pencroff's ill humor did not last long. The bits of wood which he had thrown away had been picked up by Herbert, who exerted himself to rub them well. The strong sailor could not help laughing at the boy's weak efforts to accomplish what he had failed in.

"Rub away, my boy; rub hard!" he cried.

"I am rubbing them," answered Herbert, laughing, "but only to take my turn at getting warm, instead of sitting here shivering; and pretty soon I will be as hot as you are, Pencroff!"

This was the case, and though it was necessary for this night to give up trying to make a fire, Spilett, stretching himself upon the sand in one of the passages, repeated for the twentieth time that Smith could not be baffled by such a trifle. The others followed his example, and Top slept at the feet of his master.

The next day, the 28th of March, when the engineer awoke, about 8 o'clock, he saw his companions beside him watching, and, as on the day before, his first words were,

"Island or continent?"

It was his one thought.

"Well, Mr. Smith," answered Pencroff, "we don't know."

"You haven't found out yet?"

"But we will," affirmed Pencroff, "when you are able to guide us in this country."

"I believe that I am able to do that now," answered the engineer, who, without much effort, rose up and stood erect.

"That is good," exclaimed the sailor.

"I am dying of hunger," responded Smith. "Give me some food, my friend, and I will feel better. You've fire, haven't you?"

This question met with no immediate answer. But after some moments the sailor said:—

"No, sir, we have no fire; at least, not now."

And be related what had happened the day before. He amused the engineer by recounting the history of their solitary match, and their fruitless efforts to procure fire like the savages.

"We will think about it," answered the engineer, "and if we cannot find something like tinder—"

"Well," asked the sailor.

"Well, we will make matches!"

"Friction matches?"

"Friction matches!"

"It's no more difficult than that," cried the reporter, slapping the sailor on the shoulder.

The latter did not see that it would be easy, but he said nothing, and all went out of doors. The day was beautiful. A bright sun was rising above the sea horizon, its rays sparkling and glistening on the granite wall. After having cast a quick look about him, the engineer seated himself upon a rock. Herbert offered him some handfuls of mussels and seaweed, saying:—

"It is all that we have, Mr. Smith."

"Thank you, my boy," answered he, "it is enough—for this morning, at least."

And he ate with appetite this scanty meal, washing it down with water brought from the river in a large shell.

His companions looked on without speaking. Then, after having satisfied himself, he crossed his arms and said:—

"Then, my friends, you do not yet know whether we have been thrown upon an island or a continent?"

"No sir," answered Herbert.

"We will find out to-morrow," said the engineer. "Until then there is nothing to do."

"There is one thing," suggested Pencroff.

"What is that?"

"Some fire," replied the sailor, who thought of nothing else.

"We will have it, Pencroff," said Smith. "But when you were carrying me here yesterday, did not I see a mountain rising in the west?"

"Yes," saidSpilett, "quite a high one."

"All right," exclaimed the engineer. "Tomorrow we will climb to its summit and determine whether this is an island or a continent; until then I repeat there is nothing to do."

"But there is; we want fire!" cried the obstinate sailor again.

"Have a little patience, Pencroff, and we will have the fire," said Spilett.

The other looked at the reporter as much as to say, "If there was only you to make it we would never taste roast meat." But he kept silent.

Smith had not spoken. He seemed little concerned about this question of fire. For some moments he remained absorbed in his own thoughts. Then he spoke as follows:—

"My friends, our situation is, doubtless, deplorable, nevertheless it is very simple. Either we are upon a continent, and, in that case, at the expense of greater or less fatigue, we will reach some inhabited place, or else we are on an island. In the latter case, it is one of two things; if the island is inhabited, we will get out of our difficulty by the help of the inhabitants; if it is deserted, we will get out of it by ourselves."

"Nothing could be plainer than that," said Pencroff.

"But," asked Spilett, "whether it is a continent or an island, whereabouts do you think this storm has thrown us, Cyrus?"

"In truth, I cannot say," replied the engineer, "but the probability is that we are somewhere in the Pacific. When we left Richmond the wind was northeast, and its very violence proves that its direction did not vary much. Supposing it unchanged, we crossed North and South Carolina, Georgia, the Gulf of Mexico, and the narrow part of Mexico, and a portion of the Pacific Ocean. I do not estimate the distance traversed by the balloon at less than 6,000 or 7,000 miles, and even if the wind had varied a half a quarter it would have carried us either to the Marquesas Islands or to the Low Archipelago; or, if it was stronger than I suppose, as far as New Zealand. If this last hypothesis is correct, our return home will be easy. English or Maoris, we shall always find somebody with whom to speak. If, on the other hand, this coast belongs to some barren island in the Micronesian Archipelago, perhaps we can reconnoitre it from the summit of this mountain, and then we will consider how to establish ourselves here as if we were never going to leave it."

"Never?" cried the reporter. "Do you say never, my dear Cyrus?"

"It is better to put things in their worst light at first," answered the engineer; "and to reserve those which are better, as a surprise."

"Well said," replied Pencroff. "And we hope that this island, if it is an island, will not be situated just outside of the route of ships; for that would, indeed, be unlucky."

"We will know how to act after having first ascended the mountain," answered Smith.

"But will you be able, Mr. Smith, to make the climb tomorrow?" asked Herbert.

"I hope so," answered the engineer, "if Pencroff and you, my boy, show yourselves to be good and ready hunters."

"Mr. Smith," said the sailor, "since you are speaking of game, if when I come back I am as sure of getting it roasted as I am of bringing it—"

"Bring it, nevertheless," interrupted Smith.

It was now agreed that the engineer and the reporter should spend the day at the Chimneys, in order to examine the shore and the plateau, while Neb, Herbert, and the sailor were to return to the forest, renew the supply of wood, and lay hands on every bird and beast that should cross their path. So, at 6 o'clock, the party left, Herbert confident. Neb happy, and Pencroff muttering to himself:—

"If, when I get back I find a fire in the house, it will have been the lightning that lit it!"

The three climbed the bank, and having reached the turn in the river, the sailor stopped and said to his companions:—

"Shall we begin as hunters or wood-choppers?"

"Hunters," answered Herbert. "See Top, who is already at it."

"Let us hunt, then," replied the sailor, "and on our return here we will lay in our stock of wood."

This said, the party made three clubs for themselves, and followed Top, who was jumping about in the high grass.

This time, the hunters, instead of following the course of the stream, struck at once into the depths of the forests. The trees were for the most part of the pine family. And in certain places, where they stood in small groups, they were of such a size as to indicate that this country was in a higher latitude than the engineer supposed. Some openings, bristling with stumps decayed by the weather, were covered with dead timber which formed an inexhaustible reserve of firewood. Then, the opening passed, the underwood became so thick as to be nearly impenetrable.

To guide oneself among these great trees without any beaten path was very difficult. So the sailor from time to time blazed the route by breaking branches in a manner easily recognizable. But perhaps they would have done better to have followed the water course, as in the first instance, as, after an hour's march, no game had been taken. Top, running under the low boughs, only flashed birds that were unapproachable. Even the couroucou were invisible, and it seemed likely that the sailor would be obliged to return to that swampy place where he had fished for tetras with such good luck.

"Well, Pencroff," said Neb sarcastically, "if this is all the game you promised to carry back to my master it won't take much fire to roast it!"

"Wait a bit, Neb," answered the sailor; "it won't be game that will be wanting on our return."

"Don't you believe in Mr. Smith?"

"Yes."

"But you don't believe be will make a fire?"

"I will believe that when the wood is blazing in the fire-place."

"It will blaze, then, for my master has said so!"

"Well, we'll see!"

Meanwhile the sun had not yet risen to its highest point above the horizon. The exploration went on and was signalized by Herbert's discovery of a tree bearing edible fruit. It was the pistachio pine, which bears an excellent nut, much liked in the temperate regions of America and Europe. These nuts were perfectly ripe, and Herbert showed them to his companions, who feasted on them.

"Well," said Pencroff, "seaweed for bread, raw mussels for meat, and nuts for dessert, that's the sort of dinner for men who haven't a match in their pocket!"

"It's not worth while complaining," replied Herbert.

"I don't complain, my boy. I simply repeat that the meat is a little too scant in this sort of meal."

"Top has seen something!" cried Neb, running toward a thicket into which the dog had disappeared barking. With the dog's barks were mingled singular gruntings. The sailor and Herbert had followed the negro. If it was game, this was not the time to discuss how to cook it, but rather how to secure it.

The hunters, on entering the brush, saw Top struggling with an animal which he held by the ear. This quadruped was a species of pig, about two feet and a half long, of a brownish black color, somewhat lighter under the belly, having harsh and somewhat scanty hair, and its toes at this time strongly grasping the soil seemed joined together by membranes.

Herbert thought that he recognized in this animal a cabiai, or water-hog, one of the largest specimens of the order of rodents. The water-hog did not fight the dog. Its great eyes, deep sank in thick layers of fat, rolled stupidly from side to side. And Neb, grasping his club firmly, was about to knock the beast down, when the latter tore loose from Top, leaving a piece of his ear in the dog's mouth, and uttering a vigorous grunt, rushed against and overset Herbert and disappeared in the wood.

"The beggar!" cried Pencroff, as they all three darted after the hog. But just as they had come up to it again, the water-hog disappeared under the surface of a large pond, overshadowed by tall, ancient pines.

The three companions stopped, motionless. Top had plunged into the water, but the cabiai, hidden at the bottom of the pond, did not appear.

"Wait,", said the boy, "he will have to come to the surface to breathe."

"Won't he drown?" asked Neb.

"No," answered Herbert, "since he is fin-toed and almost amphibious. But watch for him."

Top remained in the water, and Pencroff and his companions took stations upon the bank, to cut off the animal's retreat, while the dog swam to and fro looking for him.

Herbert was not mistaken. In a few minutes the animal came again to the surface. Top was upon him at once, keeping him from diving again, and a moment later, the cabiai, dragged to the shore, was struck down by a blow from Neb's club.

"Hurrah!" cried Pencroff with all his heart. "Nothing but a clear fire, and this gnawer shall be gnawed to the bone."

Pencroff lifted the carcase to his shoulder, and judging by the sun that it must be near 2 o'clock, he gave the signal to return.

Top's instinct was useful to the hunters, as, thanks to that intelligent animal, they were enabled to return upon their steps. In half an hour they had reached the bend of the river. There, as before, Pencroff quickly constructed a raft, although, lacking fire, this seemed to him a useless job, and, with the raft keeping the current, they returned towards the Chimneys. But the sailor had not gone fifty paces when he stopped and gave utterance anew to a tremendous hurrah, and extending his hand towards the angle of the cliff—

"Herbert! Neb! See!" he cried.

Smoke was escaping and curling above the rocks!

CHAPTER X.

THE ENGINEER'S INVENTION—ISLAND OR
CONTINENT?—DEPARTURE FOR THE MOUNTAIN—
THE FOREST—VOLCANIC SOIL—THE TRAGOPANS—
THE MOUFFLONS—THE FIRST PLATEAU—
ENCAMPING FOR THE NIGHT—THE SUMMIT OF
THE CONE.

A few minutes afterwards, the three hunters were seated before a sparkling fire. Beside them sat Cyrus Smith and the reporter. Pencroff looked from one to the other without saying a word, his cabiai in his hand.

"Yes, my good fellow," said the reporter, "a fire, a real fire, that will roast your game to a turn."

"But who lighted it?" said the sailor.

"The sun."

The sailor could not believe his eyes, and was too stupefied to question the engineer.

"Had you a burning-glass, sir?" asked Herbert of Cyrus Smith.

"No, my boy," said he, "but I made one."

And he showed his extemporized lens. It was simply the two glasses, from his own watch and the reporter's, which he had taken out, filled with water, and stuck together at the edges with a little clay. Thus he had made a veritable burning-glass, and by concentrating the solar rays on some dry moss had set it on fire.

The sailor examined the lens; then he looked at the engineer without saying a word, but his face spoke for him. If Smith was not a magician to him, he was certainly more than a man. At last his speech returned, and he said:—

"Put that down, Mr. Spilett, put that down in your book!"

"I have it down," said the reporter.

Then, with the help of Neb, the sailor arranged the spit, and dressed the cabiai for roasting, like a sucking pig, before the sparkling fire, by whose warmth, and by the restoration of the partitions, the Chimneys had been rendered habitable.

The engineer and his companion had made good use of their day. Smith had almost entirely recovered his strength, which he had tested by climbing the plateau above. From thence his eye, accustomed to measure heights and distances, had attentively examined the cone whose summit he proposed to reach on the morrow. The mountain, situated about six miles to the northwest, seemed to him to reach about 3,500 feet above the level of the sea, so that an observer posted at its summit, could command a horizon of fifty miles at least. He hoped, therefore, for an easy solution of the urgent question, "Island or continent?"

They had a pleasant supper, and the meat of the cabiai was proclaimed excellent; the sargassum and pistachio-nuts completed the repast. But the engineer said little; he was planning for the next day. Once or twice Pencroff talked of some project for the future, but Smith shook his head.

"To-morrow," he said, "we will know how we are situated, and we can act accordingly."

After supper, more armfuls of wood were thrown on the fire, and the party lay down to sleep. The morning found them fresh and eager for the expedition which was to settle their fate.

Everything was ready. Enough was left of the cabiai for twenty-four hours' provisions, and they hoped to replenish their stock on the way. They charred a little linen for tinder, as the watch glasses bad been replaced, and flint abounded in this volcanic region.

At half-past 7 they left the Chimneys, each with a stout cudgel. By Pencroff's advice, they took the route of the previous day, which was the shortest way to the mountain. They turned the southern angle, and followed the left bank of the river, leaving it where it bent to the southwest. They took the beaten path under the evergreens, and soon reached the northern border of the forest. The soil, flat and swampy, then dry and sandy, rose by a gradual slope towards the interior. Among the trees appeared a few shy animals, which rapidly took flight before Top. The engineer called his dog back; later, perhaps, they might hunt, but now nothing could distract him from his great object. He observed neither the character of the ground nor its products; he was going straight for the top of the mountain.

At 10 o'clock they were clear of the forest, and they halted for a while to observe the country. The mountain was composed of two cones. The first was truncated about 2,500 feet up, and supported by fantastic spurs, branching out like the talons of an immense claw, laid upon the ground. Between these spurs were narrow valleys, thick set with trees, whose topmost foliage was level with the flat summit of the first cone. On the northeast side of the mountain, vegetation was more scanty, and the ground was seamed here and there, apparently with currents of lava.

On the first cone lay a second, slightly rounded towards the summit. It lay somewhat across the other, like a huge hat cocked over the ear. The surface seemed utterly bare, with reddish rocks often protruding. The object of the expedition was to reach the top of this cone, and their best way was along the edge of the spurs.

"We are in a volcanic country," said Cyrus Smith, as they began to climb, little by little, up the side of the spurs, whose winding summit would most readily bring them out upon the lower plateau. The ground was strewn with traces of igneous convulsion. Here and there lay blocks, debris of basalt, pumice-stone, and obsidian. In isolated clumps rose some few of those conifers, which, some hundreds of feet lower, in the narrow gorges, formed a gigantic thicket, impenetrable to the sun. As they climbed these lower slopes, Herbert called attention to the recent marks of huge paws and hoofs on the ground.

"These brutes will make a fight for their territory," said Pencroff.

"Oh well," said the reporter, who had hunted tigers in India and lions in Africa, "we shall contrive to get rid of them. In the meanwhile, we must be on our guard."

While talking they were gradually ascending. The way was lengthened by detours around the obstacles which could not be directly surmounted. Sometimes, too, deep crevasses yawned across the ascent, and compelled them to return upon their track for a long distance, before they could find an available pathway. At noon, when the little company halted to dine at the foot of a great clump of firs, at whose foot babbled a tiny brook, they were still half way from the first plateau, and could hardly reach it before nightfall. From this point the sea stretched broad beneath their feet; but on the right their vision was arrested by the sharp promontory of the southeast, which left them in doubt whether there was land beyond. On the left they could see directly north for several miles; but the northwest was concealed from them by the crest of a fantastic spur, which formed a massive abutment to the central cone. They could, therefore, make no approach as yet to the solving of the great question.

At 1 o'clock, the ascent was again begun. The easiest route slanted upwards towards the southwest, through the thick copse. There, under the trees, were flying about a number of gallinaceæ of the pheasant family. These were "tragopans," adorned with a sort of fleshy wattles hanging over their necks and with two little cylindrical horns behind their eyes. Of these birds, which were about the size of a hen, the female was invariably brown, while the male was resplendent in a coat of red, with little spots of white. With a well-aimed stone Spilett killed one of the tragopans, which the hungry Pencroff looked at with longing eyes.

Leaving the copse, the climbers, by mounting on each other's shoulders, ascended for a hundred feet up a very steep hill, and reached a terrace, almost bare of trees, whose soil was evidently volcanic. From hence, their course was a zigzag towards the east, for the declivity was so steep that they had to take every point of vantage. Neb and Herbert led the way, then came Smith and the reporter; Pencroff was last. The animals who lived among these heights, and whose traces were not wanting, must have the sure foot and the supple spine of a chamois or an izard. They saw some to whom Pencroff gave a name of his own—"Sheep," he cried.

They all had stopped fifty feet from half-a-dozen large animals, with thick horns curved backwards and flattened at the end, and with woolly fleece, hidden under long silky fawn-colored hair. They were not the common sheep, but a species widely distributed through the mountainous regions of the temperate zone. Their name, according to Herbert, was *Moufflon.*

"Have they legs and chops?" asked the sailor.

"Yes," replied Herbert.

"Then they're sheep," said Pencroff. The animals stood motionless and astonished at their first sight of man. Then, seized with sudden fear, they fled, leaping away among the rocks.

"Good-bye till next time," cried Pencroff to them, in a tone so comical that the others could not forbear laughing.

As the ascension continued, the traces of lava were more frequent, and little sulphur springs intercepted their route. At some points sulphur had been deposited in crystals, in the midst of the sand and whitish cinders of feldspar which generally precede the eruption of lava. As they neared the first plateau, formed by the truncation of the lower cone, the ascent became very difficult. By 4 o'clock the last belt of trees had been passed. Here and there stood a few dwarfed and distorted pines, which had survived the attacks of the furious winds. Fortunately for the engineer and his party, it was a pleasant, mild day; for a high wind, at that altitude of 3,000 feet, would have interfered with them sadly. The sky overhead was extremely bright and clear. A perfect calm reigned around them. The sun was hidden by the upper mountain, which cast its shadow, like a vast screen, westward to the edge of the sea. A thin haze began to appear in the east, colored with all the rays of the solar spectrum.

There were only 500 feet between the explorers and the plateau where they meant to encamp for the night, but these 500 were increased to 2,000 and more by the tortuous route. The ground, so to speak, gave way under their feet. The angle of ascent was often so obtuse that they slipped upon the smooth-worn lava. Little by little the evening set in, and it was almost night when the party, tired out by a seven hours' climb, arrived at the top of the first cone.

Now they must pitch their camp, and think of supper and sleep. The upper terrace of the mountain rose upon a base of rocks, amid which they could soon find a shelter. Firewood was not plenty, yet the moss and dry thistles, so abundant on the plateau, would serve their turn. The sailor built up a fireplace with huge stones, while Neb and Herbert went after the combustibles. They soon came back with a load of thistles; and with flint and steel, the charred linen for tinder, and Neb to blow the fire, a bright blaze was soon sparkling behind the rocks. It was for warmth only, for they kept the pheasant for the next day, and supped off the rest of the cabiai and a few dozen pistachio-nuts.

It was only half-past 6 when the meal was ended. Cyrus Smith resolved to explore, in, the semi-obscurity, the great circular pediment which upheld the topmost cone of the mountain. Before taking rest, he was anxious to know whether the base of the cone could be passed, in case its flanks should prove too steep for ascent. So, regardless of fatigue, he left Pencroff and Neb to make the sleeping arrangements, and Spilett to note down the incidents of the day, and taking Herbert with him, began to walk around the base of the plateau towards the north.

The night was beautiful and still; and not yet very dark. They walked together in silence. Sometimes the plateau was wide and easy, sometimes so encumbered with rubbish that the two could not walk abreast. Finally, after twenty minutes tramp, they were brought to a halt. From this point the slant of the two cones was equal. To walk around the mountain upon an acclivity whose angle was nearly seventy-five degrees was impossible.

But though they had to give up their flank movement, the chance of a direct ascent was suddenly offered to them. Before them opened an immense chasm in the solid rock. It was the mouth of the upper crater, the gullet, so to speak, through which, when the volcano was active, the eruption took place. Inside, hardened lava and scoriæ formed a sort of natural staircase with enormous steps, by which they might possibly reach the summit. Smith saw the opportunity at a glance, and followed by the boy, he walked unhesitatingly into the huge crevasse, in the midst of the gathering darkness.

There were yet 1,000 feet to climb. Could they scale the interior wall of the crater? They would try, at all events. Fortunately, the long and sinuous declivities described a winding staircase, and greatly helped their ascent. The crater was evidently exhausted. Not a puff of smoke, not a glimmer of fire, escaped; not a sound or motion in the dark abyss, reaching down, perhaps, to the centre of the globe. The air within retained no taint of sulphur. The volcano was not only quiet, but extinct.

Evidently the attempt was to succeed. Gradually, as the two mounted the inner walls, they saw the crater grow larger over their heads. The light from the outer sky visibly increased. At each step, so to speak, which they made, new stars entered the field of their vision: The magnificent constellations of the southern sky shone resplendent. In the zenith glittered the splendid Antares of the Scorpion, and not far off that Beta of the Centaur, which is believed to be the nearest star to our terrestrial globe. Then, as the crater opened, appeared Fomalhaut of the Fish, the Triangle, and at last, almost at the Antarctic pole, the glowing Southern Cross.

It was nearly 8 o'clock when they set foot on the summit of the cone. The darkness was by this time complete, and they could hardly see a couple of miles around them. Was the land an island, or the eastern extremity of a continent? They could not yet discover. Towards the west a band of cloud, clearly defined against the horizon, deepened the obscurity, and confounded sea with sky.

But at one point of the horizon suddenly appeared a vague light, which slowly sank as the clouds mounted to the zenith. It was the slender crescent of the moon, just about to disappear. But the line of the horizon was now cloudless, and as the moon touched it, the engineer could see her face mirrored for an instant on a liquid surface. He seized the boy's hand—

"An island!" said he, as the lunar crescent disappeared behind the waves.

CHAPTER XI.

AT THE SUMMIT OF THE CONE—THE INTERIOR
OF THE CRATER—SEA EVERYWHERE—NO LAND
IN SIGHT—A BIRD'S EYE VIEW OF THE COAST—
HYDROGRAPHY AND OROGRAPHY—IS THE ISLAND
INHABITED?—A GEOGRAPHICAL BAPTISM—
LINCOLN ISLAND.

A half hour later they walked back to the camp. The engineer contented himself with saying to his comrades that the country was an island, and that to-morrow they would consider what to do. Then each disposed himself to sleep, and in this basalt cave, 2,500 feet above sea-level, they passed a quiet night in profound repose. The next day, March 30, after a hurried breakfast on roast trajopan, they started out for the summit of the volcano. All desired to see the isle on which perhaps they were to spend their lives, and to ascertain how far it lay from other land, and how near the course of vessels bound for the archipelagoes of the Pacific.

It was about 7 o'clock in the morning when they left the camp. No one seemed dismayed by the situation. They had faith in themselves, no doubt; but the source of that faith was not the same with Smith as with his companions. They trusted in him, he in his ability to extort from the wilderness around them all the necessaries of life. As for Pencroff, he would not have despaired, since the rekindling of the fire by the engineer's lens, if he had found himself upon a barren rock, if only Smith was with him.

"Bah!" said he, "we got out of Richmond without the permission of the authorities, and it will be strange if we can't get away some time from a place where no one wants to keep us!"

They followed the route of the day before, flanking the cone till they reached the enormous crevasse. It was a superb day, and the southern side of the mountain was bathed in sunlight. The crater, as the engineer had supposed, was a huge shaft gradually opening to a height of 1,000 feet above the plateau. From the bottom of the crevasse large currents of lava meandered down the flanks of the mountain, indicating the path of the eruptive matter down to the lower valleys which furrowed the north of the island.

The interior of the crater, which had an inclination of thirty-five or forty degrees, was easily scaled. They saw on the way traces of ancient lava, which had probably gushed from the summit of the cone before the lateral opening had given it a new way of escape. As to the volcano chimney which communicated with the subterranean abyss, its depth could not be estimated by the eye, for it was lost in obscurity; but there seemed no doubt that the volcano was completely extinct. Before 8 o'clock, the party were standing at the summit of the crater, on a conical elevation of the northern side.

"The sea! the sea everywhere!" was the universal exclamation. There it lay, an immense sheet of water around them on every side. Perhaps Smith had hoped that daylight would reveal some neighboring coast or island. But nothing appeared to the horizon-line, a radius of more than fifty miles. Not a sail was in sight. Around the island stretched a desert infinity of ocean.

Silent and motionless, they surveyed every point of the horizon. They strained their eyes to the uttermost limit of the ocean. But even Pencroff, to whom Nature had given a pair of telescopes instead of eyes, and who could have detected land even in the faintest haze upon the sea-line, could see nothing. Then they looked down upon their island, and the silence was broken by Spilett:—

"How large do you think this island is?"

It seemed small enough in the midst of the infinite ocean.

Smith thought awhile, noticed the circumference of the island, and allowed for the elevation.

"My friends," he said, "if I am not mistaken, the coast of the island is more than 100 miles around."

"Then its surface will be—"

"That is hard to estimate; the outline is so irregular."

If Smith was right, the island would be about the size of Malta or Zante in the Mediterranean; but it was more irregular than they, and at the same time had fewer capes, promontories, points, bays, and creeks. Its form was very striking. When Spilett drew it they declared it was like some fantastic sea beast, some monstrous pteropode, asleep on the surface of the Pacific.

The exact configuration of the island may thus be described:—The eastern coast, upon which the castaways had landed, was a decided curve, embracing a large bay, terminating at the southeast in a sharp promontory, which the shape of the land had hidden from Pencroff on his first exploration. On the northeast, two other capes shut in the bay, and between them lay a narrow gulf like the half-open jaws of some formidable dog-fish. From northeast to northwest the coast was round and flat, like the skull of a wild beast; then came a sort of indeterminate hump, whose centre was occupied by the volcanic mountain. From this point the coast ran directly north and south. For two-thirds of its length it was bordered by a narrow creek; then it finished in along cue, like the tail of a gigantic alligator. This cue formed a veritable peninsula, which extended more than thirty miles into the sea, reckoning from the southeastern cape before mentioned. These thirty miles, the southern coast of the island, described an open bay. The narrowest part of the island, between the Chimneys and the creek, on the west, was ten miles wide, but its greatest length, from the jaw in the northeast to the extremity of the southwestern peninsula, was not less than thirty miles.

The general aspect of the interior was as follows:—The southern part, from the shore to the mountain, was covered with woods; the northern part was arid and sandy. Between the volcano and the eastern coast the party were surprised to see a lake, surrounded by evergreens, whose existence they had not suspected. Viewed from such a height it seemed to be on the same level with the sea, but, on reflection, the engineer explained to his companions that it must be at least 300 feet higher, for the plateau on which it lay was as high as that of the coast.

"So, then, it is a fresh water lake?" asked Pencroff.

"Yes," said the engineer, "for it must be fed by the mountain streams."

"I can see a little river flowing into it," said Herbert, pointing to a narrow brook whose source was evidently in the spurs of the western cliff.

"True," said Smith, "and since this brook flows into the lake, there is probably some outlet towards the sea for the overflow. We will see about that when we go back."

This little winding stream and the river so familiar to them were all the watercourses they could see. Nevertheless, it was possible that under those-masses of trees which covered two-thirds of the island, other streams flowed towards the sea. This seemed the more probable from the fertility of the country and its magnificent display of the flora of the temperate zone. In the northern section there was no indication of running water; perhaps there might be stagnant pools in the swampy part of the northeast, but that was all; in the main this region was composed of arid sand-hills and downs, contrasting strongly with the fertility of the larger portion.

The volcano did not occupy the centre of the island. It rose in the northwest, and seemed to indicate the dividing line of the two zones. On the southwest, south, and southeast, the beginnings of the spurs were lost in masses of verdure. To the north, on the contrary, these ramifications were plainly visible, subsiding gradually to the level of the sandy plain.

On this side, too, when the volcano was active, the eruptions had taken place, and a great bed of lava extended as far as the narrow jaw which formed the northeastern gulf.

They remained for an hour at the summit of the mountain. The island lay stretched before them like a plan in relief, with its different tints, green for the forests, yellow for the sands, blue for the water. They understood the configuration of the entire island; only the bottoms of the shady valleys and the depths of the narrow gorges between the spurs of the volcano, concealed by the spreading foliage, escaped their searching eye.

There remained a question of great moment, whose answer would have a controlling influence upon the fortunes of the castaways. Was the island inhabited? It was the reporter who put this question, which seemed already to have been answered in the negative by the minute examination which they had just made of the different portions of the island. Nowhere could they perceive the handiwork of man; no late settlement on the beach, not even a lonely cabin or a fisherman's hut. No smoke, rising on the air, betrayed a human presence. It is true, the observers were thirty miles from the long peninsula which extended to the southwest, and upon which even Pencroff's eye could hardly have discovered a dwelling. Nor could they raise the curtain of foliage which covered three-fourths of the island to see whether some village lay sheltered there. But the natives of these little islands in the Pacific usually live on the coast, and the coast seemed absolutely desert. Until they should make a more complete exploration, they might assume that the island was uninhabited. But was it ever frequented by the inhabitants of neighboring islands? This question was difficult to answer. No land appeared within a radius of fifty miles. But fifty miles could easily be traversed by Malay canoes or by the larger pirogues of the Polynesians. Everything depended upon the situation of the island—on its isolation in the Pacific, or its proximity to the archipelagoes. Could Smith succeed, without his instruments, in determining its latitude and longitude? It would be difficult, and in the uncertainty, they must take precautions against an attack from savage neighbors.

The exploration of the island was finished, its configuration determined, a map of it drawn, its size calculated, and the distribution of its land and water ascertained. The forests and the plains had been roughly sketched upon the reporter's map. They had only now to descend the declivities of the mountain, and to examine into the animal, vegetable, and mineral resources of the country. But before giving the signal of departure, Cyrus Smith, in a calm, grave voice, addressed his companions.

"Look, my friends, upon this little corner of the earth, on which the hand of the Almighty has cast us. Here, perhaps, we may long dwell. Perhaps, too, unexpected help will arrive, should some ship chance to pass. I say *chance*, because this island is of slight importance, without even a harbor for ships. I fear it is situated out of the usual course of vessels, too far south for those which frequent the archipelagoes of the Pacific, too far north for those bound to Australia round Cape Horn. I will not disguise from you our situation."

"And you are right, my dear Cyrus," said the reporter, eagerly. "You are dealing with men. They trust you, and you can count on them. Can he not, my friends?"

"I will obey you in everyting [sic], Mr. Smith," said Herbert, taking the engineer's hand.

"May I lose my name," said the sailor, "if I shirk my part! If you choose, Mr. Smith, we will make a little America here. We will build cities, lay railroads, establish telegraphs, and some day, when the island is transformed and civilized, offer her to the United States. But one thing I should like to ask."

"What Is that?" said the reporter.

"That we should not consider ourselves any longer as castaways, but as colonists."

Cyrus Smith could not help smiling, and the motion was adopted. Then Smith thanked his companions, and added that he counted upon their energy and upon the help of Heaven.

"Well, let's start for the Chimneys," said Pencroff.

"One minute, my friends," answered the engineer; "would it not be well to name the island, as well as the capes, promontories, and water-courses, which we see before us?"

"Good," said the reporter. "That will simplify for the future the instructions which we may have to give or to take."

"Yes," added the sailor, "it will be something gained to be able to say whence we are coming and where we are going. We shall seem to be somewhere."

"At the Chimneys, for instance," said Herbert.

"Exactly," said the sailor. "That name has been quite convenient already, and I was the author of it. Shall we keep that name for our first encampment, Mr. Smith?"

"Yes, Pencroff, since you baptized it so."

"Good! the others will be easy enough," resumed the sailor, who was now in the vein. "Let us give them names like those of the Swiss family Robinson, whose story Herbert has read me more than once:— 'Providence Bay,' 'Cochalot Point,' 'Cape Disappointment.'"

"Or rather Mr. Smith's name, Mr. Spilett's, or Neb's," said Herbert.

"My name!" cried Neb, showing his white teeth.

"Why not?" replied Pencroff, "'Port Neb' would sound first-rate! And 'Cape Gideon'—"

"I would rather have names, taken from our country," said the reporter, "which will recall America to us."

"Yes," said Smith, "the principal features, the bays and seas should be so named. For instance, let us call the great bay to the east Union Bay, the southern indentation Washington Bay, the mountain on which we are standing Mount Franklin, the lake beneath our feet Lake Grant. These names will recall our country and the great citizens who have honored it;

but for the smaller features, let us choose names which will suggest their especial configuration. These will remain in our memory and be more convenient at the same time. The shape of the island is so peculiar that we shall have no trouble in finding appropriate names. The streams, the creeks, and the forest regions yet to be discovered we will baptize as they come. What say you, my friends?"

The engineer's proposal was unanimously applauded. The inland bay unrolled like a map before their eyes, and they had only to name the features of its contour and relief. Spilett would put down the names over the proper places, and the geographical nomenclature of the island would be complete. First, they named the two bays and the mountain as the engineer had suggested.

"Now," said the reporter, "to that peninsula projecting from the southwest I propose to give the name of Serpentine Peninsula, and to call the twisted curve at the termination of it Reptile End, for it is just like a snake's tail."

"Motion carried," said the engineer.

"And the other extremity of the island," said Herbert, "the gulf so like an open pair of jaws, let us call it Shark Gulf."

"Good enough," said Pencroff, "and we may complete the figure by calling the two sides of the gulf Mandible Cape."

"But there are two capes," observed the reporter.

"Well, we will have them North Mandible and South Mandible."

"I've put them down," said Spilett.

"Now we must name the southwestern extremity of the island," said Pencroff.

"You mean the end of Union Bay?" asked. Herbert.

"Claw Cape," suggested Neb, who wished to have his turn as godfather. And he had chosen an excellent name; for this Cape was very like the powerful claw of the fantastic animal to which they had compared the island. Pencroff was enchanted with the turn things were taking, and their active imaginations soon supplied other names. The river which furnished them with fresh water, and near which the balloon had cast them on shore, they called the Mercy, in gratitude to Providence. The islet on which they first set foot, was Safety Island; the plateau at the top of the high granite wall above the Chimneys, from which the whole sweep of the bay was visible, Prospect Plateau; and, finally, that mass of impenetrable woods which covered Serpentine Peninsula, the Forests of the Far West.

The engineer bad approximately determined, by the height and position of the sun, the situation of the island with reference to the cardinal points, and had put Union Bay and Prospect Plateau to the east; but on the morrow, by taking the exact time of the sun's rising and setting, and noting its situation at the time exactly intermediate, he expected to ascertain precisely the northern point of the island; for, on account of its situation on the Southern Hemisphere, the sun at the moment of its culmination would pass to the north, and not to the south, as it does in the Northern Hemisphere.

All was settled, and the colonists were about to descend the mountain, when Pencroff cried:—

"Why, what idiots we are!"

"Why so?" said Spilett, who had gotten up and closed his note-book.

"We have forgotten to baptize our island!"

Herbert was about to propose to give it the name of the engineer, and his companions would have applauded the choice, when Cyrus Smith said quietly:—

"Let us give it the name of a great citizen, my friends, of the defender of American unity! Let us call it Lincoln Island!"

They greeted the proposal with three hurrahs.

CHAPTER XII.

REGULATION OF WATCHES—PENCROFF IS
SATISFIED—A SUSPICIOUS SMOKE—THE COURSE
OF RED CREEK—THE FLORA OF THE ISLAND—
ITS FAUNA—MOUNTAIN PHEASANTS—A KANGAROO
CHASE—THE AGOUTI—LAKE GRANT—RETURN TO
THE CHIMNEYS.

The colonists of Lincoln Island cast a last look about them and walked once around the verge of the crater. Half an hour afterwards they were again upon the lower plateau, at their encampment of the previous night. Pencroff thought it was breakfast time, and so came up the question of regulating the watches of Smith and Spilett. The reporter's chronometer was uninjured by the sea water, as he had been cast high up on the sand beyond the reach of the waves. It was an admirable time-piece, a veritable pocket chronometer, and Spilett had wound it up regularly every day. The engineer's watch, of course, had stopped while he lay upon the downs. He now wound it up, and set it at 9 o'clock, estimating the time approximately by the height of the sun. Spilett was about to do the same, when the engineer stopped him.

"Wait, my dear Spilett," said he. "You have the Richmond time, have you not?"

"Yes."

"Your watch, then, is regulated by the meridian of that city, which is very nearly that of Washington?"

"Certainly."

"Well, keep it so. Wind it up carefully, but do not touch the hands. This may be of use to us."

"What's the use of that?" thought the sailor.

They made such a hearty meal, that little was left of the meat and pistachio-nuts; but Pencroff did not trouble himself about that. Top, who had not been forgotten in the feast, would certainly find some new game in the thicket. Besides, the sailor had made up his mind to ask Smith to make some powder and one or two shot-guns, which, he thought, would be an easy matter.

As they were leaving the plateau, Smith proposed to his companions to take a new road back to the Chimneys. He wished to explore Lake Grant, which lay surrounded so beautifully with trees. They followed the crest of one of the spurs in which the creek which fed the lake probably had its source. The colonists employed in conversation only the proper names which they had just devised, and found that they could express themselves much more easily. Herbert and Pencroff, one of whom was young and the other something of a child, were delighted, and the sailor said as they walked along:—

"Well, Herbert, this is jolly! We can't lose ourselves now, my boy, since, whether we follow Lake Grant or get to the Mercy through the woods of the Far West, we must come to Prospect Plateau, and so to Union Bay."

It had been agreed that, without marching in a squad, the colonists should not keep too far apart. Dangerous wild beasts surely inhabited the forest recesses, and they must be on their guard. Usually Pencroff, Herbert, and Neb walked in front, preceded by Top, who poked his nose into every corner. The reporter and engineer walked together, the former ready to note down every incident, the latter seldom speaking, and turning aside only to pick up sometimes one thing, sometimes another, vegetable or mineral, which he put in his pocket without saying a word.

"What, the mischief, is he picking up?" muttered Pencroff. "There's no use in looking; I see nothing worth the trouble of stooping for."

About 10 o'clock the little company descended the last declivities of Mount Franklin. A few bushes and trees were scattered over the ground. They were walking on a yellowish, calcined soil, forming a plain about a mile long, which extended to the border of the wood. Large fragments of that basalt which, according to Bischof's theory, has taken 350,000,000 years to cool, strewed the uneven surface of the plain. Yet there was no trace of lava, which had especially found an exit down the northern declivities. Smith thought they should soon reach the creek, which he expected to find flowing under the trees by the plain, when he saw Herbert running back, and Neb and the sailor hiding themselves behind the rocks.

"What's the matter, my boy?" said Spilett.

"Smoke," answered Herbert. "We saw smoke ascending from among the rocks, a hundred steps in front."

"Men in this region!" cried the reporter.

"We must not show ourselves till we know with whom we have to deal," answered Smith. "I have more fear than hope of the natives, if there are any such on the island. Where is Top?"

"Top is on ahead."

"And has not barked?"

"No."

"That is strange. Still, let us try to call him back."

In a few moments the three had rejoined their companions, and had hidden themselves, like Neb and Pencroff, behind the basalt rubbish. Thence they saw, very evidently, a yellowish smoke curling into the air. Top was recalled by a low whistle from his master, who motioned to his comrades to wait, and stole forward under cover of the rocks. In perfect stillness the party awaited the result, when a call from Smith summoned them forward. In a moment they were by his side, and were struck at once by the disagreeable smell which pervaded the atmosphere. This odor, unmistakable as it was, had been sufficient to reassure the engineer.

"Nature is responsible for that fire," he said, "or rather for that smoke. It is nothing but a sulphur spring, which will be good for our sore throats."

"Good!" said Pencroff; "what a pity I have not a cold!"

The colonists walked towards the smoke. There they beheld a spring of sulphate of soda, which flowed in currents among the rocks, and whose waters, absorbing the oxygen of the air, gave off a lively odor of sulpho-hydric acid. Smith dipped his hand into the spring and found it oily. He tasted it, and perceived a sweetish savor. Its temperature he estimated at 95° Fahrenheit; and when Herbert asked him on what he based his estimate:—

"Simply, my boy," said he, "because when I put my hand into this water, I have no sensation either of heat or of cold. Therefore, it is at the same temperature as the human body, that is, about 95°."

Then as the spring of sulphur could be put to no present use, the colonists walked towards the thick border of the forest, a few hundred paces distant. There, as they had thought, the brook rolled its bright limpid waters between high, reddish banks, whose color betrayed the presence of oxide of iron. On account of this color, they instantly named the water course Red Creek. It was nothing but a large mountain brook, deep and clear, here, flowing quietly over the lands, there, gurgling amid rocks, or falling in a cascade, but always flowing towards the lake. It was a mile and a half long; its breadth varied from thirty to forty feet. Its water was fresh, which argued that those of the lake would be found the same—a fortunate occurrence, in case they should find upon its banks a more comfortable dwelling than the Chimneys.

The trees which, a few hundred paces down stream overshadowed the banks of the creek, belonged principally to the species which abound in the temperate zone of Australia or of Tasmania, and belong to those conifers which clothed the portion of the island already explored, some miles around Prospect Plateau. It was now the beginning of April, a month which corresponds in that hemisphere to our October, yet their leaves had not begun to fall. They were, especially, casuarinæ and eucalypti, some of which, in the ensuing spring, would furnish a sweetish manna like that of the East. Clumps of Australian cedars rose in the glades, covered high with that sort of moss which the New-Hollanders call *tussocks*; but the cocoa-palm, so abundant in the archipelagoes of the Pacific, was conspicuous by its absence. Probably the latitude of the island was too low.

"What a pity!" said Herbert, "such a useful tree and such splendid nuts!"

There were flocks of birds on the thin boughs of the eucalypti and the casuarinæ, which gave fine play to their wings. Black, white, and grey cockatoos, parrots and parroquets of all colors, king-birds, birds of paradise, of brilliant green, with a crowd of red, and blue lories, glowing with every prismatic color, flew about with deafening clamors. All at once, a strange volley of discordant sounds seemed to come from the thicket. The colonists heard, one after another, the song of birds, the cries of four-footed beasts, and a sort of clucking sound strangely human. Neb and Herbert rushed towards the thicket, forgetting the most elementary rules of prudence. Happily, there was neither formidable wild beast nor savage native, but merely half-a-dozen of those mocking birds which they recognized as "mountain pheasants." A few skillfully aimed blows with a stick brought this parody to an end, and gave them excellent game for dinner that evening. Herbert also pointed out superb pigeons with bronze-colored wings, some with a magnificent crest, others clad in green, like their congeners at Port-Macquarie; but like the troops of crows and magpies which flew about, they were beyond reach. A load of small-shot would have killed hosts of them; but the colonists had nothing but stones and sticks, very insufficient weapons. They proved even more inadequate when a troop of quadrupeds leaped away through the underbrush with tremendous bounds thirty feet long, so that they almost seemed to spring from tree to tree, like squirrels.

"Kangaroos!" cried Herbert.

"Can you eat them?" said Pencroff.

"They make a delicious stew," said the reporter.

The words had hardly escaped his lips, when the sailor, with Neb and Herbert at his heels, rushed after the kangaroos. Smith tried in vain to recall them, but equally in vain did they pursue the game, whose elastic leaps left them far behind. After five minutes' chase, they gave it up, out of breath.

"You see, Mr. Smith," said Pencroff, "that guns are a necessity. Will it be possible to make them?"

"Perhaps," replied the engineer; "but we will begin by making bows and arrows, and you will soon use them as skilfully as the Australian hunters."

"Bows and arrows!" said Pencroff, with a contemptuous look. "They are for children!"

"Don't be so proud, my friend," said the reporter. "Bows and arrows were sufficient for many centuries for the warfare of mankind. Powder is an invention of yesterday, while war, unhappily, is as old as the race."

"That's true, Mr. Spilett," said the sailor. "I always speak before I think. Forgive me."

Meanwhile Herbert, with his Natural History always uppermost in his thoughts, returned to the subject of kangaroos.

"Those which escaped us," he said, "belong to the species most difficult to capture—very large, with long grey hair, but I am sure there are black and red kangaroos, rock-kangaroos, kangaroo-rats—"

"Herbert," said the sailor, "for me there is only one kind—the 'kangaroo-on-the-spit'—and that is just what we haven't got."

They could not help laughing at Professor Pencroff's new classification. He was much cast down at the prospect of dining on mountain-phesants; but chance was once more kind to him. Top, who felt his dinner at stake, rushed hither and thither, his instinct quickened by sharp appetite. In fact, he would have left very little of what he might catch or any one else, had not Neb watched him shrewdly. About 3 o'clock he disappeared into the rushes, from which came grunts and growls which indicated a deadly tustle. Neb rushed in, and found Top greedily devouring an animal, which in ten seconds more would have totally disappeared. But the dog had luckily fallen on a litter, and two more rodents—for to this species did the beasts belong—lay strangled on the ground. Neb reappeared in triumph with a rodent in each hand. They had yellow hair, with patches of green, and the rudiments of a tail. They were a sort of agouti, a little larger than their tropical congeners, true American hares, with long ears and five molar teeth on either side.

"Hurrah!" cried Pencroff, "the roast is here; now we can go back to the house."

The journey was resumed. Red Creek still rolled its limped waters under the arching boughs of casuarence, bankseas and gigantic gum trees. Superb liliaceæ rose, to a height of twenty feet, and other arborescent trees of species unknown to the young naturalist, bent over the brook, which murmered gently beneath its leafy cradle. It widened sensibly, nevertheless, and the mouth was evidently near. As the party emerged from a massive thicket of fine trees, the lake suddenly appeared before them.

They were now on its left bank, and a picturesque region opened to their view. The smooth sheet of water, about seven miles in circumference and 250 acres in extent, lay sleeping among the trees. Towards the east, across the intermittent screen of verdure, appeared a shining horizon of sea. To the north the curve of the lake was concave, contrasting with the sharp outline of its lower extremity. Numerous aquatic birds frequented the banks of this little Ontario, in which the "Thousand Isles" of its American original were represented by a rock emerging from its surface some hundreds of feet from the southern bank. There lived in harmony several couples of kingfishers, perched upon rocks, grave and motionless, watching for fish; then they would plunge into the water and dive with a shrill cry, reappearing with the prey in their beaks. Upon the banks of the lake and the island were constantly strutting wild ducks, pelicans, water-hens and red-beaks. The waters of the lake were fresh and limpid, somewhat dark, and from the concentric circles on its surface, were evidently full of fish.

"How beautiful this lake is!" said Spilett. "We could live on its banks."

"We will live there!" answered Smith.

The colonists, desiring to get back to the Chimneys by the shortest route, went down towards the angle formed at the south by the junction of the banks. They broke a path with much labor through the thickets and brush wood, hitherto untouched by the hand of man, and walked towards the seashore, so as to strike it to the north of Prospect Plateau. After a two miles' walk they came upon the thick turf of the plateau, and saw before them the infinite ocean.

To get back to the Chimneys they had to walk across the plateau for a mile to the elbow formed by the first bend of the Mercy. But the engineer was anxious to know how and where the overflow of the lake escaped. It was probable that a river existed somewhere pouring through a gorge in the granite. In fine, the lake was an immense receptacle gradually filled at the expense of the creek, and its overflow must somehow find a way down to the sea. Why should they not utilize this wasted store of water-power? So they walked up the plateau, following the banks of Lake Grant, but after a tramp of a mile, they could find no outlet.

It was now half-past 4, and dinner had yet to be prepared. The party returned upon its track, and reached the Chimneys by the left bank of the Mercy. Then the fire was lighted, and Neb and Pencroff, on whom devolved the cooking, in their respective characters of negro and sailor, skilfully broiled the agouti, to which the hungry explorers did great honor. When the meal was over, and just as they were settling themselves to sleep, Smith drew from his pocket little specimens of various kinds of minerals, and said quietly,

"My friends, this is iron ore, this pyrites, this clay, this limestone, this charcoal. Nature gives us these as her part in the common task. To-morrow we must do our share!"

CHAPTER XIII.

TOP'S CONTRIBUTION—MAKING BOWS AND ARROWS—A BRICK-KILN—A POTTERY—DIFFERENT COOKING UTENSILS—THE FIRST BOILED MEAT—MUGWORT—THE SOUTHERN CROSS—AN IMPORTANT ASTRONOMICAL OBSERVATION.

"Now then, Mr. Smith, where shall we begin?" asked Pencroff the next morning.

"At the beginning," answered the engineer.

And this, indeed, was necessary, as the colonists did not even possess implements with which to make implements. Neither were they in that condition of nature which "having time," economizes effort; the necessities of life must be provided for at once, and, if profiting by experience they had nothing to invent, at least they had everything to make. Their iron and steel was in the ore, their pottery was in the clay, their linen and clothes were still to be provided.

It must be remembered, however, that these colonists were *men*, in the best sense of the word. The engineer Smith could not have been aided by comrades more intelligent, or more devoted and zealous. He had questioned them, and knew their ability.

The reporter, having learned everything so as to be able to speak of everything, would contribute largely from his knowledge and skill towards the settlement of the island. He would not shirk work; and, a thorough sportsman, he would follow as a business what he had formerly indulged in as a pastime. Herbert, a manly lad, already well versed in natural science, would contribute his share to the common cause. Neb was devotion personified. Adroit, intelligent, indefatigable, robust, of iron constitution, knowing something of the work in a smithy, his assistance would be considerable. As to Pencroff, he had sailed every sea, had been a carpenter in the Brooklyn yards, an assistant tailor on board ship, and, during hie leaves of absence, a gardener, farmer, etc.; in short, like every sailor, he was a Jack-of-all-trades.

Indeed, it would have been hard to bring together five men, more able to struggle against fate, and more certain to triumph in the end.

"At the beginning," Smith had said. And this beginning was the construction of an apparatus which would serve to transform the natural substances. Every one knows what an important part heat plays in these transformations. Therefore, as wood and coal were already provided it was only necessary to make an oven to utilize them.

"What good is an oven," asked Pencroff.

"To make the pottery that we want," replied Smith.

"And how will we make an oven?"

"With bricks."

"And how will we make the bricks?"

"With the clay. Come, friends. We will set up our factory at the place of production, so as to avoid carriage. Neb will bring the provisions, and we shall not lack fire to cook food."

"No," replied the reporter, "but suppose we lack food, since we have no hunting implements?"

"If we only had a knife!" cried the sailor,

"What, then?" asked Smith.

"Why, I would make a bow and arrows. And game would be plenty in the larder."

"A knife. Something that will cut," said the engineer, as if talking to himself.

Suddenly his face brightened:

"Come here, Top," he called.

The dog bounded to his master, and Smith having taken off the collar which the animal had around his neck, broke it into halves, saying:—

"Here are two knives, Pencroff."

For all response, the sailor gave a couple of cheers. Top's collar was made from a thin piece of tempered steel. All that was therefore necessary was to rub it to an edge upon a sand-stone, and then to sharpen it upon one of finer grain. These kind of stones were readily procurable upon the beach, and in a couple of hours the implements of the colony consisted of two strong blades, which it was easy to fasten into solid handles. The overcoming of this first difficulty was greeted as a triumph and it was indeed a fortunate event.

On setting out, it was the intention of the engineer to return to the western bank of the lake, where he had noticed the clay, of which he had secured a specimen. Following the bank of the Mercy they crossed Prospect Plateau, and after a walk of about five miles, they arrived at a glade some 200 paces distant from Lake Grant.

On the way, Herbert had discovered a tree from which the South American Indians make bows. It was the "crejimba," of the palm family. From it they cut long straight branches, which they peeled and shaped into bows. For cords they took the fibres of the "hibiscus heterophyltus" (Indian hemp), a malvaceous plant, the fibres of which are as strong as the tendons of an animal. Pencroff, having thus provided bows, only needed arrows. Those were easily made from straight, stiff branches, free from knots, but it was not so easy to arm them with a substitute for iron. But Pencroff said that he had accomplished this much, and that chance would do the rest.

The party had reached the place discovered the day before. The ground was composed of that clay which is used in making bricks and tiles, and was therefore just the thing for their purpose. The labor was not difficult. It was only necessary to scour the clay with sand, mould the bricks, and then bake them before a wood fire.

Usually, bricks are pressed in moulds, but the engineer contented himself with making these by hand. All this day and the next was employed in this work. The clay, soaked in water, was kneaded by the hands and feet of the manipulators, and then divided into blocks of equal size. A skilled workman can make, without machinery, as many as 10,000 bricks in twelve hours; but in the two days the brickmakers of Lincoln Island had made but 3,000, which were piled one upon the other to await the time when they would be dry enough to bake, which would be in three or four days.

On the 2d of April, Smith occupied himself in determining the position of the island.

The day before he had noted the precise minute at which the sun had set, allowing for the refraction. On this morning, he ascertained with equal precision the time of its rising. The intervening time was twelve hours and twenty-four minutes. Therefore six hours and twelve minutes after rising the sun would pass the meridian, and the point in the sky which it would occupy at that instant would be north.

At the proper hour Smith marked this point, and by getting two trees in line obtained a meridian for his future operations.

During the two days preceding the baking they occupied themselves by laying in a supply of firewood. Branches were cut from the edge of the clearing, and all the dead wood under the trees was picked up. And now and then they hunted in the neighborhood, the more successfully, as Pencroff had some dozens of arrows with very sharp points. It was Top who had provided these points by bringing in a porcupine, poor game enough, but of an undeniable value, thanks to the quills with which it bristled. These quills were firmly fastened to the ends of the arrows, and their flight was guided by feathering them with the cockatoo's feathers. The reporter and Herbert soon became expert marksmen, and all kinds of game, such as cabiais, pigeons, agoutis, heath-cock, etc., abounded at the Chimneys. Most of these were killed in that part of the forest upon the left bank of the Mercy, which they had called Jacamar Wood, after the kingfisher which Pencroff and Herbert had pursued there during their first exploration.

The meat was eaten fresh, but they preserved the hams of the cabiai by smoking them before a fire of green wood, having made them aromatic with odorous leaves. Thus, they had nothing but roast after roast, and they would have been glad to have heard a pot singing upon the hearth; but first they must have the pot, and for this they must have the oven.

During these excursions, the hunters noticed the recent tracks of large animals, armed with strong claws, but they could not tell their species; and Smith cautioned them to be prudent, as, doubtless, there were dangerous beasts in the forest.

He was right. For one day Spilett and Herbert saw an animal resembling a jaguar. But, fortunately, the beast did not attack them, as they could hardly have killed it without being themselves wounded. But, Spilett promised, if he should ever obtain a proper weapon, such as one of the guns Pencroff begged for, that he would wage relentless war on all ferocious beasts and rid the island of their presence.

They did not do anything to the Chimneys, as the engineer hoped to discover, or to build, if need be, a more convenient habitation, but contented themselves by spreading fresh quantities of moss and dry leaves upon the sand in the corridors, and upon these primitive beds the tired workmen slept soundly. They also reckoned the days already passed on Lincoln Island, and began keeping a calendar. On the 5th of April, which was a Wednesday, they had been twelve days upon the island.

On the morning of the 6th, the engineer with his companions met at the place where the bricks were to be baked. Of course the operation was to be conducted in the open air, and not in an oven, or, rather, the pile of bricks would in itself form a bake-oven. Carefully-prepared faggots were laid upon the ground, surrounding the tiers of dry bricks, which formed a great cube, in which air-holes had been left. The work occupied the whole day, and it was not until evening that they lit the fire, which all night long they kept supplied with fuel.

The work lasted forty-eight hours, and succeeded perfectly. Then, as it was necessary to let the smoking mass cool, Neb and Pencroff, directed by Mr. Smith, brought, on a hurdle made of branches, numerous loads of limestone which they found scattered in abundance to the north of the lake. These stones, decomposed by heat, furnished a thick quick-lime, which increased in bulk by slacking, and was fully as pure as if it had been produced by the calcination of chalk or marble. Mixed with sand in order to diminish its shrinkage while drying, this lime made an excellent mortar.

By the 9th of April the engineer had at his disposal a quantity of lime, all prepared, and some thousands of bricks. They, therefore, began at once the construction of an oven, in which to bake their pottery. This was accomplished without much difficulty; and, five days later, the oven was supplied with coal from the open vein, which the engineer had discovered near the mouth of Red Creek, and the first smoke escaped from a chimney twenty feet high. The glade was transformed into a manufactory, and Pencroff was ready to believe that all the products of modern industry would be produced from this oven.

Meantime the colonists made a mixture of the clay with lime and quartz, forming pipe-clay, from which they moulded pots and mugs, plates and jars, tubs to hold water, and cooking vessels. Their form was rude and defective, but after they had been baked at a high temperature, the kitchen of the Chimneys found itself provided with utensils as precious as if they were composed of the finest kaolin.

We must add that Pencroff, desirous of knowing whether this material deserved its name of pipe-clay, made some large pipes, which he would have found perfect, but for the want of tobacco. And, indeed, this was a great privation to the sailor.

"But the tobacco will come like everything else," he would say in his hopeful moments.

The work lasted until the 15th of April, and the time was well spent. The colonists having become potters, made nothing but pottery. When it would suit the engineer to make them smiths they would be smiths. But as the morrow would be Sunday, and moreover Easter Sunday, all agreed to observe the day by rest. These Americans were religious men, scrupulous observers of the precepts of the Bible, and their situation could only develop their trust in the Author of all things.

On the evening of the 15th they returned permanently to the Chimneys, bringing the rest of the pottery back with them, and putting out the oven fire until there should be use for it again. This return was marked by the fortunate discovery by the engineer of a substance that would answer for tinder, which, we know, is the spongy, velvety pulp of a mushroom of the polypore family. Properly prepared it is extremely inflammable, especially when previously saturated with gunpowder, or nitrate or chlorate of potash. But until then they had found no polypores, nor any fungi that would answer instead. Now, the engineer, having found a certain plant belonging to the mugwort family, to which belong wormwood, mint, etc., broke off some tufts, and, handing them to the sailor, said:—

"Here, Pencroff, is something for you."

Pencroff examined the plant, with its long silky threads and leaves covered with a cotton-like down.

"What is it, Mr. Smith?" he asked. "Ah, I know! It's tobacco!"

"No," answered Smith; "it is Artemesia wormwood, known to science as Chinese mugwort, but to us it will be tinder."

This mugwort, properly dried, furnished a very inflammable substance, especially after the engineer had impregnated it with nitrate of potash, which is the same as saltpetre, a mineral very plenty on the island.

This evening the colonists, seated in the central chamber, supped with comfort. Neb had prepared some agouti soup, a spiced ham, and the boiled corms of the "caladium macrorhizum," an herbaceous plant of the arad family, which under the tropics takes a tree form. These corms, which are very nutritious, had an excellent flavor, something like that of Portland sago, and measurably supplied the place of bread, which the colonists were still without.

Supper finished, before going to sleep the party took a stroll upon the beach. It was 8 o'clock, and the night was magnificent. The moon, which had been full five days before, was about rising, and in the zenith, shining resplendent above the circumpolar constellations, rode the Southern Cross. For some moments the engineer gazed at it attentively. At its summit and base were two stars of the first magnitude, and on the left arm and the right, stars, respectively, of the second magnitude and the third. Then, after some reflection, he said:—

"Herbert, is not to-day the 15th of April?"

"Yes, sir," answered the lad.

"Then, if I am not mistaken, to-morrow will be one of the four days in the year when the mean and real time are the same; that is to say, my boy, that to-morrow, within some seconds of noon by the clocks, the sun will pass the meridian. If, therefore, the weather is clear, I think I will be able to obtain the longitude of the island within a few degrees."

"Without a sextant or instruments?" asked Spilett.

"Yes," replied the engineer. And since it is so clear, I will try to-night to find our latitude by calculating the height of the Cross, that is, of the Southern Pole, above the horizon. You see, my friends, before settling down, it will not do to be content with determining this land to be an island; we must find out its locality."

"Indeed, instead of building a house, it will be better to build a ship, if we are within a hundred miles of an inhabited land."

"That is why I am now going to try to get the latitude of the place, and to-morrow noon to calculate the longitude."

If the engineer had possessed a sextant, the work would have been easy, as this evening, by taking the height of the pole, and to-morrow by the sun's passage of the meridian, he would have the co-ordinates of the island. But, having no instruments he must devise something. So returning to the Chimneys, he made, by the light of the fire, two little flat sticks which he fastened together with a thorn, in a way that they could be opened and shut like compasses, and returned with them to the beach. But as the sea horizon was hidden from this point by Claw Cape, the engineer determined to make his observation from Prospect Plateau, leaving, until the next day, the computation of the height of the latter, which could easily be done by elementary geometry.

The colonists, therefore, went to the edge of the plateau which faced the southeast, overlooking the fantastic rocks bordering the shore. The place rose some fifty feet above the right bank of the Mercy, which descended, by a double slope, to the end of Claw Cape and to the southern boundary of the island. Nothing obstructed the vision, which extended over half the horizon from the Cape to Reptile Promontory. To the south, this horizon, lit by the first rays of the moon, was sharply defined against the sky. The Cross was at this time reversed, the star Alpha being nearest the pole. This constellation is not situated as near to the southern as the polar star is to the northern pole; Alpha is about 27° from it, but Smith knew this and could calculate accordingly. He took care also to observe it at the instant when it passed the meridian under the pole, thus simplifying the operation.

The engineer opened the arms of his compass so that one pointed to the horizon and the other to the star, and thus obtained the angle of distance which separated them. And in order to fix this distance immovably, he fastened these arms, respectively, by means of thorns, to a cross piece of wood. This done, it was only necessary to calculate the angle obtained, bringing the observation to the level of the sea so as to allow for the depression of the horizon caused by the height of the plateau. The measurement of this angle would thus give the height of Alpha, or the pole, above the horizon; or, since the latitude of a point on the globe is always equal to the height of the pole above the horizon at that point, the latitude of the island.

This calculation was postponed until the next day, and by 10 o'clock everybody slept profoundly.

CHAPTER XIV.

THE MEASURE OF THE GRANITE WALL—
AN APPLICATION OF THE THEOREM OF SIMILAR
TRIANGLES—THE LATITUDE OF THE ISLAND—
AN EXCURSION TO THE NORTH—AN OYSTER-BED—
PLANS FOR THE FUTURE—THE SUN'S PASSAGE
OF THE MERIDIAN—THE CO-ORDINATES OF
LINCOLN ISLAND.

At daybreak the next day, Easter Sunday, the colonists left the Chimneys and went to wash their linen and clean their clothing. The engineer intended to make some soap as soon as he could obtain some soda or potash and grease or oil. The important question of renewing their wardrobes would be considered in due time. At present they were strong, and able to stand hard wear for at least six months longer. But everything depended on the situation of the island as regarded inhabited countries, and that would be determined this day, providing the weather permitted.

The sun rising above the horizon, ushered in one of those glorious days which seem like the farewell of summer. The first thing to be done was to measure the height of Prospect Plateau above the sea.

"Do you not need another pair of compasses?" asked Herbert, of the engineer.

"No, my boy," responded the latter, "this time we will try another and nearly as precise a method."

Pencroff, Neb, and the reporter were busy at other things; but Herbert, who desired to learn, followed the engineer, who proceeded along the beach to the base of the granite wall.

Smith was provided with a pole twelve feet long, carefully measured off from his own height, which he knew to a hair. Herbert carried a plumb-line made from a flexible fibre tied to a stone. Having reached a point 20 feet from the shore and 500 feet from the perpendicular granite wall, Smith sunk the pole two feet in the sand, and, steadying it carefully, proceeded to make it plumb with the horizon. Then, moving back to a spot where, stretched upon the sand, he could sight over the top of the pole to the edge of the cliff, bringing the two points in line, he carefully marked this place with a stone. Then addressing Herbert,

"Do you know the first principles of geometry?" said he.

"Slightly, sir," answered Herbert, not wishing to seem forward.

"Then you remember the relation of similar triangles?"

"Yes, sir," answered Herbert. "Their like sides are proportional."

"Right, my boy. And I have just constructed two similar right angled triangles:—the smaller has for its sides the perpendicular pole and the distances from its base and top to the stake; the second has the wall which we are about to measure, and the distances from its base and summit to the stake, which are only the prolongation of the base and hypothenuse of the first triangle.

"I understand," cried Herbert. "As the distance from the stake to the pole is proportional to the distance from the stake to the base of the wall, so the height of the wall is proportional to the height of the rod."

"Exactly," replied the engineer, "and after measuring the first two distances, as we know the height of the pole, we have only to calculate the proportion in order to find the height of the wall."

The measurements were made with the pole and resulted in determining the distances from the stake to the foot of the pole and the base of the wall to be 15 and 500 feet respectively. The engineer and Herbert then returned to the Chimneys, where the former, using a flat stone and a bit of shell to figure with, determined the height of the wall to be 333.33 feet.

Then taking the compasses, and carefully measuring the angle which he had obtained the night before, upon a circle which he had divided into 360 parts, the engineer found that this angle, allowing for the differences already explained, was 53°. Which, subtracted from 90°—the distance of the pole from the equator—gave 37° as the latitude of Lincoln Island. And making an allowance of 5° for the imperfections of the observations, Smith, concluded it to be situated between the 35th and the 40th parallel of south latitude.

But, in order to establish the co-ordinates of the island, the longitude also must be taken. And this the engineer determined to do when the sun passed the meridian at noon.

They therefore resolved to spend the morning in a walk, or rather an exploration of that part of the island situated to the north of Shark Gulf and the lake; and, if they should have time, to push on as far as the western side of South Mandible Cape. They would dine on the downs and not return until evening.

At half-past 8 the little party set out, following the edge of the channel. Opposite, upon Safety Islet, a number of birds of the sphemiscus family strutted gravely about. There were divers, easily recognizable, by their disagreeable cry, which resembled the braying of an ass. Pencroff, regarding them with gastronomic intent, was pleased to learn that their flesh, though dark colored, was good to eat. They could also see amphibious animals, which probably were seals, crawling over the sand. It was not possible to think of these as food, as their oily flesh is detestable; nevertheless Smith observed them carefully, and without disclosing his plans to the others, he announced that they would very soon, make a visit to the island. The shore followed by the colonists was strewn with mollusks, which would have delighted a malacologist. But, what was more important, Neb discovered, about four miles from the Chimneys, among the rocks, a bed of oysters, left bare by the tide.

"Neb hasn't lost his day," said Pencroff, who saw that the bed extended some distance.

"It is, indeed, a happy discovery," remarked the reporter. "And when we remember that each oyster produces fifty or sixty thousand eggs a year, the supply is evidently inexhaustable."

"But I don't think the oyster is very nourishing," said Herbert.

"No," answered Smith. "Oysters contain very little azote, and it would be necessary for a man living on them alone to eat at least fifteen or sixteen dozen every day."

"Well," said Pencroff, "we could swallow dozens and dozens of these and not exhaust the bed. Shall we have some for breakfast?"

And, without waiting for an answer, which he well knew would be affirmative, the sailor and Neb detached a quantity of these mollusks from the rocks, and placed them with the other provisions for breakfast, in a basket which Neb had made from the hibiscus fibres. Then they continued along the shore between the downs and the sea.

From time to time Smith looked at his watch, so as to be ready for the noon observation.

All this portion of the island, as far as South Mandible Cape, was desert, composed of nothing but sand and shells, mixed with the debris of lava. A few sea birds, such as the sea-gulls and albatross, frequented the shore, and some wild ducks excited the covetousness of Pencroff. He tried to shoot some, but unsuccessfully, as they seldom lit, and he could not hit them flying.

This made the sailor say to the engineer:—

"You see, Mr. Smith, how much we need guns!"

"Doubtless, Pencroff," answered the reporter, "but it rests with you. You find iron for the barrels, steel for the locks, saltpetre, charcoal and sulphur for the powder, mercury and nitric acid for the fulminate, and last of all, lead for the balls, and Mr. Smith will make us guns of the best quality."

"Oh, we could probably find all these substances on the island," said the engineer. "But it requires fine tools to make such a delicate instrument as a firearm. However, we will see after awhile."

"Why, why did we throw the arms and everything else, even our penknives, out of the balloon?" cried Pencroff.

"If we hadn't, the balloon would have thrown us into the sea," answered Herbert.

"So it would, my boy," answered the sailor; and then another idea occurring to him:—

"I wonder what Mr. Forster and his friend thought," he said, "the next day, when they found they balloon had escaped?"

"I don't care what they thought," said the reporter.

"It was my plan," cried Pencroff, with a satisfied air.

"And a good plan it was, Pencroff," interrupted the reporter, laughing, "to drop us here!"

"I had rather be here than in the hands of the Southerners!" exclaimed the sailor, "especially since Mr. Smith has been kind enough to rejoin us!"

"And I, too," cried the reporter. "After all, what do we lack here? Nothing."

"That means—everything," answered the sailor, laughing and shrugging his shoulders. "But some day we will get away from this place."

"Sooner, perhaps, than you think, my friends," said the engineer, "if Lincoln Island is not very far from an inhabited archipelego or a continent. And we will find that out within an hour. I have no map of the Pacific, but I have a distinct recollection of its southern portion. Yesterday's observation places the island in the latitude of New Zealand and Chili. But the distance between these two countries is at least 6,000 miles. We must therefore determine what point in this space the island occupies, and that I hope to get pretty soon from the longitude."

"Is not the Low Archipelago nearest us in latitude," asked Herbert.

"Yes," replied the engineer, "but it is more than 1,200 miles distant."

"And that way?" inquired Neb, who followed the conversation with great interest, pointing towards the south.

"Nothing!" answered Pencroff.

"Nothing, indeed," added the engineer.

"Well, Cyrus," demanded the reporter, "if we find Lincoln Island to be only 200 or 300 miles from New Zealand or Chili?"

"We will build a ship instead of a house, and Pencroff shall command it."

"All right, Mr. Smith," cried the sailor; "I am all ready to be captain, provided you build something seaworthy."

"We will, if it is necessary," answered Smith.

While these men, whom nothing could discourage, were talking, the hour for taking the observation approached. Herbert could not imagine how Mr. Smith would be able to ascertain the time of the sun's passage of the meridian of the island without a single instrument. It was 11 o'clock, and the party, halting about six miles from the Chimneys, not far from the place where they had found the engineer after his inexplicable escape, set about preparing breakfast. Herbert found fresh water in a neighboring brook, and brought some back in a vessel which Neb had with him.

Meantime, the engineer made ready for his astronomical observation. He chose a smooth dry place upon the sand, which the sea had left perfectly level. It was no more necessary, however, for it to be horizontal, than for the rod which he stuck in the sand to be perpendicular. Indeed, the engineer inclined the rod towards the south or away from the sun, as it must not be forgotten that the colonists of Lincoln Island, being in the Southern Hemisphere, saw the orb of day describe his diurnal arc above the northern horizon.

Then Herbert understood how by means of the shadow of the rod on the sand, the engineer would be able to ascertain the culmination of the sun, that is to say, its passage of the meridian of the island, or, in other words, the *time* of the place. For the moment that the shadow obtained its minimum length it would be noon, and all they had to do was to watch carefully the end of the shadow. By inclining the rod from the sun Smith had made the shadow longer, and therefore its changes could be the more readily noted.

When he thought it was time, the engineer knelt down upon the sand and began marking the decrease in the length of the shadow by means of little wooden pegs. His companions, bending over him, watched the operation with the utmost interest.

The reporter, chronometer in hand, stood ready to mark the minute when the shadow would be shortest. Now, as this 16th of April was a day when the true and mean time are the same, Spilett's watch would give the true time of Washington, and greatly simplify the calculation.

Meantime the shadow diminished little by little, and as soon as Smith perceived it begin to lengthen he exclaimed:—

"Now!"

"One minute past 5," answered the reporter.

Nothing then remained but the easy work of summing up the result. There was, as we have seen, five hours difference between the meridian of Washington and that of the island. Now, the sun passes around the earth at the rate of 15° an hour. Fifteen multiplied by five gives seventy-five. And as Washington is in 77° 3' 11" from the meridian of Greenwich, it follows that the island was in the neighborhood of longitude 152° west.

Smith announced this result to his companions, and, making the same allowance as before, he was able to affirm that the bearing of the island was between the 35° and 37° of south latitude, and between the 150° and 155° of west longitude.

The difference in this calculation, attributable to errors in observation, was placed, as we have seen, at 5° or 300 miles in each direction. But this error did not influence the conclusion that Lincoln Island was so far from any continent or archipelago that they could not attempt to accomplish the distance in a small boat.

In fact, according to the engineer, they were at least 1,200 miles from Tahiti and from the Low Archipelago, fully 1,800 miles from New Zealand, and more than 4,500 miles from the coast of America.

And when Cyrus Smith searched his memory, he could not remember any island in the Pacific occupying the position of Lincoln Island.

CHAPTER XV.

WINTER SETS IN—THE METALLUGRIC QUESTION—
THE EXPLORATION OF SAFETY ISLAND—A SEAL
HUNT—CAPTURE OF AN ECHIDNA—THE AI—
THE CATALONIAN METHOD—MAKING IRON
AND STEEL.

The first words of the sailor, on the morning of the 17th of April, were:—

"Well, what are we going to do to-day?"

"Whatever Mr. Smith chooses," answered the reporter.

The companions of the engineer, having been brickmakers and potters, were about to become metal-workers.

The previous day, after lunch, the party had explored as far as the extremity of Mandible Cape, some seven miles from the Chimneys. The extensive downs here came to an end and the soil appeared volcanic. There were no longer high walls, as at Prospect Plateau, but the narrow gulf between the two capes was enframed by a fantastic border of the mineral matter discharged from the volcano. Having reached this point, the colonists retraced their steps to the Chimneys, but they could not sleep until the question whether they should look forwards to leaving Lincoln Island had been definitely settled.

The 1,200 miles to the Low Archipelago was a long distance. And now, at the beginning of the stormy season, a small boat would certainly not be able to accomplish it. The building of a boat, even when the proper tools are provided, is a difficult task, and as the colonists had none of these, the first thing to do was to make hammers, hatchets, adzes, saws, augers, planes, etc., which would take some time. It was therefore decided to winter on Lincoln Island, and to search for a more comfortable dwelling than the Chimneys in which to live during the inclement weather.

The first thing was to utilize the iron ore which the engineer had discovered, by transforming it into iron and steel.

Iron ore is usually found in combination with oxygen or sulphur. And it was so in this instance, as of the two specimens brought back by Cyrus Smith one was magnetic iron, and the other pyrites or sulphuret of iron. Of these, it was the first kind, the magnetic ore, or oxide of iron, which must be reduced by coal, that is to say, freed from the oxygen, in order to obtain the pure metal. This reduction is performed by submitting the ore to a great heat, either by the Catalonian method, which has the advantage of producing the metal at one operation, or by means of blast furnaces which first smelt the ore, and then the iron, carrying off the 3 or 4 per cent of coal combined with it.

The engineer wanted to obtain iron in the shortest way possible. The ore he had found was in itself very pure and rich. Such ore is found in rich grey masses, yielding a black dust crystallized in regular octahedrons, highly magnetic, and in Europe the best quality of iron is made from it. Not far from this vein was the coal field previously explored by the colonists, so that every facility existed for the treatment of the ore.

"Then, sir, are we going to work the iron?" questioned Pencroff. "Yes, my friend," answered the engineer.

"But first we will do something I think you will enjoy—have a seal hunt on the island."

"A seal hunt!" cried the sailor, addressing Spilett "Do we need seals to make iron?"

"It seems so, since Cyrus has said it," replied the reporter.

But as the engineer had already left the Chimneys, Pencroff prepared for the chase without gaining an explanation.

Soon the whole party were gathered upon the beach at a point where the channel could be forded at low water without wading deeper than the knees. This was Smith's first visit to the islet upon which his companions had been thrown by the balloon. On their landing, hundreds of penguins looked fearlessly at them, and the colonists armed with clubs could have killed numbers of these birds, but it would have been useless slaughter, and it would not do to frighten the seals which were lying on the sand some cable lengths away. They respected also certain innocent-looking sphemiscus, with flattened side appendages, mere apologies for wings, and covered with scale-like vestiges of feathers.

The colonists marched stealthily forward over ground riddled with holes which formed the nests of aquatic birds. Towards the end of the island, black objects, like moving rocks, appeared above the surface of the water, they were the seals the hunters wished to capture.

It was necessary to allow them to land, as, owing to their shape, these animals, although capital swimmers and difficult to seize in the sea, can move but slowly on the shore. Pencroff, who knew their habits, counselled waiting until the seals were sunning themselves asleep on the sand. Then the party could manage so as to cut off their retreat and despatch them with a blow on the muzzle. The hunters therefore hid themselves behind the rocks and waited quietly.

In about an hour half a dozen seals crawled on to the sand, and Pencroff and Herbert went off round the point of the island so as to cut off their retreat, while the three others, hidden by the rocks, crept forward to the place of encounter.

Suddenly the tall form of the sailor was seen. He gave a shout, and the engineer and his companions hurriedly threw themselves between the seals and the sea. They succeeded in beating two of the animals to death, but the others escaped.

"Here are your seals, Mr. Smith," cried the sailor, coming forward.

"And now we will make bellows," replied the engineer.

"Bellows!" exclaimed the sailor. "These seals are in luck."

It was, in effect, a huge pair of bellows, necessary in the reduction of the ore, which the engineer expected to make from the skins of the seals. They were medium-sized, about six feet long, and had heads resembling those of dogs. As it was useless to burden themselves with the whole carcass, Neb and Pencroff resolved to skin them on the spot, while Smith and the reporter made the exploration of the island.

The sailor and the negro acquitted themselves well, and three hours later Smith had at his disposal two seal skins, which he intended to use just as they were, without tanning.

The colonists, waiting until low water, re-crossed the channel and returned to the Chimneys.

It was no easy matter to stretch the skins upon the wooden frames and to sew them so as to make them sufficiently air-tight. Smith had nothing but the two knives to work with, yet he was so ingenious and his companions aided him so intelligently, that, three days later, the number of implements of the little colony was increased by a bellows intended to inject air into the midst of the ore during its treatment by heat—a requisite to the success of the operation.

It was on the morning of the 20th of April that what the reporter called in his notes the "iron age" began. The engineer had decided to work near the deposits of coal and iron, which were situated at the base of the northeasterly spurs of Mount Franklin, six miles from the Chimneys. And as it would not be possible to go back and forth each day, it was decided to camp upon the ground in a temporary hut, so that they could attend to the important work night and day.

This settled, they left in the morning, Neb and Pencroff carrying the bellows and a stock of provisions, which latter they would add to on the way.

The road led through the thickest part of Jacamar Wood, in a northwesterly direction. It was as well to break a path which would henceforth be the most direct route between Prospect Plateau and Mount Franklin. The trees belonging to the species already recognized were magnificent, and Herbert discovered another, the dragon tree, which Pencroff designated as an "overgrown onion," which, notwithstanding its height, belongs to the same family of liliaceous plants as the onion, the civet, the shallot, or the asparagus. These dragon trees have ligneous roots which, cooked, are excellent, and which, fermented, yield a very agreeable liquor. They therefore gathered some.

It took the entire day to traverse the wood, but the party were thus able to observe its fauna and flora. Top, specially charged to look after the fauna, ran about in the grass and bushes, flushing all kinds of game. Herbert and Spilett shot two kangaroos and an animal which was like a hedge-hog, in that it rolled itself into a ball and erected its quills, and like an ant-eater, in that it was provided with claws for digging, a long and thin snout terminating in a beak, and an extensile tongue furnished with little points, which enabled it to hold insects.

"And what does it look like boiling in the pot?" asked Pencroff, naturally.

"Like an excellent piece of beef," answered Herbert.

"We don't want to know any more than that," said the sailor.

During the march they saw some wild boars, but they did not attempt to attack the little troupe, and it seemed that they were not going to have any encounter with savage beasts, when the reporter saw in a dense thicket, among the lower branches of a tree, an animal which he took to be a bear, and which he began tranquilly to sketch. Fortunately for Spilett, the animal in question did not belong to that redoubtable family of plantigrades. It was an ai, better known as a sloth, which has a body like that of a large dog, a rough and dirty-colored skin, the feet armed with strong claws which enable it to grasp the branches of trees and feed upon the leaves. Having identified the animal without disturbing it, Spilett struck out "bear" and wrote "ai" under his drawing and the route was resumed.

At 5 o'clock Smith called a halt. They were past the forest and at the beginning of the massive spurs which buttressed Mount Franklin towards the east. A few hundred paces distant was Red Creek; so drinking water was not wanting.

The camp was made. In less than an hour a hut, constructed from the branches of the tropical bindweed, and stopped with loam, was erected under the trees on the edge of the forest. They deferred the geological work until the next day. Supper was prepared, a good fire blazed before the hut, the spit turned, and at 8 o'clock, while one of the party kept the fire going, in case some dangerous beast should prowl around, the others slept soundly.

The next morning, Smith, accompanied by Herbert, went to look for the place where they had found the specimen of ore. They found the deposit on the surface, near the sources of the creek, close to the base of one of the northeast buttresses. This mineral, very rich in iron, enclosed in its fusible vein-stone, was perfectly suited to the method of reduction which the engineer intended to employ, which was the simplified Catalonian process practised in Corsica.

This method properly required the construction of ovens and crucibles in which the ore and the coal, placed in alternate layers, were transformed and reduced. But Smith proposed to simplify matters by simply making a huge cube of coal and ore, into the centre of which the air from the bellows would be introduced. This was, probably, what Tubal Cain did. And a process which gave such good results to Adam's grandson would doubtless succeed with the colonists of Lincoln Island.

The coal was collected with the same facility as the ore, and the latter was broken into little pieces and the impurities picked from it. Then the coal and ore were heaped together in successive layers—just as a charcoal-burner arranges his wood. Thus arranged, under the influence of the air from the bellows, the coal would change into carbonic acid, then into oxide of carbon, which would release the oxygen from the oxide of iron.

The engineer proceeded in this manner. The sealskin bellows, furnished with a pipe of refractory earth (an earth difficult of fusion), which had previously been prepared at the pottery, was set up close to the heap of ore. And, moved by a mechanism consisting of a frame, fibre-cords, and balance-weight, it injected into the mass a supply of air, which, by raising the temperature, assisted the chemical transformation which would give the pure metal.

The operation was difficult. It took all the patience and ingenuity of the colonists to conduct it properly; but finally it succeeded, and the result was a pig of iron in a spongy state, which must be cut and forged in order to expel the liquified gangue. It was evident that these self-constituted smiths wanted a hammer, but they were no worse off than the first metallurgist, and they did as he must have done.

The first pig, fastened to a wooden handle, served as a hammer with which to forge the second upon an anvil of granite, and they thus obtained a coarse metal, but one which could be utilized.

At length, after much trouble and labor, on the 25th of April, many bars of iron had been forged and turned into crowbars, pincers, pickaxes, mattocks, etc., which Pencroff and Neb declared to be real jewels.

But in order to be in its most serviceable state, iron must be turned into steel. Now steel, which is a combination of iron and carbon, is made in two ways: first from cast iron, by decarburetting the molten metal, which gives natural or puddled steel; and, second, by the method of cementation, which consists in carburetting malleable iron. As the engineer had iron in a pure state, he chose the latter method, and heated the metal with powdered charcoal in a crucible made from refractory earth.

This steel, which was malleable hot and cold, he worked with the hammer. And Neb and Pencroff, skillfully directed, made axe-heads, which, heated red-hot and quickly plunged in cold water, took an excellent temper.

Other instruments, such as planes and hatchets, were rudely fashioned, and bands of steel were made into saws and chisels; and from the iron, mattocks, shovels, pickaxes, hammers, nails, etc., were manufactured.

By the 5th of May the first metallurgic period was ended, the smiths returned to the Chimneys, and new work would soon authorize their assumption of a new title.

CHAPTER XVI.

THE QUESTION OF A DWELLING DISCUSSED AGAIN—
PENCROFF'S IDEAS—AN EXPLORATION TO THE
NORTH OF THE LAKE—THE WESTERN BOUNDARY
OF THE PLATEAU—THE SERPENTS—THE OUTLET OF
THE LAKE—TOP'S ALARM—TOP SWIMMING—A FIGHT
UNDER WATER—THE DUGONG.

It was the 6th of May, corresponding to the 6th of November in the Northern Hemisphere. For some days the sky had been cloudy, and it was important to make provision against winter. However, the temperature had not lessened much, and a centigrade thermometer transported to Lincoln Island would have averaged 10° or 12° above zero. This would not be surprising, since Lincoln Island, from its probable situation in the Southern Hemisphere, was subject to the same climatic influences as Greece or Sicily in the Northern. But just as the intense cold in Greece and Sicily sometimes produces snow and ice, so, in the height of winter, this island would probably experience sudden changes in the temperature against which it would be well to provide.

At any rate, if the cold was not threatening, the rainy season was at hand, and upon this desolate island, in the wide Pacific, exposed to all the inclemency of the elements, the storms would be frequent, and, probably, terrible.

The question of a more comfortable habitation than the Chimneys ought, therefore, to be seriously considered, and promptly acted upon.

Pencroff having discovered the Chimneys, naturally had a predilection for them; but he understood very well that another place must be found. This refuge had already been visited by the sea, and it would not do to expose themselves to a like accident.

"Moreover," added Smith, who was discussing these things with his companions, "there are some precautions to take."

"Why? The island is not inhabited," said the reporter.

"Probably not," answered the engineer, "although we have not yet explored the whole of it; but if there are no human beings, I believe dangerous beasts are numerous. So it will be better to provide a shelter against a possible attack, than for one of us to be tending the fire every night. And then, my friends, we must foresee everything. We are here in a part of the Pacific often frequented by Malay pirates—"

"What, at this distance from land?" exclaimed Herbert.

"Yes, my boy, these pirates are hardy sailors as well as formidable villains, and we must provide for them accordingly."

"Well," said Pencroff, "we will fortify ourselves against two and four-footed savages. But, sir, wouldn't it be as well to explore the island thoroughly before doing anything else?"

"It would be better," added Spilett; "who knows but we may find on the opposite coast one or more of those caves which we have looked for here in vain."

"Very true," answered the engineer, "but you forget, my friends, that we must be somewhere near running water, and that from Mount Franklin we were unable to see either brook or river in that direction. Here, on the contrary, we are between the Mercy and Lake Grant, which is an advantage not to be neglected. And, moreover, as this coast faces the east, it is not as exposed to the trade winds, which blow from the northwest in this hemisphere."

"Well, then, Mr. Smith," replied the sailor, "let us build a house on the edge of the lake. We are no longer without bricks and tools. After having been brickmakers, potters, founders, and smiths, we ought to be masons easily enough."

"Yes, my friend; but before deciding it will be well to look about. A habitation all ready made would save us a great deal of work, and would, doubtless, offer a surer retreat, in which we would be safe from enemies, native as well as foreign?"

"But, Cyrus," answered the reporter, "have we not already examined the whole of this great granite wall without finding even a hole?"

"No, not one!" added Pencroff. "If we could only dig a place in it high out of reach, that would be the thing! I can see it now, on the part overlooking the sea, five or six chambers—"

"With windows!" said Herbert, laughing.

"And a staircase!" added Neb.

"Why do you laugh?" cried the sailor. "Haven't we picks and mattocks? Cannot Mr. Smith make powder to blow up the mine. You will be able, won't you, sir, to make powder when we want it?"

The engineer had listened to the enthusiastic sailor developing these imaginative projects. To attack this mass of granite, even by mining, was an Herculean task, and it was truly vexing that nature had not helped them in their necessity. But he answered Pencroff, by simply proposing to examine the wall more attentively, from the mouth of the river to the angle which ended it to the north. They therefore went out and examined it most carefully for about two miles. But everywhere it rose, uniform and upright, without any visible cavity. The rock-pigeons flying about its summit had their nests in holes drilled in the very crest, or upon the irregularly cut edge of the granite.

To attempt to make a sufficient excavation in such a massive wall even with pickaxe and powder was not to be thought of. It was vexatious enough. By chance, Pencroff had discovered in the Chimneys, which must now be abandoned, the only temporary, habitable shelter on this part of the coast.

When the survey was ended the colonists found themselves at the northern angle of the wall, where it sunk by long declivities to the shore. From this point to its western extremity it was nothing more than a sort of talus composed of stones, earth, and sand bound together by plants, shrubs, and grass, in a slope of about 45°. Here and there the granite thrust its sharp points out from the cliff. Groups of trees grew over these slopes and there was a thin carpet of grass. But the vegetation extended but a short distance, and then the long stretch of sand, beginning at the foot of the talus, merged into the beach.

Smith naturally thought that the over flow of the lake fell in this direction, as the excess of water from Red Creek must be discharged somewhere, and this point had not been found less on the side already explored, that is to say from the mouth of the creek westward as far as Prospect Plateau.

The engineer proposed to his companions that they clamber up the talus and return to the Chimneys by the heights, exploring the eastern and western shores of the lake. The proposition was accepted, and, in a few minutes, Herbert and Neb had climbed to the plateau, the others following more leisurely.

Two hundred feet distant the beautiful sheet of water shone through the leaves in the sunlight. The landscape was charming. The trees in autumn tints, were harmoniously grouped. Some huge old weatherbeaten trunks stood out in sharp relief against the green turf which covered the ground, and brilliant cockatoos, like moving, prisms, glanced among the branches, uttering their shrill screams.

The colonists, instead of proceeding directly to the north bank of the lake, bore along the edge of the plateau, so as to come back to the mouth of the creek, on its left bank. It was a circuit of about a mile and a half. The walk was easy, as the trees, set wide apart, left free passage between them. They could see that the fertile zone stopped at this point, and that the vegetation here, was less vigorous than anywhere between the creek and the Mercy.

Smith and his companions moved cautiously over this unexplored neighborhood. Bows and arrows and iron-pointed sticks were their sole weapons. But no beast showed itself, and it was probable that the animals kept to the thicker forests in the south. The colonists, however, experienced a disagreeable sensation in seeing Top stop before a huge serpent 14 or 15 feet long. Neb killed it at a blow. Smith examined the reptile, and pronounced it to belong to the species of diamond-serpents eaten by the natives of New South Wales and not venomous, but it was possible others existed whose bite was mortal, such as the forked-tail deaf viper, which rise up under the foot, or the winged serpents, furnished with two ear-like appendages, which enable them to shoot forward with extreme rapidity. Top having gotten over his surprise, pursued these reptiles with reckless fierceness, and his master was constantly obliged to call him in.

The mouth of Red Creek, where it emptied into the lake, was soon reached. The party recognized on the opposite bank the point visited on their descent from Mount Franklin. Smith ascertained that the supply of water from the creek was considerable; there therefore must be an outlet for the overflow somewhere. It was this place which must be found, as, doubtless, it made a fall which could be utilized as a motive power.

The colonists, strolling along, without, however, straying too far from each other, began to follow round the bank of the lake, which was very abrupt. The water was full of fishes, and Pencroff promised himself soon to manufacture some apparatus with which to capture them.

It was necessary first to double the point at the northeast. They had thought that the discharge would be here, as the water flowed close to the edge of the plateau. But as it was not here, the colonists continued along the bank, which, after a slight curve, followed parallel with the sea-shore.

On this side the bank was less wooded, but clumps of trees, here and there, made a picturesque landscape. The whole extent of the lake, unmoved by a single ripple, was visible before, them. Top, beating the bush, flushed many coveys of birds, which Spilett and Herbert saluted with their arrows. One of these birds, cleverly hit by the lad, dropped in the rushes. Top rushing after it, brought back a beautiful slate-colored water fowl. It was a coot, as large as a big partridge, belonging to the group of machio-dactyls, which form the division between the waders and the palmipedes. Poor game and bad tasting, but as Top was not as difficult to please as his masters, it was agreed that the bird would answer for his supper.

Then the colonists, following the southern bank of the lake, soon came to the place they had previously visited. The engineer was very much surprised, as he had seen no indication of an outlet to the surplus water. In talking with the reporter and the sailor, he did not conceal his astonishment.

At this moment, Top, who had been behaving himself quietly, showed signs of alarm. The intelligent animal, running along the bank, suddenly stopped, with one foot raised, and looked into the water as if pointing some invisible game. Then he barked furiously, questioning it, as it were, and again was suddenly silent.

At first neither Smith nor his companions paid any attention to the dog's actions, but his barking became so incessant, that the engineer noticed it.

"What is it, Top?" he called.

The dog bounded towards his master, and, showing a real anxiety, rushed back to the bank. Then, suddenly, he threw himself into the lake.

"Come back here, Top," cried the engineer, not wishing his dog to venture in those supicious waters.

"What's going on under there?" asked the sailor examining the surface of the lake.

"Top has smelt something amphibious," answered Herbert.

"It must be an alligator," said the reporter.

"I don't think so," answered Smith. "Alligators are not met with in this latitude."

Meantime, Top came ashore at the call of his master, but he could not be quiet; he rushed along the bank, through the tall grass, and, guided by instinct, seemed to be following some object, invisible under the water, which was hugging the shore. Nevertheless the surface was calm and undisturbed by a ripple. Often the colonists stood still on the bank and watched the water, but they could discover nothing. There certainly was some mystery here, and the engineer was much perplexed.

"We will follow out this exploration," he said.

In half an hour all had arrived at the southeast angle of the lake, and were again upon Prospect Plateau. They had made the circle of the bank without the engineer having discovered either where or how the surplus water was discharged.

"Nevertheless, this outlet exists," he repeated, "and, since it is not outside, it must penetrate the massive granite of the coast!"

"And why do you want to find that out?" asked Spilett.

"Because," answered the engineer, "if the outlet is through the solid rock it is possible that there is some cavity, which could be easily rendered habitable, after having turned the water in another direction."

"But may not the water flow into the sea, through a subterranean outlet at the bottom of the lake?" asked Herbert.

"Perhaps so," answered Smith, "and in that case, since Nature has not aided us, we must build our house ourselves."

As it was 5 o'clock, the colonists were thinking of returning to the Chimneys across the plateau, when Top again became excited, and, barking with rage, before his master could hold him, he sprang a second time into the lake. Every one ran to the bank. The dog was already twenty feet off, and Smith called to him to come back, when suddenly an enormous head emerged from the water.

Herbert instantly recognized it, the comical face, with huge eyes and long silky moustaches.

"A manatee," he cried.

Although not a manatee, it was a dugong, which belongs to the same species.

The huge monster threw himself upon the dog. His master could do nothing to save him, and, before Spilett or Herbert could draw their bows, Top, seized by the dugong, had disappeared under the water.

Neb, spear in hand, would have sprung to the rescue of the dog, and attacked the formidable monster in its own element, had he not been held back by his master.

Meanwhile a struggle was going on under the water—a struggle which, owing to the powerlessness of the dog, was inexplicable; a struggle which, they could see by the agitation of the surface, was becoming more terrible each moment; in short, a struggle which could only be terminated by the death of the dog. But suddenly, through the midst of a circle of foam, Top appeared, shot upward by some unknown force, rising ten feet in the air, and falling again into the tumultuous waters, from which he escaped to shore without any serious wounds, miraculously saved.

Cyrus Smith and his companions looked on amazed. Still more inexplicable, it seemed as if the struggle under water continued. Doubtless the dugong, after having seized the dog, bad been attacked by some more formidable animal, and had been obliged to defend itself.

But this did not last much longer. The water grew red with blood, and the body of the dugong, emerging from the waves, floated on to a little shoal at the southern angle of the lake.

The colonists ran to where the animal lay, and found it dead. Its body was enormous, measuring between 15 and 16 feet long and weighing between 3,000 and 4,000 pounds. On its neck, yawned a wound, which seemed to have been made by some sharp instrument.

What was it that had been able, by this terrible cut, to kill the formidable dugong? None of them could imagine, and, preoccupied with these incidents, they returned to the Chimneys.

CHAPTER XVII.

A VISIT TO THE LAKE—THE DIRECTION OF THE
CURRENT—THE PROSPECTS OF CYRUS SMITH—
THE DUGONG FAT—THE USE OF THE SCHISTOUS
LIMESTONE—THE SULPHATE OF IRON—
HOW GLYCERINE IS MADE—SOAP—SALTPETRE—
SULPHURIC ACID—NITRIC ACID—THE NEW OUTLET.

The next day, the 7th of May, Smith and Spilett, leaving Neb to prepare the breakfast, climbed the plateau, while Herbert and Pencroff went after a fresh supply of wood.

The engineer and the reporter soon arrived, at the little beach where the dugong lay stranded. Already flocks of birds had gathered about the carcass, and it was necessary to drive them off with stones, as the engineer wished to preserve the fat for the use of the colony. As to the flesh of the dugong, it would undoubtedly furnish excellent food, as in certain portions of the Malay archipelago it is reserved for the table of the native princes. But it was Neb's affair to look after that.

Just now, Cyrus Smith was thinking of other things. The incident of the day before was constantly presenting itself. He wanted to solve the mystery of that unseen combat, and to know what congener of the mastodons or other marine monster had given the dugong this strange wound.

He stood upon the border of the lake, looking upon its tranquil surface sparkling under the rays of the rising sun. From the little beach where the dugong lay, the waters deepened slowly towards the centre, and the lake might be likened to a large basin, filled by the supply from Red Creek.

"Well, Cyrus," questioned the reporter, "I don't see anything suspicious in this?"

"No, my dear fellow, and I am at a loss how to explain yesterday's affair."

"The wound on this beast is strange enough, and I can't understand how Top could have been thrown out of the water in that way. One would suppose that it had been done by a strong arm, and that that same arm, wielding a poignard, had given the dugong his death-wound."

"It would seem so," answered the engineer, who had become thoughtful. "There is something here which I cannot understand. But neither can we explain how I myself was saved; how I was snatched from the waves and borne to the downs. Therefore, I am sure there is some mystery which we will some day discover. In the mean time, let us take care not to discuss these singular incidents before our companions, but keep our thoughts for each other, and continue our work."

It will be remembered that Smith had not yet discovered what became of the surplus water of the lake, and as there was no indication of its ever overflowing, an outlet must exist somewhere. He was surprised, therefore, on noticing a slight current just at this place. Throwing in some leaves and bits of wood, and observing their drift, he followed this current, which brought him to the southern end of the lake. Here he detected a slight depression in the waters, as if they were suddenly lost in some opening below.

Smith listened, placing his ear to the surface of the lake, and distinctly heard the sound of a subterranean fall.

"It is there," said he, rising, "there that the water is discharged, there, doubtless, through a passage in the massive granite that it goes to join the sea, through cavities which we will be able to utilize to our profit! Well! I will find out!"

The engineer cut a long branch, stripped off its leaves, and, plunging it down at the angle of the two banks, he found that there was a large open hole a foot below the surface. This was the long-sought-for outlet, and such was the force of the current that the branch was snatched from his hands and disappeared.

"There can be no doubt of it now," repeated the engineer. "It is the mouth of the outlet, and I am going to work to uncover it.

"How?" inquired Spilett.

"By lowering the lake three feet."

"And how will you do that?"

"By opening another vent larger than this."

"Whereabouts, Cyrus?"

"Where the bank is nearest the coast."

"But it is a granite wall," exclaimed Spilett,

"Very well," replied Smith. "I will blow up the wall, and the waters, escaping, will subside so as to discover the orifice—"

"And will make a waterfall at the cliff," added the reporter.

"A fall that we will make use of!" answered Cyrus. "Come, come!"

The engineer hurried off his companion, whose confidence in Smith was such that he doubted not the success of the undertaking. And yet, this wall of granite, how would they begin: how, without powder, with but imperfect tools, could they blast the rock? Had not the engineer undertaken a work beyond his skill to accomplish?

When Smith and the reporter re-entered the Chimneys, they found Herbert and Pencroff occupied in unloading their raft.

"The wood-choppers have finished, sir," said the sailor, laughing, "and when you want masons—"

"Not masons, but chemists," interrupted the engineer.

"Yes," added Spilett, "we are going to blow up the island."

"Blow up the island?" cried the sailor.

"A part of it, at least," answered the reporter.

"Listen to me, my friends," said the engineer, who thereupon made known the result of his observations. His theory was, that a cavity, more or less considerable, existed in the mass of granite which upheld Prospect Plateau, and he undertook to penetrate to it. To do this, it was first necessary to free the present opening, in other words to lower the level of the lake by giving the water a larger issue. To do this they must manufacture an explosive with which to make a drain in another part of the bank. It was this Smith was going to attempt to do, with the minerals Nature had placed at his disposal.

All entered into the proposal with enthusiasm. Neb and Pencroff were at once detailed to extract the fat from the dugong and to preserve the flesh for food; and soon after their departure the others, carrying the hurdle, went up the shore to the vein of coal, where were to be found the schistous pyrites of which Smith had procured a specimen.

The whole day was employed in bringing a quantity of these pyrites to the Chimneys, and by evening they had several tons.

On the next day, the 8th of May, the engineer began his manipulations. The schistous pyrites were principally composed of carbon, of silica, of alumina, and sulphuret of iron,—these were in excess,—it was necessary to separate the sulphuret and change it into sulphate by the quickest means. The sulphate obtained, they would extract the Sulphuric acid, which was what they wanted.

Sulphuric acid is one of the agents in most general use, and the industrial importance of a nation can be measured by its consumption. In the future this acid would be of use to the colonists in making candles, tanning skins, etc., but at present the engineer reserved it for another purpose.

Smith chose, behind the Chimneys, a place upon which the earth was carefully levelled. On this he made a pile of branches and cut wood, on which were placed pieces of schistous pyrites leaning against each other, and then all was covered over with a thin layer of pyrites previously reduced to the size of nuts.

This done, they set the wood on, fire, which in turn inflamed the schist, as it contained carbon and sulphur. Then new layers of pyrites were arranged so as to form an immense heap, surrounded with earth, and grass, with air-holes left here and there, just as is done in reducing a pile of wood to charcoal.

Then they left the transformation to complete itself. It would take ten or twelve days for the sulphuret of iron and the alumina to change into sulphates, which substances were equally soluble; the others—silica, burnt carbon, and cinders—were not so.

While this chemical process was accomplishing itself, Smith employed his companions upon other branches of the work, which they undertook with the utmost zeal.

Neb and Pencroff had taken the fat from the dugong, which had been placed in large earthen jars. It was necessary to separate the glycerine from this fat by saponifying it. It was sufficient, in order to do this, to treat it with chalk or soda. Chalk was not wanting, but by this treatment the soap would be calcareous and useless, while by using soda, a soluble soap, which could be employed for domestic purposes, would be the result. Cyrus Smith, being a practical man, preferred to try to get the soda. Was this difficult? No, since many kinds of marine plants abounded on the shore, and all those fucaceæ which form wrack. They therefore gathered a great quantity of these seaweed, which were first dried, and, afterwards, burnt in trenches in the open air. The combustion of these plants was continued for many days, so that the heat penetrated throughout, and the result was the greyish compact mass, long known as "natural soda."

This accomplished, the engineer treated the fat with the soda, which gave both a soluble soap and the neutral substance, glycerine.

But this was not all. Smith wanted, in view of his future operations, another substance, nitrate of potash, better known as saltpetre.

He could make this by treating carbonate of potash, which is easily extracted from vegetable ashes, with nitric acid. But this acid, which was precisely what he wanted in order to complete his undertaking successfully, he did not have. Fortunately, in this emergency, Nature furnished him with saltpetre, without any labor other than picking it up. Herbert had found a vein of this mineral at the foot of Mount Franklin, and all they had to do was to purify the salt.

These different undertakings, which occupied eight days, were finished before the sulphate of iron was ready. During the interval the colonists made some refractory pottery in plastic clay, and constructed a brick furnace of a peculiar shape, in which to distil the sulphate of iron. All was finished on the 18th of May, the very day the chemical work was completed.

The result of this latter operation, consisting of sulphate of iron, sulphate of alumina, silica, and a residue of charcoal and cinders, was placed, in a basin full of water. Having stirred up the mixture, they let it settle, and at length poured off a clear liquid holding the sulphates of iron and alumina in solution. Finally, this liquid was partly evaporated, the sulphate of iron crystalized, and the mother-water was thrown away.

Smith had now a quantity of crystals, from which the sulphuric acid was to be extracted.

In commerce this acid is manufactured in large quantities and by elaborate processes. The engineer had no such means at his command, but he knew that in Bohemia an acid known as Nordhausen is made by simpler means, which has, moreover, the advantage of being non-concentrated. For obtaining the acid in this way, all the engineer had to do was to calcinize the crystals in a closed jar in such a manner that the sulphuric acid distilled in vapor, which would in turn produce the acid by condensation.

It was for this that the refractory jars and the furnace had been made. The operation was a success; and on the 20th of May, twelve days after having begun, Smith was the possessor of the agent which he expected to use later in different ways.

What did he want with it now? Simply to produce nitric acid, which was perfectly easy, since the saltpetre, attacked by the sulphuric acid, would give it by distillation.

But how would he use this acid? None of the others knew, as he had spoken no word on the subject.

The work approached completion, and one more operation would procure the substance which had required all this labor. The engineer mixed the nitric acid with the glycerine, which latter had been previously concentrated by evaporation in a water-bath, and without employing any freezing mixture, obtained many pints of an oily yellow liquid.

This last operation Smith had conducted alone, at some distance from the Chimneys, as he feared an explosion, and when he returned, with a flagon of this liquid, to his friends, he simply said:—"Here is some nitro-glycerine!"

It was, in truth, that terrible product, whose explosive power is, perhaps, ten times as great as that of gunpowder, and which has caused so many accidents! Although, since means have been found of transforming it into dynamite, that is, of mixing it with clay or sugar or some solid substance sufficiently porous to hold it, the dangerous liquid can be used with more safety. But dynamite was not known when the colonists were at work on Lincoln Island.

"And is that stuff going to blow up the rocks?" asked Pencroff, incredulously.

"Yes, my friend," answered the engineer, "and it will do all the better since the granite is very hard and will oppose more resistance to the explosion."

"And when will we see all this, sir?"

"To-morrow," when we have drilled a hole," answered the engineer.

Early the next morning, the 21st of May, the miners betook themselves to a point which formed the east bank of Lake Grant, not more than 500 feet from the coast. At this place the plateau was lower than the lake, which was upheld by the coping of granite. It was plain that could they break this the waters would escape by this vent, and, forming a stream, flow over the inclined surface of the plateau, and be precipitated in a waterfall over the cliff on to the shore. Consequently, there would be a general lowering of the lake, and the orifice of the water would be uncovered—this was to be the result.

The coping must be broken. Pencroff, directed by the engineer, attacked its outer facing vigorously. The hole which he made with his pick began under a horizontal edge of the bank, and penetrated obliquely so as to reach a level lower than the lake's surface. Thus the blowing up of the rocks would permit the water to escape freely and consequently lower the lake sufficiently.

The work was tedious, as the engineer, wishing to produce a violent shock, had determined to use not less than two gallons of nitro-glycerine in the operation. But Pencroff and Neb, taking turns at the work, did so well, that by 4 o'clock in the afternoon it was achieved.

Now came the question of igniting the explosive. Ordinarily, nitro-glycerine is ignited by the explosion of fulminated caps, as, if lighted without percussion, this substance burns and does not explode.

Smith could doubtless make a cap. Lacking fulminate, he could easily obtain a substance analogous to gun-cotton, since he had nitric acid at hand. This substance pressed in a cartridge, and introduced into the nitro-glycerine, could be lighted with a slow match, and produce the explosion.

But Smith knew that their liquid had the property of exploding under a blow. He determined, therefore, to make use of this property, reserving the other means in case this experiment failed.

The blow of a hammer upon some drops of the substance spread on a hard stone, suffices to provoke an explosion. But no one could give those blows without being a victim to the operation. Smith's idea was to suspend a heavy mass of iron by means of a vegetable fibre to an upright post, so as to have the iron hang directly over the hole. Another long fibre, previously soaked in sulphur, was to be fastened to the middle of the first and laid along the ground many feet from this excavation. The fire was to be applied to this second fibre, it would burn till it reached the first and set it on fire, then the latter would break and the iron be precipitated upon the nitro-glycerine.

The apparatus was fixed in place; then the engineer, after having made his companions go away, filled the hole so that the fluid overflowed the opening, and spread some drops underneath the mass of suspended iron.

This done, Smith lit the end of the sulfured fibre, and, leaving the place, returned with his companions to the Chimneys.

Twenty-five minutes after a tremendous explosion was heard. It seemed as if the whole island trembled to its base. A volley of stones rose into the air as if they had been vomited from a volcano. The concussion was such that it shook the Chimneys. The colonists, though two miles away, were thrown to the ground. Rising again, they clambered up to the plateau and hurried towards the place.

A large opening had been torn in the granite coping. A rapid stream of water escaped through it, leaping and foaming across the plateau, and, reaching the brink, fell a distance of 300 feet to the shore below.

CHAPTER XVIII.

PENCROFF DOUBTS NO MORE—THE OLD OUTLET
OF THE LAKE—A SUBTERRANEAN DESCENT—
THE WAY THROUGH THE GRANITE—TOP HAS
DISAPPEARED—THE CENTRAL CAVERN—THE LOWER
WELL—MYSTERY—THE BLOWS WITH THE PICK—
THE RETURN.

Smith's project had succeeded; but, as was his manner, he stood motionless, absorbed, his lips closed, giving no sign of satisfaction. Herbert was all enthusiasm; Neb jumped with joy; Pencroff, shaking his head, murmured:—

"Indeed, our engineer does wonders!"

The nitro-glycerine had worked powerfully. The opening was so great that at least a three times greater volume of water escaped by it than by the former outlet. In a little while, therefore, the level of the lake would be lowered two feet or more.

The colonists returned to the Chimneys, and collecting some picks, spears, ropes, a steel and tinder, returned to the plateau. Top went with them.

On the way the sailor could not resist saying to the engineer:—

"But do you really think, Mr. Smith, that one could blow up the whole island with this beautiful liquid of yours?"

"Doubtless," replied the other, "island, continents, the world itself. It is only a question of quantity."

"Couldn't you use this nitro-glycerine to load firearms."

"No, Pencroff, because it is too shattering. But it would be easy to make gun-cotton, or even common powder, as we have the material. Unfortunately, the guns themselves are wanting."

"But with a little ingenuity!—"

Pencroff had erased "impossible" from his vocabulary.

The colonists having reached Prospect Plateau, hastened at once to the old outlet of the lake, which ought now to be uncovered. And when the water no longer poured through it, it would, doubtless, be easy to explore its interior arrangement.

In a few moments they reached the lower angle of the lake, and saw at a glance what the result was.

There, in the granite wall of the lake, above the water-level, appeared the long-looked for opening. A narrow ledge, left bare, by the subsidence of the water, gave them access to it. The opening was twenty feet wide, though only two feet high. It was like the gutter-mouth in a pavement. It was not open enough for the party to get in, but Neb and Pencroff, with their picks, in less than an hour had given it a sufficient height.

The engineer looked in and saw that the walls of the opening in its upper part showed a slope of from 30° to 35°. And, therefore, unless they became much steeper it would be easy to descend, perhaps, to the level of the sea. And if, as was probable, some vast cavern existed in the interior of the massive granite, it was possible that they could make use of it.

"What are we waiting for, Mr. Smith," cried the sailor, all impatience to begin the exploration, "Top, you see, has gone ahead!"

"We must have some light," said the engineer. "Go, Neb, and cut some resinous branches."

The negro and Herbert ran to some pine and evergreens growing upon the bank, and soon returned with branches which were made into torches. Having lit them, the colonists, with Smith leading, entered the dark passage, but recently filled with water.

Contrary to their expectation, the passage grew higher as they advanced, until soon they were able to walk upright. The granite walls, worn, by the water, were very slippery, and the party had to look out for falls. They, therefore, fastened themselves together with a cord, like mountain climbers. Fortunately, some granite steps made the descent less perilous. Drops of water, still clinging to the rocks, glistened like stalactites in the torchlight. The engineer looked carefully at this black granite. He could not see a stratum or a flaw. The mass was compact and of fine grain, and the passage must have been coeval with the island. It had not been worn little by little by the constant action of water. Pluto, and not Neptune, had shaped it; and the traces of igneous action were still visible upon its surface.

The colonists descended but slowly. They experienced some emotion in thus adventuring into the depths of the earth, in being its first human visitants. No one spoke, but each was busied with his own reflections and the thought occurred to more than one, that perhaps some pulp or other gigantic cephalopod might inhabit the interior cavities which communicated with the sea. It was, therefore, necessary to advance cautiously.

Top was ahead of the little troop and they could rely on the dog's sagacity to give the alarm on occasion. After having descended 100 feet, Smith halted, and the others came up with him. They were standing in a cavern of moderate size. Drops of water fell from the roof, but they did not ooze through the rocks, they were simply the last traces of the torrent which had so long roared through this place, and the air, though humid, emitted no mephitic vapor.

"Well, Cyrus," said Spilett, "here is a retreat sufficiently unknown and hidden in the depths, but it is uninhabitable."

"How, uninhabitable?" asked the sailor.

"Why, it is too small and too dark."

"Cannot we make it bigger, blast it out, and make openings for the light and air?" answered Pencroff, who now thought nothing impracticable.

"Let us push on," said Smith. "Perhaps lower down, nature will have spared us this work."

"We are only a third of the way down," observed Herbert.

"But 100 feet," responded Cyrus; "and it is possible that 100 feet lower—."

"Where is Top?" asked Neb, interrupting his master.

They looked about the cavern. The dog was not there.

"Let us overtake him," said Smith, resuming the march. The engineer noted carefully all the deviations of the route, and easily kept a general idea of their direction, which was towards the sea. The party had not descended more than fifty feet further, when their attention was arrested by distant sounds coming from the depths of the rock. They stopped and listened. These sounds, borne along the passage, as the voice through an acoustic tube, were distinctly heard.

"Its Top's barking!" cried Herbert.

"Yes, and the brave dog is barking furiously," added Pencroff.

"We have our spears," said Smith. "Come on, and be ready."

"It is becoming more and more interesting," whispered Spilett to the sailor, who nodded assent.

They hurried to the rescue of the dog. His barks grew more distinct. They could hear that he was in a strange rage. Had he been captured by some animal whom he had disturbed? Without thinking of the danger, the colonists felt themselves drawn on by an irresistible curiosity, and slipped rather than ran down the passage. Sixteen feet lower they came up with the dog.

There, the corridor opened out into a vast and magnificent cavern. Top, rushing about, was barking furiously. Pencroff and Neb, shaking their torches, lit up all the inequalities of the granite, and the others, with their spears ready, held themselves prepared for any emergency.

But the enormous cavern was empty. The colonists searched everywhere; they could find no living thing. Nevertheless, Top continued barking, and neither threats nor caresses could stop him.

"There must be some place where the water escaped to the sea," said the engineer.

"Yes, and look out for a hole," answered Pencroff.

"On, Top, on," cried Smith, and the dog, encouraged by his master, ran towards the end of the cavern, and redoubled his barking.

Following him, they saw by the light of the torches the opening of what looked like a well in the granite. Here, undoubtedly, was the place where the water had found its way out of the cavern, but this time, instead of being a corridor sloping and accessible, it was a perpendicular well, impossible to descend.

The torches were waved above the opening. They saw nothing. Smith broke off a burning branch and dropped it into the abyss. The resin, fanned by the wind of its fall, burned brightly and illuminated the interior of the pit, but showed nothing else. Then the flame was extinguished with a slight hiss, which indicated that it had reached the water, which must be the sea level.

The engineer calculated, from the time taken in the fall, that the depth was about ninety feet. The floor of the cavern was therefore that distance above the sea.

"Here is our house," said Smith.

"But it was preoccupied," said Spilett, whose curiosity was unsatisfied.

"Well, the thing that had it, whether amphibious or not, has fled by this outlet and vacated in our favor," replied the engineer.

"Any how, I should like to have been Top a quarter of an hour ago," said the sailor, "for he does not bark at nothing."

Smith looked at his dog, and those who were near him heard him murmur:—

"Yes, I am convinced that Top knows more than we do about many things!"

However, the wishes of the colonists had been in a great measure realized. Chance, aided by the marvelous acuteness of their chief, had done them good service. Here they had at their disposal a vast cavern, whose extent could not be estimated In the insufficient light of the torches, but which could certainly be easily partitioned off with bricks into chambers, and arranged, if not as a house, at least as a spacious suite of rooms. The water having left it, could not return. The place was free.

But two difficulties remained, the possibility of lighting the cavern and the necessity of rendering it easier of access. The first could not be done from above as the enormous mass of granite was over them; but, perhaps, they would be able to pierce the outer wall which faced the sea. Smith, who during the descent had kept account of the slope, and therefore of the length of the passage, believed that this part of the wall could not be very thick. If light could be thus obtained, so could entrance, as it was as easy to pierce a door as windows, and to fix a ladder on the outside.

Smith communicated his ideas to his companions.

"Then let us set to work!" answered Pencroff; "I have my pick and will I soon make daylight in the granite! Where shall I begin?"

"Here," answered the engineer, showing the strong sailor a considerable hollow in the wall, which greatly diminished its thickness.

Pencroff attacked the granite, and for half an hour, by the light of the torches, made the splinters fly about him. Then Neb took his place, and Spilett after Neb. The work continued, two hours longer, and, when it seemed as if the wall could not be thicker than the length of the pick, at the last stroke of Spilett the implement, passing through, fell on the outside.

"Hurrah forever!" cried Pencroff.

The wall was but three feet thick.

Smith looked through the opening, which was eighty feet above the ground. Before him extended the coast, the islet, and, beyond, the boundless sea.

Through the hole the light entered in floods, inundating the splendid cavern and producing a magical effect. While on the left hand it measured only thirty feet in height and one hundred in length, to the right it was enormous, and its vault rose to a height of more than eighty feet. In some places, granite pillars, irregularly disposed, supported the arches as in the nave of a cathedral. Resting upon a sort of lateral piers, here, sinking into elliptic arches, there, rising in ogive mouldings, losing itself in the dark bays, half seen in the shadow through the fantastic arches, ornamented by a profusion of projections which seemed like pendants, this vaulted roof afforded a picturesque blending of all the architectures—Byzantine, Roman, Gothic—that the hand of man has produced. And this was the work of nature! She alone had constructed this magic Alhambra in a granite rock!

The colonists were overcome with admiration. Expecting to find but a narrow cavern, they found themselves in a sort of marvellous palace, and Neb had taken off his hat as if he had been transported into a temple!

Exclamations of pleasure escaped from their lips, and the hurrahs echoed and reechoed from the depths of the dark nave.

"My friends," cried Smith, "when we shall have lighted the interior of this place, when we shall have arranged our chambers, our store-rooms, our offices in the left-hand portion, we will still have this splendid cavern, which shall be our study and our museum!

"And we will call it—" asked Herbert.

"Granite House," answered Smith; and his companions saluted the name with their cheers.

By this time the torches were nearly consumed, and as, in order to return, it was necessary to regain the summit of the plateau and to remount the corridor, it was decided to postpone until the morrow the work of arranging their new home.

Before leaving, Smith leaned over the dark pit once more and listened attentively. But there was no sound from these depths save that of the water agitated by the undulations of the surge. A resinous torch was again thrown in, lighting up anew for an instant the walls of the well, but nothing suspicions was revealed. If any marine monster had been inopportunely surprised by the retreat of the waters, he had already regained the open sea by the subterranean passage which extended under the shore.

Nevertheless the engineer stood motionless, listening attentively, his gaze plunged in the abyss, without speaking.

Then the sailor approached him, and, touching his arm:—

"Mr. Smith," he said.

"What is it, my friend," responded the engineer, like one returning from the land of dreams.

"The torches are nearly out."

"Forward!" said Smith; and the little troop left the cavern and began the ascent through the dark weir. Top walked behind, still growling in an odd way. The ascension was sufficiently laborious, and the colonists stopped for a few minutes at the upper grotto, which formed a sort of landing half way up the long granite stairway. Then they began again to mount, and pretty soon they felt the fresh air. The drops, already evaporated, no longer shone on the walls. The light of the torches diminished; Neb's went out, and they had to hasten in order to avoid having to grope their way through, the profound darkness. A little before 4 o'clock, just as the torch of the sailor was burnt out, Smith and his companions emerged from the mouth of the passage.

CHAPTER XIX.

SMITH'S PLAN—THE FRONT OF GRANITE HOUSE—
THE ROPE LADDER—PENCROFF'S IDEAS—
THE AROMATIC HERBS—A NATURAL WARREN—
GETTING WATER—THE VIEW FROM THE WINDOWS
OF GRANITE HOUSE.

On the next day, May 22, the colonists proceeded to take possession of their new abode. They longed to exchange their insufficient shelter for the vast retreat in the rock, impenetrable to wind and wave. Still they did not intend altogether to abandon the Chimneys, but to make a workshop of it.

Smith's first care was to ascertain exactly over what point rose the face of Granite House. He went down on the shore to the foot of the immense wall, and, as the pickaxe, which slipped from the reporter's hands, must have fallen perpendicularly, he could ascertain, by finding this pickaxe, the place where the granite had been pierced. And, in fact, when the implement was found, half buried in the sand, the hole in the rock could be seen eighty feet above it, in a straight line. Rock pigeons were already fluttering in and out by this narrow opening. They evidently thought Granite House had been discovered for their benefit.

The engineer intended to divide the right portion of the cavern into several chambers opening upon an entrance-corridor, and lighted by five windows and a door cut in the face of the rock. Pencroff agreed with him as to the window, but could not understand the use of the door, since the old weir furnished a natural staircase to Granite House.

"My friend," said Smith, "if we could get to our abode by the weir, so can others. I want to block up this passage at its month, to seal it hermetically, and even, if necessary, to conceal the entrance by damming up the lake."

"And how shall we get in?" said the sailor.

"By a rope ladder from the outside," answered Smith, "which we can pull up after us."

"But why take so many precautions?" said Pencroff. "So far, the animals we have found here have not been formidable; and there are certainly no natives."

"Are you so sure, Pencroff?" said the engineer, looking steadily at the sailor.

"Of course we shall not be perfectly sure till we have explored every part."

"Yes," said Smith, "for we know as yet only a small portion. But even if there are no enemies upon the island, they may come from the outside, for this part of the Pacific is a dangerous region. We must take every precaution."

So the facade of Granite House was lighted with five windows, and with a door opening upon the "apartments," and admitting plenty of light into that wonderful nave which was to serve as their principal hallroom. This facade, eighty feet above the ground, was turned to the east, and caught the first rays of the morning sun. It was protected by the slope of the rock from the piercing northeast wind. In the meantime, while the sashes of the windows were being made, the engineer meant to close the openings with thick shutters, which would keep out wind and rain, and which could be readily concealed. The first work was to hollow out these windows. But the pickaxe was at a disadvantage among these hard rocks, and Smith again had recourse to the nitro-glycerine, which, used in small quantities, had the desired effect. Then the work was finished by the pick and mattock—the five ogive windows, the bay, the bull's-eyes, and the door—and, some days after the work was begun, the sun shone in upon the innermost recesses of Granite House.

According to Smith's plan, the space had been divided into five compartments looking out upon the sea; upon the right was the hall, opposite to the door from which the ladder was to hang, then a kitchen thirty feet long, a dining-room forty feet long, a sleeping-room of the same size, and last a "guest chamber," claimed by Pencroff; and bordering on the great hall.

These rooms, or rather this suite of rooms, in which they were to live, did not occupy the full depth of the cave. They opened upon a corridor which ran between them and a long storehouse, where were kept their utensils and provisions. All the products of the island, animal and vegetable, could be kept there in good condition and free from damp. They had room enough, and there was a place for everything. Moreover, the colonists still had at their disposal the little grotto above the large cavern, which would serve them as a sort of attic. This plan agreed upon, they became brickmakers again, and brought their bricks to the foot of Granite House.

Until that time the colonists had had access to the cavern only by the old weir. This mode of communication compelled them first to climb up Prospect Plateau, going round by the river, to descend 200 feet through the passage, and then to ascend the same distance when they wanted to regain the plateau. This involved fatigue and loss of time. Smith resolved to begin at once the construction of a strong rope ladder, which, once drawn up after them, would render the entrance to Granite House absolutely inaccessible. This ladder was made with the greatest care, and its sides were twisted of fibres by means of a shuttle. Thus constructed, it had the strength of a cable. The rungs were made of a kind of red cedar, with light and durable branches; and the whole was put together by the practised hand of Pencroff.

Another kind of tackle was made of vegetable fibre, and a sort of derrick was setup at the door of Granite House. In this way the bricks could easily be carried to the level of Granite House; and when some thousands of them were on the spot, with abundance of lime, they began work on the interior. They easily set up the wood partitions, and in a short time the space was divided into chambers and a store-house, according to the plan agreed upon.

These labors went on quickly under the direction of the engineer, who himself wielded hammer and trowel. They worked confidently and gaily. Pencroff, whether carpenter, ropemaker, or mason, always had a joke ready, and all shared in his good humor. His confidence in the engineer was absolute. All their wants would be supplied in Smith's own time. He dreamed of canals, of quarries, of mines, of machinery, even of railroads, one day, to cover the island. The engineer let Pencroff talk. He knew how contagious is confidence; he smiled to hear him, and said nothing of his own inquietude. But in his heart he feared that no help could come from the outside. In that part of the Pacific, out of the track of ships, and at such a distance from other land that no boat could dare put out to sea, they had only themselves to rely upon.

But, as the sailor said, they were far ahead of the Swiss Family Robinson, for whom miracles were always being wrought. In truth they knew Nature; and he who knows Nature will succeed when others would lie down to die.

Herbert especially distinguished himself in the work. He understood at a word and was prompt in execution. Smith grew fonder of him every day and Herbert was devoted to the engineer. Pencroff saw the growing friendship, but the honest sailor was not jealous. Neb was courage, zeal, and self-denial in person. He relied on his master as absolutely as Pencroff, but his enthusiasm was not so noisy. The sailor and he were great friends. As to Spilett, his skill and efficiency were a daily wonder to Pencroff. He was the model of a newspaper man—quick alike to understand and to perform.

The ladder was put in place May 28. It was eighty feet high, and consisted of 100 rungs; and, profiting by a projection in the face of the cliff, about forty feet up, Smith had divided it into two parts. This projection served as a sort of landing-place for the head of the lower ladder, shortening it, and thus lessening its swing. They fastened it with a cord so that it could easily be raised to the level of Granite House. The upper ladder they fastened at top and bottom. In this way the ascent was much more easy. Besides, Smith counted upon putting up at some future time a hydraulic elevator, which would save his companions much fatigue and loss of time.

The colonists rapidly accustomed themselves to the use of this ladder. The sailor, who was used to shrouds and ratlines, was their teacher. The great trouble was with Top, whose four feet were not intended for ladders. But Pencroff was persevering, and Top at last learned to run up and down as nimbly as his brothers of the circus. We cannot say whether the sailor was proud of this pupil, but he sometimes carried Top up on his back, and Top made no complaints.

All this time, the question of provisions was not neglected. Every day Herbert and the reporter spent some hours in the chase. They hunted only through Jacamar Woods, on the left of the river, for, in the absence of boat or bridge, they had not yet crossed the Mercy. The immense woody tracts which they had named the Forests of the Far West were entirely unexplored. This important excursion was set apart for the first five days of the coming spring. But Jacamar Woods were not wanting in game; kangaroos and boars were plenty there, and the iron-tipped spears, the bows and arrows of the hunters did wonders. More than this, Herbert discovered, at the southwest corner of, the lagoon, a natural warren, a sort of moist meadow covered with willows and aromatic herbs, which perfumed the air, such as thyme, basil, and all sorts of mint, of which rabbits are so fond. The reporter said that when the feast was spread for them it would be strange if the rabbits did not come; and the hunters explored the warren carefully. At all events, it produced an abundance of useful plants, and would give a naturalist plenty of work. Herbert gathered a quantity of plants possessing different medicinal properties, pectoral, astringent, febrifuge, anti-rheumatic. When Pencroff asked of what good were all this collection of herbs:—

"To cure us when we are sick," answered the boy.

"Why should we be sick, since there are no doctors on the island?" said Pencroff, quite seriously.

To this no reply could be made, but the lad went on gathering his bundle, which was warmly welcomed at Granite House; especially as he had found some Mountain Mint, known in North America as "Oswego Tea," which produces a pleasant beverage.

That day the hunters, in their search, reached the site of the warren. The ground was perforated with little holes like a colander.

"Burrows!" cried Herbert.

"But are they inhabited?"

"That is the question."

A question which was quickly resolved. Almost immediately, hundreds of little animals, like rabbits, took to flight in every direction, with such rapidity that Top himself was distanced. But the reporter was determined not to quit the place till he had captured half a dozen of the little beasts. He wanted them now for the kitchen: domestication would come later. With a few snares laid at the mouth of the burrows, the affair would be easy; but there were no snares, nor materials for snares; so they patiently rummaged every form with their sticks, until four rodents were taken.

They were rabbits, much like their European congeners, and commonly known as "American hares." They were brought back to Granite Home, and figured in that evening's meal. Delicious eating they were; and the warren bade fair to be a most valuable reserve for the colonists.

On May 31, the partitions were finished, and nothing remained but to furnish the rooms, which would occupy the long days of winter. A chimney was built in the room which served as a kitchen. The construction of the stove-pipe gave them a good deal of trouble. The simplest material was clay; and as they did not wish to have any outlet on the upper plateau, they pierced a hole above the kitchen window, and conducted the pipe obliquely to this hole. No doubt during an eastern gale the pipe would smoke, but the wind rarely blew from that quarter, and head-cook Neb was not particular

When these domestic arrangements had been made, the engineer proceeded to block up the mouth of the old weir by the lake, so as to prevent any approach from that quarter. Great square blocks were rolled to the opening, and strongly cemented together. Smith did not yet attempt to put in execution his project of damming up the waters of the lake so as to conceal this weir; he was satisfied with concealing the obstruction he had placed there by means of grass, shrubs, and thistles, which were planted in the interstices of the rocks, and which by the next spring would sprout up luxuriantly. Meanwhile he utilized the weir in conducting to their new abode a little stream of fresh water from the lake. A little drain, constructed just below its level, had the effect of supplying them with twenty-five or thirty gallons a day; so there was likely to be no want of water at Granite House.

At last, all was finished, just in time for the tempestuous season. They closed the windows with thick shutters till Smith should have time to make glass from the sand. In the rocky projections around the windows Spilett had arranged, very artistically, plants of various kinds and long floating grasses, and thus the windows were framed picturesquely in green. The denizens of this safe and solid dwelling could but be delighted with their work. The windows opened upon a limitless horizon, shut in only by the two Mandible Capes on the north and by Claw Cape at the south. Union Bay spread magnificently before them. They had reason enough to be satisfied, and Pencroff did not spare his praises of what he called "his suite on the fifth floor."

CHAPTER XX.

THE RAINY SEASON—WHAT TO WEAR-A
SEAL-HUNT—CANDLE-MAKING—-WORK IN THE
GRANITE HOUSE—THE TWO CAUSEWAYS—RETURN
FROM A VISIT TO THE OYSTER-BED—WHAT HERBERT
FOUND IS HIS POCKET.

The winter season began in earnest with the month of June, which corresponded with December in our northern hemisphere. Showers and storms succeeded each other without an intermission, and the inmates of the Granite House could appreciate the advantages of a dwelling impervious to the weather. The Chimneys would indeed have proved a miserable shelter against the inclemency of the winter; they feared even lest the high tides driven by the sea-wind should pour in and destroy their furnaces and their foundry. All this month of June was occupied with various labors, which left plenty of time for hunting and fishing, so that the reserve stock of food was constantly kept up. Pencroff intended, as soon as he had time, to set traps, from which he expected great results. He had made snares of ligneous fibre, and not a day passed but some rodent was captured from the warren. Neb spent all his time in smoking and salting meat.

The question of clothes now came up for serious discussion. The colonists had no other garments than those which they wore when the balloon cast them on shore. These, fortunately, were warm and substantial; and by dint of extreme care, even their linen had been kept clean and whole; but everything would soon wear out, and moreover, during a vigorous winter, they would suffer severely from cold. Here Smith was fairly baffled. He had been occupied in providing for their most urgent wants, food and shelter, and the winter was upon them before the clothes problem could be solved. They must resign themselves to bear the cold with fortitude, and when the dry season returned would undertake a great hunt of the moufflons, which they had seen on Mount Franklin, and whose wool the engineer could surely make into warm thick cloth. He would think over the method.

"Well, we must toast ourselves before the fire!" said Pencroff." There's plenty of fire wood, no reason for sparing it."

"Besides," added Spilett, "Lincoln Island is not in very high latitude, and the winters are probably mild. Did you not say, Cyrus that the thirty-fifth parallel corresponded with that of Spain in the other hemisphere?"

"Yes," said the engineer, "but the winter in Spain is sometimes very cold, with snow and ice, and we may have a hard time of it. Still we are on an island, and have a good chance for more moderate weather."

"Why, Mr. Smith?" said Herbert.

"Because the sea, my boy, may be considered as an immense reservoir, in which the summer heat lies stored. At the coming of winter this heat is again given out, so that the neighboring regions have always a medium temperature, cooler in summer and warmer in winter."

"We shall see," said Pencroff. "I am not going to bother myself about the weather. One thing is certain, the days are getting short already and the evenings long. Suppose we talk a little about candles."

"Nothing is easier," said Smith.

"To talk about?" asked the sailor.

"To make."

"And when shall we begin?"

"To-morrow, by a seal-hunt."

"What! to make dips?"

"No, indeed, Pencroff, candles."

Such was the engineer's project, which was feasible enough, as he had lime and sulphuric acid, and as the amphibia of the island would furnish the necessary fat. It was now June 4, and Pentecost Sunday, which they kept as a day of rest and thanksgiving. They were no longer miserable castaways, they were colonists. On the next day, June 5, they started for the islet. They had to choose the time of low tide to ford the channel; and all determined that, somehow or other, they must build a boat which would give them easy communication with all parts of the island, and would enable them to go up the Mercy, when they should undertake that grand exploration of the southwestern district which they had reserved for the first good weather.

Seals were numerous, and the hunters, armed with their iron-spiked spears, easily killed half a dozen of them, which Neb and Pencroff skinned. Only the hides and fat were carried back to Granite House, the former to be made into shoes. The result of the hunt was about 300 pounds of fat, every pound of which could be used in making candles. The operation was simple enough, and the product, if not the best of its kind, was all they needed. Had Smith had at his disposition nothing but sulphuric acid, he could, by heating this acid with neutral fats, such as the fat of the seal, separate the glycerine, which again could be resolved, by means of boiling water, into oleine, margarine, and stearine. But, to simplify the operation, he preferred to saponify the fat by lime. He thus obtained a calcareous soap, easily decomposed by sulphuric acid, which precipitated the lime as a sulphate, and freed the fatty acids. The first of these three acids (oleine, margarine, and stearine) was a liquid which he expelled by pressure. The other two formed the raw material of the candles.

In twenty-four hours the work was done. Wicks were made, after some unsuccessful attempts, from vegetable fibre, and were steeped in the liquified compound. They were real stearine candles, made by hand, white and smooth.

During all this month work was going on inside their new abode. There was plenty of carpenter's work to do. They improved and completed their tools, which were very rudimentary. Scissors were made, among other things, so that they were able to cut their hair, and, if not actually to shave their beards, at least to trim them to their liking. Herbert had no beard, and Neb none to speak of, but the others found ample employment for the scissors.

They had infinite trouble in making a hand-saw; but at last succeeded in shaping an instrument which would cut wood by a rigorous application. Then they made tables, chairs and cupboards to furnish the principal rooms, and the frames of beds whose only bedding was mattrasses of wrack-grass. The kitchen, with its shelves, on which lay the terra-cotta utensils, its brick furnace, and its washing-stone, looked very comfortable, and Neb cooked with the gravity of a chemist in his laboratory.

But joiners work had to give place to carpentry. The new weir created by the explosion rendered necessary the construction of two causeways, one upon Prospect Plateau, the other on the shore itself. Now the plateau and the coast were transversely cut by a water-course which the colonists had to cross when ever they wished to reach the northern part of the island. To avoid this they had to make a considerable detour, and to walk westward as far as the sources of Red creek. Their best plan therefore was to build two causeways, one on the plateau and one on the shore, twenty to twenty-five feet long, simply constructed of trees squared by the axe. This was the work of some days. When these bridges had been built, Neb and Pencroff profited by them to go to the oyster-bed which had been discovered off the down. They dragged after them a sort of rough cart which had taken the place of the inconvenient hurdle; and they brought back several thousand oysters, which, were readily acclimated among the rocks, and formed a natural preserve at the mouth of the Mercy. They were excellent of their kind, and formed an almost daily article of diet. In fact, Lincoln Island, though the colonists had explored but a small portion of it, already supplied nearly all their wants, while it seemed likely that a minute exploration of the western forests would reveal a world of new treasures.

Only one privation still distressed the colonists. Azotic food they had in plenty, and the vegetables which corrected it; from the ligneous roots of the dragon-trees, submitted to fermentation, they obtained a sort of acidulated beer. They had even made sugar, without sugar-cane or beet-root, by collecting the juice which distills from the "acer saccharinum," a sort of maple which flourishes in all parts of the temperate zone, and which abounded on the island. They made a very pleasant tea from the plant brought from the warren; and, finally, they had plenty of salt, the only mineral component necessary to food—but bread was still to seek.

Perhaps, at some future time, they would have been able to replace this aliment by some equivalent, sago flour, or the breadfruit tree, which they might possibly have discovered in the woods of the southwest; but so far they had not met with them. Just at this time a little incident occurred which brought about what Smith, with all his ingenuity, could not have achieved.

One rainy day the colonists were together in the large hall of Granite House, when Herbert suddenly cried,

"See, Mr. Smith, a grain of corn."

And he showed his companions a single gram which had got into the lining of his waistcoat through a hole in his pocket. Pencroff had given him some ring-doves in Richmond, and in feeding them one of the grains had remained in his pocket.

"A grain of corn?" said the engineer, quickly.

"Yes, sir; but only one."

"That's a wonderful help," said Pencroff, laughing. "The bread that grain will make will never choke us."

Herbert was about to throw away the grain, when Cyrus Smith took it, examined it, found that it was in good condition, and said quietly to the sailor:—

"Pencroff, do you know how many ears of corn will spring from one grain?"

"One, I suppose," said the sailor, surprised at the question.

"Ten, Pencroff. And how many grains are there to an ear?"

"Faith, I don't know."

"Eighty on an average," said Smith. "So then, if we plant this grain, we shall get from it a harvest of 800 grains; from them in the second year 640,000; in the third, 512,000,000; in the fourth, more than 400,000,000,000. That is the proportion."

His companions listened in silence. The figures stupefied them.

"Yes, my friend," resumed the engineer. "Such is the increase of Nature. And what is even this multiplication of a grain of corn whose ears have only 800 grains, compared with the poppy plant, which has 32,000 seeds, or the tobacco plant, which has 360,000? In a few years, but for the numerous enemies which destroy them, these plants would cover the earth. And now, Pencroff," he resumed, "do you know how many bushels there are in 400,000,000,000 grains?"

"No," answered the sailor, "I only know that I am an idiot!"

"Well, there will be more than 3,000,000, at 130,000 the bushel!"

"Three millions!" cried Pencroff.

"Three millions."

"In four years?"

"Yes," said Smith, "and even in two, if, as I hope, we can get two harvests a year in this latitude."

Pencroff answered with a tremendous hurrah.

"So, Herbert," added the engineer, "your discovery is of immense importance. Remember, my friends, that everything may be of use to us in our present situation."

"Indeed, Mr. Smith, I will remember it," said Pencroff, "and if ever I find one of those grains of tobacco which increase 360,000 times, I'll take care not to throw it away. And now what must we do?"

"We must plant this grain," said Herbert.

"Yes," added Spilett, "and with the greatest care, for upon it depend our future harvests!"

"Provided that it grows," said the sailor.

"It will grow," answered Smith.

It was now the 20th of June, a good time for planting the precious grain. They thought at first of planting it in a pot; but upon consideration, they determined to trust it frankly to the soil. The same day it was planted, with the greatest precaution. The weather clearing a little, they walked up to the plateau above Granite House, and chose there a spot well sheltered from the wind, and exposed to the midday fervor of the sun. This spot was cleared, weeded, and even dug, so as to destroy insects and worms; it was covered with a layer of fresh earth, enriched with a little lime; a palissade was built around it, and then the grain was covered up in its moist bed.

They seemed to be laying the corner-stone of an edifice. Pencroff was reminded of the extreme care with which they had lighted their only match; but this was a more serious matter. The castaways could always have succeeded in obtaining fire by some means or other; but no earthly power could restore that grain of corn, if, by ill fortune, it should perish!

CHAPTER XXI.

SEVERAL DEGREES BELOW ZERO—EXPLORATION OF
THE SWAMP REGION TO THE SOUTHEAST—THE VIEW
OF THE SEA—A CONVERSATION CONCERNING THE
FUTURE OF THE PACIFIC OCEAN—THE INCESSANT
LABOR OF THE INFUSORIA—WHAT WILL BECOME
OF THIS GLOBE—THE CHASE—THE SWAMP OF
THE TADORNS.

From this moment Pencroff did not let a day pass without visiting what he called with perfect gravity, his "corn field." And alas, for any insects that ventured there, no mercy would be shown them. Near the end of the month of June, after the interminable rains, the weather became decidedly cold, and on the 29th, a Fahrenheit thermometer would certainly have stood at only 20° above zero.

The next day, the 30th of June, the day which corresponds to the 31st of December in the Northern Hemisphere, was a Friday. Neb said the year ended on an unlucky day, but Pencroff answered that consequently the new year began on a lucky one, which was more important. At all events, it began with a very cold snap. Ice accumulated at the mouth of the Mercy, and the whole surface of the lake was soon frozen over.

Fresh firewood had continually to be procured. Pencroff had not waited for the river to freeze to convey enormous loads of wood to their destination. The current was a tireless motor, and conveyed the floating wood until the ice froze around it. To the fuel, which the forest so plentifully furnished, were added several cartloads of coal, which they found at the foot of the spurs of Mount Franklin. The powerful heat from the coal was thoroughly appreciated in a temperature which on the 4th of July fell to eight degrees above zero. A second chimney had been set up in the dining-room, where they all worked together. During this cold spell Cyrus Smith could not be thankful enough that he had conducted to Granite House a small stream of water from Lake Grant. Taken below the frozen surface, then conducted through the old weir, it arrived unfrozen at the interior reservoir, which had been dug at the angle of the storehouse, and which, when too full, emptied itself into the sea. About this time the weather being very dry, the colonists, dressing as warmly as possible, determined to devote a day to the exploration of that part of the island situated to the southeast, between the Mercy and Claw Cape. It was a large swampy district and might offer good hunting, as aquatic birds must abound there. They would have eight or nine miles to go and as far to return, consequently the whole day must be given up. As it concerned the exploration of an unknown portion of the island, every one had to take part.

Therefore, on the 5th of July, at 6 o'clock in the morning, before the sun had fairly risen, the whole party, armed with spears, snares, bows and arrows, and furnished with enough provisions for the day, started from Granite House, preceded by Top, who gambolled before them. They took the shortest route, which was to cross the Mercy on the blocks of ice which then obstructed it.

"But," as the reporter very truly observed, "this cannot supply the place of a real bridge."

So the construction of a "real" bridge was set down as work for the future. This was the first time that the colonists had set foot on the right bank of the Mercy and had plunged into the forest of large and magnificent firs, then covered with snow. But they had not gone half a mile when the barking of Top frightened from a dense thicket where they had taken up their abode, a whole family of quadrupeds.

"Why they look like foxes," said Herbert, when he saw them scampering quickly away.

And they were foxes, but foxes of enormous size. They made a sort of bark which seemed to astonish Top, for he stopped in his chase and gave these swift animals time to escape. The dog had a right to be surprised, for he knew nothing of natural history; but by this barking, the greyish-red color of their hair, and their black tails, which ended in a white tuft, these foxes had betrayed their origin. So Herbert gave them without hesitation their true name of culpeux. These culpeux are often met with in Chili, in the Saint Malo group, and in all those parts of America lying between the 30th and 40th parallels.

Herbert was very sorry that Top had not caught one of these carnivora.

"Can we eat them?" asked Pencroff, who always considered the fauna of the island from that special point of view.

"No," said Herbert, "but zoologists have not yet ascertained whether the pupil of the eye of this fox is diurnal or nocturnal, or whether the animal would come under the genus "canine.""

Smith could not help smiling at this remark of the boy, which showed thoughtfulness beyond his years. As for the sailor, from the moment these foxes ceased to belong to the edible species, they ceased to interest him. Ever since the kitchen had been established at Granite House he had been saying that precautions ought to be taken against these four-footed plunderers. A fact which no one denied.

Having turned Jetsam Point the party came upon a long reach washed by the sea. It was then 8 o'clock in the morning. The sky was very clear, as is usual in prolonged cold weather; but, warmed by their work, Smith and his companions did not suffer from the sharpness of the atmosphere. Besides, there was no wind, the absence of which always renders a low temperature more endurable. The sun, bright but cold, rose from the ocean, and his enormous disc was poised in the horizon. The sea was a calm, blue sheet of water, like a land-locked sea under a clear sky. Claw

Cape, bent in the shape of an ataghan, was clearly defined about four miles to the southeast. To the left, the border of the swamp was abruptly intercepted by a little point which shone brightly against the sun. Certainly in that part of Union Bay, which was not protected from the open sea, even by a sand bank, ships beaten by an east wind could not have found shelter.

By the perfect calm of the sea, with no shoals to disturb its waters, by its uniform color, with no tinge of yellow, and, finally, by the entire absence of reefs, they knew that this side was steep, and that here the ocean was fathoms deep. Behind them, in the west, at a distance of about four miles, they saw the beginning of the Forests of the Far West. They could almost have believed themselves upon some desolate island in the Antarctic regions surrounded by ice.

The party halted here for breakfast; a fire of brushwood and seaweed was lighted, and Neb prepared the meal of cold meat, to which he added some cups of Oswego tea. While eating they looked around them. This side of Lincoln island was indeed barren, and presented a strong contrast to the western part.

The reporter thought that if the castaways had been thrown upon this coast, they would have had a very melancholy impression of their future home.

"I do not believe we could even have reached it," said the engineer, "for the sea is very deep here, and there is not even a rock which would have served as a refuge; before Granite House there were shoals, at least, and a little island which multiplied our chances of safety; here is only the bottomless sea."

"It is curious enough," said Spilett, "that this island, relatively so small, presents so varied a soil. This diversity of appearance belongs, logically, only to continents of a considerable area. One would really think that the western side of Lincoln Island, so rich and fertile, was washed by the warm waters of the Gulf of Mexico, and that the northern and southern coasts extended into a sort of Arctic Sea."

"You are right, my dear Spilett," replied the engineer, "I have observed the same thing. I have found this island curious both in its shape and in its character. It has all the peculiarities of a continent, and I would not be surprised if it had been a continent formerly."

"What! a continent in the middle of the Pacific!" cried Pencroff.

"Why not?" answered Smith. "Why should not Australia, New Ireland, all that the English geographers call Australasia, joined to the Archipelagoes of the Pacific Ocean, have formed in times past a sixth part of the world as important as Europe or Asia, Africa or the two Americas. My mind does not refuse to admit that all the islands rising from this vast ocean are the mountains of a continent now engulphed, but which formerly rose majestically from these waters."

"Like Atlantis?" asked Herbert. "Yes. my boy, if that ever existed." "And Lincoln Island may have been a part of this continent?" asked Pencroff. "It is probable," replied Smith. "And that would explain the diversity of products upon the surface, and the number of animals which still live here," added Herbert.

"Yes, my boy," answered the engineer, "and that gives me a new argument in support of my theory. It is certain after what we have seen that the animals in the island are numerous, and what is more curious, is that the species are extremely varied. There must be a reason for this, and mine is, that Lincoln Island was formerly a part of some vast continent, which has, little by little, sunk beneath the surface of the Pacific." "Then," said Pencroff, who did not seem entirely convinced, "what remains of this old continent may disappear in its turn and leave nothing between America and Asia." "Yes," said Smith, "there will be new continents which millions upon millions of animalculæ are building at this moment." "And who are these masons?" inquired Pencroff. "The coral insects," answered Smith. "It is these who have built by their constant labor the Island of Clermont Tonnerre, the Atolls and many other coral islands which abound in the Pacific. It takes 47,000,000 of these insects to deposit one particle; and yet with the marine salt which they absorb, and the solid elements of the water which they assimilate, these animalculæ produce limestone, and limestone forms those enormous submarine structures whose hardness and solidity is equal to that of granite.

Formerly, during the first epochs of creation, Nature employed heat to produce land by upheaval, but now she lets these microscopic insects replace this agent, whose dynamic power at the interior of this globe has evidently diminished. This fact is sufficiently proved by the great number of volcanoes actually extinct on the surface of the earth. I verily believe that century after century, and infusoria after infusoria will change the Pacific some day into a vast continent, which new generations will, in their turn, inhabit and civilize."

"It will take a long time," said Pencroff. "Nature has time on her side," replied the engineer. "But what is the good of new continents?" asked Herbert. "It seems to me that the present extent of habitable countries is enough for mankind. Now Nature does nothing in vain." "Nothing in vain, indeed," replied the engineer; "but let us see how we can explain the necessity of new continents in the future, and precisely in these tropical regions occupied by these coral islands. Here is an explanation, which seems to me at least plausible."

"We are listening, Mr. Smith," replied Herbert.

"This is my idea: Scientists generally admit that some day the globe must come to an end, or rather the animal and vegetable life will be no longer possible, on account of the intense cold which will prevail. What they cannot agree upon is the cause of this cold. Some think that it will be produced by the cooling of the sun in the course of millions of years; others by the gradual extinction of the internal fires of our own globe, which have a more decided influence than is generally supposed. I hold to this last hypothesis, based upon the fact that the moon is without doubt a refrigerated planet, which is no longer habitable, although the sun continues to pour upon its surface the same amount of heat. If then, the moon is refrigerated, it is because these internal fires, to which like all the stellar world it owes its origin, are entirely extinct. In short, whatever be the cause, our world will certainly some day cool; but this cooling will take place gradually. What will happen then? Why, the temperate zones, at a time more or less distant, will be no more habitable than are the Polar regions now. Then human, as well as animal life, will be driven to latitudes more directly under the influence of the solar rays. An immense emigration will take place. Europe, Central Asia, and North America will little by little be abandoned, as well as Australasia and the lower parts of South America. Vegetation will follow the human emigration. The flora will move towards the equator at the same time with the fauna, the central parts of South America and Africa will become the inhabited continent. The Laplanders and the Samoyedes will find the climate of the Polar Sea on the banks of the Mediterranean. Who can tell but that at this epoch, the equatorial regions will not be too small to contain and nourish the population of the globe. Now, why should not a provident nature, in order from this time, to provide a refuge for this animal and vegetable emigration, lay the foundation, under the equator, of a new continent, and charge these infusoria with the building of it? I have often thought of this, my friends, and I seriously believe that, some day, the aspect of our globe will be completely transformed, that after the upheaval of new continents the seas will cover the old ones, and that in future ages some Columbus will discover in the islands of Chimborazo or the Himalaya, or Mount Blanc, all that remains of an America, an Asia, and a Europe. Then at last, these new continents, in their turn, will become uninhabitable. The heat will die out as does the heat from a body whose soul has departed, and life will disappear from the globe, if not forever, at least for a time. Perhaps then our sphere will rest from its changes, and will prepare in death to live again under nobler conditions.

"But all this my friends, is with the Creator of all things. From the talking of the work of these infusoria I have been led into too deep a scrutiny of the secrets of the future."

"My dear Cyrus," said the reporter, "these theories are to me prophesies. Some day they will be accomplished."

"It is a secret with the Almighty," replied Smith.

"All this is well and good," said Pencroff, who had listened with all his ears, "but will you tell me, Mr. Smith, if Lincoln Island has been constructed by these infusoria."

"No," replied Smith, "it is of purely volcanic origin."

"Then it will probably disappear some day. I hope sincerely we won't be here."

"No, be easy, Pencroff, we will get away."

"In the meantime," said Spilett, "let us settle ourselves as if forever. It is never worth while to do anything by halves."

This ended the conversation. Breakfast was over, the exploration continued, and the party soon arrived at the beginning of the swampy district.

It was, indeed, a marsh which extended as far as the rounded side forming the southeastern termination of the island, and measuring twenty square miles. The soil was formed of a silicious clay mixed with decayed vegetation. It was covered by confervæ, rushes, sedges, and here and there by beds of herbage, thick as a velvet carpet. In many places frozen pools glistened under the sun's rays. Neither rains, nor any river swollen by a sudden increase could have produced this water. One would naturally conclude that this swamp was fed by the infiltration of water through the soil. And this was the fact. It was even to be feared that the air here during hot weather, was laden with that miasma which engenders the marsh fever. Above the aquatic herbs on the surface of the stagnant waters, a swarm of birds were flying. A hunter would not have lost a single shot. Wild ducks, teal, and snipe lived there in flocks, and it was easy to approach these fearless creatures. So thick were these birds that a charge of shot would certainly have brought down a dozen of them, but our friends had to content themselves with their bows and arrows. The slaughter was less, but the quiet arrow had the advantage of not frightening the birds, while the sound of fire-arms would have scattered them to every corner of the swamp. The hunters contented themselves this time with a dozen ducks, with white bodies, cinnamon-colored belts, green heads, wings black, white, and red, and feathered beaks. These Herbert recognized as the "Tadorns." Top did his share well in the capture of these birds, whose name was given this swampy district.

The colonists now had an abundant reserve of aquatic game. When the time should come the only question would be how to make a proper use of them, and it was probable that several species of these birds would be, if not domesticated, at least acclimated, upon the borders of the lake, which would bring them nearer to the place of consumption.

About 5 o'clock in the afternoon Smith and his companions turned their faces homewards. They crossed Tadorn's Fens, and re-crossed the Mercy upon the ice, arriving at Granite House at 8 o'clock in the evening.

CHAPTER XXII.

THE TRAPS—THE FOXES—THE PECCARIES—
THE WIND VEERS TO THE NORTHWEST—
THE SNOW-STORM—THE BASKET-MAKERS—
THE COLDEST SNAP OF WINTER—
CRYSTALLIZATION OF THE SUGAR-MAPLE—
THE MYSTERIOUS SHAFTS—THE PROJECTED
EXPLORATION—THE PELLET OF LEAD.

The intense cold lasted until the 15th of August, the thermometer never rising above the point hitherto observed. When the atmosphere was calm this low temperature could be easily borne; but when the wind blew, the poor fellows suffered much for want of warmer clothing. Pencroff regretted that Lincoln Island, instead of harboring so many foxes and seals, with no fur to speak of, did not shelter some families of bears.

"Bears," said he, "are generally well dressed; and I would ask nothing better for the winter than the loan of their warm cloaks.".

"But perhaps," said Neb, laughing "These bears would not consent to give you their cloak. Pencroff, these fellows are no Saint Martins."

"We would make them, Neb, we would make them," answered Pencroff in a tone of authority.

But these formidable carnivora did not dwell on the island, or if they did, had not yet shown themselves. Herbert, Pencroff, and the reporter were constantly at work getting traps on Prospect Plateau and on the borders of the forest. In the sailor's opinion any animal whatever would be a prize, and rodents or carnivora, whichever these new traps should entice, would be well received at Granite House. These traps were very simple. They were pits dug in the ground and covered with branches and grass, which hid the openings. At the bottom they placed some bait, whose odor would attract the animals. They used their discretion about the position of their traps, choosing places where numerous footprints indicated the frequent passage of quadrupeds. Every day they went to look at them, and at three different times during the first few days they found in them specimens of those foxes which had been already seen on the right bank of the Mercy.

"Pshaw! there are nothing but foxes in this part of the world," said Pencroff, as, for the third time, he drew one of these animals out of the pit. "Good-for-nothing beasts;"

"Stop," said Spilett; "they are good for something."

"For what?"

"To serve as bait to attract others!"

The reporter was right, and from this time the traps were baited with the dead bodies of foxes. The sailor had made snares out of the threads of curry-jonc, and these snares were more profitable than the traps. It was a rare thing for a day to pass without some rabbit from the warren being captured. It was always a rabbit, but Neb knew how to vary his sauces, and his companions did not complain. However, once or twice in the second week in August, the traps contained other and more useful animals than the foxes. There were some of those wild boars which had been already noticed at the north of the lake. Pencroff had no need to ask if these animals were edible, that was evident from their resemblance to the hog of America and Europe.

"But these are not hogs, let me tell you," said Herbert.

"My boy," replied the sailor, handing over the trap and drawing out one of these representatives of the swine family by the little appendage which served for a tail, "do let me believe them to be hogs."

"Why?"

"Because it pleases me."

"You are fond of hogs, then, Pencroff?"

"I am very fond of them," replied the sailor, "especially of their feet, and if any had eight instead of four I would like them twice as much."

These animals were peccaries, belonging to one of the four genera, which make up that family. This particular species were the "tajassans," known by there dark color and the absence of those long fangs which belong to the others of their race. Peccaries generally live in herds, and it was likely that these animals abounded in the woody parts of the island. At all events they were edible from head to foot, and Pencroff asked nothing more.

About the 15th of August the weather moderated suddenly by a change of wind to the northwest. The temperature rose several degrees higher, and the vapors accumulated in the air were soon resolved into snow. The whole island was covered with a white mantle, and presented a new aspect to its inhabitants. It snowed hard for several days and the ground was covered two feet deep. The wind soon rose with great violence and from the top of Granite House they could hear the sea roaring against the reefs.

At certain angles the wind made eddies in the air, and the snow, forming itself into high whirling columns, looked like those twisting waterspouts which vessels attack with cannon. The hurricane, coming steadily from the northwest, spent its force on the other side of the island, and the eastern lookout of Granite House preserved it from a direct attack.

During this snow-storm, as terrible as those of the polar regions, neither Smith nor his companions could venture outside. They were completely housed for five days, from the 20th to the 25th of August. They heard the tempest roar though Jacamar Woods, which must have suffered sadly. Doubtless numbers of trees were uprooted, but Pencroff comforted himself with the reflection that there would be fewer to cut down.

"The wind will be wood-cutter; let it alone," said he.

How fervently now the inhabitants of Granite House must have thanked Heaven for having given to them this solid and impenetrable shelter! Smith had his share of their gratitude, but after all, it was nature which had hollowed out this enormous cave, and he had only discovered it. Here all were in safety, the violence of the tempest could not reach them. If they had built a house of brick and wood on Prospect Plateau, it could not have resisted the fury of this hurricane. As for the Chimneys, they heard the billows strike them with such violence that they knew they must be uninhabitable, for the sea, having entirely covered their islet, beat upon them with all its force.

But here at Granite House, between these solid walls which neither wind nor water could effect, they had nothing to fear. During this confinement the colonists were not idle. There was plenty of wood in the storehouse cut into planks, and little by little they completed their stock of furniture. As far as tables and chairs went they were certainly solid enough, for the material was not spared. This furniture was a little too heavy to fulfil its essential purpose of being easily moved, but it was the pride of Neb and Pencroff, who would not have exchanged it for the handsomest Buhl.

Then the carpenters turned basket-makers, and succeeded remarkably well at this new occupation.

They had discovered at the northern part of the lake a thick growth of purple osiers. Before the rainy season, Pencroff and Herbert had gathered a good many of these useful shrubs; and their branches, being now well seasoned, could be used to advantage. Their first specimens were rough; but, thanks to the skill and intelligence of the workmen consulting together, recalling the models they had seen, and rivalling each other in their efforts, hampers and baskets of different sizes here soon added to the stock of the colony. The storehouse was filled with them, and Neb set away in special baskets his stock of pistachio nuts and roots of the dragon tree.

During the last week in August the weather changed again, the temperature fell a little, and the storm was over. The colonists at once started out. There must have been at least two feet of snow on the shore, but it was frozen over the top, which made it easy to walk over. Smith and his companions climbed up Prospect Plateau. What a change they beheld! The woods which they had left in bloom, especially the part nearest to them where the conifers were plenty, were now one uniform color.

Everything was white, from the top of Mount Franklin to the coast—forests, prairie, lake, river, beach. The waters of the Mercy ran under a vault of ice, which cracked and broke with a loud noise at every change of tide. Thousands of birds—ducks and wood-peckers—flew over the surface of the lake. The rocks between which the cascade plunged to the borders of the Plateau were blocked up with ice. One would have said that the water leaped out of a huge gargoyle, cut by some fantastic artist of the Renaissance. To calculate the damage done to the forest by this hurricane would be impossible until the snow had entirely disappeared.

Spilett, Pencroff, and Herbert took this opportunity to look after their traps and had hard work finding them under their bed of snow. There was danger of their falling in themselves; a humiliating thing to be caught in one's own trap! They were spared this annoyance, however, and found the traps had been untouched; not an animal had been caught, although there were a great many footprints in the neighborhood, among others, very clearly impressed marks of claws.

Herbert at once classified these carnivora among the cat tribe, a circumstance which justified the engineer's belief in the existence of dangerous beasts on Lincoln Island. Doubtless these beasts dwelt in the dense forests of the Far West; but driven by hunger, they had ventured as far as Prospect Plateau. Perhaps they scented the inhabitants of Granite House.

"What, exactly, are these carnivora?" asked Pencroff.

"They are tigers," replied Herbert.

"I thought those animals were only found in warm countries."

"In the New World," replied the lad, "they are to be found from Mexico to the pampas of Buenos Ayres. Now, as Lincoln Island is in almost the same latitude as La Plata, it is not surprising that tigers are found here."

"All right, we will be on our guard," replied Pencroff.

In the meantime, the temperature rising, the snow began to melt, it came on to rain, and gradually the white mantle disappeared. Notwithstanding the bad weather the colonists renewed their stock of provisions, both animal and vegetable.

This necessitated excursions into the forest, and thus they discovered how many trees had been beaten down by the hurricane. The sailor and Neb pushed forward with their wagon as far as the coal deposit in order to carry back some fuel. They saw on their way that the chimney of the pottery oven had been much damaged by the storm; at least six feet had been blown down.

They also renewed their stock of wood as well as that of coal, and the Mercy having become free once more, they employed the current to draw several loads to Granite House. It might be that the cold season was not yet over.

A visit had been made to the Chimneys also, and the colonists could not be sufficiently grateful that this had not been their home during the tempest. The sea had left undoubted signs of its ravages. Lashed by the fury of the wind from the offing, and rushing over Safety Island, it spent its full force upon these passages, leaving them half full of sand and the rocks thickly covered with seaweed.

While Neb, Herbert, and Pencroff spent their time in hunting and renewing their supply of fuel, Smith andSpilett set to work to clear out the Chimneys. They found the forge and furnaces almost unhurt, so carefully protected had they been by the banks of sand which the colonists had built around them.

It was a fortunate thing that they laid in a fresh supply of fuel, for the colonists had not yet seen the end of the intense cold. It is well known that in the Northern Hemisphere, the month of February is noted for its low temperature. The same rule held good in the Southern Hemisphere, and the end of August, which is the February of North America, did not escape from this climatic law.

About the 25th, after another snow and rain storm, the wind veered to the southeast, and suddenly the cold became intense. In the engineer's opinion, a Fahrenheit thermometer would have indicated about eight degrees below zero, and the cold was rendered more severe by a cutting wind which lasted for several days.

The colonists were completely housed again, and as they were obliged to block up all their windows, only leaving one narrow opening for ventilation, the consumption of candles was considerable. In order to economize them, the colonists often contented themselves with only the light from the fire; for fuel was plenty.

Once or twice some of them ventured to the beach, among the blocks of ice which were heaped up there by every fresh tide. But they soon climbed up to Granite House again. This ascent was very painful, as their hands were frostbitten by holding on to the frozen sides of the ladder.

There were still many leisure hours to be filled up during this long confinement, so Smith undertook another indoor occupation.

The only sugar which they had had up to this time was a liquid substance which they had procured by making deep cuts in the bark of the maple tree. They collected this liquid in jars and used it in this condition for cooking purposes. It improved with age, becoming whiter and more like a syrup in consistency. But they could do better than this, and one day Cyrus Smith announced to his companions that he was going to turn them into refiners.

"Refiners! I believe that's a warm trade?" said Pencroff.

"Very warm!" replied the engineer.

"Then it will suit this season!" answered the sailor.

Refining did not necessitate a stock of complicated tools or skilled workmen; it was a very simple operation.

To crystallize this liquid they first clarified it, by putting it on the fire in earthenware jars, and submitting it to evaporation. Soon a scum rose to the surface, which, when it began to thicken, Neb removed carefully with a wooden ladle. This hastened the evaporation, and at the same time prevented it from scorching.

After several hours boiling over a good fire, which did as much good to the cooks as it did to the boiling liquid, it turned into a thick syrup. This syrup was poured into clay moulds which they had made beforehand, in various shapes in the same kitchen furnace.

The next day the syrup hardened, forming cakes and loaves. It was sugar of a reddish color, but almost transparent, and of a delicious taste.

The cold continued until the middle of September, and the inmates of Granite House began to find their captivity rather tedious. Almost every day they took a run out-doors, but they always soon returned. They were constantly at work over their household duties, and talked while they worked.

Smith instructed his companions in everything, and especially explained to them the practical applications of science.

The colonists had no library at their disposal, but the engineer was a book, always ready, always open at the wished-for page. A book which answered their every question, and one which they often read. Thus the time passed, and these brave man had no fear for the future.

However, they were all anxious for the end of their captivity, and longed to see, if not fine weather, at least a cessation of the intense cold. If they had only had warmer clothing, they would have attempted excursions to the downs and to Tadorns' Fens, for game would have been easy to approach, and the hunt would assuredly have been fruitful. But Smith insisted that no one should compromise his health, as he had need of every hand; and his advice was taken.

The most impatient of the prisoners, after Pencroff, was Top. The poor dog found himself in close quarters in Granite House, and ran from room to room, showing plainly the uneasiness he felt at this confinement.

Smith often noticed that whenever he approached the dark well communicating with the sea, which had its opening in the rear of the storehouse, Top whined in a most curious manner, and ran around and around the opening, which had been covered over with planks of wood. Sometimes he even tried to slip his paws under the planks, as if trying to raise them up, and yelped in a way which indicated at the same time anger and uneasiness.

The engineer several times noticed this strange behavior, and wondered what there could be in the abyss to have such a peculiar effect upon this intelligent dog.

This well, of course, communicated with the sea. Did it then branch off into narrow passages through the rock-work of the island? Was it in communication with other caves? Did any sea-monsters come into it from time to time from the bottom of these pits?

The engineer did not know what to think, and strange thoughts passed through his mind. Accustomed to investigate scientific truths, he could not pardon himself for being drawn into the region of the mysterious and supernatural; but how explain why Top, the most sensible of dogs, who never lost his time in barking at the moon, should insist upon exploring this abyss with nose and ear, if there was nothing there to arouse his suspicions?

Top's conduct perplexed Smith more than he cared to own to himself. However, the engineer did not mention this to any one but Spilett, thinking it useless to worry his companions with what might be, after all, only a freak of the dog.

At last the cold spell was over. They had rain, snow-squalls, hail-storms, and gales of wind, but none of these lasted long. The ice thawed and the snow melted; the beach, plateau, banks of the Mercy, and the forest were again accessible. The return of spring rejoiced the inmates of

Granite House, and they soon passed all their time in the open air, only returning to eat and sleep.

They hunted a good deal during the latter part of September, which led Pencroff to make fresh demands for those fire-arms which he declared Smith had promised him. Smith always put him off, knowing that without a special stock of tools it would be almost impossible to make a gun which would be of any use to them.

Besides, he noticed that Herbert and Spilett had become very clever archers, that all sorts of excellent game, both feathered and furred—agoutis, kangaroos, cabiais, pigeons, bustards, wild ducks, and snipe—fell under their arrows; consequently the firearms could wait. But the stubborn sailor did not see it in this light, and constantly reminded the engineer that he bad not provided them with guns; and Gideon Spilett supported Pencroff.

"If," said he, "the island contains, as we suppose, wild beasts, we must consider how to encounter and exterminate them. The time may come when this will be our first duty."

But just now it was not the question of firearms which occupied Smith's mind, but that of clothes. Those which the colonists were wearing had lasted through the winter, but could not hold out till another. What they must have at any price was skins of the carnivora, or wool of the ruminants; and as moufflons (mountain goats), were plenty, they must consider how to collect a flock of them which they could keep for the benefit of the colony. They would also lay out a farm yard in a favorable part of the island, where they could have an enclosure for domestic animals and a poultry yard.

These important projects must be carried out during the good weather. Consequently, in view of these future arrangements, it was important to undertake a reconnoissance into the unexplored part of Lincoln Island, to wit:—the high forests which extended along the right bank of the Mercy, from its mouth to the end of Serpentine Peninsula. But they must be sure of their weather, and a month must yet elapse before it would be worth while to undertake this exploration. While they were waiting impatiently, an incident occurred which redoubled their anxiety to examine the whole island.

It was now the 24th of October. On this day Pencroff went to look after his traps which he always kept duly baited. In one of them, he found three animals, of a sort welcome to the kitchen. It was a female peccary with her two little ones. Pencroff returned to Granite House, delighted with his prize, and, as usual, made a great talk about it.

"Now, we'll have a good meal, Mr Smith," cried he, "and you too, Mr. Spilett, must have some."

"I shall be delighted," said the reporter, "but what is it you want me to eat?"

"Sucking pig," said Pencroff.

"Oh, a sucking-pig! To hear you talk one would think you had brought back a stuffed partridge!"

"Umph," said Pencroff, "so you turn up your nose at my sucking pig?"

"No," answered Spilett coolly, "provided one does not get too much of them—"

"Very well, Mr. Reporter!" returned the sailor, who did not like to hear his game disparaged. "You are getting fastidious! Seven months ago, when we were cast upon this island, you would have been only too glad to have come across such game."

"Well, well," said the reporter, "men are never satisfied."

"And now," continued Pencroff, "I hope Neb will distinguish himself. Let us see; these little peccaries are only three months old, they will be as tender as quail. Come, Neb, I will superintend the cooking of them myself."

The sailor, followed by Neb, hastened to the kitchen, and was soon absorbed over the oven. The two prepared a magnificent repast; the two little peccaries, kangaroo soup, smoked ham, pistachio nuts, dragon-tree wine, Oswego tea; in a word, everything of the best. But the favorite dish of all was the savory peccaries made into a stew. At 5 o'clock, dinner was served in the dining-room of Granite House. The kangaroo soup smoked upon the table. It was pronounced excellent.

After the soup came the peccaries, which Pencroff begged to be allowed to carve, and of which he gave huge pieces to every one. These sucking pigs were indeed delicious, and Pencroff plied his knife and fork with intense earnestness, when suddenly a cry and an oath escaped him.

"What's the matter?" said Smith.

"The matter is that I have just lost a tooth!" replied the sailor.

"Are there pebbles in your peccaries, then?" said Spilett.

"It seems so," said the sailor, taking out of his mouth the object which had cost him a grinder.

It was not a pebble, it was a leaden pellet.

PART II

THE ABANDONED

CHAPTER XXIII.

CONCERNING THE LEADEN PELLET—MAKING A
CANOE—HUNTING—IN THE TOP OF A KAURI—
NOTHING TO INDICATE THE PRESENCE OF
MAN—THE TURTLE ON ITS BACK—THE TURTLE
DISAPPEARS—SMITH'S EXPLANATION.

It was exactly seven months since the passengers in the balloon had been thrown upon Lincoln Island. In all this time no human being had been seen. No smoke had betrayed the presence of man upon he island. No work of man's hands, either ancient or modern, had attested his passage. Not only did it seem uninhabited at present, but it appeared to have been so always. And now all the framework of deductions fell before a little bit of metal found in the body of a pig.

It was certainly a bullet from a gun, and what but a human being would be so provided?

When Pencroff had placed it upon the table, his companions looked at it with profound astonishment. The possibilities suggested by this seemingly trivial incident flashed before them. The sudden appearance of a supernatural being could not have impressed them more.

Smith instantly began to reason upon the theories which this incident, as surprising as it was unexpected, suggested. Taking the bit of lead between his fingers he turned it round and about for some time before he spoke.

"You are sure, Pencroff," he asked, at length, "that the peccary was hardly three months old?"

"I'm sure, sir," answered the sailor. "It was sucking its mother when I found it in the ditch."

"Well, then, that proves that within three months a gun has been fired upon Lincoln Island."

"And that the bullet has wounded, though not mortally, this little animal," added Spilett.

"Undoubtedly," replied Smith; "and now let us see what conclusions are to be drawn from this incident. Either the island was inhabited before our arrival, or men have landed here within three months. How these men arrived, whether voluntarily or involuntarily, whether by landing or by shipwreck, cannot be settled at present. Neither have we any means of determining whether they are Europeans or Malays, friends or enemies; nor do we know whether they are living here at present or whether they have gone. But these questions are too important to be allowed to remain undecided."

"No!" cried the sailor springing from the table. "There can be no men besides ourselves on Lincoln Island. Why, the island is not large: and if it had been inhabited, we must have met some one of its people before this."

"It would, indeed, be astonishing if we had not," said Herbert.

"But it would be much more astonishing, I think," remarked the reporter, "if this little beast had been born with a bullet in his body!"

"Unless," suggested Neb, seriously, "Pencroff had had it—"

"How's that, Neb?" interrupted the sailor, "I, to have had a bullet in my jaw for five or six months, without knowing it? Where would it have been?" he added, opening his mouth and displaying the thirty-two splendid teeth that ornamented it. "Look, Neb, and if you can find one broken one in the whole set you may pull out half-a-dozen!"

"Neb's theory is inadmissible," said Smith, who, in spite of the gravity of his thoughts, could not restrain a smile. "It is certain that a gun has been discharged on the island within three months. But I am bound to believe that the persons on this island have been here but a short time, or else simply landed in passing; as, had the island had inhabitants when we made the ascent of Mount Franklin, we must have seen them or been seen. It is more probable, that within the past few weeks some people have been shipwrecked somewhere upon the coast; the thing, therefore, to do is to discover this point."

"I think we should act cautiously," said the reporter.

"I think so, too," replied Smith, "as I fear that they must be Malay pirates."

"How would it do, Mr. Smith," said the sailor, "to build A canoe so that we could go up this river, or, if need be, round the coast? It won't do to be taken unawares."

"It's a good idea," answered the engineer; "but we have not the time now. It would take at least a month to build a canoe—"

"A regular one, yes," rejoined the sailor; "but we don't want it to stand the sea. I will guarantee to make one in less than five days that will do to use on the Mercy."

"Build a boat in five days," cried Neb.

"Yes, Neb, one of Indian fashion."

"Of wood?" demanded the negro, still incredulous.

"Of wood, or what is better, of bark," answered Pencroff. "Indeed, Mr. Smith, it could be done in five days!"

"Be it so, then," answered the engineer. "In five days."

"But we must look out for ourselves in the meantime!" said Herbert.

"With the utmost caution, my friends," answered Smith. "And be very careful to confine your hunting expeditions to the neighborhood of Granite House."

The dinner was finished in lower spirits than Pencroff had expected. The incident of the bullet proved beyond doubt that the island had been, or was now, inhabited by others, and such a discovery awakened the liveliest anxiety in the breasts of the colonists.

Smith and Spilett, before retiring, had a long talk about these things. They questioned, if by chance this incident had an connection with the unexplained rescue of the engineer, and other strange events which they had encountered in so many ways. Smith, after having discussed the pros and cons of the question, ended by saying:—

"In short, Spilett, do you want to know my opinion?"

"Yes, Cyrus."

"Well, this is it. No matter how minutely we examine the island, we will find nothing!"

Pencroff began his work the next day. He did not mean to build a boat with ribs and planks, but simply a flat bottomed float, which would do admirably in the Mercy, especially in the shallow water and its sources. Strips of bark fastened together would be sufficient for their purpose, and in places where a portage would be necessary the affair would be neither heavy nor cumbersome. The sailor's idea was to fasten the strips of bark together with clinched nails, and thus to make the craft staunch.

The first thing was to select trees furnishing a supple and tough bark. Now, it had happened that the last storm had blown down a number of Douglass pines, which were perfectly adapted to this purpose. Some of these lay prone upon the earth, and all the colonists had to do was to strip them of their bark, though this indeed was somewhat difficult, on account of the awkwardness of their tools.

While the sailor, assisted by the engineer was thus occupied, Herbert and Spilett, who had been made purveyors to the colony, were not idle. The reporter could not help admiring the young lad, who had acquired a remarkable proficiency in the use of the bow and arrows, and who exhibited, withal, considerable hardiness and coolness. The two hunters, remembering the caution of the engineer, never ventured more than two miles from Granite House, but the outskirts of the forest furnished a sufficient supply of agoutis, cabiais, kangaroos, peccaries, etc., and although the traps had not done so well since the cold had abated, the warren furnished a supply sufficient for the wants of the colonists.

Often, while on these excursions, Herbert conversed with Spilett about the incident of the bullet and of the engineer's conclusions, and one day—the 26th of October—he said:—

"Don't you think it strange, Mr. Spilett, that any people should have been wrecked on this island, and never have followed up the coast to Granite House?"

"Very strange if they are still here," answered the reporter, "but not at all astonishing if they are not."

"Then you think they have gone again?"

"It is likely, my boy, that, if they had staid any time, or were still here, something would have discovered their presence."

"But if they had been able to get off again they were not really shipwrecked."

"No, Herbert, they were what I should call shipwrecked temporarily. That is, it is possible that they were driven by stress of weather upon the island, without having to abandon their vessel, and when the wind moderated they set out again."

"One thing is certain," said Herbert, "and that is, that Mr. Smith has always seemed to dread, rather than to desire, the presence of human beings on our island."

"The reason is, that he knows that only Malays frequent these seas, and these gentlemen are a kind of rascals that had better be avoided."

"Is it not possible, sir, that some time we will discover traces of their landing and, perhaps, be able to settle this point?"

"It is not unlikely, my boy. An abandoned camp or the remains of a fire, we would certainly notice, and these are what we will look for on our exploration."

The hunters, talking in this way, found themselves in a portion of the forest near the Mercy, remarkable for its splendid trees. Among others, were those magnificent conifera, called by the New Zealanders "kauris," rising mere than 200 feet in height.

"I have an idea, Mr. Spilett," said Herbert, "supposing I climb to the top of one of these kauris, I could see, perhaps, for a good ways."

"It's a good idea," answered the other, "but can you climb one of these giants?"

"I am going to try, anyhow," exclaimed the boy, springing upon the lower branches of one, which grew in such a manner as to make the tree easy to mount. In a few minutes he was in its top, high above all the surrounding leafage of the forest.

From this height, the eye could take in all the southern portion of the island between Claw Cape on the southeast and Reptile Promontory on the southwest. To the northwest rose Mount Franklin, shutting out more than one-fourth of the horizon.

But Herbert, from his perch, could overlook the very portion of the island which was giving, or had given, refuge to the strangers whose presence they suspected. The lad looked about him with great attention, first towards the sea, where not a sail was visible, although it was possible that a ship, and especially one dismasted, lying close in to shore, would be concealed from view by the trees which hid the coast. In the woods of the Far West nothing could be seen. The forest formed a vast impenetrable dome many miles in extent, without an opening or glade. Even the course of the Mercy could not be seen, and it might be that there were other streams flowing westward, which were equally invisible.

But, other signs failing, could not the lad catch in the air some smoke that would indicate the presence of man? The atmosphere was pure, and the slightest vapor was sharply outlined against the sky. For an instant Herbert thought he saw a thin film rising in the west, but a more careful observation convinced him that he was mistaken. He looked again, however, with all care, and his sight was excellent. No, certainly, it was nothing.

Herbert climbed down the tree, and he and the reporter returned to Granite House. There Smith listened to the lad's report without comment.

212

It was plain he would not commit himself until after the island had been explored.

Two days later—the 28th of October—another unaccountable incident happened.

In strolling along the beach, two miles from Granite House, Herbert and Neb had been lucky enough to capture a splendid specimen of the chelonia mydas (green turtle), whose carapace shone with emerald reflections. Herbert had caught sight of it moving among the rocks towards the sea.

"Stop him, Neb, stop him!" he cried.

Neb ran to it.

"It's a fine animal," said Neb, "but how are we going to keep it?"

"That's easy enough, Neb. All we have to do is to turn it on its back, and then it cannot get away. Take your spear and do as I do."

The reptile had shut itself in its shell, so that neither its head nor eyes were visible, and remained motionless as a rock. The lad and the negro placed their spears underneath it, and, after some difficulty, succeeded in turning it over. It measured three feet in length, and must have weighed at least 400 pounds.

"There, that will please Pencroff," cried Neb.

Indeed, the sailor could not fail to be pleased, as the flesh of these turtles, which feed upon eel-grass, is very savory.

"And now what can we do with our game?" asked Neb; "we can't carry it to Granite House."

"Leave it here, since it cannot turn back again," answered Herbert, "and we will come for it with the cart."

Neb agreed, and Herbert, as an extra precaution, which the negro thought useless, propped up the reptile with large stones. Then the two returned to Granite House, following the beach, on which the tide was down. Herbert, wishing to surprise Pencroff, did not tell him of the prize which was lying on its back upon the sand; but two hours later Neb and he returned with the cart to where they had left it, and—the "splendid specimen of chelonia mydas" was not there!

The two looked about them. Certainly, this was where they had left it. Here were the stones he had used, and, therefore, the lad could not be mistaken.

"Did the beast turn over, after all?" asked Neb.

"It seems so," replied Herbert, puzzled, and examining the stones scattered over the sand.

"Pencroff will be disappointed."

"And Mr. Smith will be troubled to explain this!" thought Herbert.

"Well," said Neb, who wished to conceal their misadventure, "we won't say anything about it."

"Indeed, we will tell the whole story," answered Herbert.

And taking with them the useless cart, they returned to Granite House.

At the shipyard they found the engineer and the sailor working together. Herbert related all that happened.

"You foolish fellows," cried the sailor, "to let at least fifty pounds of soup, escape!"

"But, Pencroff," exclaimed Neb, "it was not our fault that the reptile got away; haven't I told you we turned it on its back?"

"Then you didn't turn it enough!" calmly asserted the stubborn sailor.

"Not enough!" cried Herbert; and he told how he had taken care to prop the turtle up with stones.

"Then it was a miracle!" exclaimed Pencroff.

"Mr. Smith," asked Herbert, "I thought that turtles once placed on their backs could not get over again, especially the very large ones?"

"That is the fact," answered Smith.

"Then how did it—"

"How far off from the sea did you leave this turtle," asked the engineer, who had stopped working and was turning this incident over in his mind.

"About fifteen feet," answered Herbert.

"And it was low water?"

"Yes, sir."

"Well," responded the engineer, "what the turtle could not do on land, he could do in water. When the tide rose over him he turned over, and—tranquilly paddled off."

"How foolish we are," cried Neb.

"That is just what I said you were," answered Pencroff.

Smith had given this explanation, which was doubtless admissible; but was he himself satisfied with it? He did not venture to say that.

CHAPTER XXIV.

TRIAL OF THE CANOE—A WRECK ON THE SHORE—
THE TOW—JETSAM POINT—INVENTORY OF THE
BOX—WHAT PENCROFF WANTED—A BIBLE—A VERSE
FROM THE BIBLE.

On the 29th of October the canoe was finished. Pencroff had kept his word, and had built, in five days, a sort of bark shell, stiffened with flexible crejimba rods. A seat at either end, another midway to keep it open, a gunwale for the thole-pins of a pair of oars, and a paddle to steer with, completed this canoe, which was twelve feet in length, and did not weigh 200 pounds.

"Hurrah!" cried the sailor, quite ready to applaud his own success. "With this we can make the tour of—"

"Of the world?" suggested Spilett.

"No, but of the island. Some stones for ballast, a mast in the bow, with a sail which Mr. Smith will make some day, and away we'll go! But now let us try our new ship, for we must see if it will carry all of us."

The experiment was made. Pencroff, by a stroke of the paddle, brought the canoe close to the shore by a narrow passage between the rocks, and he was confident that they could at once make a trial trip of the craft by following the bank as far as the lower point where the rocks ended.

As they were stepping in, Neb cried:—

"But your boat leaks, Pencroff."

"Oh, that's nothing, Neb," answered the sailor. "The wood has to drink! But in two days it will not show, and there will be as little water in our canoe as in the stomach of a drunkard! Come, get in!"

They all embarked, and Pencroff pushed off. The weather was splendid, the sea was as calm as a lake, and the canoe could venture upon it with as much security as upon the tranquil current of the Mercy.

Neb and Herbert took the oars, and Pencroff sat in the stern with the paddle as steersman.

The sailor crossed the channel, and rounded the southern point of the islet. A gentle breeze was wafted from the south. There were no billows, but the canoe rose and fell with the long undulations of the sea, and they rowed out half a mile from the coast so as to get a view of the outline of Mount Franklin. Then, putting about, Pencroff returned towards the mouth of the river, and followed along the rounded shore which hid the low marshy ground of Tadorn's Fen. The point, made longer by the bend of the coast, was three miles from the Mercy, and the colonists resolved to go past it far enough to obtain a hasty glance at the coast as far as Claw Cape.

The canoe followed along the shore, keeping off some two cables length so as to avoid the line of rocks beginning to be covered by the tide. The cliff, beginning at the mouth of the river, lowered as it approached the promontory. It was a savage-looking, unevenly-arranged heap of granite blocks, very different from the curtain of Prospect Plateau. There was not a trace of vegetation on this sharp point, which projected two miles beyond the forest, like a giant's arm, thrust out from a green sleeve.

The canoe sped easily along. Spilett sketched the outline of the coast in his note-book, and Neb, Pencroff, and Herbert discussed the features of their new domain; and as they moved southward the two Mandible Capes seemed to shut together and enclose Union Bay. As to Smith, he regarded everything in silence, and from his distrustful expression it seemed as if he was observing some suspicious land.

The canoe had reached the end of the point and was about doubling it, when Herbert rose, and pointing out a black object, said:—

"What is that down there on the sand?"

Every one looked in the direction indicated.

"There is something there, indeed," said the reporter. "It looks like a wreck half buried in the sand."

"Oh, I see what it is!" cried Pencroff.

"What?" asked Neb.

"Barrels! they are barrels, and, may be, they are full!"

"To shore, Pencroff!" said Smith.

And with a few strokes the canoe was driven into a little cove, and the party went up the beach.

Pencroff was not mistaken. There were two barrels half buried in the sand; but firmly fastened to them was a large box, which, borne up by them, had been floated on to the shore.

"Has there been a shipwreck here?" asked Herbert.

"Evidently," answered Spilett.

"But what is in this box?" exclaimed Pencroff, with a natural impatience. "What is in this box? It is closed, and we have nothing with which to raise the lid. However, with a stone—"

And the sailor picked up a heavy rock, and was about to break one of the sides, when the engineer, stopping him, said:—

"Cannot you moderate your impatience for about an hour, Pencroff?"

"But, think, Mr. Smith! May be there is everything we want in it!"

"We will find out, Pencroff," answered the engineer, "but do not break the box, as it will be useful. Let us transport it to Granite House, where we can readily open it without injuring it. It is all prepared for the voyage, and since it has floated here, it can float again to the river month."

"You are right, sir, and I am wrong," answered the sailor, "but one is not always his own master!"

The engineer's advice was good. It was likely that the canoe could not carry the things probably enclosed in the box, since the latter was so heavy that it had to be buoyed up by two empty barrels. It was, therefore, better to tow it in this condition to the shore at the Granite House.

And now the important question was, from whence came this jetsam? Smith and his companions searched the beach for several hundred paces, but there was nothing else to be seen. They scanned the sea, Herbert and Neb climbing up a high rock, but not a sail was visible on the horizon.

Nevertheless, there must have been a shipwreck, and perhaps this incident was connected with the incident of the bullet. Perhaps the strangers had landed upon another part of the island. Perhaps they were still there. But the natural conclusion of the colonists was that these strangers could not be Malay pirates, since the jetsam was evidently of European or American production.

They all went back to the box, which measured five feet by three. It was made of oak, covered with thick leather, studded with copper nails. The two large barrels, hermetically sealed, but which sounded empty, were fastened to its sides by means of strong ropes, tied in what Pencroff recognized to be "sailor's knots." That it was uninjured seemed to be accounted for by the fact of its having been thrown upon the sand instead of the rocks. And it was evident that it had not been long either in the sea or upon the beach. It seemed probable, also, that the water had not penetrated, and that its contents would be found uninjured. It therefore looked as if this box must have been thrown overboard from a disabled ship making for the island. And, in the hope that it would reach the island, where they would find it later, the passengers had taken the precaution to buoy it up.

"We will tow this box to Granite House," said the engineer, "and take an inventory of its contents; then, if we discover any of the survivors of this supposed shipwreck, we will return them what is theirs. If we find no one—"

"We will keep the things ourselves!" cried the sailor. "But I wish I knew what is in it."

The sailor was already working at the prize, which would doubtless float at high water. One of the ropes which was fastened to the barrels was partly untwisted and served to fasten these latter to the canoe. Then, Neb and Pencroff dug out the sand with their oars, and soon the canoe, with the jetsam in tow, was rounding the promontory to which they gave the name of Jetsam Point. The box was so heavy that the barrels just sufficed to sustain it above the water; and Pencroff feared each moment that it would break loose and sink to the bottom. Fortunately his fears were groundless, and in an hour and a half the canoe touched the bank before Granite House.

The boat and the prize were drawn upon the shore, and as the tide was beginning to fall, both soon rested on dry ground. Neb brought some tools so as to open the box without injury, and the colonists forthwith proceeded to examine its contents.

Pencroff did not try to hide his anxiety. He began by unfastening the barrels, which would be useful in the future, then the fastenings were forced with pincers, and the cover taken off. A second envelope, of zinc, was enclosed within the case, in such a manner that its contents were impervious to moisture.

"Oh!" cried Pencroff, "they must be preserves which are inside."

"I hope for something better than that," answered the reporter.

"If it should turn out that there was—" muttered the sailor.

"What?" asked Neb.

"Nothing!"

The zinc cover was split, lengthwise and turned back, and, little by little, many different objects were lifted out on the sand. At each new discovery Pencroff cheered, Herbert clapped his hands, and Neb danced. There were books which made the lad crazy with pleasure, and cooking implements which Neb covered with kisses.

In truth the colonists had reason to be satisfied, as the following inventory, copied from Spilett's note-book, will show:—

TOOLS.—3 pocket-knives, with-several blades, 2 wood-chopper's hatchets, 2 carpenter's hatchets, 3 planes, I adzes, 1 axe, 6 cold chisels, 2 files, 3 hammers, 3 gimlets, 2 augers, 10 bags of nails and screws, 3 saws of different sizes, 2 boxes of needles.

ARMS.—2 flint-lock guns, 2 percussion guns, 2 central-fire carbines; 5 cutlasses, 4 boarding sabres, 2 barrels of powder, holding 15 pounds each, 12 boxes of caps.

INSTRUMENTS.—1 sextant, 1 opera-glass, 1 spyglass, 1 box compass, 1 pocket compass, 1 Fahrenheit thermometer, 1 aneroid barometer, 1 box containing a photographic apparatus, together with glasses, chemicals, etc.

CLOTHING.—2 dozen shirts of a peculiar material resembling wool, though evidently a vegetable substance; 3 dozen stockings of the same material.

UTENSILS.—1 Iron pot, 6 tinned copper stewpans, 3 iron plates, 10 aluminium knives and forks, 2 kettles, 1 small portable stove. 5 table knives.

BOOKS.-1 Bible, 1 atlas, 1 dictionary of Polynesian languages, 1 dictionary of the Natural Sciences, 3 reams of blank paper, 2 blank books.

"Unquestionably," said the reporter, after the inventory had been taken, "the owner of this box was a practical man! Tools, arms, instruments, clothing, utensils, books, nothing is wanting. One would say that he had made ready for a shipwreck before-hand!"

"Nothing, Indeed, is wanting," murmured Smith, thoughtfully.

"And it is a sure thing," added Herbert, "that the ship that brought this box was not a Malay pirate!"

"Unless its owner had been taken prisoner," said Pencroff.

"That is not likely," answered the reporter. "It is more probable that an American or European ship has been driven to this neighborhood, and that the passengers, wishing to save what was, at least, necessary, have prepared this box and have thrown it overboard."

"And do you think so, Mr. Smith?" asked Herbert.

"Yes, my boy," answered the engineer, "that might have been the case. It is possible, that, anticipating a ship wreck, this chest has been prepared, so that it might be found again on the coast—"

"But the photographic apparatus!" observed the sailor incredulously.

"As to that," answered the engineer, "I do not see its use; what we, as well as any other ship wrecked person, would have valued more, would have been a greater assortment of clothing and more ammunition!"

"But have none of these things any mark by which we can tell where they came from," askedSpilett.

They looked to see. Each article was examined attentively, but, contrary to custom, neither books, instruments, nor arms had any name or mark; nevertheless, they were in perfect order, and seemed never to have been used. So also with the tools and utensils; everything was new, and this went to prove that the things had not been hastily thrown together in the box, but that their selection had been made thoughtfully and with care. This, also, was evident from the zinc case which had kept everything watertight, and which could not have been soldered in a moment.

The two dictionaries and the Bible were in English, and the latter showed that it had been often read. The Atlas was a splendid work, containing maps of every part of the world, and many charts laid out on Mercator's Projection. The nomenclature in this book was in French, but neither in it, nor in any of the others, did the name of the editor or publisher appear.

The colonists, therefore, were unable to even conjecture the nationality of the ship that had so recently passed near them. But no matter where it came from, this box enriched the party on Lincoln Island. Until now, in transforming the products of nature, they had created everything for themselves, and had succeeded by their own intelligence. Did it not now seem as if Providence had intended to reward them by placing these divers products of human industry in their hands? Therefore, with one accord, they all rendered thanks to Heaven.

Nevertheless, Pencroff was not entirely satisfied. It appeared that the box did not contain something to which he attached an immense importance, and as its contests lessened, his cheers had become less hearty, and when the inventory was closed, he murmured:—

"That's all very fine, but you see there is nothing for me here!"

"Why, what did you expect, Pencroff?" exclaimed Neb.

"A half pound of tobacco," answered the sailor, "and then I would have been perfectly happy!"

The discovery of this jetsam made the thorough exploration of the island more necessary than ever. It was, therefore, agreed that they should set out early the next morning, proceeding to the western coast via the Mercy. If anyone had been shipwrecked on that part of the island, they were doubtless without resources, and help must be given them at once.

During the day the contents of the box were carried to Granite House and arranged in order in the great hall. And that evening—the 29th of October—Herbert before retiring asked Mr. Smith to read some passages from the Bible.

"Gladly," answered the engineer, taking the sacred book in his hands; when Pencroff checking him, said:—

"Mr. Smith, I am superstitious. Open the book at random and read the first verse which you meet with. We will see if it applies to our situation."

Smith smiled at the words of the sailor, but yielding to his wishes he opened the Bible where the marker lay between the leaves. Instantly his eye fell upon a red cross made with a crayon, opposite the 8th verse of the seventh chapter of St. Matthew.

He read these words:—

"For every one that asketh, receiveth; and he that seeketh, findeth."

CHAPTER XXV.

THE DEPARTURE—THE RISING TIDE—ELMS
AND OTHER TREES—DIFFERENT PLANTS—
THE KINGFISHER—APPEARANCE OF THE FOREST—
THE GIGANTIC EUCALYPTI—WHY THEY ARE CALLED
FEVER-TREES—MONKEYS—THE WATERFALL—
ENCAMPMENT FOR THE NIGHT.

The next day—the 30th of October—everything was prepared for the proposed exploration, which these last events had made so necessary. Indeed, as things had turned out, the colonists could well imagine themselves in a condition to give, rather than to receive, help.

It was agreed that they ascend the Mercy as far as practicable. They would thus be able to transport their arms and provisions a good part of the way without fatigue.

It was also necessary to think, not only of what they now carried, but of what they might perhaps bring back to Granite House. If, as all thought, there had been a shipwreck on the coast, they would find many things they wanted on the shore, and the cart would doubtless have proved more convenient than the canoe. But the cart was so heavy and unwieldy that it would have been too hard work to drag it, which fact made Pencroff regret that the box had not only held his half-pound of tobacco, but also a pair of stout New Jersey horses, which would have been so useful to the colony.

The provisions, already packed by Neb, consisted of enough dried meat, beer, and fermented liquor to last them for the three days which Smith expected they would be absent. Moreover, they counted on being able to replenish their stock at need along the route, and Neb had taken care not to forget the portable stove.

They took the two wood-choppers' hatchets to aid in making their way through the thick forest, and also the glass and the pocket compass.

Of the arms, they chose the two flint-lock guns in preference to the others, as the colonists could always renew the flints; whereas the caps could not be replaced. Nevertheless, they took one of the carbines and some cartridges. As for the powder, the barrels held fifty pounds, and it was necessary to take a certain amount of that; but the engineer expected to manufacture an explosive substance, by which it could be saved in the future. To the firearms they added the five cutlasses, in leather scabbards. And thus equipped, the party could venture into the forest with some chance of success.

Armed in this manner, Pencroff, Herbert, and Neb had all they could desire, although Smith made them promise not to fire a shot unnecessarily.

At 6 o'clock the party, accompanied by Top, started for the mouth of the Mercy. The tide had been rising half an hour, and there were therefore some hours yet of the flood which they could make use of. The current was strong, and they did not need to row to pass rapidly up between the high banks and the river. In a few minutes the explorers had reached the turn where, seven months before, Pencroff had made his first raft. Having passed this elbow, the river, flowing from the southwest, widened out under the shadow of the grand ever-green conifers; and Smith and his companions could not but admire the beautiful scenery. As they advanced the species of forest trees changed. On the right bank rose splendid specimens of ulmaceæ, those valuable elms so much sought after by builders, which have the property of remaining sound for a long time in water. There was, also, numerous groups belonging to the same family, among them the micocouliers, the root of which produces a useful oil. Herbert discovered some lardizabalaceæ, whose flexible branches, soaked in water, furnish excellent ropes, and two or three trunks of ebony of a beautiful black color, curiously veined.

From time to time, where a landing was easy, the canoe stopped, and Spilett, Herbert, and Pencroff, accompanied by Top, explored the bank. In addition to the game, Herbert thought that he might meet with some useful little plant which was not to be despised, and the young naturalist was rewarded by discovering a sort of wild spinach and numerous specimens of the genus cabbage, which would, doubtless, bear transplanting; they were cresses, horse-radishes, and a little, velvety, spreading plant, three-feet high, bearing brownish-colored seeds.

"Do you know what this is?" asked Herbert of the sailor.

"Tobacco!" cried Pencroff, who had evidently never seen the plant which he fancied so much.

"No, Pencroff," answered Herbert, "It is not tobacco, it is mustard."

"Only mustard!" exclaimed the other. "Well if you happen to come across a tobacco plant, my boy, do not pass it by."

"We will find it someday," said Spilett.

"All right," cried Pencroff, "and then I will be able to say that the island lacks nothing!"

These plants were taken up carefully and carried back to the canoe, where Cyrus Smith had remained absorbed in his own thoughts.

The reporter, Herbert, and Pencroff, made many of these excursions, sometimes on the right bank of the Mercy and sometimes upon the left. The latter was less abrupt, but more wooded. The engineer found, by reference to the pocket-compass, that the general direction of the river from its bend was southwest, and that it was nearly straight for about three miles. But it was probable that the direction would change further up, and that it would flow from the spurs of Mount Franklin, which fed its waters in the northwest.

During one of these excursions Spilett caught a couple of birds with long, slim beaks, slender necks, short wings, and no tails, which Herbert called tinamous, and which they resolved should be the first occupants of the future poultry-yard.

But the first report of a gun that echoed through the forests of the Far West, was provoked by the sight of a beautiful bird, resembling a kingfisher.

"I know it," cried Pencroff.

"What do you know?" asked the reporter.

"That bird! It is the bird which escaped on our first exploration, the one after which we named this part of the forest!"

"A jacamar!" exclaimed Herbert.

It was, indeed, one of those beautiful birds, whose harsh plumage is covered with a metallic lustre. Some small shot dropped it to the earth, and Top brought it, and also some touracolories, climbing birds, the size of pigeons, to the canoe. The honor of this first shot belonged to the lad, who was pleased enough with the result. The touracolories were better game than the jacamar, the flash of the latter being tough, but it would have been hard to persuade Pencroff that they had not killed the most delicious of birds.

It was 10 o'clock when the canoe reached the second bend of the river, some five miles from the mouth. Here they stopped half an hour, under the shadow of the trees, for breakfast.

The river measured from sixty to seventy feet in width, and was five or six feet deep. The engineer had remarked its several affluents, but they were simply unnavigable streams. The Forests of the Far West, or Jacamar Wood, extended farther than they could see, but no where could they detect the presence of man. If, therefore, any persons had been shipwrecked on the island, they had not yet quitted the shore, and it was not in those thick coverts that search must be made for the survivors.

The engineer began to manifest some anxiety to get to the western coast of the island, distant, as he calculated, about five miles or less. The journey was resumed, and, although the course of the Mercy, sometimes towards the shore, was oftener towards the mountain, it was thought better to follow it as long as possible, on account of the fatigue and loss of time incident to hewing a way through the wood. Soon, the tide having attained its height, Herbert and Neb took the oars, and Pencroff the paddle, wad they continued the ascent by rowing.

It seemed as if the forest of the Far West began to grow thinner. But, as the trees grew farther apart, they profited by the increased space, and attained a splendid growth.

"Eucalypti!" cried Herbert, descrying some of these superb plants, the loftiest giants of the extra-tropical zone, the congeners of the eucalypti of Australia and New Zealand, both of which countries were situated in the same latitude as Lincoln Island. Some rose 200 feet in height and measured twenty feet in circumference, and their bark, five fingers in thickness, exuded an aromatic resin. Equally wonderful were the enormous specimens of myrtle, their leaves extending edgewise to the sun, and permitting its rays to penetrate and fall upon the ground.

"What trees!" exclaimed Neb. "Are they good for anything?"

"Pshaw!" answered Pencroff. "They are like overgrown men, good for nothing but to show in fairs!"

"I think you're wrong, Pencroff," said Spilett, "the eucalyptus wood is beginning to be extensively used in cabinet work."

"And I am sure," added Herbert, "that it belongs to a most useful family," and thereupon the young naturalist enumerated many species of the plant and their uses.

Every one listened to the lad's lesson in botany, Smith smiling, Pencroff with an indescribable pride. "That's all very well, Herbert," answered the sailor, "but I dare swear that of all these useful specimens none are as large as these!"

"That is so."

"Then, that proves what I said," replied the sailor, "that giants are good for nothing."

"There's where you are wrong, Pencroff," said the engineer, "these very eucalypti are good for something."

"For what?"

"To render the country healthy about them. Do you know what they call them In Australia and New Zealand?"

"No sir."

"They call them 'fever' trees."

"Because they give it?"

"No; because they prevent it!"

"Good. I shall make a note of that," said the reporter.

"Note then, my dear Spilett, that it has been proved that the presence of these trees neutralizes marsh miasmas. They have tried this natural remedy in certain unhealthy parts of Europe, and northern Africa, with the best results. And there are no intermittent fevers in the region of these forests, which is a fortunate thing for us colonists of Lincoln Island."

"What a blessed island!" cried Pencroff. "It would lack nothing—if it was not—"

"That will come, Pencroff, we will find it," answered the reporter; "but now let us attend to our work and push on as far as we can get with the canoe."

They continued on through the woods two miles further, the river becoming more winding, shallow, and so narrow that Pencroff pushed along with a pole. The sun was setting, and, as it would be impossible to pass in the darkness through the five or six miles of unknown woods which the engineer estimated lay between them and the coast, it was determined to camp wherever the canoe was obliged to stop.

They now pushed on without delay through the forest, which grew more dense, and seemed more inhabited, because, if the sailor's eyes did not deceive him, he perceived troops of monkeys running among the underbrush. Sometimes, two or three of these animals would halt at a distance from the canoe and regard its occupants, as if, seeing men for the first time, they had not then learned to fear them. It would have been easy to have shot some of these quadrumanes, but Smith was opposed to the useless slaughter. Pencroff, however, looked upon the monkey from a gastronomic point of view, and, indeed, as these animals are entirely herberiferous, they make excellent game; but since provisions abounded, it was useless to waste the ammunition.

Towards 4 o'clock the navigation of the Mercy became very difficult, its course being obstructed by rocks and aquatic plants. The banks rose higher and higher, and, already, the bed of the stream was confined between the outer spurs of Mount Franklin. Its sources could not be far off, since the waters were fed by the southern watershed of that mountain.

"Before a quarter of an hour we will have to stop, sir," said Pencroff.

"Well, then, we will make a camp for the night."

"How far are we from Granite House?" asked Herbert.

"About seven miles, counting the bends of the river, which have taken us to the northwest."

"Shall we keep on?" asked the reporter.

"Yes, as far as we can get," answered the engineer. "To-morrow, at daylight, we will leave the canoe, and traverse, in two hours I hope, the distance which separates us from the coast, and then we will have nearly the whole day in which to explore the shore."

"Push on," cried Pencroff.

Very soon the canoe grated on the stones at the bottom of the river, which was not more than twenty feet wide. A thick mass of verdure overhung and descended the stream, and they heard the noise of a waterfall, which indicated that some little distance further on there existed a natural barrier.

And, indeed, at the last turn in the river, they saw the cascade shining through the trees. The canoe scraped over the bottom and then grounded on a rock near the right bank.

It was 5 o'clock, and the level rays of the setting sun illuminated the little fall. Above, the Mercy, supplied from a secret source, was hidden by the bushes. The various streams together had made it a river, but here it was but a shallow, limpid brook.

They made camp in this lovely spot. Having disembarked, a fire was lighted under a group of micocouliers, in whose branches Smith and his companions could, if need be, find a refuge for the night.

Supper was soon finished, as they were very hungry, and then there was nothing to do but to go to sleep. But some suspicious growling being heard at nightfall, the fire was so arranged as to protect the sleepers by its flames. Neb and Pencroff kept it lit, and perhaps they were not mistaken in believing to have seen some moving shadows among the trees and bushes; but the night passed without accident, and the next day—the 31st of October—by 5 o'clock all were on foot ready for the start.

CHAPTER XXVI.

GOING TOWARD THE COAST—TROOPS OF
MONKEYS—A NEW WATER-COURSE—WHY THE
TIDE WAS NOT FELT—A FOREST ON THE SHORE—
REPTILE PROMONTORY—SPILETT MAKES HERBERT
ENVIOUS—THE BAMBOO FUSILADE.

It was 6 o'clock when the colonists, after an early breakfast, started with the intention of reaching the coast by the shortest route. Smith had estimated that it would take them two hours, but it must depend largely on the nature of the obstacles in the way. This part of the Far West was covered with trees, like an immense thicket composed of many different species. It was, therefore, probable that they would have to make a way with hatchets in hand—and guns also, if they were to judge from the cries heard over night.

The exact position of the camp had been determined by the situation of Mount Franklin, and since the volcano rose less than three miles to the north, it was only necessary to go directly toward the southwest to reach the west coast.

After having seen to the mooring of the canoe, the party started, Neb and Pencroff carrying sufficient provisions to last the little troop for two days at least. They were no longer hunting, and the engineer recommended his companions to refrain from unnecessary firing, so as not to give warning of their presence on the coast. The first blows of the hatchet were given in the bushes just above the cascade, while

Smith, compass in hand, indicated the route. The forest was, for the most part, composed of such trees as had already been recognized about the lake and on Prospect Plateau. The colonists could advance but slowly, and the engineer believed that in time their route would join with that of Red Creek.

Since their departure, the party had descended the low declivities which constituted the orography of the island, over a very dry district, although the luxuriant vegetation suggested either a hydrographic network permeating the ground beneath, or the proximity to some stream. Nevertheless, Smith did not remember having seen, during the excursion to the crater, any other water courses than Bed Creek and the Mercy.

During the first few hours of the march, they saw troops of monkeys, who manifested the greatest astonishment at the sight of human beings. Spilett laughingly asked if these robust quadrumanes did not look upon their party as degenerate brethren; and, in truth, the simple pedestrians, impeded at each step by the bushes, entangled in the lianas, stopped by tree trunks, did not compare favorably with these nimble animals, which bounded from branch to branch, moving about without hindrance. These monkeys were very numerous, but, fortunately, they did not manifest any hostile disposition.

They saw, also, some wild-boars, some agoutis, kangaroos, and other rodents, and two or three koulas, which latter Pencroff would have been glad to shoot.

"But," said he, "the hunt has not begun. Play now, my friends, and we will talk to you when we come back."

At half-past 9, the route, which bore directly southwest, was suddenly interrupted by a rapid stream, rushing over rocks, and pent in between banks but thirty or forty feet apart. It was deep and clear, but absolutely unnavigable.

"We are stopped!" cried Neb.

"No," replied Herbert; "we can swim such a brook as this."

"Why should we do that?" answered Smith. "It is certain that this creek empties into the sea. Let us keep to this bank and I will be astonished if it does not soon bring us to the coast. Come on!"

"One minute," said the reporter. "The name of this creek, my friends? We must not leave our geography incomplete."

"True enough," said Pencroff.

"You name it, my boy," said the engineer, addressing Herbert.

"Will not it be better to wait till we have discovered its mouth?" asked Herbert.

"Right," replied Smith, "let us push on."

"Another minute," exclaimed Pencroff.

"What more?" demanded the reporter.

"If hunting is forbidden, fishing is allowed, I suppose," said the sailor.

"We haven't the time to waste," answered the engineer.

"But just five minutes," pleaded Pencroff; "I only want five minutes for the sake of breakfast!" And lying down on the bank he plunged his arms in the running waters and soon brought up several dozen of the fine crawfish which swarmed between the rocks.

"These will be good!" cried Neb, helping the sailor.

"Did not I tell you that the island had everything but tobacco?" sighed the sailor.

It took but five minutes to fill a sack with these little blue crustaceæ, and then the journey was resumed.

By following the bank the colonists moved more freely. Now and then they found traces of large animals which came to the stream for water, but they found no sign of human beings, and they were not yet in that part of the Far West where the peccary had received the leaden pellet which cost Pencroff a tooth.

Smith and his companions judged, from the fact that the current rushed towards the sea with such rapidity, that they must be much farther from, the coast than they imagined, because at this time the tide was rising, and its' effect would have been visible near the mouth of the creek. The engineer was greatly astonished, and often consulted his compass to be sure that the stream, was not returning towards the depths of the forest. Meantime, its waters, gradually widening, became less tumultuous. The growth of trees on the right bank was much denser than on the left, and it was impossible to see through this thicket; but these woods were certainly not inhabited, or Top would have discovered it. At half-past 10, to the extreme surprise of Smith, Herbert, who was walking some paces ahead, suddenly stopped, exclaiming, "The sea!"

And a few minutes later the colonists, standing upon the border of the forest, saw the western coast of the island spread before them.

But what a contrast was this coast to the one on which chance had thrown them! No granite wall, no reef in the offing, not even a beach. The forest formed the shore, and its furthermost trees, washed by the waves, leaned over the waters. It was in no sense such a beach as is usually met with, composed of vast reaches of sand or heaps of rocks, but a fine border of beautiful trees. The bank was raised above the highest tides, and upon this rich soil, supported by a granite base, the splendid monarchs of the forest seemed to be as firmly set as were those which stood in the interior of the island.

The colonists stood in a hollow by a tiny rivulet, which served as a neck to the other stream; but, curiously enough, these waters, instead of emptying into the sea by a gently sloping opening, fell from a height of more than forty feet—which fact explained why the rising tide did not affect the current. And, on this account, they were unanimous in giving this water-course the name of Fall River.

Beyond, towards the north, the forest shore extended for two miles; then the trees became thinner, and, still further on, a line of picturesque heights extended from north to south. On the other hand, all that part of the coast comprised between Fall River and the promontory of Reptile End was bordered by masses of magnificent trees, some upright and others leaning over the sea, whose waves lapped their roots. It was evidently, therefore, on this part of the coast that the exploration must be continued, as this shore offered to the castaways, whoever they might be, a refuge, which the other, desert and savage, had refused.

The weather was beautiful, and from the cliff where the breakfast had been prepared, the view extended far and wide. The horizon was perfectly distinct, without a sail in sight, and upon the coast, as far as could be seen, there was neither boat nor wreck, but the engineer was not willing to be satisfied in this respect, until they had explored the whole distance as far as Serpentine Peninsula.

After a hurried breakfast he gave the signal to start. Instead of traversing a beach, the colonists followed along the coast, under the trees. The distance to Reptile End was about twelve miles, and, had the way been clear, they could have accomplished it in four hours, but the party were constantly obliged to turn out from the way, or to cut branches, or to break through thickets, and these hindrances multiplied as they proceeded. But they saw no signs of a recent shipwreck on the shore; although, as Spilett observed, as the tide was up, they could not say with certainty that there had not been one.

This reasoning was just, and, moreover, the incident of the bullet proved, indubitably, that within three months a gun had been fired on the island.

At 5 o'clock the extremity of the peninsula was still two miles distant, and it was evident that the colonists would have to camp for the night on the promontory of Reptile End. Happily, game was as plenty here as on the other coast, and birds of different kinds abounded. Two hours later, the party, tired out, reached the promontory. Here the forest border ended, and the shore assumed the usual aspect of a coast. It was possible that an abandoned vessel might be here, but, as the night was falling, it was necessary to postpone the exploration until the morrow.

Pencroff and Herbert hastened to find a suitable place for a camp. The outskirts of the forest died away here, and near them the lad found a bamboo thicket.

"Good," said he, "this is a valuable discovery."

"Valuable?" asked Pencroff.

"Yes, indeed, I need not tell you, Pencroff, all its uses, such as for making baskets, paper, and water-pipes; that the larger ones make excellent building material and strong jars. But—"

"But?"

"But perhaps you do not know that in India they eat bamboo as we do asparagus."

"Asparagus thirty feet high?" cried, Pencroff. "And is it good?"

"Excellent," answered the lad. "But they eat only the young sprouts."

"Delicious!" cried Pencroff.

"And I am sure that the pith of young plants preserved in vinegar makes an excellent condiment."

"Better and better."

"And, lastly, they exude a sweet liquor which makes a pleasant drink."

"Is that all?" demanded the sailor.

"That's all."

"Isn't it good to smoke?"

"No, my poor Pencroff, you cannot smoke it!"

They did not have to search far for a good place for the camp. The rocks, much worn by the action of the sea, had many hollows that would afford shelter from the wind. But just as they were about to enter one of these cavities they were arrested by formidable growlings.

"Get back!" cried Pencroff, "we have only small shot in our guns, and these beasts would mind it no more than salt!"

And the sailor, seizing Herbert, dragged him behind some rocks, just as a huge jaguar appeared at the mouth of the cavern. Its skin was yellow, striped with black, and softened off with white under its belly. The beast advanced, and looked about. Its hair was bristling, and its eyes sparkling as if it was not scenting man for the first time.

Just then Spilett appeared, coming round the high rocks, and Herbert, thinking he had not seen the jaguar, was about rushing towards him, when the reporter, motioning with his hand, continued his approach. It was not his first tiger.

Advancing within ten paces of the animal, he rested motionless, his gun at his shoulder, not a muscle quivering. The jaguar, crouching back, made a bound towards the hunter, but as it sprung a bullet struck it between the eyes, dropping it dead.

Herbert and Pencroff rushed to it, and Smith and Neb coming up at the moment, all stopped to look at the splendid animal lying at length upon the sand.

"Oh, Mr. Spilett, how I envy you!" cried Herbert, in an excess of natural enthusiasm.

"Well, my boy, you would have done as well," answered the reporter.

"I have been as cool as that!"

"Only imagine, Herbert, that a jaguar is a hare, and you will shoot him as unconcernedly as anything in the world! And now," continued the reporter, "since the jaguar has left his retreat I don't see, my friends, why we should not occupy the place during the night"

"But some others may return!" said Pencroff.

"We will only have to light a fire at the entrance of the cavern," said the reporter, "and they will not dare to cross the threshold."

"To the jaguar house, then," cried the sailor, dragging the body of the animal after him.

The colonists went to the abandoned cave, and, while Neb was occupied in skinning the carcass, the others busied themselves with piling a great quantity of dry wood around the threshold. This done they installed themselves in the cave, whose floor was strewn with bones; the arms were loaded for an emergency; and, having eaten supper, as soon as the time for sleep was come, the fire at the entrance was lit.

Immediately a tremendous fusilade ensued! It was the bamboo which, in burning, exploded like fire-works! The noise, in itself, would have been sufficient to frighten off the bravest beasts.

CHAPTER XXVII.

PROPOSAL TO RETURN BY THE SOUTH COAST—
ITS CONFIGURATION—SEARCH FOR THE
SHIPWRECKED—A WAIF IN THE AIR—DISCOVERY OF
A SMALL NATURAL HARBOR—MIDNIGHT ON THE
MERCY—A DRIFTING CANOE.

Smith and his companions slept like mice in the cavern which the jaguar had so politely vacated, and, by sunrise, all were on the extremity of the promontory, and scrutinizing the horizon visible on either hand. No ship or wreck was to be seen, and not even with the spy-glass could any suspicious object be discerned. It was the same along the shore, at least on all that portion, three miles in length, which formed the south side of the promontory; as, beyond that, a slope of the land concealed the rest of the coast, and even from the extremity of Serpentine Peninsula, Claw Cape was hidden by high rocks.

The southern bank of the island remained to be explored. Had they not better attempt this at once, and give up this day to it? This procedure had not entered into their first calculations, as, when the canoe was left at the sources of the Mercy, the colonists thought that, having explored the west coast, they would return by the river; Smith having then believed that this coast sheltered either a wreck or a passing ship. But as soon as this shore disclosed no landing place, it became necessary to search the south side of the island for those whom they had failed to discover on the west.

It was Spilett who proposed continuing the exploration so as to settle definitely the question of the supposed shipwreck, and he inquired how far it would be to Claw Cape.

"About thirty miles," answered the engineer, "if we allow for the irregularity of the shore."

"Thirty miles!" exclaimed Spilett, "that would be a long walk. Nevertheless, I think we should return to Granite House by the south coast."

"But," observed Herbert, "from Claw Cape to Granite House is at least ten miles further."

"Call it forty miles altogether," answered the reporter, "and do not let us hesitate to do it. At least we will have seen this unknown shore, and will not have it to explore over again."

"That is so," said Pencroff. "But how about the canoe?"

"The canoe can stay where it is for a day or two," replied Spilett. "We can hardly say that the island is infested with thieves!"

"Nevertheless, when I remember that affair of the turtle, I am not so confident."

"The turtle! the turtle!" cried the reporter, "don't you know that the sea turned it over?"

"Who can say?" murmured the engineer.

"But—," began Neb, who, it was evident, wished to say something.

"What is it, Neb?" questioned the engineer.

"If we do return by the shore to Claw Cape, after having gone round it, we will be stopped—"

"By the Mercy!" cried Herbert. "And we have no bridge or boat!"

"Oh!" answered Pencroff, "we can cross it readily enough with some logs."

"Nevertheless," said Spilett, "it would be well to build a bridge some time if we wish to have ready access to the Far West."

"A bridge!" cried Pencroff. "Well isn't Mr. Smith State Engineer? If we shall need a bridge we will have one. As to carrying you over the

Mercy to-night without getting wet, I will look out for that. We still have a day's provision, which is all that is necessary, and, besides, the game may not give out to-day as It did yesterday. So let us go."

The proposal of the reporter, strongly seconded by the sailor, obtained general approval, as every one wished to end their doubts, and by returning by Claw Cape the exploration would be complete. But no time was to be lost, for the tramp was long, and they counted on reaching Granite House that night. So by 6 o'clock the little party was on its way, the guns loaded with ball in case of an encounter, and Top, who went ahead, ordered to search the edge of the forest.

The first five miles of the distance was rapidly traversed, and not the slightest sign of any human being was seen. When the colonists arrived at the point where the curvature of the promontory ended, and Washington Bay began, they were able to take in at one view the whole extent of the southern coast. Twenty-five miles distant the shore was terminated by Claw Cape, which was faintly visible through the morning mists, and reproduced as a mirage in mid-air. Between the place occupied by the colonists and the upper end of the Great Bay the shore began with a flat and continuous beach, bordered in the background by tall trees; following this, it became very irregular, and thrust sharp points into the sea, and finally a heap of black rocks, thrown together in picturesque disorder, completed the distance to Claw Cape.

"A ship would surely be lost on these sands and shoals and reefs," said Pencroff.

"It is poor quarters!"

"But at least a portion of her would be left," observed the reporter.

"Some bits of wood would remain on the reefs, nothing on the sands," answered the sailor.

"How is that?"

"Because the sands are even more dangerous than the rocks, and swallow up everything that is thrown upon them; a few days suffice to bury out of sight the hull of a ship of many tons measurement."

"Then, Pencroff," questioned the engineer, "if a vessel had been lost on these banks, it would not be surprising if there was no trace left?"

"No, sir, that is after a time or after a tempest. Nevertheless, it would be surprising, as now, that no spars or timbers were thrown upon the shore beyond the reach of the sea."

"Let us continue our search," replied Smith.

By 1 o'clock the party had accomplished twenty miles, having reached the upper end of Washington Bay, and they stopped to lunch.

Here began an irregular shore, oddly cut into by a long line of rocks, succeeding the sand banks, and just beginning to show themselves by long streaks of foam, above the undulations of the receding waves. From this point to Claw Cape the beach was narrow and confined between the reef of rocks and the forest, and the march would therefore be more difficult. The granite wall sunk more and more, and above it the tops of the trees, undisturbed by a breath of air, appeared in the background.

After half an hour's rest the colonists took up the march again, on the lookout for any sign of a wreck, but without success. They found out, however, that edible mussels were plenty on this beach, although they would not gather them until means of transport between the two banks of the river should have been perfected.

Towards 3 o'clock, Smith and his companions reached a narrow inlet, unfed by any water-course. It formed a veritable little natural harbor, invisible from without, and approached by a narrow passage guarded by the reefs. At the upper end of this creek some violent convulsion had shattered the rock, and a narrow, sloping passage gave access to the upper plateau, which proved to be ten miles from Claw Cape, and therefore four miles in a direct line from Prospect Plateau.

Spilett proposed to his companions to halt here, and, as the march had sharpened their appetites, although it was not dinner time, no one objected to a bit of venison, and with this lunch they would be able to await supper at Granite House.

Soon the colonists, seated under a group of splendid pines, were eating heartily of the provisions which Neb had brought out from his haversack. The place was some fifty or sixty feet above the sea, and the view, extending beyond the furthest rock of the cape, was lost in Union Bay. But the islet and Prospect Plateau were invisible, as the high ground and the curtain of high trees shut out the horizon to the north. Neither over the extent of sea nor on that part of the coast which it was still necessary to explore could they discover even with the spyglass any suspicious object.

"Well" said Spilett, "we can console ourselves by thinking that no one is disputing the island with us."

"But how about the pellet?" said Herbert. "It was not a dream."

"Indeed it was not!" cried Pencroff, thinking of his missing tooth.

"Well, what are we to conclude?" asked the reporter.

"This," said Smith, "that within three months a ship, voluntarily or otherwise, has touched—"

"What! You will admit, Cyrus, that it has been swallowed up without leaving any trace?" cried the reporter.

"No, my dear Spilett; but you must remember that while it is certain that a human being has been here, it seems just as certain that he is not here now."

"Then, if I understand you sir," said Herbert, "the ship has gone again?"

"Evidently."

"And we have lost, beyond return, a chance to get home?" said Neb.

"I believe without return."

"Well then, since the chance is lost, let us push on," said Pencroff, already home-sick for Granite House.

"But, just as they were rising, Top's barking was heard, and the dog burst from the forest, holding in his mouth a soiled rag.

Neb took it from him. It was a bit of strong cloth. Top, still barking, seemed by his motions to invite his master to follow into the wood.

"Here is something which will explain my bullet," cried Pencroff.

"A shipwrecked person!" answered Herbert.

"Wounded, perhaps!" exclaimed Neb.

"Or dead!" responded the reporter.

And all holding their arms in readiness, hurried after the dog through the outskirts of the forests. They advanced some distance into the wood, but, to their disappointment, they saw no tracks. The underbrush and lianas were uninjured and had to be cut away with the hatchet, as in the depths of the forest. It was hard to imagine that any human creature had passed there, and yet Top's action showed no uncertainty, but was more like that of a human being having a fixed purpose.

In a few minutes the dog stopped. The colonists, who had arrived at a sort of glade surrounded by high trees, looked all about them, but neither in the underbrush or between the tree trunks could they discover a thing.

"What is it, Top?" said Smith.

Top, barking louder, ran to the foot of a gigantic pine.

Suddenly Pencroff exclaimed:—

"This is capital!"

"What's that," asked Spilett.

"We've been hunting for some waif on the sea or land—"

"Well?"

"And here it is in the air!"

And the sailor pointed out a mass of faded cloth caught on the summit of the pine, a piece of which Top had found on the ground.

"But that is no waif!" exclaimed Spilett.

"Indeed it is," answered Pencroff.

"How is it!"

"It is all that is left of our balloon, of our ship which is stranded on the top of this tree."

Pencroff was not mistaken, and he added, with a shout:—

245

"And there is good stuff in it which will keep us in linen for years. It will make us handkerchiefs and shirts. Aha, Mr. Spilett! what do you say of an island where shirts grow on the trees?"

It was, indeed, a fortunate thing for the colonists that the aerostat, after having made its last bound into the air, had fallen again on the island. They could, either keep the envelope in its present shape, in case they might desire to attempt a new flight through the air, or, after having taken off the varnish, they could make use of its hundreds of ells of good cotton cloth. At these thoughts all shared Pencroff's joy.

It was no easy task to take down this envelope from the tree top. But Neb, Herbert, and the sailor climbed up to it, and after two hours of hard work not only the envelope, with its valve, springs, and leather mountings, but the net, equivalent to a large quantity of cordage and ropes, together with the iron ring and the anchor, lay upon the ground. The envelope, excepting the rent, was in good order, and only its lower end had been torn away.

It was a gift from heaven.

"Nevertheless, Mr. Smith," said the sailor, "if we ever do decide to leave the island it won't be in a balloon, I hope. These air ships don't always go the way you want them to, as we have found out. If you will let me have my way, we will build a ship of twenty tons, and you will allow me to cut from this cloth a foresail and jib. The rest of it will do for clothes."

"We will see about it, Pencroff," answered Smith.

"And meanwhile it must all be put away carefully," said Neb.

In truth, they could not think of carrying all this weight of material to Granite House; and while waiting for a proper means of removing it, it was important not to leave it exposed to the weather. The colonists, uniting their efforts, succeeded in dragging it to the shore, where they discovered a cave so situated that neither wind, rain, nor sea could get at it.

"It is a wardrobe," said Pencroff; "but since it does not kick, it will be prudent to hide the opening, not, perhaps from two-footed, but from four-footed thieves!"

By 6 o'clock everything was stored away, and after having named the little inlet, Balloon, Harbor, they took the road for Claw Cape. Pencroff and the engineer discussed several projects, which it would be well to attend to at once. The first thing was to build a bridge across the Mercy, and, as the canoe was too small, to bring the balloon over in the cart. Then to build a decked launch, which Pencroff would make cutter-rigged, and in which they could make voyages of circumnavigation—around the island; then, etc.

In the meantime the night approached, and it was already dark, when the colonists reached Jetsam Point, where they had discovered the precious box. But here, as elsewhere, there was nothing to indicate a shipwreck, and it became necessary to adopt the opinions expressed by Smith.

The four miles from Jetsam Point to Granite House were quickly traversed, but it was midnight when the colonists arrived at the first bend above the mouth of the Mercy. There the river was eighty feet wide, and Pencroff, who had undertaken to overcome the difficulty of crossing it, set to work. It must be admitted that the colonists were fatigued. The tramp had been long, and the incident of the balloon had not rested their arms or legs. They were therefore anxious to get back to Granite House to supper and bed, and if they had only had the bridge, in a quarter of an hour they could have been at home.

The night was very dark. Pencroff and Neb, armed with the hatchets, chose two trees near the bank, and began cutting them down, in order to make a raft. Smith and Spilett, seated on the ground, waited to assist their companions, and Herbert sauntered about, doing nothing.

All at once the lad, who had gone up the stream, returned hurriedly, and, pointing back, exclaimed:—

"What is that drifting there?"

Pencroff stopped work and perceived an object resting motionless in the gloom.

"A canoe!" he exclaimed.

All came up and saw, to their astonishment, a boat following the current.

"Canoe, ahoy!" shouted Pencroff from force of habit, forgetting that it might be better to keep quiet.

There was no answer. The boat continued to drift, and it was not more than a dozen paces off, when the sailor exclaimed:—

"Why, it's our canoe! She has broken away and drifted down with the current. Well, we must admit that she comes in the nick of time!"

"Our canoe!" murmured the engineer.

Pencroff was right. It was indeed their canoe, which had doubtless broken loose and drifted all the way from the headwaters of the Mercy! It was important to seize it in passing before it should be drawn into the rapid current at the mouth of the river, and Pencroff and Neb, by the aid of a long pole, did this, and drew the canoe to the bank.

The engineer stepped in first, and, seizing the rope, assured himself that it had been really worn in two against the rocks.

"This," said the reporter in an undertone; "this is a coincidence—"

"It is very strange!" answered the engineer.

At least it was fortunate, and while no one could doubt that the rope had been broken by friction, the astonishing part of the affair was that the canoe had arrived at the moment when the colonists were there to seize it, for a quarter of an hour later, and it would have been carried out to sea. Had there been such things as genii, this incident would have been sufficient to make the colonists believe that the island was inhabited by a supernatural being, who placed his power at their disposal.

With a few strokes the party arrived at the mouth of the Mercy. The canoe was drawn on shore at the Chimneys, and all took their way to the ladder at Granite House.

But, just then, Top began barking furiously, and Neb, who was feeling for the lower rung, cried out:—

"The ladder's gone!"

CHAPTER XXVIII.

PENCROFF'S HALLOOS—A NIGHT IN THE
CHIMNEYS—HERBERT'S ARROW—SMITH'S PLAN—
AN UNEXPECTED SOLUTION—WHAT HAD HAPPENED
IN GRANITE HOUSE—HOW THE COLONISTS
OBTAINED A NEW DOMESTIC.

Smith stood silent. His companions searched in the obscurity along the wall, over the ground, for the broken part of the ladder, supposing it had been torn off by the wind. But the ladder had certainly disappeared, although it was impossible to tell in the darkness whether a gust of wind had not carried it up and lodged it on the first ledge.

"If this is a joke, it's a pretty poor one," cried Pencroff. "To get home and not be able to find the staircase, won't do for tired men."

Neb stood in open-mouthed amazement.

"It could not have been carried away by the wind!" said Herbert.

"I'm beginning to think that strange things happen in Lincoln Island!" said Pencroff.

"Strange?" rejoined Spilett. "Why no, Pencroff, nothing is more natural. Somebody has come while we have been absent, and has taken possession of the house and drawn up the ladder!".

"Some one!" cried the sailor. "Who could it be?"

"Why, the man who shot the bullet," answered the reporter "How else can you explain it?"

"Very well, if any one is up there," replied Pencroff, beginning to get angry, "I will hail him, and he had better answer."

And in a voice of thunder the sailor gave a prolonged "Ohe," which was loudly repeated by the echoes.

The colonists listened, and thought that they heard a sort of chuckling proceed from Granite House. But there was no answering voice to the sailor, who repeated his appeal in vain.

Here was an event that would have astonished people the most indifferent, and from their situation the colonists could not be that. To them, the slightest incident was of moment, and certainly during their seven months' residence nothing equal to this had happened.

They stood there at the foot of Granite House not knowing what to do or to say. Neb was disconsolate at not being able to get back to the kitchen, especially as the provisions taken for the journey had all been eaten, and they had no present means of renewing them.

"There is but one thing to do, my friends," said Smith, "to wait until daylight, and then to be governed by circumstances. Meanwhile let us go to the Chimneys, where we will be sheltered, and, even if we cannot eat, we can sleep."

"But who is the ill-mannered fellow that has played us this trick?" asked Pencroff again, who thought it no joke.

Whoever he was, there was nothing to do but to follow the engineer's advice. Top having been ordered to lie down under the windows of Granite House, took his place without complaint. The brave dog remained at the foot of the wall, while his master and his companions took shelter among the rocks.

The colonists, tired as they were, slept but little. Not only were their beds uncomfortable, but it was certain that their house was occupied at present, and they were unable to get into it. Now Granite House was not only their dwelling, it was their storehouse. Everything they possessed was stored there. It would be a serious thing if this should be pillaged and they should have again to begin at the beginning. In their anxiety, one or the other went out often to see if the dog remained on watch. Smith, alone, waited with his accustomed patience, although he was exasperated at finding himself confronted by something utterly inexplicable, and his reason shrank from the thought that around him, over him, perhaps, was exercising an influence to which he could give no name. Spilett sharing his thoughts, they conversed together in an undertone of those unaccountable events which defied all their knowledge and experience. Certainly, there was a mystery about this island, but how discover it? Even Herbert did not know what to think, and often questioned Smith. As to Neb, he said that this was his master's business and not his; and if he had not feared offending his companions, the brave fellow would have slept this night as soundly as if he had been in his bed in Granite House.

Pencroff, however, was very much put out.

"It's a joke," he said. "It's a joke that is played on us. Well, I don't like such jokes, and the joker won't like it, if I catch him!"

At dawn the colonists, well armed, followed along the shore to the reefs. By 5 o'clock the closed windows of Granite House appeared through their leafy curtain. Everything, from this side, appeared to be in order, but an exclamation escaped from the colonists when they perceived that the door which they had left closed was wide open. There could be no more doubt that some one was in Granite House, The upper ladder was in its place; but the lower had been drawn up to the threshold. It was evident that the intruders wished to guard against a surprise. As to telling who or how many they were, that was still impossible, as none had yet shown themselves.

Pencroff shouted again, but without answer.

"The beggars!" he exclaimed, "to sleep as soundly as if they were at home! Halloo! pirates! bandits! corsairs! sons of John Bull!"

When Pencroff, as an American, called any one a "son of John Bull," he had reached the acme of insult.

Just then, the day broke and the facade of Granite House was illuminated by the rays of the rising sun. But inside as well as without all was still and calm. It was evident from the position of the ladder that whoever bad been inside the house had not come out. But how could they get up to them?

Herbert conceived the idea of shooting an arrow attached to a cord between the lower rungs of the ladder which were hanging from the doorway: They would thus be able by means of the cord to pull this ladder down, and gain access to Granite House. There was evidently nothing else to do, and with a little skill this attempt might prove successful. Fortunately there were bows and arrows at the Chimneys, and they found there, also, some twenty fathoms of light hibiscus cord. Pencroff unrolled this, and fastened the end to a well-feathered arrow. Then Herbert having placed the arrow in his bow took careful aim at the hanging part of the ladder.

The others stationed themselves some distance in the background to observe what might happen, and the reporter covered the doorway with his carbine.

The bow bent, the arrow shot upward with the cord, and passed between the two lower rungs of the ladder. The operation had succeeded. But just as Herbert, having caught the end of the cord, was about giving it a pull to make the ladder fall, an arm thrust quickly between the door and the wall seized the ladder and drew it within Granite House.

"You little beggar!" cried Pencroff. "If a ball would settle you, you would not have to wait long!"

"But what is it?" demanded Neb.

"What! didn't you see?"

"No."

"Why, it's a monkey, a macauco, a sapajo, an orang, a baboon, a gorilla, a sagoin! Our house has been invaded by monkeys, which have climbed up the ladder while we were away."

And at the moment, as if to prove the truth of what the sailor said, three or four quadrumana threw open the window shutters and saluted the true proprietors of the place with a thousand contortions and grimaces.

"I knew all the time it was a joke," cried Pencroff, "But here's one of the jokers that will pay for the others!" he added, covering a monkey with his gun and firing. All disappeared but, this one, which, mortally wounded, fell to the ground.

This monkey was very large and evidently belonged to the first order of quadrumana. Whether a chimpanzee, an orang, a gorilla, or a gibbon, it ranked among these anthropomorphi, so called on account of their likeness to the human race. Herbert declared it was an orang-outang, and we all know that the lad understood zoology.

"What a fine beast!" cried Neb.

"As fine as you choose!" answered the reporter, "but I don't see yet how we are going to get in!"

"Herbert is a good shot," said the reporter, "and his bow is sure! We will try again—"

"But these monkeys are mischievous," cried Pencroff, "and if they don't come to the windows, we cannot shoot them; and when I think of the damage they can do in the rooms and, in the magazine—"

"Have patience," answered Smith. "These animals cannot hold us in check, very long."

"I will be sure of that when they are out of there, "rejoined Pencroff, "Can you say how many dozens of these fools there may be?"

It would hare been hard to answer Pencroff, but it was harder to try again the experiment of the arrow, as the lower end of the ladder had been drawn within the doorway, and when they pulled on the cord again, it broke, and the ladder remained, as before.

It was, Indeed, vexatious. Pencroff was in a fury, and, although the situation had a certain comic aspect, he did not think it funny at all. It was evident that the colonists would, eventually, get back into their house and drive out the monkeys, but when and how they could not say.

Two hours passed, during which the monkeys avoided showing themselves; but they were there, for all that, and, two or three times, a muzzle or paw slipped by the door or the windows, and was saluted by a shot.

"Let us conceal ourselves," said the engineer, at length. "And then the monkeys will think we have gone off, and will show themselves again. Let Herbert and Spilett remain hidden behind the rocks and fire on any that appear.

The directions of the engineer were followed, and while the reporter and the lad, who were the best shots in the party, took their positions, the others went over the plateau to the forest to shoot some game, as it was breakfast time and they had no food.

In half an hour the hunters returned with some wild pigeons, which would be pretty good roasted. Not a monkey had shown itself.

Spilett and Herbert went to their breakfast, while Top kept watch under the windows. Then they returned to their post. Two hours later the situation was unchanged. The quadrumana gave no sign of existence, and it seemed as if they must have disappeared; but it was more likely that, frightened by the death of one of their number and the detonations of the guns, they kept themselves hidden in the chambers or the store-room of Granite House. And, when the colonists thought of all that was stored in this latter room, the patience which the engineer had recommended turned into irritation, and indeed they could not be blamed for it.

"It is too bad!" exclaimed the reporter, at length; "and is there no way we can put an end to this?"

"We must make these beggars give up!" cried Pencroff. "We can readily do it, even if there are twenty of them, in a hand-to hand fight! Oh, is there no way we can get at them?"

"Yes," replied Smith, struck by an idea.

"Only one?" rejoined Pencroff. "Well, that's better than none at all. What is it?"

"Try to get into Granite House by the old weir," answered the engineer.

"Why in the mischief didn't I think of that!" cried the sailor.

This was, indeed, the only way to get into Granite House, in order to fight the band and drive them out. It is true that, if they tore down the cemented wall which closed the weir, the work would have all to be done over again; but, fortunately, Smith had not yet effected his design of hiding this opening by covering it again with the lake, as that operation necessitated a good deal of time.

It was already past noon when the colonists, well armed and furnished with picks and mattocks, left the Chimneys, passed under the windows of Granite House, and, having ordered Top to remain at his post, made ready to climb the left bank of the Mercy, so as to reach Prospect Plateau. But they had hardly gone fifty paces, when they heard the loud barkings of the dog, as if making a desperate appeal. All halted.

"Let us run back," cried Pencroff. And all did as proposed as fast as possible.

Arrived at the turn, the whole situation was changed. The monkeys, seized with a sudden fright, startled by some unknown cause, were trying to escape. Two or three were running and springing from window to window, with the agility of clowns. In their fright they seemed to have forgotten to replace the ladder, by which they could easily have descended. In a moment half a dozen were in such a position that they could be shot, and the colonists, taking aim, fired. Some fell, wounded or killed, within the chambers, uttering sharp cries. Others, falling to the ground without, were crushed by the fall, and a few moments afterwards it seemed as if there was not one living quadrumana in Granite House.

"Hurrah," said Pencroff, "hurrah, hurrah!"

"Don't cheer yet," saidSpilett.

"Why not," asked Pencroff. "Ain't they all killed."

"Doubtless: but that does not give us the means of getting in."

"Let us go the weir!" exclaimed Pencroff.

"We will have to," said the engineer. "Nevertheless it would have been preferable—"

And at the instant, as if in answer to the observation of the engineer, they saw the ladder slide over the door-sill and roll over to the ground.

"By the thousand pipes, but that is lucky!" cried Pencroff, looking at Smith.

"Too lucky!" muttered Smith, springing up the ladder.

"Take care, Mr. Smith!" exclaimed Pencroff, "if there should be any sojourners—"

"We will soon see," responded the other.

All his companions followed him and in a moment were within the doorway.

They searched everywhere. No one was in the chambers or in the storeroom, which remained undisturbed by the quadrumana.

"And the ladder," said Pencroff; "where is the gentleman who pushed it down to us?"

But just then a cry was heard, and a huge monkey, that had taken refuge in the corridor, sprang into the great hall, followed by Neb.

"Ah, the thief!" cried Pencroff, about to spring with his hatchet at the head of the animal, when Smith stopped him.

"Spare it, Pencroff."

"What, spare this black ape?"

"Yes, it is he that has thrown us the ladder," said the engineer, in a voice so strange, that it was hard to say whether he was in earnest or not.

Nevertheless, all threw themselves on the monkey, which, after a brave resistance, was thrown down and tied.

"Ugh!" exclaimed Pencroff; "and now what will we do with it?"

"Make a servant of it," answered Herbert, half in earnest, as the lad knew how great was the intelligence of this race of quadrumana.

The colonists gathered round the monkey and examined it attentively. It appeared to belong to that species of anthropomorphi in which the facial angle is not visibly inferior to that of the Australians or Hottentots. He was an orang of the kind which has neither the ferocity of the baboon nor the macauco, nor the thoughtlessness of the sagoin, nor the impatience of the magot, nor the bad instincts of the cynocephalous. It was of a family of anthropomorphi which has traits indicating a half-human intelligence. Employed in houses, they can wait on the table, do chamberwork, brush clothes, black boots, clean the knives and forks, and—empty the bottles, as well as the best trained flunkey. Buffon possessed one of these monkeys, which served him a long time as a zealous and faithful servant.

The one at present tied in the hall of Granite House was a big fellow, six feet high, deep-chested, and finely built, a medium-sized head, with a sharp facial angle, a well-rounded skull, and a prominent nose, and a skin covered with smooth hair, soft and shining,—in short, a finished type of anthropomorphi. Its eyes, somewhat smaller than those of a human being, sparkled with intelligence; its teeth glistened beneath its moustache, and it wore a small nut-brown beard.

"He is a fine chap," said Pencroff. "If we only understood his language, one might talk with him!"

"Then," said Neb, "are they in earnest, my master? Will we take it as a domestic?"

"Yes, Neb," said the engineer, smiling. "But you need not be jealous."

"And I hope it will make an excellent servant. As it is young its education will be easy, and we will not have to use force to make it mind, nor to pull out its teeth as is sometimes done. It cannot fail to become attached to masters who only treat it well."

"And we will do that," said Pencroff, who having forgotten his recent wrath against the "jokers," approached the orang and accosted him with:—

"Hullo, my boy, how goes it?"

The orang responded with a little grunt, which seemed to denote a not bad temper.

"You want to join the colony, do you? Would you like to enter the service of Mr. Smith?"

The monkey gave another affirmative grunt.

"And you'll be satisfied with your board as wages?"

A third affirmative grunt.

"His conversation is a little monotonous," observed Spilett.

"Well," replied Pencroff, "the best domestics are those that speak least. And then, no wages! Do you hear, my boy? At first we give you no wages, but we will double them later, if you suit us!"

Thus the colonists added to their number one who had already done them a service. As to a name, the sailor asked that he should be called, in remembrance of another monkey, Jupiter, or by abbreviation, Jup. And thus, without more ado, Master Jup was installed in Granite House.

CHAPTER XXIX.

PROJECTS TO BE CARRIED OUT—A BRIDGE OVER
THE MERCY—TO MAKE AN ISLAND OF PROSPECT
PLATEAU—THE DRAW-BRIDGE—THE CORN
HARVEST—THE STREAM—THE CAUSEWAY—
THE POULTRY YARD—THE PIGEON-HOUSE—
THE TWO WILD ASSES—HARNESSED TO THE
WAGON—EXCURSION TO BALLOON HARBOR.

The colonists had now reconquered their domicile without having been obliged to follow the weir. It was, indeed, fortunate, that at the moment they decided to destroy their masonry, the band of monkeys, struck by a terror not less sudden than inexplicable, had rushed from Granite House. Had these animals a presentiment that a dangerous attack was about to be made on them from another direction? This was the only way to account for their retreat.

The rest of the day was occupied in carrying the dead monkeys to the wood and burying them there, and in repairing the disorder made by the intruders,—disorder and not damage, as, though they had upset the furniture in the rooms, they had broken nothing. Neb rekindled the range, and the supply in the pantry furnished a substantial repast that was duly honored.

Jup was not forgotten, and he ate with avidity the pistachio nuts and the roots of the sumach, with which he saw himself abundantly provided.

Pencroff had unfastened his arms, although he thought it best to keep the monkey's legs bound until they could be sure he had surrendered.

Seated at the table, before going to bed, Smith and his companions discussed three projects, the execution of which was urgent. The most important and the most pressing was the establishment of a bridge across the Mercy, then the building of a corral, designed for the accommodation of moufflons or other woolly animals which they had agreed to capture. These two plans tended to solve the question of clothing, which was then the most serious question.

It was Smith's intention to establish this corral at the sources of Red Creek, where there was abundant pasturage. Already the path between there and Prospect Plateau was partially cleared, and with a better constructed cart, carriage would be easy, especially if they should capture some animal that could draw it.

But while it would not be inconvenient to have the corral some distance from Granite House, it was different with the poultry-yard, to which Neb called attention. It was necessary that the "chickens" should be at the hand of the cook, and no place seemed more favorable for an establishment of this kind than that portion of the lake shore bordering on the former weir. The aquatic birds also would thrive there, and the pair of tinamons, taken in the last excursion, would serve as a beginning.

The next day—the 3d of November—work was begun on the bridge, and all hands were required on the important undertaking. Laden with tools the colonists descended to the shore.

Here Pencroff reflected as follows:—

"Supposing while we are away Master Jup takes the notion of hauling up the ladder, which he so gallantly unrolled for us yesterday."

"We would be dependent on his tail!" answered Spilett.

The ladder was therefore made fast to two stakes driven firmly into the ground. The colonists ascended the river, and soon arrived at its narrow bend, where they halted to examine whether the bridge could not be thrown across at this place. The situation was suitable, as from this point to Balloon Harbor the distance was three miles and a half, and a wagon road connecting Granite House with the southern part of the island, could easily be constructed.

Then Smith communicated to his companions a project which he had had in view for some time. This was to completely isolate Prospect Plateau, so as to protect it from all attacks of quadrupeds or quadrumana. By this means Granite House, the Chimneys, the poultry yard, and all the upper part of the plateau destined for sowing would be protected against the depredations of animals.

Nothing could be easier than to do this, and the engineer proposed to accomplish it as follows:—The plateau was already protected on three sides by either natural or artificial water courses. On the northwest, by the bank of Lake Grant, extending from the angle against the former weir to the cut made in the east bank to draw off the water. On the north, by this new water course which had worn itself a bed both above and below the fall, which could be dug out sufficiently to render the passage impracticable to animals. And upon the east, by the sea itself, from the mouth of this new creek to the mouth of the Mercy. Therefore the only part remaining open was the western part of the plateau included between the bend in the river and the southern angle of the lake, a distance of leas than a mile. But nothing could be easier than to dig a ditch, wide and deep, which would be filled from the lake, and flow into the Mercy. Doubtless the level of the lake would be lowered somewhat by this new drain on its resources, but Smith had assured himself that the flow of Red Creek was sufficient for his purpose.

"Thus," added the engineer, "Prospect Plateau will be a veritable island, unconnected with the rest of our domain, save by the bridge which we will throw over the Mercy, by the two causeways already built above and below the fall, and by the two others which are to be constructed, one over the proposed ditch, and the other over the left bank of the Mercy. Now if this bridge and the causeways can be raised at will, Prospect Plateau will be secured from surprise."

Smith, in order to make his companions comprehend clearly his plans, had made a plot of the plateau, and his project was rendered perfectly plain. It met with unanimous approval; and Pencroff, brandishing his hatchet, exclaimed:—

"And first, for the bridge!"

This work was the most urgent. Trees were selected, felled, lopped, and cut into beams, planks, and boards. The bridge was to be stationary on the right bank of the Mercy, but on the left it was to be so constructed as to raise by means of counterweights, as in some draw-bridges.

It will be seen that this work, even if it could be easily accomplished, would take considerable time, as the Mercy was eighty feet wide at this point. It was first necessary to drive piles in the bed of the river, to sustain the flooring of the bridge, and to set up a pile-driver to drive the piles, so as to form two arches capable of supporting heavy weights.

Fortunately they lacked neither the necessary tools for preparing the timber, nor the iron work, to bind it together, nor the ingenuity of a man who was an adept at this sort of work, nor, finally, the zeal of his companions who in these seven months had necessarily acquired considerable manual skill. And it should be added that Spilett began to do nearly as well as the sailor himself "who would never have expected so much from a newspaper man!"

It took three weeks of steady work to build this bridge. And as the weather was fine they lunched on the ground, and only returned to Granite House for supper.

During this period it was observed that Master Jup took kindly to and familiarized himself with his new masters, whom he watched with the greatest curiosity. Nevertheless, Pencroff was careful not to give him complete liberty until the limits of the plateau had been rendered impassible. Top and he were the best possible friends, and got on capitally together although Jup took everything gravely.

The bridge was finished on the 20th of November. The movable part balanced perfectly with the counterpoise, and needed but little effort to raise it; between the hinge and crossbeam on which the draw rested when closed, the distance was twenty feet, a gap sufficiently wide to prevent animals from getting across.

It was next proposed to go for the envelope of the balloon, which the colonists were anxious to place in safety; but in order to bring it, the cart would have to be dragged to Balloon Harbor, necessitating the breaking of a road through the dense underwood of the Far West, all of which would take time. Therefore Neb and Pencroff made an excursion to the harbor, and as they reported that the supply of cloth was well protected in the cave, it was decided that the works about the plateau should not be discontinued.

"This," said Pencroff, "will enable us to establish the poultry-yard under the most advantageous conditions, since we need have no fear of the visits of foxes or other noxious animals."

"And also," added Neb, "we can clear the plateau, and transplant wild plants"—

"And make ready our second corn-field," continued the sailor with a triumphant air.

Indeed the first corn-field, sowed with a single grain, had prospered admirably, thanks to the care of Pencroff. It had produced the ten ears foretold by the engineer, and as each ear had eighty grains, the colonists found themselves possessed of 800 grains—in six months—which promised them a double harvest each year. These 800 grains, excepting fifty which it was prudent to reserve, were now about to be sowed in a new field with as much care as the first solitary specimen.

The field was prepared, and inclosed with high, sharp-pointed palisades, which quadrupeds would have found very difficult to surmount. As to the birds, the noisy whirligigs and astonishing scarecrows, the product of Pencroff's genius, were enough to keep them at a distance. Then the 750 grains were buried in little hills, regularly disposed, and Nature was left to do the rest.

On the 21st of November, Smith began laying out the ditch which was to enclose the plateau on the west. There were two or three feet of vegetable earth, and beneath that the granite. It was, therefore, necessary to manufacture some more nitro-glycerine, and the nitro-glycerine had its accustomed effect. In less than a fortnight a ditch, twelve feet wide and six feet deep was excavated in the plateau. A new outlet was in like manner made in the rocky border of the lake, and the waters rushed into this new channel, forming a small stream, to which they gave the name of Glycerine Creek. As the engineer had foreseen the level of the lake was lowered but very slightly. Finally, for completing the enclosure, the bed of the stream across the beach was considerably enlarged, and the sand was kept up by a double palisade.

By the middle of December all these works were completed, and Prospect Plateau, shaped something like an irregular pentagon, having a perimeter of about four miles, was encircled with a liquid belt, making it absolutely safe from all aggression.

During this month the heat was very great. Nevertheless, the colonists, not wishing to cease work, proceeded to construct the poultry-yard. Jup, who since the enclosing of the plateau had been given his liberty, never quitted his masters nor manifested the least desire to escape. He was a gentle beast, though possessing immense strength and wonderful agility. No one could go up the ladder to Granite House as he could. Already he was given employment; he was instructed to fetch wood and carry off the stones which had been taken from the bed of Glycerine Creek.

"Although he's not yet a mason, he is already a 'monkey,'" said Herbert, making a joking allusion to the nickname masons give their apprentices. And if ever a name was well applied, it was so in this instance!

The poultry-yard occupied an area of 200 square yards on the southeast bank of the lake. It was enclosed with a palisade, and within were separate divisions for the proposed inhabitants, and huts of branches divided into compartments awaiting their occupants.

The first was the pair of tinamons, who were not long in breeding numerous little ones. They had for companions half-a-dozen ducks, who were always by the water-side. Some of these belonged to that Chinese variety whose wings open like a fan, and whose plumage rivals in brilliance that of the golden pheasant. Some days later, Herbert caught a pair of magnificent curassows, birds of the gallinaceæ family, with long rounding tails. These soon bred others, and as to the pellicans, the kingfishers, the moorhens, they came of themselves to the poultry-yard. And soon, all this little world, after some disputing, cooing, scolding, clucking, ended by agreeing and multiplying at a rate sufficient for the future wants of the colony.

Smith, in order to complete his work, established a pigeon-house in the corner of the poultry-yard, and placed therein a dozen wild pigeons. These birds readily habituated themselves to their new abode, and returned there each evening, showing a greater propensity to domestication than the wood pigeons, their congeners, which do not breed except in a savage state.

And now the time was come to make use of the envelope in the manufacture of clothing, for to keep it intact in order to attempt to leave the island by risking themselves in a balloon filled with heated air over a sea, which might be called limitless, was only to be thought of by men deprived of all other resources, and Smith, being eminently practical, did not dream of such a thing.

It was necessary to bring the envelope to Granite House, and the colonists busied themselves in making their heavy cart less unwieldly and lighter. But though the vehicle was provided, the motor was still to be found! Did not there exist in the island some ruminant of indiginous species which could replace the horse, ass, ox, or cow? That was the question.

"Indeed," said Pencroff, "a draught animal would be very useful to us, while we are waiting until Mr. Smith is ready to build a steam-wagon or a locomotive, though doubtless, some day we will have a railway to Balloon Harbor, with a branch road up Mount Franklin!"

And the honest sailor, in talking thus, believed what he said. Such is the power of imagination combined with faith!

But, in truth, an animal capable of being harnessed would have just suited Pencroff, and as Fortune favored him, she did not let him want.

One day, the 23d of December, the colonists, busy at the Chimneys, heard Neb crying and Top barking in such emulation, that dreading some terrible accident, they ran to them.

What did they see? Two large, beautiful animals, which had imprudently ventured upon the plateau, the causeways not having been closed. They seemed like two horses, or rather two asses, male and female, finely shaped, of a light bay color, striped with black on the head, neck, and body, and with white legs and tail. They advanced tranquilly, without showing any fear, and looked calmly on these men in whom they had not yet recognized their masters.

"They are onagers," cried Herbert. "Quadrupeds of a kind between the zebra and the quagga."

"Why aren't they asses?" asked Neb.

"Because they have not long ears, and their forms are more graceful."

"Asses or horses," added Pencroff—"they are what Mr. Smith would call "motors," and it will be well to capture them!"

The sailor, without startling the animals, slid through the grass to the causeway over Glycerine Creek, raised it, and the onagers were prisoners. Should they be taken by violence, and made to submit to a forced domestication? No. It was decided that for some days they would let these animals wander at will over the plateau where the grass was abundant, and a stable was at once constructed near to the poultry-yard in which the onagers would find a good bedding, and a refuge for the night.

The fine pair were thus left entirely at liberty, and the colonists avoided approaching them. In the meantime the onagers often tried to quit the plateau, which was too confined for them, accustomed to wide ranges and deep forests. The colonists saw them following around the belt of water impossible to cross, whinnying and galloping over the grass, and then resting quietly for hours regarding the deep woods from which they were shut off.

In the meantime, harness had been made from vegetable fibres, and some days after the capture of the onagers, not only was the cart ready, but a road, or rather a cut, had been made through the forest all the way from the bend in the Mercy to Balloon Harbor. They could therefore get to this latter place with the cart, and towards the end of the month the onagers were tried for the first time.

Pencroff had already coaxed these animals so that they ate from his hand, and he could approach them without difficulty, but, once harnessed, they reared and kicked, and were with difficulty kept from breaking loose, although it was not long before they submitted to this new service.

This day, every one except Pencroff, who walked beside his team, rode in the cart to Balloon Harbor. They were jolted about a little over this rough road, but the cart did not break down, and they were able to load it, the same day, with the envelope and the appurtenances to the balloon.

By 8 o'clock in the evening, the cart, having recrossed the bridge, followed down the bank of the Mercy and stopped on the beach. The onagers were unharnessed, placed in the stable, and Pencroff, before sleeping, gave a sigh of satisfaction that resounded throughout Granite House.

CHAPTER XXX.

CLOTHING—SEAL-SKIN BOOTS—MAKING
PYROXYLINE—PLANTING—THE FISH—TURTLES'
EGGS—JUP'S EDUCATION—THE CORRAL-HUNTING
MOUFFLONS—OTHER USEFUL ANIMALS AND
VEGETABLES—HOME THOUGHTS.

The first week In January was devoted to making clothing. The needles found in the box were plied by strong, if not supple fingers, and what was sewed, was sewed strongly. Thread was plenty, as Smith had thought of using again that with which the strips of the balloon had been fastened together. These long bands bad been carefully unripped by Spilett and Herbert with commendable patience, since Pencroff had thrown aside the work, which bothered him beyond measure; but when it came to sewing again the sailor was unequalled.

The varnish was then removed from the cloth by means of soda procured as before, and the cloth was afterwards bleached in the sun. Some dozens of shirts and socks—the latter, of course, not knitted, but made of sewed strips—were thus made. How happy it made the colonists to be clothed again in white linen—linen coarse enough, it is true, but they did not mind that—and to lie between sheets, which transformed the banks of Granite House into real beds! About this time they also made boots from seal leather, which were a timely substitute for those brought from America. They were long and wide enough, and never pinched the feet of the pedestrians.

In the beginning of the year (1866) the hot weather was incessant, but the hunting in the woods, which fairly swarmed with birds and beasts, continued; and Spilett and Herbert were too good shots to waste powder. Smith had recommended them to save their ammunition, and that they might keep it for future use the engineer took measures to replace it by substances easily renewable. How could he tell what the future might have in store for them in case they left the island? It behooved them, therefore, to prepare for all emergencies.

As Smith had not discovered any lead in the island he substituted iron shot, which were easily made. As they were not so heavy as leaden ones they had to be made larger, and the charges contained a less number, but the skill of the hunters counterbalanced this defect. Powder he could have made, since he had all the necessary materials but as its preparation requires extreme care, and as without special apparatus it is difficult to make it of good quality, Smith proposed to manufacture pyroxyline, a kind of gun-cotton, a substance in which cotton is not necessary, except as cellulose. Now cellulose is simply the elementary tissue of vegetables, and is found in almost a pure state not only in cotton, but also in the texile fibres of hemp and flax, in paper and old rags, the pith of the elder, etc. And it happened that elder trees abounded in the island towards the mouth of Red Creek:—the colonists had already used its shoots and berries in place of coffee.

Thus they had the cellulose at hand, and the only other substance necessary for the manufacture of pyroxyline was nitric acid, which Smith could easily produce as before. The engineer, therefore, resolved to make and use this combustible, although he was aware that it had certain serious inconveniences, such as inflaming at 170° instead of 240°, and a too instantaneous deflagration for firearms. On the other hand, pyroxyline had these advantages—it was not affected by dampness, it did not foul the gun-barrels, and its explosive force was four times greater than that of gunpowder.

In order to make the pyroxyline, Smith made a mixture of three parts of nitric acid with five of concentrated sulphuric acid, and steeped the cellulose in this mixture for a quarter of an hour; afterwards it was washed in fresh water and left to dry. The operation succeeded perfectly, and the hunters had at their disposal a substance perfectly prepared, and which, used with discretion, gave excellent results.

About this time the colonists cleared three acres of Prospect Plateau, leaving the rest as pasture for the onagers. Many excursions were made into Jacamar Wood and the Far West, and they brought back a perfect harvest of wild vegetables, spinach, cresses, charlocks, and radishes, which intelligent culture would greatly change, and which would serve to modify the flesh diet which the colonists had been obliged to put up with. They also hauled large quantities of wood and coal, and each excursion helped improve the roads by grinding down its inequalities under the wheels.

The warren always furnished its contingent of rabbits, and as it was situated without Glycerine creek, its occupants could not reach nor damage the new plantations. As to the oyster-bed among the coast rocks, it furnished a daily supply of excellent mollusks. Further, fish from the lake and river were abundant, as Pencroff had made set-lines on which they often caught trout and another very savory fish marked with small yellow spots on a silver-colored body. Thus Neb, who had charge of the culinary department, was able to make an agreeable change in the menu of each repast. Bread alone was wanting at the colonists' table, and they felt this privation exceedingly.

Sometimes the little party hunted the sea-turtles, which frequented the coast at Mandible Cape. At this season the beach was covered with little mounds enclosing the round eggs, which were left to the sun to hatch; and as each turtle produces two hundred and fifty eggs annually, their number was very great.

"It is a true egg-field," said Spilett, "and all we have to do is to gather them."

But they did not content themselves with these products; they hunted also the producers, and took back to Granite House a dozen of these reptiles, which were excellent eating. Turtle soup, seasoned with herbs, and a handful of shell-fish thrown in, gained high praise for its concoctor, Neb.

Another fortunate event, which permitted them to make new provision for winter, must be mentioned. Shoals of salmon ascended the Mercy for many miles, in order to spawn. The river was full of these fish, which measured upwards of two feet in length, and it was only necessary to place some barriers in the stream in order to capture a great many. Hundreds were caught in this way, and salted down for winter, when the ice would stop the fishing.

Jup, during this time, was elevated to the position of a domestic. He had been clothed in a jacket, and short trowsers, and an apron with pockets, which were his joy, as he kept his hands in them and allowed no one to search them. The adroit orang had been wonderfully trained by Neb, and one would have said they understood each other's conversation. Jup had, moreover, a real affection for the Negro, which was reciprocated. When the monkey was not wanted to carry wood or to climb to the top of some tree, he was passing his time in the kitchen, seeking to imitate Neb in all that he was doing. The master also showed great patience and zeal in instructing his pupil, and the pupil showed remarkable intelligence in profiting by these lessons.

Great was the satisfaction one day when Master Jup, napkin on arm, came without having been called to wait on the table. Adroit and attentive, he acquitted himself perfectly, changing the plates, bringing the dishes, and pouring the drink, all with a gravity which greatly amused the colonists, and completely overcame Pencroff.

"Jup, some more soup! Jup, a bit more agouti! Jup, another plate! Jup, brave, honest Jup!"

Jup, not in the least disconcerted, responded to every call, looked out for everything, and nodded his head intelligently when the sailor, alluding to his former pleasantry said:—

"Decidedly, Jup, we must double your wages!"

The orang had become perfectly accustomed, to Granite House, and often accompanied his masters to the forest without manifesting the least desire to run off. It was laughable to see him march along with a stick of Pencroff's on his shoulder, like a gun. If any one wanted some fruit gathered from a treetop how quickly be was up there. If the wagon wheels stuck in the mire, with what strength he raised it onto the road again.

"What a Hercules!" exclaimed Pencroff. "If he was as mischievous as he is gentle we could not get along with him."

Towards the end of January the colonists undertook great work in the interior of the island. It had been decided that they would establish at the foot of Mount Franklin, near the sources of Red Creek, the corral destined to contain the animals whose presence would have been unpleasant near Granite House, and more particularly the moufflons, which were to furnish wool for winter clothing. Every morning all the colonists, or oftener Smith, Herbert, and Pencroff, went with the onagers to the site, five miles distant, over what they called Corral Road. There an extensive area had been chosen opposite the southern slope of the mountain. It was a level plain, having here and there groups of trees, situated at the base of one of the spurs, which closed it in on that side. A small stream, rising close by, crossed it diagonally, and emptied into Red Creek. The grass was lush, and the position of the trees allowed the air to circulate freely. All that was necessary was to build a palisade around to the mountain spur sufficiently high to keep in the animals. The enclosure would be large enough to contain one hundred cattle, moufflons or wild goats and their young.

The line of the corral was marked out by the engineer, and they all set to work to cut down the trees necessary for the palisade. The road which they had made furnished some hundred trees, which were drawn to the place and set firmly in the ground. At the back part of the palisade they made an entranceway, closed by a double gate made from thick plank, which could be firmly fastened on the outside.

The building of this corral took all of three weeks, as, besides the work on the palisades, Smith put up large sheds for the animals. These were made of planks, and, indeed, everything had to be made solidly and strong, as moufflons have great strength, and their first resistance was to be feared. The uprights, pointed at the end and charred, had been bolted together, and the strength of the whole had been augmented by placing braces at intervals.

The corral finished, the next thing was to inaugurate a grand hunt at the pasturages, near the foot of Mount Franklin, frequented by the animals. The time chosen was the 7th of February, a lovely summer day, and everybody took part in the affair. The two onagers, already pretty well trained, were mounted by Spilett and Herbert and did excellent service. The plan was to drive together the moufflons and goats by gradually narrowing the circle of the chase around them. Smith, Pencroff, Neb, and Jup posted themselves in different parts of the wood, while the two horsemen and Top scoured the country for half a mile around the corral. The moufflons were very numerous in this neighborhood. These handsome animals were as large as deer, with larger horns than those of rams, and a greyish-colored wool, mingled with long hair, like argali.

The hunt, with its going and coming, the racing backwards and forwards, the shouting and hallooing, was fatiguing enough. Out of a hundred animals that were driven together many escaped, but little by little some thirty moufflons and a dozen wild goats were driven within the corral, whose open gate seemed to offer a chance of escape. The result was, therefore, satisfactory; and as many of these moufflons were females with young, it was certain that the herd would prosper, and milk and skins be plenty in the future.

In the evening the hunters returned to Granite House nearly tired out. Nevertheless the next day they went back to look at the corral. The prisoners had tried hard to break down the palisade, but, not succeeding, they had soon become quiet.

Nothing of any importance happened during February. The routine of daily work continued, and while improving the condition of the existing roads, a third, starting from the enclosure, and directed towards the southern coast, was begun. This unknown portion of Lincoln Island was one mass of forest, such as covered Serpentine Peninsula, giving shelter to the beasts from whose presence Spilett proposed to rid their domain.

Before the winter returned careful attention was given to the cultivation of the wild plants which had been transplanted to the plateau, and Herbert seldom returned from an excursion without bringing back some useful vegetable. One day it was a kind of succory, from the seed of which an excellent oil can be pressed; another time, it was the common sorrel, whose anti-scorbutic properties were not to be neglected; and again, it was some of those valuable tubercles which have always been cultivated in South America, those potatoes, of which more than two hundred species are known at present. The kitchen garden, already well enclosed, well watered, and well defended against the birds, was divided into small beds of lettuce, sorrel, radish, charlock, and other crucifers; and as the soil upon the plateau was of wonderful richness, abundant crops might be anticipated.

Neither were various drinks wanting, and unless requiring wine, the most fastidious could not have complained. To the Oswego tea, made from the mountain mint, and the fermented liquor made from the roots of the dragon-tree, Smith added a genuine beer; this was made from the young shoots of the "abies nigra," which, after having been boiled and fermented, yielded that agreeable and particularly healthful drink, known to Americans as "spring beer," that is, spruce beer.

Toward the close of summer the poultry yard received a fine pair of bustards belonging to the species "houbara," remarkable for a sort of short cloak of feathers and a membranous pouch extending on either side of the upper mandible; also some fine cocks, with black skin, comb, and wattles, like those of Mozambique, which strutted about the lake shore.

Thus the zeal of these intelligent and brave men made every thing prosper. Providence, doubtless, assisted them; but, faithful to the precept, they first helped themselves, and Heaven helped them accordingly.

In the evenings, during this warm summer weather, after the day's work was ended, and when the sea breeze was springing up, the colonists loved to gather together on the edge of Prospect Plateau in an arbor of Neb's building, covered with climbing plants. There they conversed and instructed each other, and planned for the future; or the rough wit of the sailor amused this little world, in which the most perfect harmony had never ceased to reign.

They talked, too, of their country, dear and grand America. In what condition was the Rebellion? It certainly could not have continued. Richmond had, doubtless, soon fallen into General Grant's hands. The capture of the Confederate capital was necessarily the last act in that unhappy struggle. By this time the North must have triumphed. How a newspaper would have been welcomed by the colonists of Lincoln Island! It was eleven months since all communication between them and the rest of the world had been interrupted, and pretty soon, the 24th of March, the anniversary of the day when the balloon had thrown them on this unknown coast, would have arrived. Then they were castaways, struggling with the elements for life. Now thanks to the knowledge of their leader, thanks to their own intelligence, they were true colonists, furnished with arms, tools, instruments, who had turned to their use the animals, vegetables and minerals of the island, the three kingdoms of nature.

As to Smith, he listened to the conversation of his companions oftener than he spoke himself. Sometimes he smiled at some thought of Herbert's, or some sally of Pencroff's, but always and above all other things, he reflected upon those inexplicable events, upon that strange enigma whose secret still escaped him.

CHAPTER XXXI.

BAD WEATHER—THE HYDRAULIC ELEVATOR—
MAKING WINDOW GLASS AND TABLE WARE—
THE BREAD TREE—FREQUENT VISITS TO THE
CORRAL—THE INCREASE OF THE HERD—
THE REPORTER'S QUESTION—THE EXACT POSITION
OF LINCOLN ISLAND—PENCROFF'S PROPOSAL.

The weather changed during the first week in March. There was a full moon in the beginning of the month, and the heat was excessive. The electricity in the air could be felt, and the stormy weather was at hand. On the 2d the thunder was very violent, the wind came out east, and the hail beat against the front of Granite House, pattering like a volley of musketry. It was necessary to fasten the doors and shutters in order to keep the rooms from being inundated. Some of the hailstones were as large as pigeons' eggs, and made Pencroff think of his cornfield. He instantly ran there, and by covering the tiny young sprouts with a large cloth was able to protect them. The sailor was well pelted, but he did not mind that.

The stormy weather lasted for eight days, and the thunder was almost continuous. The heavens were full of lightning, and many trees in the forest were struck, and also a huge pine growing upon the border of the lake. Two or three times the electric fluid struck the beach, melting and vitrifying the sand. Finding these fulgurites, Smith conceived the idea that it would be possible to furnish the windows of Granite House with glass thick and solid enough to resist the wind and rain and hail.

The colonists, having no immediate out-of-doors work, profited by the bad weather to complete and perfect the interior arrangements of Granite House. The engineer built a lathe with which they were able to turn some toilette articles and cooking utensils, and also some buttons, the need of which had been pressing. They also made a rack for the arms, which were kept with the utmost care. Nor was Jup forgotten; he occupied a chamber apart, a sort of cabin with a frame always full of good bedding, which suited him exactly.

"There's no such thing as fault-finding with Jup," said Pencroff. "What a servant he is, Neb!"

"He is my pupil and almost my equal!"

"He's your superior," laughed the sailor, "as you can talk, Neb, and he cannot!"

Jup had by this time become perfectly familiar with all the details of his work. He brushed the clothes, turned the spit, swept the rooms, waited at table, and—what delighted Pencroff—never laid down at night before he had tucked the worthy sailor in his bed.

As to the health of the colony, bipeds and bimana, quadrupeds and quadrumana, it left nothing to be desired. With the out-of-doors work, on this salubrious soil, under this temperate zone, laboring with head and hand, they could not believe that they could ever be sick, and all were in splendid health. Herbert had grown a couple of inches during the year; his figure had developed and knitted together, and he promised to become a fine man physically and morally. He profited by the lessons which he learned practically and from the books in the chest, and he found in the engineer and the reporter masters pleased to teach him. It was the engineer's desire to teach the lad all he himself knew.

"If I die," thought Smith, "he will take my place."

The storm ended on the 9th of March, but the sky remained clouded during the remainder of the month, and, with the exception of two or three fine days, rainy or foggy.

About this time a little onager was born, and a number of moufflons, to the great joy of Neb and Herbert, who had each their favorites among these new comers.

The domestication of piccaries was also attempted—a pen being built near the poultry-yard, and a number of the young animals placed therein under Neb's care. Jup was charged with taking them their daily nourishment, the kitchen refuse, and he acquitted himself conscientiously of the task. He did, indeed, cut off their tails, but this was a prank and not naughtiness, because those little twisted appendages amused him like a toy, and his instinct was that of a child.

One day in March, Pencroff, talking with the engineer, recalled to his mind a promise made some time before.

"You have spoken of something to take the place of our long ladder, Mr. Smith. Will you make it some day?"

"You mean a kind of elevator?" answered Smith.

"Call it an elevator if you wish," responded the sailor. "The name does not matter, provided we can get to our house easily."

"Nothing is easier, Pencroff; but is it worth while?"

"Certainly, sir, it is. After we have the necessaries, let us think of the conveniences. For people this will be a luxury, if you choose; but for things, it is indispensable. It is not so easy to climb a long ladder when one is heavily loaded."

"Well, Pencroff, we will try to satisfy you," answered Smith.

"But you haven't the machine."

"We will make one."

"To go by steam?"

"No, to go by water."

Indeed, a natural force was at hand. All that was necessary was to enlarge the passage which furnished Granite House with water, and make a fall at the end of the corridor. Above this fall the engineer placed a paddle-wheel, and wrapped around its axle a strong rope attached to a basket. In this manner, by means of a long cord which reached to the ground, they could raise or lower the basket by means of the hydraulic motor.

On the 17th of March the elevator was used for the first time, and after that everything was hoisted into Granite House by its means. Top was particularly pleased by this improvement, as he could not climb like Jup, and he had often made the ascent on the back of Neb or of the orang.

Smith also attempted to make glass, which was difficult enough, but after numerous attempts he succeeded in establishing a glass-works at the old pottery, where Herbert and Spilett spent several days. The substances entering into the composition of glass—sand, chalk, and soda—the engineer had at hand; but the "cane" of the glassmaker, an iron tube five or six feet long, was wanting. This Pencroff, however, succeeded in making, and on the 28th of March the furnace was heated.

One hundred parts of sand, thirty-five of chalk, forty of sulphate of soda, mixed with two of three parts of powdered charcoal, composed the substance which was placed in earthen vessels and melted to a liquid, or rather to the consistency of paste. Smith "culled" a certain quantity of this paste with his cane, and turned it back and forth on a metal plate so placed that it could be blown on; then he passed the cane to Herbert, telling him to blow in it.

"As you do to make soap bubbles?"

"Exactly."

So Herbert, puffing out his cheeks, blew through the cane, which he kept constantly turning about, in such a manner as to inflate the vitreous mass. Other quantities of the substance in fusion were added to the first, and the result was a bubble, measuring a foot in diameter. Then Smith took the cane again, and swinging it like a pendulum, he made this bubble lengthen into the shape of cylinder.

This cylinder was terminated at either end by two hemispherical caps, which were easily cut off by means of a sharp iron dipped in cold water; in the same way the cylinder was cut lengthwise, and after having been heated a second time it was spread on the plate and smoothed with a wooden roller.

Thus the first glass was made, and by repeating the operation fifty times they had as many glasses, and the windows of Granite House were soon garnished with transparent panes, not very clear, perhaps, but clear enough.

As to the glassware, that was mere amusement. They took whatever shape happened to come at the end of the cane. Pencroff had asked to be allowed to blow in his turn and he enjoyed it, but he blew so hard that his products took the most diverting forms, which pleased him amazingly.

During one of the excursions undertaken about this time a new tree was discovered, whose products added much to the resources of the colony.

Smith and Herbert, being out hunting one day, went into the forests of the Far West, and as usual the lad asked the engineer a thousand questions, and as Smith was no sportsman, and Herbert was deep in physics and chemistry, the game did not suffer; and so it fell out that the day was nearly ended, and the two hunters were likely to have made a useless excursion, when Herbert, stopping suddenly, exclaimed joyfully:—

"Oh, Mr. Smith, do you see that tree?"

And he pointed out a shrub rather than a tree, as it was composed of a single stem with a scaly bark, and leaves striped with small parallel veins.

"It looks like a small palm. What is it?" asked Smith.

"It is a "cycas revoluta," about which I have read in our Dictionary of Natural History."

"But I see no fruit on this shrub?"

"No, sir, but its trunk contains a flour which Nature furnishes all ground."

"Is it a bread-tree?"

"That's it, exactly."

"Then, my boy, since we are waiting for our wheat crop, this is a valuable discovery. Examine it, and pray heaven you are not mistaken."

Herbert was not mistaken. He broke the stem of the cycas, which was composed of a glandular tissue containing a certain quantity of farinaceous flour, traversed by ligneous fibres and separated by concentric rings of the same substance. From the fecula oozed a sticky liquid of a disagreeable taste, but this could readily be removed by pressure. The substance itself formed a real flour of superior quality, extremely nourishing, and which used to be forbidden exportation by the laws of Japan.

Smith and Herbert, after baring carefully noted the location of the cycas, returned to Granite House and made known their discovery, and the next day all the colonists went to the place, and, Pencroff, jubilant, asked the engineer:—

"Mr Smith, do you believe there are such things as castaways' islands?"

"What do you mean, Pencroff?."

"Well, I mean islands made especially for people to be shipwrecked upon, where the poor devils could always get along!"

"Perhaps," said the engineer, smiling.

"Certainly!" answered the sailor, "and just as certainly Lincoln Island is one of them!"

They returned to Granite House with an ample supply of cycas stems, and the engineer made a press by which the liquid was expelled, and they obtained a goodly quantity of flour which Neb transformed into cakes and puddings. They had not yet real wheaten bread, but it was the next thing to do.

The onager, the goats, and the sheep in the corral furnished a daily supply of milk to the colony, and the cart, or rather a light wagon, which had taken its place, made frequent trips to the corral. And when Pencroff's turn came, he took Jup along, and made him drive, and Jup, cracking his whip, acquitted himself with his usual intelligence. Thus everything prospered, and the colonists, if they had not been so far from their country, would have had nothing to complain of. They liked the life and they were so accustomed to the island that they would have left it with regret. Nevertheless, such is man's love of country, that had a ship hove in sight the colonists would have signalled it, have gone aboard and departed. Meantime, they lived this happy life and they had rather to fear than to wish for any interruption of its course.

But who is able to flatter himself that he has attained his fortune and reached the summit of his desires?

The colonists often discussed the nature of their Island, which they had inhabited for more than a year, and one day a remark was made which, was destined, later, to bring about the most serious result.

It was the 1st of April, a Sunday, and the Pascal feast, which Smith and his companions had sanctified by rest and prayer. The day had been lovely, like a day in October in the Northern Hemisphere. Towards evening all were seated in the arbor on the edge of the plateau, watching the gradual approach of night, and drinking some of Neb's elderberry coffee. They had been talking of the island and its isolated position in the Pacific, when something made Spilett say:—

"By the way, Cyrus, have you ever taken the position of the island again since you have had the sextant?"

"No," answered the engineer.

"Well, wouldn't it be well enough to do so?".

"What would be the use?" asked Pencroff. "The island is well enough where it is."

"Doubtless," answered Spilett, "but it is possible that the imperfections of the other instruments may have caused an error in that observation, and since, it is easy to verify it exactly—"

"You are right, Spilett," responded the engineer, "and I would have made this verification before, only that if I have made an error it cannot exceed five degrees in latitude or longitude."

"Who knows," replied the reporter, "who knows but that we are much nearer an inhabited land than we believe?"

"We will know to-morrow," responded the engineer," and had it not been for the other work, which has left us no leisure, we would have known already."

"Well," said Pencroff, "Mr. Smith is too good an observer to have been mistaken, and if the island has not moved, it is just where he put it!"

So the next day the engineer made the observations with the sextant with the following result:—Longitude 150° 30' west; latitude 34° 57' south. The previous observation had given the situation of the island as between longitude 150° and 155° west, and latitude 36° and 35° south, so that, notwithstanding the rudeness of his apparatus, Smith's error had not been more than five degrees.

"Now," said Spilett, "since, beside a sextant, we have an atlas, see, my dear Cyrus, the exact position of Lincoln Island in the Pacific."

Herbert brought the atlas, which it will be remembered gave the nomenclature in the French language, and the volume was opened at the map of the Pacific. The engineer, compass in hand, was about to determine their situation, when, suddenly he paused, exclaiming:—

"Why, there is an island marked in this part of the Pacific!"

"An island?" cried Pencroff.

"Doubtless it is ours." added Spilett.

"No." replied Smith. "This island is situated in 153° of longitude and 37° 11' of latitude."

"And what's the name?" asked Herbert.

"Tabor Island."

"Is it important?"

"No, it is an island lost in the Pacific, and which has never, perhaps, been visited."

"Very well, we will visit it," said Pencroff.

"We?"

"Yes, sir; We will build a decked boat, and I will undertake to steer her. How far are we from this Tabor Island?"

"A hundred and fifty miles to the northeast."

"Is that all?" responded Pencroff.

"Why in forty-eight hours, with a good breeze, we will be there!"

"But what would be the use?" asked the reporter.

"We cannot tell till we see it!"

And upon this response it was decided that a boat should be built so that it might be launched by about the next October, on the return of good weather.

CHAPTER XXXII.

SHIP BUILDING—THE SECOND HARVEST—
AI HUNTING—A NEW PLANT—A WHALE—
THE HARPOON FROM THE VINEYARD—CUTTING
UP THIS CETACEA—USE OF THE WHALEBONE—
THE END OF MAY—PENCROFF IS CONTENT.

When Pencroff was possessed of an idea, he would not rest till it was executed. Now, he wanted to visit Tabor Island, and as a boat of some size was necessary, therefore the boat must be built. He and the engineer accordingly determined upon the following model:—

The boat was to measure thirty-five feet on the keel by nine feet beam—with the lines of a racer—and to draw six feet of water, which would be sufficient to prevent her making leeway. She was to be flush-decked, with the two hatchways into two holds separated by a partition, and sloop-rigged with mainsail, topsail, jib, storm-jib and brigantine, a rig easily handled, manageable in a squall, and excellent for lying close in the wind. Her hull was to be constructed of planks, edge to edge, that is, not overlapping, and her timbers would be bent by steam after the planking had been adjusted to a false frame.

On the question of wood, whether to use elm or deal, they decided on the latter as being easier to work, and supporting immersion in water the better.

These details having been arranged, it was decided that, as the fine weather would not return before six months, Smith and Pencroff should do this work alone. Spilett and Herbert were to continue hunting, and Neb and his assistant, Master Jup, were to attend to the domestic cares as usual.

At once trees were selected and cut down and sawed into planks, and a week later a ship-yard was made in the hollow between Granite House and the Cliff, and a keel thirty-five feet long, with stern-post and stem lay upon the sand.

Smith had not entered blindly upon this undertaking. He understood marine construction as he did almost everything else, and he had first drawn the model on paper. Moreover, he was well aided by Pencroff, who had worked as a ship-carpenter. It was, therefore, only after deep thought and careful calculation that the false frame was raised on the keel.

Pencroff was very anxious to begin the new enterprise, and but one thing took him away, and then only for a day, from the work. This was the second harvest, which was made on the 15th of April. It resulted as before, and yielded the proportion of grains calculated.

"Five bushels, Mr. Smith," said Pencroff, after having scrupulously measured these riches.

"Five bushels," answered the engineer, "or 650,000 grains of corn."

"Well, we will sow them all this time, excepting a small reserve."

"Yes, and if the next harvest is proportional to this we will have 4,000 bushels."

"And we will eat bread."

"We will, indeed."

"But we must build a mill?"

"We will build one."

The third field of corn, though incomparably larger than the others, was prepared with great care and received the precious seed. Then Pencroff returned to his work.

In the meantime, Spilett and Herbert hunted in the neighborhood, or with their guns loaded with ball, adventured into the unexplored depths of the Far West. It was an inextricable tangle of great trees growing close together. The exploration of those thick masses was very difficult and the engineer never undertook it without taking with him the pocket compass, as the sun was rarely visible through the leaves. Naturally, game was not plenty in these thick undergrowths, but three ai were shot during the last fortnight in April, and their skins were taken to Granite House, where they received a sort of tanning with sulfuric acid.

On the 30th of April, a discovery, valuable for another reason, was made by Spilett. The two hunters were deep in the south-western part of the Far West when the reporter, walking some fifty paces ahead of his companion, came to a sort of glade, and was surprised to perceive an odor proceeding from certain straight stemmed plants, cylindrical and branching, and bearing bunches of flowers and tiny seeds. The reporter broke off some of these stems, and, returning to the lad, asked him if he knew what they were.

"Where did you find this plant?" asked Herbert.

"Over there in the glade; there is plenty of it."

"Well, this is a discovery that gives you Pencroff's everlasting gratitude."

"Is it tobacco?"

"Yes, and if it is not first quality it is all the same, tobacco."

"Good Pencroff, how happy he'll be. But he cannot smoke all. He'll have to leave some for us."

"I'll tell you what, sir. Let us say nothing to Pencroff until the tobacco has been prepared, and then some fine day we will hand him a pipe full."

"And you may be sure, Herbert, that on that day the good fellow will want nothing else in the world."

The two smuggled a good supply of the plant into Granite House with as much precaution as if Pencroff had been the strictest of custom house officers. Smith and Neb were let into the secret, but Pencroff never suspected any thing during the two months it took to prepare the leaves, as he was occupied all day at the ship-yard.

On the 1st of May the sailor was again interrupted at his favorite work by a fishing adventure, in which all the colonists took part.

For some days they had noticed an enormous animal swimming in the sea some two or three miles distant from the shore. It was a huge whale, apparently belonging to the species *australis*, called "cape whales."

"How lucky for us if we could capture it!" cried the sailor. "Oh, if we only had a suitable boat and a harpoon ready, so that I could say:—Let's go for him! For he's worth all the trouble he'll give us!"

"Well, Pencroff, I should like to see you manage a harpoon. It must be interesting."

"Interesting and somewhat dangerous," said the engineer, "but since we have not the means to attack this animal, it is useless to think about him."

"I am astonished to see a whale in such comparatively high latitude."

"Why, Mr. Spilett, we are in that very part of the Pacific which whalers call the 'whale-field,' and just here whales are found in the greatest number."

"That is so," said Pencroff, "and I wonder we have not seen one before, but it don't matter much since we cannot go to it."

And the sailor turned with a sigh to his work, as all sailors are fishermen; and if the sport is proportionate to the size of the game, one can imagine what a whaler must feel in the presence of a whale. But, aside from the sport, such spoil would have been very acceptable to the colony, as the oil, the fat, and the fins could be turned to various uses.

It appeared as if the animal did not wish to leave these waters. He kept swimming about in Union Bay for two days, now approaching the shore, when his black body could be seen perfectly, and again darting through the water or spouting vapor to a vast height in the air. Its presence continually engaged the thoughts of the colonists, and Pencroff was like a child longing for some forbidden object.

Fortune, however, did for the colonists what they could not have done for themselves, and on the 3d of May, Neb looking from his kitchen shouted that the whale was aground on the island.

Herbert and Spilett, who were about starting on a hunt, laid aside their guns, Pencroff dropped his hatchet, and Smith and Neb, joining their companions, hurried down to the shore. It had grounded on Jetsam Point at high water, and it was not likely that the monster would be able to get off easily; but they must hasten in order to cut off its retreat if necessary. So seizing some picks and spears they ran across the bridge, down the Mercy and along the shore, and in less than twenty minutes the party were beside the huge animal, above whom myriads of birds were already hovering.

"What a monster!" exclaimed Neb.

And the term was proper, as it was one of the largest of the southern whales, measuring forty-five feet in length and weighing not less than 150,000 pounds.

Meantime the animal, although the tide was still high, made no effort to get off the shore, and the reason for this was explained later when at low water the colonists walked around its body.

It was dead, and a harpoon protruded from its left flank.

"Are there whalers in our neighborhood?" asked Spilett.

"Why do you ask?"

"Since the harpoon is still there—"

"Oh that proves nothing, sir," said Pencroff. "Whales sometimes go thousands of miles with a harpoon in them, and I should not be surprised if this one which came to die here had been struck in the North Atlantic."

"Nevertheless"—began Spilett, not satisfied with Pencroff's affirmation.

"It is perfectly possible," responded the engineer, "but let us look at the harpoon. Probably it will have the name of the ship on it."

Pencroff drew out the harpoon, and read this inscription:—

Maria-Stella Vineyard.

"A ship from the Vineyard! A ship of my country!" be cried. "The Maria-Stella! a good whaler! and I know her well! Oh, my friends, a ship from the Vineyard! A whaler from the Vineyard!"

And the sailor, brandishing the harpoon, continued to repeat that name dear to his heart, the name of his birthplace.

But as they could not wait for the Maria-Stella to come and reclaim their prize, the colonists resolved to cut it up before decomposition set in. The birds of prey were already anxious to become possessors of the spoil, and it was necessary to drive them away with gunshots.

The whale was a female, and her udders furnished a great quantity of milk, which, according to Dieffenbach, resembles in taste, color, and density, the milk of cows.

As Pencroff had served on a whaler he was able to direct the disagreeable work of cutting up the animal—an operation which lasted during three days. The blubber, cut in strips two feet and a half thick and divided into pieces weighing a thousand pounds each, was melted down in large earthen vats, which had been brought on to the ground. And such was its abundance, that notwithstanding a third of its weight was lost by melting, the tongue alone yielded 6,000 pounds of oil. The colonists were therefore supplied with an abundant supply of stearine and glycerine, and there was, besides, the whalebone, which would find its use, although there were neither umbrellas nor corsets in Granite House.

The operation ended, to the great satisfaction of the colonists, the rest of the animal was left to the birds, who made away with it to the last vestiges, and the daily routine of work was resumed. Still, before going to the ship-yard, Smith worked on certain affairs which excited the curiosity of his companions. He took a dozen of the plates of baleen (the solid whalebone), which he cut into six equal lengths, sharpened at the ends.

"And what is that for?" asked Herbert, when they were finished.

"To kill foxes, wolves, and jaguars," answered the engineer.

"Now?"

"No, but this winter, when we have the ice."

"I don't understand," answered Herbert.

"You shall understand, my lad," answered the engineer. "This is not my invention; it is frequently employed by the inhabitants of the Aleutian islands. These whalebones which you see, when the weather is freezing I will bend round and freeze in that position with a coating of ice; then having covered them with a bit of fat, I will place them in the snow. Supposing a hungry animal swallows one of these baits? The warmth will thaw the ice, and the whalebone, springing back, will pierce the stomach."

"That is ingenious!" said Pencroff.

"And it will save powder and ball," said Smith.

"It will be better than the traps."

"Just wait till winter comes."

The ship-building continued, and towards the end of the month the little vessel was half-finished. Pencroff worked almost too hard, but his companions were secretly preparing a recompense for all his toil, and the 31st of May was destined to be one of the happiest times in his life.

After dinner on that day, just as he was leaving table, Pencroff felt a hand on his shoulder and heard Spilett saying to him:—

"Don't go yet awhile, Pencroff. You forget the dessert."

"Thank you, Spilett, but I must get back to work."

"Oh, well, have a cup of coffee."

"Not any."

"Well, then, a pipe?"

Pencroff started up quickly, and when he saw the reporter holding him a pipe full of tobacco, and Herbert with a light, his honest, homely face grew pale, and he could not say a word; but taking the pipe, he placed it to his lips, lit it, and drew five or six long puffs, one after the other.

A fragrant, blueish-colored smoke filled the air, and from the depths of this cloud came a voice, delirious with joy, repeating,

"Tobacco! real tobacco!"

"Yes, Pencroff," answered Smith, "and good tobacco at that."

"Heaven be praised!" ejaculated the sailor. "Nothing now is wanting in our island. And he puffed and puffed and puffed.

"Who found it?" he asked, at length. "It was you, Herbert, I suppose?"

"No, Pencroff, it was Mr. Spilett."

"Mr. Spilett!" cried the sailor, hugging the reporter, who had never been treated that way before.

"Yes, Pencroff,"—taking advantage of a cessation in the embrace to get his breath—"But include in your thanksgiving Herbert, who recognized the plant, Mr. Smith, who prepared it, and Neb, who has found it hard to keep the secret."

"Well, my friends, I will repay you for this some day! Meanwhile I am eternally grateful!."

CHAPTER XXXIII.

WINTER—FULLING CLOTH—THE MILL—PENCROFF'S
FIXED PURPOSE—THE WHALEBONES—THE USE OF
AN ALBATROSS—TOP AND JUP—STORMS—DAMAGE
TO THE POULTRY-YARD—AN EXCURSION TO THE
MARSH—SMITH ALONE—EXPLORATION OF THE PITS.

Winter came with June, and the principal work was the making of strong warm clothing. The moufflons had been clipped, and the question was how to transform the wool into cloth.

Smith, not having any mill machinery, was obliged to proceed in the simplest manner, in order to economize the spinning and weaving. Therefore he proposed to make use of the property possessed by the filaments of wool of binding themselves together under pressure, and making by their mere entanglement the substance known as felt. This felt can be obtained by a simple fulling, an operation which, while it diminishes the suppleness of the stuff, greatly augments its heat-preserving qualities; and as the moufflons' wool was very short it was in good condition for felting.

The engineer, assisted by his companions, including Pencroff—who had to leave his ship again—cleansed the wool of the grease and oil by soaking it in warm water and washing it with soda, and, when it was partially dried by pressure it was in a condition to be milled, that is, to produce a solid stuff, too coarse to be of any value in the industrial centres of Europe, but valuable enough in the Lincoln Island market.

The engineer's professional knowledge was of great service in constructing the machine destined to mill the wool, as he knew how to make ready use of the power, unemployed up to this time, in the waterfall at the cliff, to move a fulling mill.

Its construction was most simple. A tree furnished with cams, which raised and dropped the vertical millers, troughs for the wool, into which the millers fell, a strong wooden building containing and sustaining the contrivance, such was the machine in question.

The work, superintended by Smith, resulted admirably. The wool, previously impregnated with a soapy solution, came from the mill in the shape of a thick felt cloth. The striæ and roughnesses of the material had caught and blended together so thoroughly that they formed a stuff equally suitable for cloths or coverings. It was not, indeed, one of the stuffs of commerce, but it was "Lincoln felt," and the island had one more industry.

The colonists, being thus provided with good clothes and warm bed-clothing, saw the winter of 1866-67 approach without any dread. The cold really began to be felt on the 20th of June, and, to his great regret, Pencroff was obliged to suspend work on his vessel, although it would certainly be finished by the next spring.

The fixed purpose of the sailor was to make a voyage of discovery to Tabor Island, although Smith did not approve of this voyage of simple curiosity, as there was evidently no succor to be obtained from that desert and half arid rock. A voyage of 150 miles in a boat, comparatively small, in the midst of unknown seas, was cause for considerable anxiety. If the frail craft, once at sea, should be unable to reach Tabor Island, or to return to Lincoln Island, what would become of her in the midst of this ocean so fertile in disasters?

Smith often talked of this project with Pencroff, and he found in the sailor a strange obstinacy to make the voyage, an obstinacy for which Pencroff himself could not account.

"Well," said the engineer one day, "you must see, Pencroff, after having said every good of Lincoln Island, and expressing the regret you would feel should you have to leave it, that you are the first to want to get away."

"Only for a day or two," answered Pencroff, "for a few days, Mr. Smith; just long enough to go and return, and see what this island is."

"But it cannot compare with ours."

"I know that.'"

"Then why go?"

"To find out what's going on there!"

"But there is nothing; there can be nothing there."

"Who knows?"

"And supposing you are caught in a storm?"

"That is not likely in that season," replied Pencroff. "But, sir, as it is necessary to foresee everything, I want your permission to take Herbert with me."

"Pencroff," said the engineer, laying his hand on the shoulder of the sailor, "If anything should happen to you and this child, whom chance has made our son, do you think that we would ever forgive ourselves?"

"Mr. Smith," responded Pencroff with unshaken confidence, "we won't discuss such mishaps. But we will talk again of this voyage when the time comes. Then, I think, when you have seen our boat well rigged, when you have seen how well she behaves at sea, when you have made the tour of the island—as we will, together—I think, I say, that you will not hesitate to let me go. I do not conceal from you that this will be a fine work, your ship."

"Say rather, our ship, Pencroff," replied the engineer, momentarily disarmed. And the conversation, to be renewed later, ended without convincing either of the speakers.

The first snow fell towards the end of the month. The corral had been well provisioned, and there was no further necessity for daily visits, but it was decided to go there at least once a week. The traps were set again, and the contrivances of Smith were tried, and worked perfectly. The bent whalebones, frozen, and covered with fat, were placed near the edge of the forest, at a place frequented by animals, and some dozen foxes, some wild boars, and a jaguar were found killed by this means, their stomachs perforated by the straightened whalebones.

At this time, an experiment, thought of by the reporter, was made. It was the first attempt of the colonists to communicate with their kindred.

Spilett had already often thought of throwing a bottle containing a writing into the sea, to be carried by the currents, perhaps, to some inhabited coast, or to make use of the pigeons. But it was pure folly to seriously believe that pigeons or bottles could cross the 1,200 miles separating the island from all lands.—

But on the 30th of June they captured, not without difficulty, an albatross, which Herbert had slightly wounded in the foot. It was a splendid specimen of its kind, its wings measuring ten feet from tip to tip, and it could cross seas as vast as the Pacific.

Herbert would have liked to have kept the bird and tamed it, but Spilett made him understand that they could not afford to neglect this chance of corresponding by means of this courier with the Pacific coasts. So Herbert gave up the bird, as, if it had come from some inhabited region, it was likely to return there if at liberty.

Perhaps, in his heart, Spilett, to whom the journalistic spirit returned sometimes, did not regret giving to the winds an interesting article relating the adventures of the colonists of Lincoln Island. What a triumph for the reporters of the New York *Herald*, and for the issue containing the chronicle, if ever the latter should reach his director, the honorable John Bennett!

Spilett, therefore, wrote out a succinct article, which was enclosed in a waterproof-cloth bag, with the request to whoever found it to send it to one of the offices of the *Herald*. This little bag was fastened around the neck of the albatross and the bird given its freedom, and it was not without emotion that the colonists saw this rapid courier of the air disappear in the western clouds.

"Where does he go that way?" asked Pencroff.

"Towards New Zealand," answered Herbert.

"May he have a good voyage," said the sailor, who did not expect much from this method of communication.

With the winter, in-door work was resumed; old clothes were repaired, new garments made, and the sails of the sloop made from the inexhaustible envelope of the balloon. During July the cold was intense, but coal and wood were abundant, and Smith had built another chimney in the great hall, where they passed the long evenings. It was a great comfort to the colonists, when, seated in this well-lighted and warm hall, a good dinner finished, coffee steaming in the cups, the pipes emitting a fragrant smoke, they listened to the roar of the tempest without. They were perfectly comfortable, if that is possible where one is far from his kindred and without possible means of communicating with them. They talked about their country, of their friends at home, of the grandeur of the republic, whose influence must increase; and Smith, who had had much to do with the affairs of the Union, entertained his hearers with his stories, his perceptions and his prophecies.

One evening as they had been sitting talking in this way for some time, they were interrupted by Top, who began barking in that peculiar way which had previously attracted the attention of the engineer, and running around the mouth of the well which opened at the end of the inner corridor.

"Why is Top barking that way again?" asked Pencroff.

"And Jup growling so?" added Herbert.

Indeed, both the dog and the orang gave unequivocal signs of agitation, and curiously enough these two animals seemed to be more alarmed than irritated.

It is evident," said Spilett, "that this well communicates directly with the sea, and that some animal comes to breathe in its depths."

"It must be so, since there is no other explanation to give. Be quiet, Top! and you, Jup! go to your room."

The animals turned away, Jup went to his bed, but Top remained in the hall, and continued whining the remainder of the evening. It was not, however, the question of this incident that darkened the countenance of the engineer.

During the remainder of the month, rain and snow alternated, and though the temperature was not as low as during the preceding winter, there were more storms and gales. On more than one occasion the Chimneys had been threatened by the waves, and it seemed as if an upraising of the sea, caused by some submarine convulsion, raised the monstrous billows and hurled them against Granite House.

During these storms it was difficult, even dangerous, to attempt using the roads on the island, as the trees were falling constantly. Nevertheless, the colonists never let a week pass without visiting the corral, and happily this enclosure, protected by the spur of the mountain, did not suffer from the storms. But the poultry-yard, from its position, exposed to the blast, suffered considerable damage. Twice the pigeon-house was unroofed, and the fence also was demolished, making it necessary to rebuild it more solidly. It was evident that Lincoln Island was situated in the worst part of the Pacific. Indeed, it seemed as if the island formed the central point of vast cyclones which whipped it as if it were a top; only in this case the top was immovable and the whip spun about.

During the first week in August the storm abated, and the atmosphere recovered a calm which it seemed never to have lost. With the calm the temperature lowered, and the thermometer of the colonists indicated 8° below zero.

On the 3d of August, an excursion, which had been planned for some time was made to Tadorn's Fen. The hunters were tempted by the great number of aquatic birds which made these marshes their home, and not only Spilett and Herbert, but Pencroff and Neb took part in the expedition. Smith alone pleaded some excuse for remaining behind at Granite House.

The hunters promised to return by evening. Top and Jup accompanied them. And when they had crossed the bridge over the Mercy the engineer left them, and returned with the idea of executing a project in which he wished to be alone. This was to explore minutely the well opening into the corridor.

Why did Top run round this place so often? Why did he whine in that strange way? Why did Jup share Top's anxiety? Had this well other branches beside the communication with the sea? Did it ramify towards other portions of the island? This is what Smith wanted to discover, and, moreover, to be alone in his discovery. He had resolved to make this exploration during the absence of his companions, and here was the opportunity.

It was easy to descend to the bottom of the well by means of the ladder, which had not been used since the elevator had taken its place. The engineer dragged this ladder to the opening of the well, and, having made fast one end, let it unroll itself into the abyss. Then, having lit a lantern, and placing a revolver and cutlass in his belt, he began to descend the rungs. The sides of the well were smooth, but some projections of rocks appeared at intervals, and by means of these projections an athlete could have raised himself to the mouth of the well. The engineer noticed this, but in throwing the light of the lantern on these points he could discover nothing to indicate that they had ever been used in that way.

Smith descended deeper, examining every part of the well, but he saw nothing suspicious. When he had reached the lowermost rung, he was at the surface of the water, which was perfectly calm. Neither there, nor in any other part of the well, was there any lateral opening. The wall, struck by the handle of Smith's cutlass, sounded solid. It was a compact mass, through which no human being could make his way. In order to reach the bottom of the well, and from thence climb to its mouth, it was necessary to traverse the submerged passage under the shore, which connected with the sea, and this was only possible for marine animals. As to knowing whereabouts on the shore, and at what depth under the waves, this passage came out, that was impossible to discover.

Smith, having ended his exploration, remounted the ladder, covered over again the mouth of the well, and returned thoughtfully to the great hall of Granite House, saying to himself:—

"I have seen nothing, and yet, there is something there."

CHAPTER XXXIV.

RIGGING THE LAUNCH—ATTACKED BY FOXES—
JUP WOUNDED—JUP NURSED—JUP CURED—
COMPLETION OF THE LAUNCH—PENCROFF'S
TRIUMPH—THE GOOD LUCK—TRIAL TRIP,
TO THE SOUTH OF THE ISLAND—
AN UNEXPECTED DOCUMENT.

The same evening the hunters returned, fairly loaded down with game, the four men having all they could carry. Top had a circlet of ducks round his neck, and Jup belts of woodcock round his body.

"See, my master," cried Neb, "see how we have used our time. Preserves, pies, we will have a good reserve! But some one must help me, and I count upon you, Pencroff."

"No, Neb," responded the sailor, "the rigging of the launch occupies my time, and you will have to do without me."

"And you, Master Herbert?"

"I, Neb, must go to-morrow to the corral."

"Then will you help me, Mr. Spilett?"

"To oblige you, I will, Neb," answered the reporter, "but I warn you that if you discover your recipes to me I will publish them."

"Whenever you choose, sir," responded Neb; "whenever you choose."

And so the next day the reporter was installed as Neb's aid in his culinary laboratory. But beforehand the engineer had given him the result of the previous day's exploration, and Spilett agreed with Smith in his opinion that, although he had found out nothing, still there was a secret to be discovered.

The cold continued a week longer, and the colonists did not leave Granite House excepting to look after the poultry-yard. The dwelling was perfumed by the good odors which the learned manipulations of Neb and the reporter emitted; but all the products of the hunt in the fen had not been made into preserves, and as the game kept perfectly in the intense cold, wild ducks and others, were eaten fresh, and declared better than any waterfowl in the world.

During the week, Pencroff, assisted by Herbert, who used the sailor's needle skilfully, worked with such diligence that the sails of the launch were finished. Thanks to the rigging which had been recovered with the envelope of the balloon, hemp cordage was not wanting. The sails were bordered by strong bolt-ropes, and there was enough left to make halliards, shrouds, and sheets. The pulleys were made by Smith on the lathe which he had set up, acting under Pencroff's instruction. The rigging was, therefore, completed before the launch was finished. Pencroff made a red, white, and blue flag, getting the dye from certain plants; but to the thirty-seven stars representing the thirty-seven States of the Union, the sailor added another star, the star of the "State of Lincoln:" as he considered his island as already annexed to the great republic.

"And," said he, "it is in spirit, if it is not in fact!"

For the present the flag was unfurled from the central window of Granite House and saluted with three cheers.

Meantime, they had reached the end of the cold season; and it seemed as if this second winter would pass without any serious event, when during the night of the 11th of August, Prospect Plateau was menaced by a complete devastation. After a busy day the colonists were sleeping soundly, when towards 4 o'clock in the morning, they were suddenly awakened by Top's barking. The dog did not bark this time at the mouth of the pit, but at the door, and he threw himself against it as if he wished to break it open. Jup, also, uttered sharp cries.

"Be quiet, Top!" cried Neb, who was the first awake.

But the dog only barked the louder.

"What's the matter?" cried Smith. And every one dressing in haste, hurried to the windows and opened them.

"Beneath them a fall of snow shone white through the darkness. The colonists could see nothing, but they heard curious barkings penetrating the night. It was evident that the shore had been invaded by a number of animals which they could not see."

"What can they be?" cried Pencroff.

"Wolves, jaguars, or monkeys!" replied Neb.

"The mischief! They can get on to the plateau!" exclaimed the reporter.

"And our poultry-yard, and our garden!" cried Herbert.

"How have they got in?" asked Pencroff.

"They have come through the causeway," answered the engineer, "which one of us must have forgotten to close!"

"In truth," said Spilett, "I remember that I left it open—"

"A nice mess you have made of it, sir!" cried the sailor.

"What is done, is done," replied Spilett. "Let us consider what it is necessary to do!"

These questions and answers passed rapidly between Smith and his companions. It was certain that the causeway had been passed, that the shore had been invaded by animals, and that, whatever they were, they could gain Prospect Plateau by going up the left bank of the Mercy. It was, therefore, necessary quickly to overtake them, and, if necessary, to fight them!

"But what are they?" somebody asked a second time, as the barking resounded more loudly.

Herbert started at the sound, and he remembered having heard it during his first visit to the sources of Red Creek.

"They are foxes! they are foxes!" he said.

"Come on!" cried the sailor. And all, armed with hatchets, carbines, and revolvers, hurried into the elevator, and were soon on the shore.

These foxes are dangerous animals, when numerous or irritated by hunger. Nevertheless, the colonists did not hesitate to throw themselves into the midst of the band, and their first shots, darting bright gleams through the darkness, drove back the foremost assailants.

It was most important to prevent these thieves from gaining Prospect Plateau, as the garden and the poultry-yard would have been at their mercy, and the result would have been immense, perhaps, irreparable damage, especially to the corn-field. But as the plateau could only be invaded by the left bank of the Mercy, it would suffice to oppose a barrier to the foxes on the narrow portion of the shore comprised between the river and the granite wall.

This was apparent to all, and under Smith's direction the party gained this position and disposed themselves so as to form an impassable line. Top, his formidable jaws open, preceded the colonists, and was followed by Jup, armed with a knotty cudgel, which he brandished like a cricket-bat.

The night was very dark, and it was only by the flash of the discharges that the colonists could perceive their assailants, who numbered at least 100, and whose eyes shone like embers.

"They must not pass!" cried Pencroff.

"They shall not pass!" answered the engineer.

But if they did not it was not because they did not try. Those behind kept pushing on those in front, and it was an incessant struggle; the colonists using their hatchets and revolvers. Already the dead bodies of the foxes were strewn over the ground, but the band did not seem to lessen; and it appeared as if reinforcements were constantly pouring in through the causeway on the shore. Meantime the colonists fought side by side, receiving some wounds, though happily but trifling. Herbert shot one fox, which had fastened itself on Neb like a tiger-cat. Top fought with fury, springing at the throats of the animals and strangling them at once. Jup, armed with his cudgel, laid about him like a good fellow, and it was useless to try to make him stay behind. Gifted, doubtless, with a sight able to pierce the darkness, he was always in the thick of the fight, uttering from time to time a sharp cry, which was with him a mark of extreme jollification. At one time he advanced so far, that by the flash of a revolver he was seen, surrounded by five or six huge foxes, defending himself with rare coolness.

At length the fight ended in a victory for the colonists, but only after two hours of resistance. Doubtless the dawn of day determined the retreat of the foxes, who scampered off toward the north across the drawbridge, which Neb ran at once to raise. When daylight lit the battlefield, the colonists counted fifty dead bodies upon the shore.

"And Jup! Where is Jup?" cried Neb.

Jup had disappeared. His friend Neb called him, and for the first time he did not answer the call. Every one began to search for the monkey, trembling lest they should find him among the dead. At length, under a veritable mound of carcasses, each one marked by the terrible cudgel of the brave animal, they found Jup. The poor fellow still held in his hand the handle of his broken weapon; but deprived of this arm, he had been overpowered by numbers, and deep wounds scored his breast.

"He's alive!" cried Neb, who knelt beside him.

"And we will save him," answered the sailor, "We will nurse him as one of ourselves!"

It seemed as if Jup understood what was said, for he laid his head on Pencroff's shoulder as if to thank him. The sailor himself was wounded, but his wounds, like those of his companions, were trifling, as thanks to their firearms, they had always been able to keep the assailants at a distance. Only the orang was seriously hurt.

Jup, borne by Neb and Pencroff, was carried to the elevator, and lifted gently to Granite House. There he was laid upon one of the beds, and his wounds carefully washed. No vital organ seemed to have been injured, but the orang was very feeble from loss of blood, and a strong fever had set in. His wounds having been dressed, a strict diet was imposed upon him, "just as for a real person," Neb said, and they gave him a refreshing draught made from herbs.

He slept at first but brokenly, but little by little, his breathing became more regular, and they left him in a heavy sleep. From time to time Top came "on tip-toe" to visit his friend, and seemed to approve of the attentions which had been bestowed upon it.

One of Jup's hands hung over the side of the bed, and Top licked it sympathetically.

The same morning they disposed of the dead foxes by dragging the bodies to the Far West and burying them there.

This attack, which might have been attended with very grave results, was a lesson to the colonists, and thenceforth they never slept before having ascertained that all the bridges were raised and that no invasion was possible.

Meantime Jup, after having given serious alarm for some days, began to grow better. The fever abated gradually, and Spilett, who was something of a physician, considered him out of danger. On the 16th of August Jup began to eat. Neb made him some nice, sweet dishes, which the invalid swallowed greedily, for if he had a fault, it was that he was a bit of a glutton, and Neb had never done anything to correct this habit.

"What would you have?" he said to Spilett, who sometimes rebuked the negro for indulging him. "Poor Jup has no other pleasure than to eat! and I am only too glad to be able to reward his services in this way!"

By the 21st of August he was about again. His wounds were healed, and the colonists saw that he would soon recover his accustomed suppleness and vigor. Like other convalescents he was seized with an excessive hunger, and the reporter let him eat what he wished, knowing that the monkey's instinct would preserve him from excess. Neb was overjoyed to see his pupil's appetite returned.

"Eat Jup," he said, "and you shall want for nothing. You have shed your blood for us, and it is right that I should help you to make it again!"

At length, on the 25th of August, the colonists seated in the great hall, were called by Neb to Jup's room.

"What is it?" asked the reporter.

"Look!" answered Neb, laughing, and what did they see but Jup, seated like a Turk within the doorway of Granite House, tranquilly and gravely smoking!

"My pipe!" cried Pencroff. "He has taken my pipe! Well, Jup, I give it to you. Smoke on my friend, smoke on!"

And Jup gravely puffed on, seeming to experience the utmost enjoyment.

Smith was not greatly astonished at this incident, and he cited numerous examples of tamed monkeys that had become accustomed to the use of tobacco.

And after this day master Jup had his own pipe hung in his room beside his tobacco-bag, and, lighting it himself with a live coal, he appeared to be the happiest of quadrumana. It seemed as if this community of taste drew closer together the bonds of friendship already existing between the worthy monkey and the honest sailor.

"Perhaps he is a man," Pencroff would sometimes say to Neb. "Would it astonish you if some day he was to speak?"

"Indeed it would not," replied Neb. "The wonder is that he don't do it, as that is all he lacks!"

"Nevertheless, it would be funny if some fine day he said to me:—Pencroff, suppose we change pipes!"

"Yes," responded Neb. "What a pity he was born mute!"

Winter ended with September, and the work was renewed with ardor. The construction of the boat advanced rapidly. The planking was completed, and as wood was plenty Pencroff proposed that they line the interior with a stout ceiling, which would insure the solidity of the craft. Smith, not knowing what might be in store for them, approved the sailor's idea of making his boat as strong as possible. The ceiling and the deck were finished towards the 13th of September. For caulking, they used some dry wrack, and the seams were then covered with boiling pitch, made from the pine trees of the forest.

The arrangement of the boat was simple. She had been ballasted with heavy pieces of granite, set in a bed of lime, and weighing 12,000 pounds. A deck was placed over this ballast, and the interior was divided into two compartments, the larger containing two bunks, which served as chests. The foot of the mast was at the partition separating the compartments, which were entered through hatchways.

Pencroff had no difficulty in finding a tree suitable for a mast. He chose a young straight fir, without knots, so that all he had to do was to square the foot and round it off at the head. All the iron work had been roughly but solidly made at the Chimneys; and in the first week of October yards, topmast, spars, oars, etc., everything, in short, was completed; and it was determined that they would first try the craft along the shores of the island, so as to see how she acted.

She was launched on the 10th of October. Pencroff was radiant with delight. Completely rigged, she had been pushed on rollers to the edge of the shore, and, as the tide rose, she was floated on the surface of the water, amid the applause of the colonists, and especially of Pencroff, who showed no modesty on this occasion. Moreover, his vanity looked beyond the completion of the craft, as, now that she was built, he was to be her commander. The title of captain was bestowed upon him unanimously.

In order to satisfy Captain Pencroff it was necessary at once to name his ship, and after considerable discussion they decided upon Good Luck—the name chosen by the honest sailor. Moreover, as the weather was fine, the breeze fresh, and the sea calm, the trial must be made at once in an excursion along the coast.

"Get aboard! Get aboard!" cried Captain Pencroff.

At half-past 10, after having eaten breakfast and put some provisions aboard, everybody, including Top and Jup, embarked, the sails were hoisted, the flag set at the masthead, and the Good Luck, with Pencroff at the helm, stood out to sea.

On going out from Union Bay they had a fair wind, and they were able to see that, sailing before it, their speed was excellent. After doubling Jetsam Point and Claw Cape, Pencroff had to lie close to the wind in order to skirt along the shore, and he observed the Good Luck would sail to within five points of the wind, and that she made but little lee-way. She sailed very well, also, before the wind, minding her helm perfectly, and gained even in going about.

The passengers were enchanted. They had a good boat, which, in case of need, could render them great service, and in this splendid weather, with the fair wind, the sail was delightful. Pencroff stood out to sea two or three miles, opposite Balloon Harbor, and then the whole varied panorama of the island from Claw Cape to Reptile Promontory was visible under a new aspect. In the foreground were the pine forests, contrasting with the foliage of the other trees, and over all rose Mt. Franklin, its head white with snow.

"How beautiful it is!" exclaimed Herbert.

"Yes, she is a pretty creature," responded Pencroff. "I love her as a mother. She received us poor and needy, and what has she denied to these five children who tumbled upon her out of the sky?"

"Nothing, captain, nothing," answered Neb. And the two honest fellows gave three hearty cheers in honor of their island.

Meantime, Spilett, seated by the mast, sketched the panorama before him, while Smith looked on in silence.

"What do you say of our boat, now, sir?" demanded Pencroff.

"It acts very well," replied the engineer.

"Good. And now don't you think it could undertake a voyage of some length?"

"Where, Pencroff?"

"To Tabor Island, for instance."

"My friend," replied the engineer, "I believe that in a case of necessity there need be no hesitancy in trusting to the Good Luck even for a longer journey; but, you know, I would be sorry to see you leave for Tabor Island, because nothing obliges you to go."

"One likes to know one's neighbors," answered Pencroff, whose mind was made up. "Tabor Island is our neighbor, and is all alone. Politeness requires that at least we make her a visit."

"The mischief!" exclaimed Spilett, "our friend Pencroff is a stickler for propriety."

"I am not a stickler at all," retorted the sailor, who was a little vexed by the engineer's opposition.

"Remember, Pencroff," said Smith, "that you could not go the island alone."

"One other would be all I would want."

"Supposing so," replied the engineer, "would you risk depriving our colony of five, of two of its colonists?"

"There are six," rejoined Pencroff. "You forget Jup."

"There are seven," added Neb. "Top is as good as another."

"There is no risk in it, Mr. Smith," said Pencroff again.

"Possibly not, Pencroff; but, I repeat, that it is exposing oneself without necessity."

The obstinate sailor did not answer, but let the conversation drop for the present. He little thought that an incident was about to aid him, and change to a work of humanity what had been merely a caprice open to discussion.

The Good Luck, after having stood out to sea, was returning towards the coast and making for Balloon Harbor, as it was important to locate the channel-way between the shoals and reefs so as to buoy them, for this little inlet was to be resting place of the sloop.

They were half a mile off shore, beating up to windward and moving somewhat slowly, as the boat was under the lee of the land. The sea was as smooth as glass. Herbert was standing in the bows indicating the channel-way. Suddenly he cried:—

"Luff, Pencroff, luff."

"What is it?" cried the sailor, springing to his feet. "A rock?"

"No—hold on, I cannot see very well—luff again—steady—bear away a little—" and while thus speaking, the lad lay down along the deck, plunged his arm quickly into the water, and then rising up again with something in his hand, exclaimed:—

"It is a bottle!"

Smith took it, and without saying a word, withdrew the cork and took out a wet paper, on which was written these words:—

"A shipwrecked man—Tabor Island:—153° W. lon.—37° 11' S. lat."

CHAPTER XXXV.

DEPARTURE DECIDED UPON—PREPARATIONS—
THE THREE PASSENGERS—THE FIRST NIGHT—
THE SECOND NIGHT—TABOR ISLAND—SEARCH ON
THE SHORE—SEARCH IN THE WOODS—NO ONE—
ANIMALS—PLANTS—A HOUSE—DESERTED.

"Some one shipwrecked!" cried Pencroff, "abandoned some hundred miles from us upon Tabor Island! Oh! Mr. Smith, you will no longer oppose my project!"

"No, Pencroff, and you must leave as soon as possible.".

"To-morrow?"

"To-morrow."

The engineer held the paper which he had taken from the bottle in his hand. He considered for a few moments, and then spoke:—

"From this paper, my friends," said he, "and from the manner in which it is worded, we must conclude that, in the first place, the person cast away upon Tabor Island is a man well informed, since he gives the latitude and longitude of his island exactly; secondly, that he is English or American, since the paper is written in English."

"That is a logical conclusion," answered Spilett, "and the presence of this person explains the arrival of the box on our coast. There has been a shipwreck, since some one has been shipwrecked. And he is fortunate in that Pencroff had the idea of building this boat and even of trying it to-day, for in twenty-four hours the bottle would have been broken on the rocks."

"Indeed,!' said Herbert, "it is a happy chance that the Good Luck passed by the very spot where this bottle was floating."

"Don't it seem to you odd?" asked Smith of Pencroff.

"It seems fortunate, that's all," replied the sailor. "Do you see anything extraordinary in it, sir? This bottle must have gone somewhere, and why not here as well as anywhere else?"

"Perhaps you are right, Pencroff," responded the engineer, "and nevertheless—"

"But," interrupted Herbert, "nothing proves that this bottle has floated in the water for a long time."

"Nothing," responded Spilett, "and moreover the paper seems to have been recently written. What do you think, Cyrus?"

"It is hard to decide." answered Smith.

Meanwhile Pencroff had not been idle. He had gone about, and the Good Luck, with a free wind, all her sails drawing, was speeding toward Claw Cape. Each one thought of the castaway on Tabor Island. Was there still time to save him? This was a great event in the lives of the colonists. They too were but castaways, but it was not probable that another had been as favored as they had been, and it was their duty to hasten at once to this one's relief. By 2 o'clock Claw Cape was doubled, and the Good Luck anchored at the mouth of the Mercy.

That evening all the details of the expedition were arranged. It was agreed that Herbert and Pencroff, who understood the management of a boat, were to undertake the voyage alone. By leaving the next day, the 11th of October, they would reach the island, supposing the wind continued, in forty-eight hours. Allowing for one day there, and three or four days to return in, they could calculate on being at Lincoln Island again on the 17th. The weather was good, the barometer rose steadily, the wind seemed as if it would continue, everything favored these brave men, who were going so far to do a humane act.

Thus, Smith, Neb, and Spilett was to remain at Granite House; but at the last moment, the latter, remembering his duty as reporter to the New York *Herald*, having declared that he would swim rather than lose such an opportunity, was allowed to take part in the voyage.

The evening was employed in putting bedding, arms, munitions, provisions, etc., on board, and the next morning, by 5 o'clock, the good-byes were spoken, and Pencroff, hoisting the sails, headed for Claw Cape, which had to be doubled before taking the route to the southeast. The Good Luck was already a quarter of a mile from shore when her passengers saw upon the heights of Granite House two men signalling farewells. They were Smith and Neb, from whom they were separating for the first time in fifteen months.

Pencroff, Herbert, and the reporter returned the signal, and soon Granite House disappeared behind the rocks of the Cape.

During the morning, the Good Luck remained in view of the southern coast of the island, which appeared like a green clump of trees, above which rose Mount Franklin. The heights, lessened by distance, gave it an appearance little calculated to attract ships on its coasts. At 1 o'clock Reptile Promontory was passed ten miles distant. It was therefore impossible to distinguish the western coast, which extended to the spurs of the mountain, and three hours later, Lincoln Island had disappeared behind the horizon.

The Good Luck behaved admirably. She rode lightly over the seas and sailed rapidly. Pencroff had set his topsail, and with a fair wind he followed a straight course by the compass. Occasionally Herbert took the tiller, and the hand of the young lad was so sure, that the sailor had nothing to correct.

Spilett chatted with one and the other, and lent a hand when necessary in manœuvring the sloop. Captain Pencroff was perfectly satisfied with his crew, and was constantly promising them an extra allowance of grog.

In the evening the slender crescent of the moon glimmered in the twilight. The night came on dark but starlit, with the promise of a fine day on the morrow. Pencroff thought it prudent to take in the topsail, which was perhaps an excess of caution in so still a night, but he was a careful sailor, and was not to be blamed.

The reporter slept during half the night, Herbert and Pencroff taking two-hour turns at the helm. The sailor had as much confidence in his pupil as he had in himself, and his trust was justified by the coolness and judgment of the lad. Pencroff set the course as a captain to his helmsman, and Herbert did not allow the Good Luck to deviate a point from her direction.

The night and the next day passed quietly and safely. The Good Luck held her southeast course, and, unless she was drawn aside by some unknown current, she would make Tabor Island exactly. The sea was completely deserted, save that sometimes an albatross or frigate-bird passed within gun-shot distance.

"And yet," said Herbert, "this is the season when the whalers usually come towards the southern part of the Pacific. I don't believe that there is a sea more deserted than this."

"It is not altogether deserted," responded Pencroff.

"What do you mean?"

"Why we are here. Do you take us for porpoises or our sloop for driftwood?" And Pencroff laughed at his pleasantry.

By evening they calculated the distance traversed at 130 miles, or three and a third miles an hour. The breeze was dying away, but they had reason to hope, supposing their course to have been correct, that they would sight Tabor Island at daylight.

No one of the three slept during this night. While waiting for morning they experienced the liveliest emotions. There was so much uncertainty in their enterprise. Were they near the island? Was the shipwrecked man still there? Who was he? Might not his presence disturb the unity of the colony? Would he, indeed, consent to exchange one prison for another? All these questions, which would doubtless be answered the next day, kept them alert, and at the earliest dawn they began to scan the western horizon.

What was the joy of the little crew when towards 6 o'clock Pencroff shouted—

"Land!"

In a few hours they would be upon its shore.

The island was a low coast, raised but a little above the waves, not more than fifteen miles away. The sloop, which had been heading south of it, was put about, and, as the sun rose, a few elevations became visible here and there.

"It is not as large as Lincoln Island," said Herbert, "and probably owes its origin to like submarine convulsions."

By 11 o'clock the Good Luck was only two miles distant from shore, and Pencroff, while seeking some place to land, sailed with extreme caution through these unknown waters. They could see the whole extent of this island, on which were visible groups of gum and other large trees of the same species as those on Lincoln Island. But, it was astonishing, that no rising smoke indicated that the place was inhabited, nor was any signal visible upon the shore. Nevertheless the paper had been precise: it stated that there was a shipwrecked man here; and he should have been upon the watch.

Meanwhile the Good Luck went in through the tortuous passages between the reefs, Herbert steering, and the sailor stationed forward, keeping a sharp lookout, with the halliards in his hand, ready to run down the sail. Spilett, with the spy-glass, examined all the shore without perceiving anything. By noon the sloop touched the beach, the anchor was let go, the sails furled, and the crew stepped on shore.

There could be no doubt that that was Tabor Island, since the most recent maps gave no other land in all this part of the Pacific.

After having securely moored the sloop, Pencroff and his companion, well armed, ascended the coast towards a round hill, some 250 feet high, which was distant about half a mile, from the summit of which they expected to have a good view of the island.

The explorers followed the edge of grassy plain which ended at the foot of the hill. Rock-pigeons and sea-swallows circled about them, and in the woods bordering the plain to the left they heard rustlings in the bushes and saw movements in the grass indicating the presence of very timid animals, but nothing, so far, indicated that the island was inhabited.

Having reached the hill the party soon climbed to its summit, and their gaze traversed the whole horizon. They were certainly upon an island, not more than six miles in circumference, in shape a long oval, and but little broken by inlets or promontories. All around it, the sea, absolutely deserted, stretched away to the horizon.

This islet differed greatly from Lincoln Island in that it was covered over its entire surface with woods, and the uniform mass of verdure clothed two or three less elevated hills. Obliquely to the oval of the island a small stream crossed a large grassy plain and emptied into the sea on the western side by a narrowed mouth.

"The place is small," said Herbert.

"Yes," replied the sailor. "It would have been too small for us."

"And," added the reporter, "it seems uninhabited."

"Nevertheless," said Pencroff, "let us go down and search."

The party returned to the sloop, and they decided to walk round the entire island before venturing into its interior, so that no place could escape their investigation.

The shore was easily followed, and the explorers proceeded towards the south, starting up flocks of aquatic birds and numbers of seals, which latter threw themselves into the sea as soon as they caught sight of the party.

"Those beasts are not looking on man for the first time. They fear what they know," said the reporter.

An hour after their departure the three had reached the southern point of the islet, which terminated in a sharp cape, and they turned towards the north, following the western shore, which was sandy, like the other, and bounded by a thick wood.

In four hours after they had set out the party had made the circuit of the island, without having seen any trace of a habitation, and not even a footprint. It was most extraordinary, to say the least, and it seemed necessary to believe that the place was not and had not been inhabited. Perhaps, after all, the paper had been in the water for many months, or even years, and it was possible, in that case, that the shipwrecked one had been rescued or that he had died from suffering.

The little party, discussing all sorts of possibilities, made a hasty dinner on board the sloop, and at 5 o'clock started to explore the woods.

Numerous animals fled before their approach, principally, indeed solely, goats and pigs, which it was easy to see were of European origin. Doubtless some whaler had left them here, and they had rapidly multiplied. Herbert made up his mind to catch two or three pairs to take back to Lincoln Island.

There was no longer any doubt that the island had previously been visited. This was the more evident as in passing through the forest they saw the traces of pathways, and the trunks of trees felled by the hatchet, and all about, marks of human handiwork; but these trees had been felled years before; the hatchet marks were velvetted with moss, and the pathways were so overgrown with grass that it was difficult to discover them.

"But," observed Spilett, "this proves that men not only landed here, but that they lived here. Now who and how many were these men, and how many remain?"

"The paper speaks of but one," replied Herbert.

"Well," said Pencroff, "if he is still here we cannot help finding him."

The exploration was continued, following diagonally across the island, and by this means the sailor and his companions reached the little stream which flowed towards the sea.

If animals of European origin, if works of human hands proved conclusively that man had once been here, many specimens of the vegetable kingdom also evidenced the fact. In certain clear places it was plain that kitchen vegetables had formerly been planted. And Herbert was overjoyed when he discovered potatoes, succory, sorrel, carrots, cabbage, and turnips, the seeds of which would enrich the garden at Granite House.

"Indeed," exclaimed Pencroff, "this will rejoice Neb. Even if we don't find the man, our voyage will not have been useless, and Heaven will have rewarded us."

"Doubtless," replied Spilett, "but from the conditions of these fields, it looks as if the place had not been inhabited for a long time."

"An inhabitant, whoever he was, would not neglect anything so important as this."

"Yes, this man has gone. It must be—"

"That the paper had been written a long time ago?"

"Undoubtedly."

"And that the bottle had been floating in the sea a good while before it arrived at Lincoln Island?"

"Why not?" said Pencroff. "But, see, it is getting dark," he added, "and I think we had better give over the search."

"We will go aboard, and to-morrow we will begin again," replied the reporter.

They were about adopting this counsel, when Herbert, pointing to something dimly visible, through the trees, exclaimed:—

"There's a house!"

All three directed their steps towards the place indicated, and they made out in the twilight that it was built of planks, covered with heavy tarpaulin. The door, half closed, was pushed back by Pencroff, who entered quickly.

The place was empty!

CHAPTER XXXVI.

THE INVENTORY—THE NIGHT—SOME LETTERS—
THE SEARCH CONTINUED—PLANTS AND ANIMALS—
HERBERT IN DANGER—ABOARD—THE DEPARTURE—
BAD WEATHER—A GLIMMER OF INTELLIGENCE—
LOST AT SEA—A TIMELY LIGHT.

Pencroff, Spilett and Herbert stood silent In darkness. Then the former gave a loud call. There was no answer. He lit a twig, and the light illuminated for a moment a small room, seemingly deserted. At one end was a large chimney, containing some cold cinders and an armful of dry wood. Pencroff threw the lighted twig into it, and the wood caught fire and gave out a bright light.

The sailor and his companions thereupon discovered a bed in disorder, its damp and mildewed covers proving that it had been long unused; in the corner of the fireplace were two rusty kettles and an overturned pot; a clothes-press with some sailors' clothing, partially moulded; on the table a tin plate, and a Bible, injured by the dampness; in a corner some tools, a shovel, a mattock, a pick, two shot guns, one of which was broken; on a shelf was a barrel full of powder, a barrel of lead, and a number of boxes of caps. All were covered with a thick coating of dust.

"There is no one here," said the reporter.

"Not a soul."

"This room has not been occupied in a long time."

"Since a very long time."

"Mr. Spilett," said Pencroff, "I think that instead of going on board we had better stay here all night."

"You are right, Pencroff, and if the proprietor returns he will not be sorry, perhaps, to find the place occupied."

"He won't come back, though," said the sailor, shaking his head.

"Do you think he has left the island?"

"If he had left the island he would have taken these things with him. You know how much a shipwrecked person would be attached to these objects. No, no," repeated the sailor, in the tone of a man perfectly convinced; "no, he has not left the island. He is surely here."

"Alive?"

"Alive or dead. But if he is dead he could not have buried himself, I am sure, and we will at least find his remains."

It was therefore agreed to pass the night in this house, and a supply of wood in the corner gave them the means of heating it. The door having been closed, the three explorers, seated upon a bench, spoke little, but remained deep in thought. They were in the mood to accept anything that might happen, and they listened eagerly for any sound from without. If the door had suddenly opened and a man had stood before them, they would not have been much surprised, in spite of all the evidence of desolation throughout the house; and their hands were ready to clasp the hands of this man, of this shipwrecked one, of this unknown friend whose friends awaited him.

But no sound was heard, the door did not open, and the hours passed by.

The night seemed interminable to the sailor and his companions. Herbert, alone, slept for two hours, as at his age, sleep is a necessity. All were anxious to renew the search of the day before, and to explore the innermost recesses of the islet. Pencroff's conclusions were certainly just, since the house and its contents had been abandoned. They determined, therefore, to search for the remains of its inhabitant, and to give them Christian burial.

As soon as it was daylight they began to examine the house. It was prettily situated under a small hill, on which grew several fine gum trees. Before it a large space had been cleared, giving a view over the sea. A small lawn, surrounded by a dilapidated fence, extended to the bank of the little stream. The house had evidently been built from planks taken from a ship. It seemed likely that a ship had been thrown upon the island, that all or at least one of the crew had been saved, and that this house had been built from the wreck. This was the more probable, as Spilett, in going round the dwelling, saw on one of the planks these half-effaced letters:—

BR . . . TAN . . . A.

"Britannia," exclaimed Pencroff, who had been called by the reporter to look at it; "that is a common name among ships, and I cannot say whether it is English or American. However, it don't matter to what country the man belongs, we will save him, if he is alive. But before we begin our search let us go back to the Good Luck."

Pencroff had been seized with a sort of anxiety about his sloop. Supposing the island was inhabited, and some one had taken it—but he shrugged his shoulders at this unlikely thought. Nevertheless the sailor was not unwilling to go on board to breakfast. The route already marked was not more than a mile in length, and they started on their walk, looking carefully about them in the woods and underbrush, through which ran hundreds of pigs and goats.

In twenty minutes the party reached the place where the Good Luck rode quietly at anchor. Pencroff gave a sigh of satisfaction.

After all, this boat was his baby, and it is a father's right to be often anxious without reason.

All went on board and ate a hearty breakfast, so as not to want anything before a late dinner; then the exploration was renewed, and conducted with the utmost carefulness. As it was likely that the solitary inhabitant of this island was dead, the party sought rather to find his remains than any traces of him living. But during all the morning they were unable to find anything; if he was dead, some animal must have devoured his body.

"We will leave to-morrow at daylight," said Pencroff to his companions, who towards 2 o'clock were resting for a few moments under a group of trees.

"I think we need not hesitate to take those things which belonged to him?" queried Herbert.

"I think not," answered Spilett; "and these arms and tools will add materially to the stock at Granite House. If I am not mistaken, what is left of the lead and powder is worth a good deal."

"And we must not forget to capture a couple of these pigs," said Pencroff.

"Nor to gather some seed," added Herbert, "which will give us some of our own vegetables."

"Perhaps it would be better to spend another day here, in order to get together everything that we want," suggested the reporter.

"No, sir;" replied the sailor. "I want to get away to-morrow morning. The wind seems to be shifting to the west, and will be in our favor going back."

"Then don't let us lose any time," said Herbert, rising.

"We will not," replied Pencroff. "Herbert, you get the seed, and Spilett and I will chase the pigs, and although we haven't Top, I think we will catch some."

Herbert, therefore, followed the path which led to the cultivated part of the island, while the others plunged at once into the forest. Although the pigs were plenty they were singularly agile, and not in the humor to be captured. However, after half an hour's chasing the hunters had captured a couple in their lair, when cries mingled with horrible hoarse sounds, having nothing human in them, were heard. Pencroff and Spilett sprang to their feet, regardless of the pigs, which escaped.

"It is Herbert!" cried the reporter.

"Hurry!" cried the sailor, as the two ran with their utmost speed towards the place from whence the cries came.

They had need to hasten, for at a turn in the path they saw the lad prostrate beneath a savage, or perhaps a gigantic ape, who was throttling him.

To throw themselves on this monster and pinion him to the ground, dragging Herbert away, was the work of a moment. The sailor had herculean strength. Spilett, too, was muscular, and, in spite of the resistance of the monster, it was bound so that it could not move.

"You are not wounded, Herbert?"

"No, oh no."

"Ah! if it bad hurt you, this ape-"

"But he is not an ape!" cried Herbert.

At these words Pencroff and Spilett looked again at the object lying on the ground. In fact, it was not an ape, but a human being—a man! But what a man! He was a savage, in all the horrible acceptation of the word; and, what was more frightful, he seemed to have fallen to the last degree of brutishness.

Matted hair, tangled beard descending to his waist, his body naked, save for a rag about his loins, wild eyes, long nails, mahogany-colored skin, feet as hard as if they had been made of horn; such was the miserable creature which it was, nevertheless, necessary to call a man. But one might well question whether this body still contained a soul, or whether the low, brutish instinct alone survived.

"Are you perfectly sure that this is what has been a man?" questioned Pencroff of the reporter.

"Alas! there can be no doubt of it," replied Spilett.

"Can he be the person shipwrecked?" asked Herbert

"Yes," responded the reporter, "but the poor creature is no longer human."

Spilett was right. Evidently, if the castaway had ever been civilized, isolation had made him a savage, a real creature of the woods. He gave utterance to hoarse sounds, from between teeth which were as sharp as those of animals living on raw flesh. Memory had doubtless long ago left him, and he had long since forgotten the use of arms and tools, and even how to make a fire. One could see that he was active and supple, but that his physical qualities had developed to the exclusion of his moral perception.

Spilett spoke to him, but he neither understood nor listened, and, looking him in the eye, the reporter could see that all intelligence had forsaken him. Nevertheless, the prisoner did not struggle or strive to break his bonds. Was he cowed by the presence of these men, whom he had once resembled? Was there in some corner of his brain a flitting remembrance which drew him towards humanity? Free, would he have fled or would he have remained? They did not know, and they did not put him to the proof. After having looked attentively at the miserable creature, Spilett said:—

"What he is, what he has been, and what he will be; it is still our duty to take him to Lincoln Island."

"Oh yes, yes," exclaimed Herbert, "and perhaps we can, with care, restore to him some degree of intelligence."

"The soul never dies," answered the reporter, "and it would be a great thing to bring back this creature of God's making from his brutishness."

Pencroff shook his head doubtfully.

"It is necessary to try at all events," said the reporter, "humanity requires it of us."

"It was, indeed, their duty as civilized and Christian beings, and they well knew that Smith would approve of their course.

"Shall we leave him bound?" inquired the sailor.

"Perhaps if we unfasten his feet he will walk," said Herbert.

"Well, let us try," replied the sailor.

And the cords binding the creature's legs were loosened, although his arms were kept firmly bound. He rose without manifesting any desire to escape. His tearless eyes darted sharp glances upon the three men who marched beside him, and nothing denoted that he remembered being or having been like them. A wheezing sound escaped from his lips, and his aspect was wild, but he made no resistance.

By the advice of the reporter, the poor wretch was taken to the house, where, perhaps, the sight of the objects in it might make some impression upon him. Perhaps a single gleam would awaken his sleeping consciousness, illuminate his darkened mind.

The house was near by, and in a few minutes they were there; but the prisoner recognized nothing—he seemed to have lost consciousness of everything. Could it be that this brutish state was due to his long imprisonment on the island? That, having come here a reasoning being, his isolation had reduced him to this state?

The reporter thought that perhaps the sight of fire might affect him, and in a moment one of those lovely flames which attract even animals lit up the fireplace. The sight of this flame seemed at first to attract the attention of the unfortunate man, but very soon he ceased regarding it. Evidently, for the present at least, there was nothing to do but take him aboard the Good Luck, which was accordingly done. He was left in charge of Pencroff, while the two others returned to the island and brought over the arms and implements, a lot of seeds, some game, and two pairs of pigs which they had caught. Everything was put on board, and the sloop rode ready to hoist anchor as soon as the next morning's tide would permit.

The prisoner had been placed in the forward hold, where he lay calm, quiet, insensible, and mute. Pencroff offering him some cooked meat to eat, he pushed it away; but, on being shown one of the ducks which Herbert had killed, he pounced on it with bestial avidity and devoured it.

"You think he'll be himself again?" asked the sailor, shaking his head.

"Perhaps," replied the reporter. "It is not impossible that our attentions will react on him, since it is the isolation that has done this; and he will be alone no longer."

"The poor fellow has doubtless been this way for a long time."

"Perhaps so."

"How old do you think he is?" asked the lad.

"That is hard to say," replied the reporter, "as his matted beard obscures his face; but he is no longer young, and I should say he was at least fifty years old."

"Have you noticed how his eyes are set deep in his head?"

"Yes, but I think that they are more human than one would suspect from his general appearance."

"Well, we will see," said Pencroff; "and I am curious to have Mr. Smith's opinion of our savage. We went to find a human being, and we are bringing back a monster. Any how, one takes what he can get."

The night passed, and whether the prisoner slept or not he did not move, although he had been unbound. He was like one of those beasts that in the first moments of their capture submit, and to whom the rage returns later.

At daybreak the next day, the 17th, the change in the weather was as Pencroff had predicted. The wind hauled round to the northwest and favored the return of the Good Luck; but at the same time it had freshened, so as to make the sailing more difficult. At 5 o'clock the anchor was raised, Pencroff took a reef in the mainsail and headed directly towards home.

The first day passed without incident. The prisoner rested quietly in the forward cabin, and, as he had once been a sailor, the motion of the sloop produced upon him a sort of salutary reaction. Did it recall to him some remembrance of his former occupation? At least he rested tranquil, more astonished than frightened.

On the 16th the wind freshened considerably, coming round more to the north, and therefore in a direction less favorable to the course of the Good Luck, which bounded over the waves. Pencroff was soon obliged to hold her nearer to the wind, and without saying so, he began to be anxious at the lookout ahead. Certainly, unless the—wind moderated, it would take much longer to go back than it had taken to come.

On the 17th they had been forty-eight hours out, and yet nothing indicated they were in the neighborhood of Lincoln Island. It was, moreover, impossible to reckon their course, or even to estimate the distance traversed, as the direction and the speed had been too irregular. Twenty-four hours later there was still no land in view. The wind was dead ahead, and an ugly sea running. On the 18th a huge wave struck the sloop, and had not the crew been lashed to the deck, they would have been swept overboard.

On this occasion Pencroff and his companions, busy in clearing things away, received an unhoped-for assistance from the prisoner, who sprang from the hatchway as if his sailor instinct bad returned to him, and breaking the rail by a, vigorous blow—with a spar, enabled the water on the deck to flow off more freely. Then, the boat cleared, without having said a word, he returned to his cabin.

Nevertheless, the situation was bad, and the sailor had cause to believe himself lost upon this vast sea, without the possibility of regaining his course. The night of the 18th was dark and cold. But about 11 o'clock the wind lulled, the sea fell, and the sloop, less tossed about, moved more rapidly. None of the crew thought of sleep. They kept an eager lookout, as either Lincoln Island must be near at hand and they would discover it at daybreak, or the sloop had been drifted from her course by the currents, and it would be next to impossible to rectify the direction.

Pencroff, anxious to the last degree, did not, however, despair; but, seated at the helm, he tried to see through the thick darkness around him. Towards 2 o'clock he suddenly started up, crying:—"A light! a light!" It was indeed a bright light appearing twenty miles to—the northeast. Lincoln Island was there, and this light, evidently lit by Smith, indicated the direction to be followed.

Pencroff, who bad been heading much too far towards the north, changed his course, and steered directly towards the light, which gleamed above the horizon like a star of the first magnitude.

CHAPTER XXXVII.

THE RETURN-DISCUSSION—SMITH AND THE UNKNOWN—BALLOON HARBOR-THE DEVOTION OF THE ENGINEER-A TOUCHING EXPERIENCE-TEARS.

At 7 o'clock the next morning the boat touched the shore at the mouth of the Mercy. Smith and Neb, who had become very anxious at the stormy weather and the prolonged absence of their companions, bad climbed, at daylight, to Prospect Plateau, and had at length perceived the sloop in the distance.

"Thank Heaven! There they are," exclaimed Smith; while Neb, dancing with pleasure, turned towards his master, and, striking his hands together, cried, "Oh, my master!"-a more touching expression than, the first polished phrase.

The engineer's first thought, on counting the number of persons on the deck of the Good Luck, was that Pencroff had found no one on Tabor Island, or that the unfortunate man had refused to exchange one prison for another.

The engineer and Neb were on the beach at the moment the sloop arrived, and before the party had leaped ashore, Smith said:—

"We have been very anxious about you, my friends. Did anything happen to you?" "No, indeed; everything went finely," replied Spilett. "We will tell you all about it."

"Nevertheless, you have failed in your search, since you are all alone.", "But, sir, there are four of us," said the sailor.

"Have you found this person?". "Yes."

"And brought him back?" "Yes." "Living?" "Where is he, and what is he, then?" "He is, or rather, he was a human being; and that is all, Cyrus, that we can say."

The engineer was thereupon, informed of everything that had happened; of the search, of the long-abandoned house, of the capture of the scarcely human inhabitant.

"And," added Pencroff," I don't know whether we have done right in bringing him here."

"Most certainly you have done right," replied the engineer.

"But the poor fellow has no sense at all." "Not now, perhaps; in a few months, he will be as much a man as any of us. "Who knows what might happen to the last one of us, after living for a long time alone on this island? It is terrible to be all alone, my friends, and it is probable that solitude quickly overthrows reason, since you have found this poor being in such a condition."

"But, Mr. Smith," asked Herbert, "what makes you think that the brutishness of this man has come on within a little while?"

"Because the paper we found had been recently written, and no one but this shipwrecked man could have written it."

"Unless," suggested Spilett, "it had been written by a companion of this man who has since died."

"That is impossible, Spilett."

"Why so?"

"Because, then, the paper would have mentioned two persons instead of one."

Herbert briefly related the incident of the sea striking the sloop, and insisted that the prisoner must then have had a glimmer of his sailor instinct.

"You are perfectly right, Herbert," said the engineer, "to attach great importance to this fact. This poor man will not be incurable; despair has made him what he is. But here he will find his kindred, and if he still has any reason, we will save it."

Then, to Smith's great pity and Neb's wonderment, the man was brought up from the cabin of the sloop, and as soon as he was on land, he manifested a desire to escape. But Smith, approaching him, laid his hand authoritatively upon his shoulder and looked at him with infinite tenderness. Thereupon the poor wretch, submitting to a sort of instantaneous power, became quiet, his eyes fell, his head dropped forward, and he made no further resistance.

"Poor shipwrecked sailor," murmured the reporter.

Smith regarded him attentively. To judge from his appearance, this miserable creature had little of the human left in him; but Smith caught in his glance, as the reporter had done, an almost imperceptible gleam of intelligence.

It was decided that the Unknown, as his new companions called him, should stay in one of the rooms of Granite House, from which he could not escape. He made no resistance to being conducted there, and with good care they might, perhaps, hope that some day he would prove a companion to them.

Neb hastened to prepare breakfast, for the voyagers were very hungry, and during the meal Smith made them relate in detail every incident of the cruise. He agreed with them in thinking that the name of the Britannia gave them reason to believe that the Unknown was either English or American; and, moreover, under all the growth of hair covering the man's face, the engineer thought he recognized the features characteristic of an Anglo-Saxon.

"But, by the way, Herbert," said the reporter, "you have never told us how you met this savage, and we know nothing, except that he would have strangled you, had we not arrived so opportunely."

"Indeed, I am not sure that I can tell just what happened," replied Herbert. "I was, I think, gathering seeds, when I heard a tremendous noise in a high tree near by. I had hardly time to turn, when this unhappy creature, who had, doubtless, been hidden crouching in the tree, threw himself upon me; and, unless Mr. Spilett and Pencroff—"

"You were in great danger, indeed, my boy," said Smith; "but perhaps, if this had not happened, this poor being would have escaped your search, and we would have been without another companion."

"You expect, then, to make him a man again?" asked the reporter.

"Yes," replied Smith.

Breakfast ended, all returned to the shore and began unloading the sloop; and the engineer examined the arms and tools, but found nothing to establish the identity of the Unknown.

The pigs were taken to the stables, to which they would soon become accustomed. The two barrels of powder and shot and the caps were a great acquisition, and it was determined to make a small powder magazine in the upper cavern of Granite House, where there would be no danger of an explosion. Meantime, since the pyroxyline answered very well, there was no present need to use this powder.

When the sloop was unloaded Pencroff said:—

"I think, Mr. Smith, that it would be better to put the Good Luck in a safe place."

"Is it not safe enough at the mouth of the Mercy?"

"No, sir," replied the sailor. "Most of the time she is aground on the sand, which strains her."

"Could not she be moored out in the stream?"

"She could, but the place is unsheltered, and in an easterly wind I am afraid she would suffer from the seas."

"Very well; where do you want to put her?"

"In Balloon Harbor," replied the sailor. "It seems to me that that little inlet, hidden by the rocks, is just the place for her."

"Isn't it too far off?"

"No, it is only three miles from Granite House, and we have a good straight road there."

"Have your way, Pencroff," replied the engineer. "Nevertheless, I should prefer to have the sloop under our sight. We must, when we have time, make a small harbor."

"Capital!" cried Pencroff. "A harbor with a light house, a breakwater, and a dry dock! Oh, indeed, sir, everything will be easy enough with you!"

"Always provided, my good man, that you assist me, as you do three fourths of the work."

Herbert and the sailor went aboard the Good Luck, and set sail, and in a couple of hours the sloop rode quietly at anchor in the tranquil water of Balloon Harbor.

During the first few days that the Unknown was at Granite House, had he given any indication of a change in his savage nature? Did not a brighter light illumine the depths of his intelligence? Was not, in short, his reason returning to him? Undoubtedly, yes; and Smith and Spilett questioned whether this reason had ever entirely forsaken him.

At first this man, accustomed to the air and liberty which he had had in Tabor Island, was seized with fits of passion, and there was danger of his throwing himself out of one of the windows of Granite House. But little by little he grew more quiet, and he was allowed to move about without restraint.

Already forgetting his carnivorous instincts, he accepted a less bestial nourishment, and cooked food did not produce in him the sentiment of disgust which he had shown on board the Good Luck.

Smith had taken advantage of a time when the man was asleep to cut the hair and beard which had grown like a mane about his face, and had given him such a savage aspect. He had also been clothed more decently, and the result was that the Unknown appeared more like a human being, and it seemed as if the expression of his eyes was softened. Certainly, sometimes, when intelligence was visible, the expression of this man had a sort of beauty.

Every day, Smith made a point of passing some hours in his company. He worked beside him, and occupied himself in various ways to attract his attention. It would suffice, if a single ray of light illuminated his reason, if a single remembrance crossed his mind. Neither did the engineer neglect to speak in a loud voice, so as to penetrate by both sound and sight to the depths of this torpid intelligence. Sometimes one or another of the party joined the engineer, and they usually talked of such matters pertaining to the sea as would be likely to interest the man. At times the Unknown gave a sort of vague attention to what was said, and soon the colonists began to think that he partly understood them. Again his expression would be dolorous, proving that he suffered inwardly. Nevertheless, he did not speak, although they thought, at times, from his actions, that words were about to pass his lips.

The poor creature was very calm and sad. But was not the calmness only on the surface, and the sadness the result of his confinement? They could not yet say. Seeing only certain objects and in a limited space, always with the colonists, to whom he had become accustomed, having no desire to satisfy, better clothed and better fed, it was natural that his physical nature should soften little by little; but was he imbued with the new life, or, to use an expression justly applicable to the case, was he only tamed, as an animal in the presence of its master? This was the important question Smith was anxious to determine, and meantime he did not wish to be too abrupt with his patient. For to him, the unknown was but a sick person. Would he ever be a convalescent?

Therefore, the engineer watched him unceasingly. How he laid in wait for his reason, so to speak, that he might lay hold of it.

The colonists followed with strong interest all the phases of this cure undertaken by Smith. All aided him in it, and all, save perhaps the incredulous Pencroff, came to share in his belief and hope.

The submission of the Unknown was entire, and it seemed as if he showed for the engineer, whose influence over him was apparent, a sort of attachment, and Smith resolved now to test it by transporting him to another scene, to that ocean which he had been accustomed to look upon, to the forest border, which would recall those woods where he had lived such a life!"

"But," said Spilett, "can we hope that once at liberty, he will not escape?"

"We must make the experiment," replied the engineer.

"All right," said Pencroff. "You will see, when this fellow snuffs the fresh air and sees the coast clear, if he don't make his legs spin!"

"I don't think it," replied the engineer.

"We will try, any how," said Spilett.

It was the 30th of October, and the Unknown had been a prisoner for nine days. It was a beautiful, warm, sunshiny day. Smith and Pencroff went to the room of the Unknown, whom they found at the window gazing out at the sky.

"Come, my friend," said the engineer to him.

The Unknown rose immediately. His eye was fixed on Smith, whom he followed; and the sailor, little confident in the results of the experiment, walked with him.

Having reached the door, they made him get into the elevator, at the foot of which the rest of the party were waiting. The basket descended, and in a few seconds all were standing together on the shore.

The colonists moved off a little distance from the Unknown, so as to leave him quite at liberty. He made some steps forward towards the sea, and his face lit up with pleasure, but he made no effort to escape. He looked curiously at the little waves, which, broken by the islet, died away on the shore.

"It is not, indeed, the ocean," remarked Spilett, "and it is possible that this does not give him the idea of escaping."

"Yes," replied Smith, "we must take him to the plateau on the edge of the forest. There the experiment will be more conclusive."

"There he cannot get away, since the bridges are all raised," said Neb.

336

"Oh, he is not the man to be troubled by such a brook as Glycerine Creek; he could leap it at a bound," returned Pencroff.

"We will see presently," said Smith, who kept his eye fixed on his patient.

And thereupon all proceeded towards Prospect Plateau. Having reached the place they encountered the outskirts of the forest, with its leaves trembling in the wind, The Unknown seemed to drink in with eagerness the perfume in the air, and a long sigh escaped from his breast.

The colonists stood some paces back, ready to seize him if he attempted to escape.

The poor creature was upon the point of plunging in the creek that separated him from the forest; he placed himself ready to spring—then all at once he turned about, dropping his arms beside him, and tears coursed down his cheeks.

"Ah!" cried Smith, "you will be a man again, since you weep!"

CHAPTER XXXVIII.

A MYSTERY TO BE SOLVED—THE FIRST WORDS
OF THE UNKNOWN—TWELVE YEARS ON THE
ISLAND—CONFESSIONS—DISAPPEARANCE—
SMITH'S CONFIDENCE—BUILDING A WIND-MILL—
THE FIRST BREAD—AN ACT OF DEVOTION—
HONEST HANDS.

Yes, the poor creature had wept. Some remembrance had flashed across his spirit, and, as Smith had said, he would be made a man through his tears.

The colonists left him for some time, withdrawing themselves, so that he could feel perfectly at liberty; but he showed no inclination to avail himself of this freedom, and Smith soon decided to take him back to Granite House.

Two days after this occurrence, the Unknown showed a disposition to enter little by little into the common life. It was evident that he heard, that he understood, but it was equally evident that he manifested a strange disinclination to speak to them. Pencroff, listening at his room, heard these words escape him:—

"No! here! I! never!"

The sailor reported this to his companions, and Smith said:—

"There must be some sad mystery here."

The Unknown had begun to do some little chores, and to work in the garden. When he rested, which was frequent, he seemed entirely self-absorbed; but, on the advice of the engineer, the others respected the silence, which he seemed desirous of keeping. If one of the colonists approached him he recoiled, sobbing as if overcome. Could it be by remorse? or, was it, as Spilett once suggested:—

"If he does not speak I believe it is because he has something on his mind too terrible to mention."

Some days later the Unknown was working on the plantation, when, of a sudden, he stopped and let his spade fall, and Smith, who was watching him from a distance, saw that he was weeping again. An irresistible pity drew the engineer to the poor fellow's side; and, touching his arm lightly,

"My friend," said he.

The Unknown tried to look away, and when Smith sought to take his hand he drew back quickly.

"My friend," said Smith, with decision, "I wish you to look at me."

The Unknown obeyed, raising his eyes and regarding the other as one does who is under the influence of magnetism. At first he wished to break away, then his whole expression changed; his eyes flashed, and, unable longer to contain himself, he muttered some incoherent words. Suddenly he crossed his arms, and in a hollow voice:—

"Who are you?" he demanded.

"Men shipwrecked as you have been," replied the engineer, greatly moved. "We have brought you here among your kindred."

"My kindred! I have none!

"You are among friends—,"

"Friends! I! Friends!" cried the Unknown, hiding his face in his hands. "Oh, no! never! Leave me! leave me!" and he rushed to the brink of the plateau overlooking the sea, and stood there, motionless, for a long time.

Smith had rejoined his companions and had related to them what had happened.

"There certainly is a mystery in this man's life," said Spilett, "and it seems as if his first human sensation was remorse."

"I don't understand what kind of a man we have brought back," says the sailor. "He has secrets—"

"Which we will respect," answered the engineer, quickly. "If he has committed some fault he has cruelly expiated it, and in our sight it is absolved."

For two hours the Unknown remained upon the shore, evidently under the influence of remembrances which brought back to him all his past, a past which, doubtless, was hateful enough, and the colonists, though keeping watch upon him, respected his desire to be alone.

Suddenly he seemed to have taken a resolution, and he returned to the engineer. His eyes were red with the traces of tears, and his face wore an expression of deep humility. He seemed apprehensive, ashamed, humiliated, and his looks were fixed on the ground.

"Sir," said he, "are you and your companions English?"

"No," replied Smith, "we are Americans."

"Ah!" murmured the Unknown, "I am glad of that."

"And what are you, my friend?" asked the engineer.

"English," he responded, as if these few words had cost him a great effort. He rushed to the shore, and traversed its length to the mouth of the Mercy, in a state of extreme agitation.

Having, at one place, met Herbert, he stopped, and in a choking voice, accosted him:—

"What month is it?"

"November," replied the lad.

"And what year?"

"1866."

"Twelve years! Twelve years!" he cried, and then turned quickly away.

Herbert related this incident to the others.

"The poor creature knew neither the month nor the year," remarked Spilett.

"And he had been twelve years on the island, when we found him."

"Twelve years," said Smith. "Twelve years of isolation, after a wicked life, perhaps; that would indeed affect a man's reason."

"I cannot help thinking," observed Pencroff, "that this man was not wrecked on that island, but that he has been left there for some crime."

"You may be right, Pencroff," replied the reporter, "and if that is the case, it is not impossible that whoever left him there may return for him some day."

"And they would not find him," said Herbert.

"But, then," exclaimed Pencroff, "he would want to go back, and—"

"My friends," interrupted Smith, "do not let us discuss this question till we know what we are talking about. I believe that this unhappy man has suffered, and that he has paid bitterly for his faults, whatever they may have been, and that he is struggling with the need of opening his heart to someone. Do not provoke him to speak; he will tell us of his own accord some day, and when we have learned all, we will see what course it will be necessary to follow. He alone can tell us if he has more than the hope, the certainty of some day being restored to his country, but I doubt it."

"Why?" asked the reporter.

"Because, had he been sure of being delivered after a fixed time, he would have awaited the hour of his deliverance, and not have thrown that paper in the sea. No, it is more likely that be was condemned to die upon this island, to never look upon his kind again."

"But there still is something which I cannot understand," said the sailor.

"What is that?"

"Why, if this man had been left on Tabor Island twelve years ago, it seems probable that he must have been in this savage condition for a long time."

"That is probable," replied the engineer.

"And, therefore, it is a long time since he wrote that paper."

"Doubtless—and yet that paper seemed to have been written recently—"

"Yes, and how account for the bottle taking so many years in coming from Tabor Island here?"

"It is not absolutely impossible," responded the reporter. "Could not it have been in the neighborhood of the island for a long time?"

"And have remained floating? No," answered the sailor, "for sooner or later it would have been dashed to pieces on the rocks."

"It would, indeed," said Smith, thoughtfully.

"And, moreover," continued the sailor, if the paper had been enclosed in the bottle for a long time, it would have been injured by the moisture, whereas, it was not damaged in the least."

The sailor's remark was just, and, moreover, this paper, recently written, gave the situation of the island with an exactness which implied a knowledge of hydrography, such as a simple sailor could not have.

"There is, as I said before, something inexplicable in all this," said the engineer, "but do not let us urge our new companion to speak, When he wishes it we will be ready to listen."

For several days after this the Unknown neither spoke nor left the plateau. He worked incessantly, digging in the garden apart from the colonists, and at meal times, although he was often asked to join them, he remained alone, eating but a few uncooked vegetables. At night, instead of returning to his room in Granite House, he slept under the trees, or hid himself, if the weather was bad, in some hollow of the rocks. Thus he returned again to that manner of life in which he had lived when he had no other shelter than the forests of Tabor Island, and all endeavor to make him modify this life having proved fruitless, the colonists waited patiently. But the moment came when, irresistibly and as if involuntarily forced from him by his conscience, the terrible avowals were made.

At dusk on the evening of the 10th of November, as the colonists were seated in the arbor, the Unknown stood suddenly before them. His eyes glowed, and his whole appearance wore again the savage aspect of former days. He stood there, swayed by some terrible emotion, his teeth chattering like those of a person in a fever. The colonists were astounded. "What was the matter with him? Was the sight of his fellow-creatures unendurable? Had he had enough of this honest life? Was he homesick for his brutish life? One would have thought so, hearing him give utterance to these incoherent phrases:-

"Why am I here? By what right did you drag me from my island? Is there any bond between you and me? Do you know who I am—what I have done—why I was there—alone? And who has told you that I was not abandoned—that I was not condemned to die there? Do you know my past? Do you know whether I have not robbed, murdered—if I am not a miserable—a wicked being—fit to live like a wild beast—far from all—say—do you know?"

The colonists listened silently to the unhappy creature, from whom these half avowals came in spite of himself. Smith, wishing to soothe him, would have gone to him, but the Unknown drew back quickly.

"No! no!" he cried. "One word only—am I free?".

"You are free," replied the engineer.

"Then, good-bye!" he cried, rushing off.

Neb, Pencroff, and Herbert ran to the border of the wood, but they returned alone.

"We must let him have his own way," said the engineer.

"He will never come back," exclaimed Pencroff.

"He will return," replied the engineer.

And after that conversation many days passed, but Smith—was it a presentiment—persisted in the fixed idea that the unhappy man would return sooner or later.

"It is the last struggle of this rude nature, which is touched by remorse, and which would be terrified by a new isolation."

In the meantime, work of all kinds was continued, both on Prospect Plateau and at the corral, where Smith proposed to make a farm. It is needless to say that the seeds brought from Tabor Island had been carefully sown. The plateau was a great kitchen-garden, well laid out and enclosed, which kept the colonists always busy. As the plants multiplied, it was necessary to increase the size of the beds, which threatened to become fields, and to take the place of the grass land. But as forage abounded in other parts of the island, there was no fear of the onagers having to be placed on rations; and it was also better to make Prospect Plateau, defended by its belt of creeks, a garden of this kind, and to extend the fields, which required no protection, beyond the belt.

On the 15th of November they made their third harvest. Here was a field which had indeed increased in the eighteen months since the first grain of corn had been sown. The second crop of 600,000 grains produced this time 4,000 bushels or more than 500,000,000 grains. The colonists were, therefore, rich in corn; as it was only necessary to sow a dozen bushels each year in order to have a supply sufficient for the nourishment of man and beast.

After harvesting they, gave up the last fortnight in the month to bread-making. They had the grain but not the flour, and a mill was therefore necessary. Smith could have used the other waterfall which fell into the Mercy, but, after discussing the question, it was decided to build a simple wind-mill on the summit of the plateau. Its construction would be no more difficult than a water-mill, and they would be sure of always having a breeze on this open elevation.

"Without counting," said Pencroff, "the fine aspect a wind-mill will give to the landscape."

They began the work by selecting timber for the cage and machinery for the mill. Some large sand-stones, which the colonists found to the north of the lake, were readily made into mill-stones, and the inexhaustible envelope of the balloon furnished the cloth necessary for the sails.

Smith made his drawings, and the site for the mill was chosen a little to the right of the poultry-yard, and close to the lake shore. The whole cage rested upon a pivot, held in position by heavy timbers, in such a manner that it could turn, with all the mechanism within it, towards any quarter of the wind.

The work progressed rapidly. Neb and Herbert had become expert carpenters, and had only to follow the plans furnished by the engineer, so that in a very short time a sort of round watch-house, a regular pepper-box, surmounted by a sharp roof, rose upon the site selected. The four wings had been firmly fastened by iron tenons to the main shaft, in such a manner as to make a certain angle with it. As for the various parts of the interior mechanism—the two mill-stones, the runner and the feeder; the hopper, a sort of huge square trough, large above and small below, permitting the grains to fall upon the mill-stones; the oscillating bucket, designed to regulate the passage of the grain; and, finally, the bolter, which, by the operation of the sieve, separated the bran from the flour—all these were easily made. And as their tools were good, the work simple, and everybody took part in it, the mill was finished by the 1st of December.

As usual, Pencroff was overjoyed by his work, and he was sure that the machine was perfection.

"Now, with a good wind, we will merrily grind our corn."

"Let it be a good wind, Pencroff, but not too strong," said the engineer.

"Bah! our mill will turn the faster."

"It is not necessary to turn rapidly," replied the engineer. "Experience has demonstrated that the best results are obtained by a mill whose wings make six times the number of turns in a minute that the wind travels feet in a second. Thus, an ordinary wind, which travels twenty-four feet in a second, will turn the wings of the mill sixteen times in a minute, which is fast enough."

"Already!" exclaimed Herbert, "there is a fine breeze from the northeast, which will be just the thing!"

There was no reason to delay using the mill, and the colonists were anxious to taste the bread of Lincoln Island; so this very morning two or three bushels of corn were ground, and the next day, at breakfast, a splendid loaf, rather heavy perhaps, which had been raised with the barm of beer, was displayed upon the table of Granite House. Each munched his portion with a pleasure perfectly inexpressible.

Meantime the Unknown had not come back again. Often Spilett and Herbert had searched the forest in the neighborhood of Granite House without finding any trace of him, and all began to be seriously alarmed at his prolonged absence. Undoubtedly the former savage of Tabor Island would not find it difficult to live in the forests of the Far West, which were so rich in game; but was it not to be feared that he would resume his former habits, and that his independence would revive in him his brutish instincts? Smith alone, by a sort of presentiment, persisted in saying that the fugitive would return.

"Yes, he will come back," he repeated with a confidence in which his companions could not share. "When this poor creature was on Tabor Island, he knew he was alone, but here, he knows that his kindred await him. Since he half-spoke of his past life, he will return to tell us everything, and on that day he will be ours."

The event proved the correctness of Cyrus Smith's reasoning.

On the 3d of December, Herbert had gone to the southern shore of the lake, to fish, and, since the dangerous animals never showed themselves in this part of the island, he had gone unarmed.

Pencroff and Neb were working in the poultry-yard, while Smith and the reporter were occupied at the Chimneys making soda, the supply of soap being low.

Suddenly sharp cries of help were heard by Neb and Pencroff, who summoned the others, and all rushed towards the lake.

But before them, the Unknown, whose presence in the neighborhood had not been suspected, leapt over Glycerine Creek and bounded along the opposite bank.

There, Herbert stood facing a powerful jaguar, like the one which had been killed at Reptile End. Taken by surprise, he stood with his back against a tree, and the animal, crouching on his haunches, was about to spring upon him, when the Unknown, with no other arm than his knife, threw himself on the brute, which turned upon its new adversary.

The struggle was short. This man, whose strength and agility was prodigious, seized the jaguar by the throat in a vice-like grip, and, not heeding the claws of the beast tearing his flesh, he thrust his knife into its heart.

The jaguar fell, and the Unknown was about turning to go away, when the colonists came up, and Herbert, catching hold of him, exclaimed:—

"No, no, you must not leave us!"

Smith walked towards the man, who frowned at his approach. The blood was flowing from a wound in his shoulder, but he did not heed it.

"My friend," said Smith, "we are in your debt. You have risked your life to save our boy."

"My life," murmured the Unknown; "what is it worth? less than nothing."

"You are wounded?"

"That does not matter."

"Will you not shake hands with me?" asked Herbert.

But on the lad's seeking to take his hand, the Unknown folded his arms, his chest heaved, and he looked about as if he wished to escape; but, making a violent effort at self-control, and in a gruff voice:—

"Who are you?" he asked, "and what are you going to do with me?"

It was their history that he thus asked for, for the first time. Perhaps, if that was related, he would tell his own. So Smith, in a few words, recounted all that had happened since their departure from Richmond; how they had succeeded, and the resources now at their disposal.

The Unknown listened with the utmost attention.

Then Smith told him who they all were, Spilett, Herbert, Pencroff, Neb, himself, and he added that the greatest happiness that had come to them since their arrival on Lincoln Island was on their return from the islet, when they could count one more companion.

At these words the other colored up, and bowing his head, seemed greatly agitated.

"And now that you know us," asked Smith, "will you give us your hand?"

"No," answered the Unknown in a hoarse voice; "no! You are honest men. But I—"

CHAPTER XXXIX.

ALWAYS APART—A BEQUEST OF THE UNKNOWN'S—
THE FARM ESTABLISHED AT THE CORRAL—
TWELVE YEARS—THE BOATSWAIN'S MATE OF THE
BRITANNIA—LEFT ON TABOR ISLAND—THE HAND
OF SMITH—THE MYSTERIOUS PAPER.

These last events justified the presentiments of the colonists. There was some terrible past in the life of this man, expiated, perhaps, in the eyes of men, but which his conscience still held unabsolved. At any rate, he felt remorse; he had repented, and his new friends would have cordially grasped that hand, but he did not feel himself worthy to offer it to honest men. Nevertheless, after the struggle with the jaguar, he did not go back to the forest, but remained within the bounds of Granite House.

What was the mystery of this life? Would he speak of it some day? The colonists thought so, but they agreed that, under no circumstances, would they ask him for his secret; and, in the meantime, to associate with him as if they suspected nothing.

For some days everything went on as usual. Smith and Spilett worked together, sometimes as chemists, sometimes as physicists, the reporter never leaving the engineer, except to hunt with Herbert, as it was not prudent to allow the young lad to traverse the forest alone. As to Neb and Pencroff, the work in the stables and poultry-yard, or at the corral, besides the chores about Granite House, kept them busy.

The Unknown worked apart from the others. He had gone back to his former habit of taking no share in the meals, of sleeping under the trees, of having nothing to do with his companions. It seemed, indeed, as if the society of those who had saved him was intolerable.

"But why, then," asked Pencroff, "did he seek succor from his fellow-creatures; why did he throw this paper in the sea?"

"He will tell us everything," was Smith's invariable answer.

"But when?"

"Perhaps sooner than you think, Pencroff."

And, indeed, on the 10th of December, a week after his return to Granite House, the Unknown accosted the engineer and in a quiet humble voice said:—

"Sir, I have a request to make."

"Speak," replied the engineer, "but, first, let me ask you a question?"

At these words the Unknown colored and drew back. Smith saw what was passing in the mind of the culprit, who feared, doubtless, that the engineer would question him upon his past.

Smith took him by the hand.

"Comrade," said he, "we are not only companions, we are friends. I wanted to say this to you first, now I will listen."

The Unknown covered his eyes with his hand; a sort of tremor seized him, and for some moments he was unable to articulate a word.

"Sir," said he, at length, "I came to implore a favor from you."

"What is it?"

"You have, four or five miles from here, at the foot of the mountain, a corral for your animals. These require looking after. Will you permit me to live over there with them?"

Smith regarded the unhappy man for some time, with deep commiseration. Then:—

"My friend," said he, "the corral has nothing but sheds, only fit for the animals—"

"It will be good enough, for me, sir."

"My friend," replied Smith, "we will never thwart you in anything. If you wish to live in the corral, you may; nevertheless, you will always be welcome at Granite House. But since you desire to stay at the corral, we will do what is necessary to make you comfortable."

"Never mind about that, I will get along well enough."

"My friend," responded Smith, who persisted in the use of this cordial title, "you must let us be the judges in that matter."

The Unknown thanked the engineer and went away. And Smith, having told his companions of the proposition that had been made, they decided to build a log house at the corral, and to make it as comfortable as possible.

The same day the colonists went, with the necessary tools, to the place, and before the week was out the house was ready for its guest. It was built twenty feet from the sheds, at a place where the herd of moufflons, now numbering twenty-four animals, could be easily overlooked. Some furniture, including a bed, table, bench, clothes-press, and chest was made, and some arms, ammunition, and tools, were carried there.

The Unknown, meanwhile, had not seen his new home, letting the colonists work without him, while he remained at the plateau, wishing, doubtless, to finish up his work there. And, indeed, by his exertion the ground was completely tilled, and ready for the sowing when the time should arrive.

On the 20th everything was prepared at the corral, aid the engineer told the Unknown that his house was ready for him, to which the other replied that he would sleep there that night.

The same evening, the colonists were all together in the great hall of Granite House. It was 8 o'clock, the time of their companion's departure; and not wishing by their presence to impose on him the leave-taking, which would, perhaps, have cost him an effort, they had left him alone and gone up into Granite House.

They had been conversing together in the hall for some minutes, when there was a light knock on the door, the Unknown entered, and without further introduction:—

"Before I leave you, sirs," said he, "it is well that you should know my history. This is it."

These simple words greatly affected Smith and companions. The engineer started up.

"We ask to hear nothing, my friend," he said. "It is your right to be silent—"

"It is my duty to speak."

"Then sit down."

"I will stand where I am."

"We are ready to hear what you have to say," said Smith.

The Unknown stood in a shadowed corner of the hall, bare-headed, his arms crossed on his breast. In this position, in a hoarse voice, speaking as one who forces himself to speak, he made the following recital, uninterrupted by any word from his auditors:—

"On the 20th of December, 1854, a steam pleasure-yacht, the Duncan, belonging to a Scotch nobleman, Lord Glenarvan, cast anchor at Cape Bernoulli, on the western coast of Australia, near the thirty-seventh parallel. On board the yacht were Lord Glenarvan, his wife, a major in the English army, a French geographer, a little boy, and a little girl. These two last were the children of Captain Grant, of the ship Britannia, which, with its cargo, had been lost the year before. The Duncan was commanded by Captain John Mangles, and was manned by a crew of fifteen men.

"This is the reason why the yacht was on the Australian coast at that season:—

"Six months before, a bottle containing a paper written in English, German, and French, had been picked up by the Duncan in the Irish Sea. This paper said, in substance, that three persons still survived from the wreck of the Britannia; that they were the captain and two of the men; that they had found refuge on a land of which the latitude and longitude was given, but the longitude, blotted by the sea water, was no longer legible.

"The latitude was 37° 11' south. Now, as the longitude was unknown, if they followed the latitude across continents and seas, they were certain to arrive at the land inhabited by Captain Grant and his companions.

"The English Admiralty, having hesitated to undertake the search, Lord Glenarvan had resolved to do everything in his power to recover the captain. Mary and Robert Grant had been in correspondence with him, and the yacht Duncan was made ready for a long voyage, in which the family of Lord Glenarvan and the children of the captain intended to participate. The Duncan, leaving Glasgow, crossed the Atlantic, passed the Straits of Magellan, and proceeded up the Pacific to Patagonia, where, according to the first theory suggested by the paper, they might believe that Captain Grant was a prisoner to the natives.

"The Duncan left its passengers on the western coast of Patagonia, and sailed for Cape Corrientes on the eastern coast, there to wait for them.

"Lord Glenarvan crossed Patagonia, following the 37th parallel, and, not having found any trace of the captain, he reembarked on the 13th of November, in order to continue his search across the ocean.

"After having visited without success the islands of Tristan d'Acunha and of Amsterdam, lying in the course, the Duncan, as I have stated, arrived at Cape Bernouilli on the 20th of December, 1854.

"It was Lord Glenarvan's intention to cross Australia, as he had crossed Patagonia, and he disembarked. Some miles from the coast was a farm belonging to an Irishman, who offered hospitality to the travellers. Lord Glenarvan told the Irishman the object which had brought him to that region, and asked if he had heard of an English three-master, the Britannia, having been lost, within two years, on the west coast of Australia.

"The Irishman had never heard of this disaster, but, to the great surprise of everybody, one of his servants, intervening, said:—

"'Heaven be praised, my lord. If Captain Grant is still alive he is in Australia.'

"'Who are you?' demanded Lord Glenarvan.

"'A Scotchman, like yourself, my lord,' answered this man, 'and one of the companions of Captain Grant, one of the survivors of the Britannia.'

"This man called himself Ayrton. He had been, in short, boatswain's mate of the Britannia, as his papers proved. But, separated from Captain Grant at the moment when the ship went to pieces on the rocks, he had believed until this moment that every one had perished but himself.

"'Only,' he added, 'it was not on the western but on the eastern coast of Australia that the Britannia was lost; and if the Captain is still living he is a prisoner to the natives, and he must be searched for there.'

"This man said these things frankly and with a confident expression. No one would have doubted what he said. The Irishman, in whose service he had been for more than a year, spoke in his favor. Lord Glenarvan believed in his loyalty, and, following his advice, he resolved to cross Australia, following the 37th parallel. Lord Glenarvan, his wife, the children, the major, the Frenchman, Captain Mangles and some sailors formed the little party under the guidance of Ayrton, while the Duncan, under the command of the mate, Tom Austin, went to Melbourne, to await further instructions.

"They left on the 23d of December, 1861.

"It is time to say that this Ayrton was a traitor. He was, indeed, the boatswain's mate of the Britannia; but, after some dispute with his captain, he had tried to excite the crew to mutiny and seize the ship, and Captain Grant had put him ashore, the 8th of April, 1832, on the west coast of Australia, and had gone off, leaving him there, which was no more than right.

"Thus this wretch knew nothing of the shipwreck of the Britannia. He had just learned it from Lord Glenarvan's recital! Since his abandonment, he had become, under the name of Ben Joyce, the leader of some escaped convicts; and, if he impudently asserted the ship had been lost on the east coast, if he urged Lord Glenarvan to go in that direction, it was in the hope of separating him from his ship, of seizing the Duncan, and of making this yacht a pirate of the Pacific."

Here the Unknown stopped for a moment. His voice trembled, but he began again in these words:—

"The expedition across Australia set out. It was naturally unfortunate, since Ayrton, or Ben Joyce, whichever you wish, led it, sometimes preceded, sometimes followed by the band of convicts, who had been informed of the plot.

"Meanwhile, the Duncan had been taken to Melbourne to await instructions. It was therefore necessary to persuade Lord Glenarvan to order her to leave Melbourne and to proceed to the east coast of Australia, where it would be easy to seize her. After having led the expedition sufficiently near this coast, into the midst of vast forests, where all resources were wanting, Ayrton obtained a letter which he was ordered to deliver to the mate of the Duncan; a letter which gave the order directing the yacht to proceed immediately to the east coast, to Twofold Bay, a place some days journey from the spot where the expedition had halted. It was at this place that Ayrton had given the rendezvous to his accomplices.

"At the moment when this letter was to have been sent, the traitor was unmasked and was obliged to flee. But this letter, giving him the Duncan, must be had at any cost. Ayrton succeeded in getting hold of it, and, in two days afterwards, he was in Melbourne.

"So far, the criminal had succeeded in his odious projects. He could take the Duncan to this Twofold Bay, where it would be easy for the convicts to seize her; and, her crew massacred, Ben Joyce would be master of the sea. Heaven stopped him in the consummation of these dark designs.

"Ayrton, having reached Melbourne, gave the letter to the mate, Tom Austin, who made ready to execute the order; but one can judge of the disappointment and the rage of Ayrton, when, the second day out, he learned that the mate was taking the ship, not to Twofold Bay on the east coast of Australia, but to the east coast of New Zealand. He wished to oppose this, but the mate showed him his order. And, in truth, by a providential error of the French geographer who had written this letter, the eastern coast of New Zealand had been named as their place of destination.

"All the plans of Ayrton had miscarried. He tried to mutiny. They put him in irons; and he was taken to the coast of New Zealand, unaware of what had become of his accomplices, or of Lord Glenarvan.

"The Duncan remained on this coast until the 3d of March. On that day, Ayrton heard firing. It was a salute from the Duncan, and, very soon, Lord Glenarvan and all his party came on board.

"This is what had happened:—

"After innumerable fatigues and dangers, Lord Glenarvan had been able to accomplish his journey and arrived at Twofold Bay. The Duncan was not there! He telegraphed to Melbourne, and received a reply:— 'Duncan sailed on the 18th. Destination unknown.'

"Lord Glenarvan could think of but one explanation, that was that the good yacht had fallen into the hands of Ben Joyce, and had become a pirate ship.

"Nevertheless, Lord Glenarvan did not wish to give up his undertaking. He was an intrepid and a generous man. He embarked on a merchant vessel, which took him to the west coast of New Zealand, and he crossed the country, following the 37th parallel without finding any trace of Captain Grant; but on the other coast, to his great surprise, and by the bounty of Heaven, he found the Duncan, commanded by the mate, which had been waiting for him for five weeks!

"It was the 3d of March, 1855. Lord Glenarvan was again on the Duncan, but Ayrton was there also. He was brought before his lordship, who wished to get from this bandit all that he knew concerning Captain Grant. Ayrton refused to speak. Lord Glenarvan told him, then, that at the first port, he would be given over to the English authorities. Ayrton remained silent.

"The Duncan continued along the thirty-seventh parallel. Meanwhile, Lady Glenarvan undertook to overcome the obstinacy of the bandit, and, finally, her influence conquered him. Ayrton, in exchange for what he would tell, proposed to Lord Glenarvan to leave him upon one of the islands in the Pacific, instead of giving him up to the English authorities. Lord Glenarvan, ready to do anything to gain information concerning Captain Grant, consented.

"Then Ayrton told the history of his life, and declared that he knew nothing about Captain Grant since the day when the latter had left him on the Australian coast.

"Nevertheless, Lord Glenarvan kept the promise he had made. The Duncan, continuing her route, arrived at Tabor Island. It was there that Ayrton was to be left, and it was there, too, that, by a miracle, they found Captain Grant and his two companions. The convict was put upon the island in their stead, and when he left the yacht, Lord Glenarvan spoke to him in these words:—

"'Here, Ayrton, you will be far from any country, and without any possible means of communicating with your fellow-men. You will not be able to leave this island. You will be alone, under the eye of a God who looks into the depths of our hearts, but you will neither be lost nor neglected, like Captain Grant. Unworthy as you are of the remembrance of men, you will be remembered. I know where you are, Ayrton, and I know where to find you. I will never forget it.'

"And the Duncan, setting sail, soon disappeared.

"This was the 18th of March, 1855.

"Ayrton was alone; but he lacked neither ammunition nor arms nor seeds. He, the convict, had at his disposal the house built by the honest Captain Grant. He had only to live and to expiate in solitude the crimes which he had committed.

"Sirs, he repented; he was ashamed of his crimes, and he was very unhappy. He said to himself that, as some day men would come to seek him on this islet, he must make himself worthy to go back with them. How he suffered, the miserable man! How he labored to benefit himself by labor! How he prayed to regenerate himself by prayer!

"For two years, for three years, it was thus. Ayrton, crushed by this isolation, ever on the watch for a ship to appear upon the horizon of his island, asking himself if the time of expiation was nearly ended, suffered as one has rarely suffered. Oh! but solitude is hard, for a soul gnawed by remorse!

"But, doubtless, Heaven found this unhappy wretch insufficiently punished, for he fell, little by little, till he became a savage! He felt, little by little, the brute nature taking possession of him. He cannot say whether this was after two or four years of abandonment, but at last he became the miserable being whom you found.

"I need not tell you, sirs, that Ayrton and Ben Joyce and I are one!"

Smith and his companions rose as this recital was finished. It is hard to say how deeply they were affected! Such misery, such grief, and such despair, had been shown to them!

"Ayrton," said Smith, "you have been a great criminal, but Heaven has, doubtless, witnessed the expiation of your crimes. This is proved, in that you have been restored to your fellow-men. Ayrton, you are pardoned! And now, will you be our companion?"

The man drew back.

"Here is my hand," said the engineer.

Ayrton darted forward and seized it, great tears streaming from his eyes.

"Do you desire to live with us?" asked Smith.

"Oh, Mr. Smith, let me have yet a little time," he answered, "let me remain alone in the house at the corral!"

"Do as you wish, Ayrton," responded Smith.

The unhappy man was about retiring, when Smith asked him a last question.

"One word more, my friend. Since it is your wish to live in solitude, why did you throw that paper, which put us in the way of finding you, into the sea?"

"A paper?" answered Ayrton, who seemed not to understand what was said.

"Yes, that paper, which we found enclosed in a bottle, and which gave the exact situation of Tabor Island?"

The man put his hand to his forehead, and, after some reflection, said:—

"I never threw any paper into the sea!"

"Never!" cried Pencroff.

"Never!"

And then, inclining his head, Ayrton left the room.

CHAPTER XL.

A TALK—SMITH AND SPILETT—THE ENGINEER'S
IDEA—THE ELECTRIC TELEGRAPH—THE WIRES—
THE BATTER-THE ALPHABET—FINE WEATHER—
THE PROSPERITY OF THE COLONY—
PHOTOGRAPHY—A SNOW EFFECT—TWO YEARS ON
LINCOLN ISLAND.

"The poor man!" said Herbert, returning from the door, after having watched Ayrton slide down the rope of the elevator and disappear in the darkness.

"He will come back," said Smith.

"What does it mean?" exclaimed Pencroff. "That he had not thrown this bottle into the sea? Then who did it?"

Certainly, if there was a reasonable question this was.

"He did it," replied Neb; "only the poor fellow was half out of his senses at the time."

"Yes," said Herbert, "and he had no knowledge of what he was doing."

"It can be explained in no other way, my friends," responded Smith, hurriedly, "and I understand, now, how Ayrton was able to give the exact situation of the island, since the events prior to his abandonment gave him that knowledge."

"Nevertheless," observed Pencroff, "he was not a brute when he wrote that paper, and if it is seven or eight years since it was thrown into the sea, how is it that the paper has not been injured by moisture?"

"It proves," said Smith, "that Ayrton retained possession of his faculties to a period much more recent than he imagines."

"That must be it," replied Pencroff, "for otherwise the thing would be inexplicable."

"Inexplicable, indeed," answered the engineer, who seemed not to wish to prolong this talk.

"Has Ayrton told the truth?" questioned the sailor.

"Yes," answered the reporter, "the history he has related is true in every particular. I remember, perfectly well, that the papers reported Lord Glenarvan's undertaking and its result."

"Ayrton has told the truth," added Smith, "without any doubt, Pencroff, since it was trying enough for him to do so. A man does not lie when he accuses himself in this way."

The next day—the 21st—the colonists went down to the beach, and then clambered up to the plateau, but they saw nothing of Ayrton. The man had gone to his house the night before, and they judged it best not to intrude upon him. Time would, doubtless, effect what sympathy would fail to accomplish.

Herbert, Pencroff, and Neb resumed their accustomed occupations; and it happened that their work brought Smith and Spilett together at the Chimneys.

"Do you know, Cyrus, that your explanation of yesterday about the bottle does not satisfy me at all? It is impossible to suppose that this unhappy creature could have written that paper, and thrown the bottle into the sea, without remembering anything about it!"

"Consequently, it is not he who threw it there, my dear Spilett!"

"Then you believe—"

"I believe nothing, I know nothing!" replied Smith, interrupting the reporter. "I place this incident with those others which I have not been able to explain!"

"In truth, Cyrus," said Spilett, "these things are incredible. Your rescue, the box thrown up on the beach, Top's adventures, and now this bottle. Will we never have an answer to these enigmas?"

"Yes," answered the engineer, earnestly, "yes, when I shall have penetrated the bowels of this island!"

"Chance will, perhaps, give us the key to this mystery."

"Chance, Spilett! I do not believe in chance any more than I believe in mystery in this world. There is a cause for everything, however inexplicable, which has happened here, and I will discover it. But, while waiting, let us watch and work."

January arrived, and the year 1867 began. The works had been pushed forward vigorously. One day Herbert and Spilett, passing the corral, ascertained that Ayrton had taken possession of his abode. He occupied himself with the large herd confided to his care, and thus saved his companions the necessity of visiting it two or three times a week. Nevertheless, in order not to leave Ayrton too much alone, they frequently went there.

It was just as well—owing to certain suspicions shared by Smith and Spilett—that this part of the island should be under a certain supervision, and Ayrton, if anything happened, would not fail to let the inhabitants of Granite House know of it.

Possibly, some sudden event might happen, which it would be important to communicate to the engineer without delay. And, aside from whatever might be connected with the mystery of the island, other things, requiring the prompt intervention of the colonists, might occur, as, for example, the discovering of a ship in the offing and in sight of the west coast, a wreck on that shore, the possible arrival of pirates, etc.

So Smith determined to place the corral in instant communication with Granite House.

It was the 10th of January when he told his project to his companions.

"How are you going to do such a thing as that, Mr. Smith?" asked Pencroff. "Maybe you propose to erect a telegraph!"

"That is precisely what I propose to do."

"Electric?" exclaimed Herbert.

"Electric," responded Smith. "We have everything necessary for making a battery, and the most difficult part will be to make the wires, but I think we can succeed."

"Well, after this," replied the sailor, "I expect some day to see us riding along on a railway!"

They entered upon the work at once, beginning with the most difficult part, that is to say, the manufacture of the wires, since, if that failed, it would be useless to make the battery and other accessories.

The iron of Lincoln Island was, as we know, of excellent quality, and, therefore, well adapted to the purpose. Smith began by making a steel plate, pierced with conical holes of different sizes, which would bring the wire to the desired size. This piece of steel, after having been tempered "through and through," was fixed firmly to a solid frame-work sunk in the ground, only a few feet distant from the waterfall—the motive power which the engineer intended to use.

And, indeed, there was the fulling-mill, not then in use, the main shaft of which turned with great force, and would serve to draw out the wire and roll it around itself.

The operation was delicate and required great care. The iron, previously made into long and thin bars, with tapering ends, having been introduced into the largest hole of the drawing-plate, was drawn out by the main shaft of the mill, rolled out to a length of 25 or 30 feet, then unrolled, and pulled, in turn, through the smaller holes; and at length, the engineer obtained wires 30 or 40 feet long, which it was easy to join together and place along the five miles between the corral and Granite House.

It took but a little while to get this work under way, and then, Smith, making his companions the wire-drawers, busied himself in the construction of his battery.

It was necessary to make a battery with a constant circuit. We know that modern batteries are usually made of a certain kind of coke, zinc, and copper. Copper the engineer was without, since, in spite of all his efforts, he had been unable to find a trace of it on the island. The coke, which is that hard deposit obtained from gas retorts could be procured, but it would be necessary to arrange a special apparatus—a difficult thing to do. As to the zinc, it will be remembered that the box found on Jetsam Point, was lined with a sheet of that metal, which could not be better utilized than at present.

Smith, after deep reflection, resolved to make a very simple battery, something like that which Becquerel invented in 1820, in which zinc alone is used. The other substances, nitric-acid and potash, he had at hand.

The manner in which he made this battery, in which the current was produced by the action of the acid and the potash on each other, was as follows:—

A certain number of glass vessels were made and filled with nitric-acid. They were corked with perforated corks, containing glass tubes reaching into the acid, and stopped: with clay plugs, connected with threads. Into these tubes the engineer poured a solution of potash—obtained from burnt plants—and thus the acid and the potash reacted on each other through the clay.

Then Smith plunged two plates of zinc, the one in the nitric acid, the other in the solution, and thus produced a circuit between the tube and jar, and as these plates had been connected by a bit of wire, the one in the tube became the positive and the other the negative pole of the apparatus. Each jar produced its currents, which, together, were sufficient to cause all the phenomena of the electric telegraph.

On the 6th of February they began to erect the poles, furnished with glass insulators, and some days later the wire was stretched, ready to produce the electric current, which travels with the speed of 100,000 kilometres a second.

Two batteries had been made, one for Granite House, and the other for the corral, as, if the corral had to communicate with Granite House, it might, also, be needful for Granite House to communicate with the corral.

As to the indicator and manipulator, they were very simple. At both stations the wire was wrapped around an electro-magnet of soft iron. Communication was established between the two poles; the current, leaving the positive pole, traversed the wire, passed into the electro-magnet, and returned under ground to the negative pole. The current closed, the attraction of the electro-magnet ceased. It was, therefore, sufficient to place a plate of soft iron before the electro-magnet which, attracted while the current is passing, falls, when it is interrupted. The movement of the plate thus obtained, Smith easily fastened to it a needle, pointing to a dial, which bore the letters of the alphabet upon its face.

Everything was finished by the 12th of February. On that day Smith, having turned on the current, asked if everything was all right at the corral, and received, in a few moments, a satisfactory reply from Ayrton.

Pencroff was beside himself with delight, and every morning and evening he sent a telegraph to the corral, which never remained unanswered.

This method of communication presented evident advantages, both in informing the colonists of Ayrton's presence at the corral, and in preventing his complete isolation. Moreover, Smith never allowed a week to pass without visiting him, and Ayrton came occasionally to Granite House, where he always found a kind reception.

Continuing their accustomed work, the fine weather passed away, and the resources of the colony, particularly in vegetables and cereals, increased from day to day, and the plants brought from Tabor Island had been perfectly acclimated. The plateau presented a most attractive appearance. The fourth crop of corn had been excellent, and no one undertook to count the 400,000,000,000 grains produced in the harvest; although Pencroff had had some such idea, until Smith informed him that, supposing he could count 300 grains a minute, or 18,000 an hour, it would take him 5,500 years to accomplish his undertaking.

The weather was superb, though somewhat warm during the day; but, in the evening, the sea-breeze sprung up, tempering the air and giving refreshing nights to the inhabitants of Granite House. Still there were some storms, which, although not long continued, fell upon Lincoln Island with extraordinary violence. For several hours at a time the lightning never ceased illuminating the heavens, and the thunder roared without cessation.

This was a season of great prosperity to the little colony. The denizens of the poultry-yard increased rapidly, and the colonists lived on this increase, as it was necessary to keep the population within certain limits. The pigs had littered, and Pencroff and Neb's attention to these animals absorbed a great part of their time. There were too young onagers, and their parents were often ridden by Spilett and Herbert, or hitched to the cart to drag wood or bring the minerals which the engineer made use of.

Many explorations were made about this time into the depths of the Far West. The explorers did not suffer from the heat, as the sun's rays could not penetrate the leafy roof above them. Thus, they visited all that part to the left of the Mercy, bordering on the route from the corral to the mouth of Fall River.

But during these excursions the colonists took care to be well armed, as they often encountered exceedingly savage and ferocious wild boars. They also waged war against the jaguars, for which animals Spilett had a special hatred, and his pupil, Herbert, seconded him well. Armed as they were, the hunters never shunned an encounter with these beasts, and the courage of Herbert was superb, while the coolness of the reporter was astonishing. Twenty magnificent skins already ornamented the hall at Granite House, and at this rate the jaguars would soon be exterminated.

Sometimes the engineer took part in explorations of the unknown portions of the island, which he observed with minute attention. There were other traces than those of animals which he sought for in the thickest places in the forests, but not once did anything suspicions appear. Top and Jup, who accompanied him, showed by their action that there was nothing there, and yet the dog had growled more than once again above that pit which the engineer had explored without result.

During this season Spilett, assisted by Herbert, took numerous views of the most picturesque portions of the island, by means of the photographic apparatus, which had not been used until now.

This apparatus, furnished with a powerful lens, was very complete. All the substances necessary in photographic work were there; the nitrate of silver, the hyposulphata of soda, the chloride of ammonium, the acetate of soda, and the chloride of gold. Even the paper was there, all prepared, so that all that was necessary, in order to use it, was to steep it for a few moments in diluted nitrate of silver.

The reporter and his assistant soon became expert operators, and they obtained fine views of the neighborhood, such as a comprehensive view of the island taken from Prospect Plateau, with Mount Franklin on the horizon, the mouth of the Mercy so picturesquely framed between its high rocks, the glade and the corral, with the lower spurs of the mountain in the background, the curious outline of Claw Cape, Jetsam Point, etc. Neither did the photographers forget to take portraits of all the inhabitants of the island, without exception.

"Its people," as Pencroff expressed it.

And the sailor was charmed to see his likeness, faithfully reproduced, ornamenting the walls of Granite House, and he stood before this display as pleased as if he had been gazing in one of the richest show-windows on Broadway.

It must be confessed, however, that the portrait, showing the finest execution, was that of master Jup. Master Jup has posed with a gravity impossible to describe, and his picture was a speaking likeness!

"One would say he was laughing!" exclaimed Pencroff.

And if Jup had not been satisfied, he must have been hard to please. But there it was, and he contemplated his image with such a sentimental air, that it was evident he was a little conceited.

The heat of the summer ended with March. The season was rainy, but the air was still warm, and the month was not as pleasant as they had expected. Perhaps it foreboded an early and a rigorous winter.

One morning, the 21st, Herbert had risen early, and, looking from the window, exclaimed:—

"Hullo, the islet is covered with snow!"

"Snow at this season!" cried the reporter, joining the lad.

Their companions were soon beside them, and every one saw that not only the islet, but that the entire beach below Granite House, was covered with the white mantle.

"It is, indeed, snow," said Pencroff.

"Or something very much like it," replied Neb.

"But the thermometer stands at 58°," said Spilett.

Smith looked at the white covering without speaking, for he was, indeed, at a loss how to explain such a phenomenon in this season and in this temperature.

"The deuce!" cried the sailor; "our crops will have been frost-bitten."

And he was about descending when Jup sprang before him and slid down the rope to the ground.

The orang had scarcely touched the earth before the immense body of snow rose and scattered itself through the air in such innumerable flocks as to darken all the heavens for a time.

"They are birds!" cried Herbert.

The effect had, indeed, been produced by myriads of sea-birds, with plumage of brilliant whiteness. They had come from hundreds of miles around on to the islet and the coast, and they now disappeared in the horizon, leaving the colonists as amazed as if they had witnessed a transformation scene, from winter to summer, in some fancy spectacle. Unfortunately, the change had been so sudden that neither the reporter nor the lad had had an opportunity of knocking over some of these birds, whose species they did not recognize.

A few days later, and it was the 26th of March. Two years had passed since the balloon had been thrown upon Lincoln Island.

CHAPTER XLI.

THOUGHTS OF HOME—CHANCES OF RETURN—
PLAN TO EXPLORE THE COAST—THE DEPARTURE OF
THE 16TH OF APRIL—SERPENTINE PENINSULA SEEN
FROM SEA—THE BASALTIC CLIFFS OF THE WESTERN
COAST—BAD WEATHER—NIGHT—A NEW INCIDENT.

Two years already! For two years the colonists had had no communication with their fellows! They knew no more of what was happening in the world, lost upon this island, than if they had been upon the most distant asteroid of the solar system.

What was going on in their country? Their fatherland was always present to their eyes, that land which, when they left it, was torn by civil strife, which perhaps was still red with rebellious blood. It was a great grief to them, this war, and they often talked about it, never doubting, however, that the cause of the North would triumph for the honor of the American confederation.

During these two years not a ship had been seen. It was evident that Lincoln Island was out of the route of vessels; that it was unknown—the maps proved this—was evident, because, although it had no harbor, yet its streams would have drawn thither vessels desiring to renew their supply of water. But the surrounding sea was always desert, and the colonists could count on no outside help to bring them to their home.

Nevertheless, one chance of rescue existed, which was discussed one day in the first week of April, when the colonists were gathered in the hall of Granite House.

They had been talking of America and of the small hope of ever seeing it again.

"Undoubtedly, there is but one way of leaving the island," said Spilett, "which is, to build a vessel large enough to make a voyage of some hundreds of miles. It seems to me, that, when one can build a shallop, they can readily build a ship."

"And that they can as easily go to the Low Archipelago as to Tabor Island," added Herbert.

"I do not say we cannot," replied Pencroff, who always had the most to say on questions of a maritime nature; "I do not say we cannot, although it is very different whether one goes far or near! If our sloop had been threatened with bad weather when we went to Tabor Island, we knew that a shelter was not far off in either direction; but 1,200 miles to travel is a long bit of road, and the nearest land is at least that distance!"

"Do you mean, supposing the case to occur, Pencroff, that you would not risk it?" questioned the reporter.

"I would undertake whatever you wished, sir," replied the sailor, "and you know I am not the man to draw back."

"Remember, moreover, that we have another sailor with us, now," said Neb.

"Who do you mean," asked Pencroff.

"Ayrton."

"That is true," responded Herbert.

"If he would join us," remarked Pencroff.

"Why," said the reporter, "do you think that if Lord Glenarvan's yacht had arrived at Tabor Island while Ayrton was living there, that he would have refused to leave?"

"You forget, my friends," said Smith, "that Ayrton was not himself during the last few years there. But that is not the question. It is important to know whether we can count on the return of this Scotch vessel as among our chances for rescue. Now, Lord Glenarvan promised Ayrton that he would return to Tabor Island, when he judged his crimes sufficiently punished, and I believe that he will return.

"Yes," said the reporter, "and, moreover, I think he will return soon, as already Ayrton has been here twelve years!"

"I, also, think this lord will come back, and, probably, very soon. But where will he come to? Not here, but to Tabor Island."

"That is as sure as that Lincoln Island is not on the maps," said Herbert.

"Therefore, my friends," replied Smith, "we must take the necessary precautions to have Ayrton's and our presence on Lincoln Island advertised on Tabor Island."

"Evidently," said the reporter, "and nothing can be easier than to place in Captain Grant's cabin a notice, giving the situation of our island."

"It is, nevertheless, annoying," rejoined the sailor, "that we forgot to do that on our first voyage to the place."

"Why should we have done so?" replied Herbert. "We knew nothing about Ayrton at that time, and when we learned his history, the season was too far advanced to allow of our going back there."

"Yes," answered Smith, "it was too late then, and we had to postpone the voyage until spring."

"But supposing the yacht comes in the meantime?" asked Pencroff.

"It is not likely," replied the engineer, "as Lord Glenarvan would not choose the winter season to adventure into these distant seas. Either it has already been to the island, in the five months that Ayrton has been with us, or it will come later, and it will be time enough, in the first fine weather of October, to go to Tabor Island and leave a notice there."

"It would, indeed, be unfortunate," said Neb, "if the Duncan has been to and left these seas within a few months."

"I hope that it is not so," answered Smith, "and that Heaven has not deprived us of this last remaining chance."

"I think," observed the reporter, "that, at least, we will know what our chances are, when we have visited the island; for those Stockmen would, necessarily, leave some trace of their visit, had they been there."

"Doubtless," answered the engineer. "And, my friends, since we have this chance of rescue, let us wait patiently, and if we find it has been taken from us, we will see then what to do."

"At any rate," said Pencroff, "it is agreed that if we do leave the inland by some way or another, it will not be on account of ill-treatment!"

"No indeed, Pencroff," replied the reporter, "it will be because we are far from everything which a man loves in this world, his family, his friends, his country!"

Everything having been thus arranged there was no longer any question of building a ship, and the colonists occupied themselves in preparing for their third winter in Granite House.

But they determined, before the bad weather set in, to make a voyage in the sloop around the island. The exploration of the coast had never been completed, and the colonists had only an imperfect idea of its western and northern portions from the mouth of Fall River to the Mandible Capes, and of the narrow bay between them.

Pencroff had proposed this excursion, and Smith had gladly agreed to it, as he wished to see for himself all that part of his domain.

The weather was still unsettled, but the barometer made no rapid changes, and they might expect fair days. So, in the first week of April, after a very low barometer, its rise was followed by a strong west wind, which lasted for five or six weeks; then the needle of the instrument became stationary at a high figure, and everything seemed propitious for the exploration.

The day of departure was set for the 16th, and the Good Luck, moored in Balloon Harbor, was provisioned for a long cruise.

Smith told Ayrton of the excursion, and proposed to him to take part in it; but as Ayrton preferred to remain on shore, it was decided that he should come to Granite House while his companions were absent. Jup was left to keep him company, and made no objection.

On the morning of the 16th all the colonists, including Top, went on board the Good Luck. The breeze blew fresh from the south-west, so that from Balloon Harbor they had to beat up against the wind in order to make Reptile End. The distance between these two points, following the coast, was twenty miles. As the wind was dead ahead, and they had had on starting but two hours of the ebb, it took all day to reach the promontory, and it was night before the point was doubled.

Pencroff proposed to the engineer that they should keep on slowly, sailing under a double-reef, but Smith preferred mooring some cable lengths from shore, in order to survey this part of the coast by daylight.

And it was agreed that henceforth, as a minute exploration of the island was to be made, they would not sail at night, but cast anchor every evening at the most available point.

The wind fell as night approached, and the silence was unbroken. The little party, excepting Pencroff, slept less comfortably than in their beds at Granite House, but still they slept; and at daylight the next morning the sailor raised anchor, and, with a free wind, skirted the shore.

The colonists knew this magnificently wooded border, as they had traversed it formerly, on foot; but its appearance excited renewed admiration. They ran as close in as possible, and moderated their speed in order to observe it carefully. Often, they would cast anchor that Spilett might take photographic views of the superb scenery.

About noon the Good Luck arrived at the mouth of the Fall River. Above, upon the right bank, the trees were less numerous, and three miles further on they grew in mere isolated groups between the western spurs of the mountain, whose arid declivities extended to the very edge of the ocean.

How great was the contrast between the southern and the northern portions of this coast! The one wooded and verdant, the other harsh and savage! It was what they call in certain countries, an "iron-bound coast," and its tempestuous aspect seemed to indicate a sudden crystallization of the boiling basalt in the geologic epochs. How appalling would this hideous mass have been to the colonists if they had chanced to have been thrown on this part of the island! When they were on Mount Franklin, their position had been too elevated for them to recognize the awfully forbidding aspect of this shore; but, viewed from the sea, it presented an appearance, the like of which cannot be seen, perhaps, in any portion of the globe.

The sloop passed for half a mile before this coast. It was composed of blocks of all dimensions from twenty to thirty feet high, and of all sorts of shapes, towers, steeples, pyramids, obelisks, and cones. The ice-bergs of the polar seas could not have been thrown together in more frightful confusion! Here, the rocks formed bridges, there, nave-like arches, of indistinguishable depth; in one place, were excavations resembling monumental vaults, in another a crowd of points outnumbering the pinnacles of a Gothic cathedral. All the caprices of nature, more varied than those of the imagination, were here displayed over a distance of eight or nine miles.

Smith and companions gazed with a surprise approaching stupefaction. But, though they rested mute, Top kept up an incessant barking, which awoke a thousand echoes. The engineer noticed the same strangeness in the dog's action as he showed at the month of the well in Granite House.

"Go alongside," said Smith.

And the Good Luck ran in as close to the rocks as possible. Perhaps there was some cavern here which it would be well to explore. But Smith saw nothing, not even a hollow which could serve as a retreat for any living thing, and the base of the rocks was washed by the surf of the sea. After a time the dog stopped barking, and the sloop kept off again at some cable lengths from the shore.

In the northwest portion of the island the shore became flat and sandy. A few trees rose above the low and swampy ground, the home of myriads of aquatic birds.

In the evening the sloop moored in a slight hollow of the shore, to the north of the island. She was close into the bank, as the water here was of great depth. The breeze died away with nightfall, and the night passed without incident.

The next morning Spilett and Herbert went ashore for a couple of hours and brought back many bunches of ducks and snipe, and by 8 o'clock the Good Luck, with a fair, freshening breeze, was speeding on her way to North Mandible Cape.

"I should not be surprised," said Pencroff, "if we had a squall. Yesterday the sun set red, and, this morning, the cats-tails foreboded no good."

These "cats-tails"—were slender cyrrhi, scattered high above, in the zenith. These feathery messengers usually announce the near disturbance of the elements.

"Very well, then," said Smith, "crowd on all sail and make for Shark Gulf. There, I think the sloop will be safe."

"Perfectly," replied the sailor, "and, moreover, the north coast is nothing but uninteresting downs."

"I shall not regret," added the engineer, "passing, not only the night, but also tomorrow in that bay, which deserves to be explored with care."

"I guess we'll have to, whether we want to or no," replied Pencroff, "as it is beginning to be threatening in the west. See how dirty it looks!"

"Any how, we have a good wind to make Mandible Cape," observed the reporter.

"First rate; but, we will have to tack to get into the gulf, and I would rather have clear weather in those parts which I know nothing about."

"Parts which are sown with reefs," added Herbert, "if I may judge from what we have seen of the coast to the south of the gulf."

"Pencroff," said Smith, "do whatever you think best, we leave everything to you."

"Rest assured, sir," responded the sailor, "I will not run any unnecessary risk. I would rather have a knife in my vitals, than that my Good Luck should run on a rock!"

"What time is it?" asked Pencroff.

"10 o'clock."

"And how far is it to the cape?"

"About fifteen miles."

"That will take two hours and a half. Unfortunately, the tide then will be going down, and it will be a hard matter to enter the gulf with wind and tide against us."

"Moreover," said Herbert, "it is full moon to-day, and these April tides are very strong."

"But, Pencroff," asked Smith, "cannot you anchor at the cape?"

"Anchor close to land, with bad weather coming on!" cried the sailor. "That would be to run ourselves ashore."

"Then what will you do?"

"Keep off, if possible, until the tide turns, which will be about 1 o'clock, and if there is any daylight left try to enter the gulf; if not, we will beat on and off until daylight."

"I have said, Pencroff, that we will leave everything to your judgment."

"Ah," said Pencroff, "if only there was a light-house on this coast it would be easier for sailors."

"Yes," answered Herbert, "and this time we have no thoughtful engineer to light a fire to guide us into harbor."

"By the way, Cyrus," said Spilett, "we have never thanked you for that; but indeed, without that fire we would not have reached—"

"A fire?" demanded Smith, astounded by the words of the reporter.

"We wish to say, sir," said Pencroff, "that we would have been in a bad fix on board the Good Luck, when we were nearly back, and that we would have passed to windward of the island unless you had taken the precaution to light a fire, on the night of the 19th of October, upon the plateau above Granite House."

"Oh, yes, yes! It was a happy thought!" replied Smith.

"And now," added Pencroff, "unless Ayrton thinks of it, there is not a soul to do us this little service."

"No—no one!" replied Smith.

And a moment or two later, being alone with Spilett, the engineer whispered to him:—

"If there is anything sure in this world, Spilett, it is that I never lit a fire on that night, either on the plateau or anywhere else!"

CHAPTER XLII.

NIGHT AT SEA—SHARK GULF—CONFIDENCES—
PREPARATIONS FOR WINTER—EARLY ADVENT
OF BAD WEATHER—COLD—IN-DOOR WORK—
SIX MONTHS LATER—A SPECK ON THE
PHOTOGRAPH—AN UNEXPECTED EVENT.

The sailor's predictions were well founded. The breeze changed to a strong blow such as would hare caused a ship in the open sea to have lowered her topmasts and sailed under close reefs. The sloop was opposite the gulf at 6 o'clock, but the tide was running out, so all that Pencroff could do was to bend the jib down to the mainmast as a stay-sail and lie to with the bows of the Good Luck pointing on shore.

Fortunately, although the wind was strong, the ocean, protected by the coast, was not very rough, and there was no danger from heavy seas, which would have tried the staunchness of the little craft. Pencroff, although he had every confidence in his boat, waited anxiously for daylight.

During the night Smith and Spilett had not another opportunity to talk alone, although the whispered words of the engineer made the reporter anxious to discuss with him again the mysterious influence which seemed to pervade Lincoln Island. Spilett could not rid himself of the thought of this new and inexplicable incident. He and his companions also had certainly seen this light, and yet Smith declared that he knew nothing about it.

He determined to return to this subject as soon as they returned home, and to urge Smith to inform their companions of these strange events. Perhaps, then, they would decide to make, altogether, a thorough search into every part of the island.

Whatever it was, no light appeared upon these unknown shores during this night, and at daylight the wind, which had moderated somewhat, shifted a couple of points, and permitted Pencroff to enter the gulf without difficulty. About 7 o'clock the Good Luck passed into these waters enclosed in a grotesque frame of lava.

"Here," said Pencroff, "is a fine roadstead, where fleets could ride at ease."

"It is curious," remarked Smith, "that this gulf has been formed by two successive streams of lava, completely enclosing its waters; and it is probable that, in the worst weather, the sea here is perfectly calm."

"It is a little too large for the Good Luck," remarked the reporter.

"I admit that," replied the sailor, "but if the navy of the United States needed a shelter in the Pacific, I don't think they could find a better roadstead than this!"

"We are in the shark's jaws," said Neb, alluding to the form of the gulf.

"We are, indeed," replied Herbert; "but, Neb, you are not afraid that they will close on us?"

"No, sir, not that; and yet I don't like the looks of the place. It has a wicked aspect."

"So Neb begins running down my roadstead just as I was thinking to offer it to the United States!" cried Pencroff.

"But are its waters deep enough?" asked the engineer.

"That is easily seen," answered the sailor, taking the sounding line, which measured fifty fathoms, and letting it down. It unrolled to the end without touching bottom.

"There," said Pencroff, "our iron-clads could come here without running aground!"

"In truth," said Smith, "this gulf is an abyss; but when we remember the plutonic origin of the island, that is not extraordinary."

"One might think," said Herbert, "that these walls had been cut with an instrument, and I believe that at their very base, even with a line six times as long, we could not reach the bottom."

"All this is very well," said the reporter, "but I would suggest that Pencroff's roadstead lacks one important element."

"What is that?"

"A cut, or pathway of some kind, by which one could go inland. I do not see a place where there is even a foothold."

And, indeed, these steep lava walls afforded no landing place on all their circumference. The Good Luck, skirting within touching distance of the lava, found no place where the passengers could disembark.

Pencroff consoled himself by saying that they could blow up the wall, if they wanted to, and then, as there was certainly nothing to be done here, he turned towards the narrow opening, which was passed at 2 o'clock.

Neb gave a long sigh of relief. It was evident that the brave negro had not been comfortable in those enormous jaws!

The sloop was now headed for Granite House, eight miles distant, and, with a fair wind, coasted along within a mile of the shore. The enormous lava rocks were soon succeeded by the oddly-disposed downs, among which the engineer had been so singularly discovered, and the place was covered with sea-birds.

Towards 4 o'clock, Pencroff, leaving the islet to the left, entered the channel separating it from the island, and an hour later cast anchor in the Mercy.

The colonists had been absent three days. Ayrton was waiting for them on the shore, and Jup came joyously to welcome them, grinning with satisfaction.

The entire exploration of the coast had been made, and nothing suspicious had been seen. So that if any mysterious being resided on the island, it must be under cover of the impenetrable woods on Serpentine Peninsula, which the colonists had not, as yet, investigated.

Spilett talked the matter over with the engineer, and it was agreed that they should call their comrades' attention to these strange events, the last one of which was the most inexplicable of all.

"Are you sure you saw it, Spilett?" asked Smith, for the twentieth time. "Was it not a partial eruption of the volcano, or some meteor?"

"No, Cyrus, it wag certainly a fire lit by the hand of man. For that matter, question Pencroff and Herbert. They saw it also, and they will confirm my words."

So, some evenings later, on the 26th of April, when all the colonists were gathered together on Prospect Plateau, Smith began:—

"My friends, I want to call your attention to certain things which are happening in our island, and to a subject on which I am anxious to have your advice. These things are almost supernatural—"

"Supernatural!" exclaimed the sailor, puffing his pipe. "Can anything be supernatural?"

"No, Pencroff, but certainly mysterious; unless, indeed, you can explain what Spilett and I have been unable to account for up to this time."

"Let us hear it, Mr. Smith," replied the sailor.

"Very well. Have you understood, then, how, after being thrown into the sea, I was found a quarter of a mile inland, without my having been conscious of getting there?"

"Possibly, having fainted,"—began the sailor.

"That is not admissible," answered the engineer; "but, letting that go, have you understood how Top discovered your retreat five miles from the place where I lay?"

"The dog's instinct," replied Herbert.

"A singular instinct," remarked the reporter, "since, in spite of the storm that was raging, Top arrived at the Chimneys dry and clean!"

"Let that pass," continued the engineer; "have you understood how our dog was so strangely thrown up from the lake, after his struggle with the dugong?"

"No! that I avow," replied Pencroff, "and the wound in the dugong which seemed to have been made by some sharp instrument, I don't understand that at all."

"Let us pass on again," replied Smith. "Have you understood, my friends, how that leaden bullet was in the body of the peccary; how that box was so fortunately thrown ashore, without any trace of a shipwreck; how that bottle, enclosing the paper, was found so opportunely; how our canoe, having broken its rope, floated down the Mercy to us at the very moment when we needed it; how, after the invasion of the monkeys, the ladder was let down from Granite House; how, finally, the document, which Ayrton pretends not to have written, came into our hands?"

Smith had thus enumerated, without forgetting one, the strange events that had happened on the island. Herbert, Pencroff, and Neb looked at each other, not knowing what to say, as this succession of events, thus grouped together, gave them the greatest surprise.

"Upon my faith," said Pencroff, at length, "you are right, Mr. Smith, and it is hard to explain those things."

"Very well, my friends," continued the engineer, "one thing more is to be added, not less incomprehensible than the others!"

"What is that?" demanded Herbert, eagerly.

"When you returned from Tabor Island, Pencroff, you say that you saw a light on Lincoln Island?"

"Certainly I did."

"And you are perfectly sure that you saw it?"

"As sure as that I see you."

"And you, Herbert?"

"Why, Mr. Smith," cried Herbert, "it shone like a star of the first magnitude!"

"But was it not a star?" insisted the engineer.

"No," replied Pencroff, "because the sky was covered with heavy clouds, and, under any circumstances, a star would not have been so low on the horizon. But Mr. Spilett saw it, and he can confirm what we say."

"I would add," said the reporter, "that it was as bright as an electric light."

"Yes, and it was certainly placed above Granite House!" exclaimed Herbert.

"Very well, my friends," replied Smith, "during all that night neither Neb nor I lit any fire at all!"

"You did not!—" cried Pencroff, so overcome with astonishment that he could not finish the sentence.

"We did not leave Granite House, and if any fire appeared upon the coast, it was lit by another hand!"

The others were stupefied with amazement. Undoubtedly a mystery existed! Some inexplicable influence, evidently favorable to the colonists, but exciting their curiosity, made itself felt upon Lincoln Island. Was there then some being hidden in its innermost retreats? They wished to know this, cost what it might!

Smith also recalled to his companions the singular actions of Top and Jup, about the mouth of the well, and he told them that he had explored its depths without discovering anything. And the conversation ended by a determination, on the part of the colonists, to make a thorough search of the island as soon as the spring opened.

After this Pencroff became moody. This island, which he had looked upon as his own, did not belong to him alone, but was shared by another, to whom, whether he would or not, the sailor felt himself inferior. Neb and he often discussed these inexplicable circumstances, and readily concluded that Lincoln Island was subject to some supernatural influence.

The bad weather began early, coming in with May; and the winter occupations were undertaken without delay. The colonists were well protected from the rigor of the season. They had plenty of felt clothing, and the moufflons had furnished a quantity of wool for its further manufacture.

Ayrton had been comfortably clothed, and when the bad weather began, he had returned to Granite House; but he remained humble and sad, never joining in the amusements of his companions.

The most of this third winter was passed by the colonists indoors at Granite House. The storms were frequent and terrible, the sea broke over the islet, and any ship driven upon the coast would have been lost without any chance of rescue. Twice the Mercy rose to such a height that the bridge and causeways were in danger of destruction. Often the gusts of wind, mingled with snow and rain, damaged the fields and the poultry-yard, and made constant repairs necessary.

In the midst of this season, some jaguars and quadrumanes came to the very border of the plateau, and there was danger of the bolder of these beasts making a descent on the fields and domestic animals of the colonists. So that a constant watch had to be kept upon these dangerous visitors, and this, together with the work indoors, kept the little party in Granite House busy.

Thus the winter passed, with now and then a grand hunt in the frozen marshes of Tadorn's Fen. The damage done to the corral during the winter was unimportant, and was soon repaired by Ayrton, who, in the latter part of October, returned there to spend some days at work.

The winter had passed without any new incident. Top and Jup passed by the well without giving any sign of anxiety, and it seemed as if the series of supernatural events had been interrupted. Nevertheless, the colonists were fixed in their determination to make a thorough exploration of the most inaccessible parts of the island, when an event of the gravest moment, which set aside all the plans of Smith and his companions, happened.

It was the 28th of October. Spring was rapidly approaching, and the young leaves were appearing on the trees on the edge of the forest. Herbert, tempted by the beauty of the day, determined to take a photograph of

Union Bay, as it lay facing Prospect Plateau, between Mandible and Claw Capes.

It was 3 o'clock, the horizon was perfectly clear, and the sea, just stirred by the breeze, scintillated with light. The instrument had been placed at one of the windows of Granite House, and the lad, having secured his negative, took the glass into the dark room, where the chemicals were kept, in order to fix it. Returning to the light, after this operation, he saw a speck on the plate, just at the horizon, which he was unable to wash out.

"It is a defect in the glass," he thought.

And then he was seized by a curiosity to examine this speck by means of a magnifying glass made from one of the lenses of the instrument.

Hardly had he given one look, when, uttering a cry of amazement, he ran with the plate and the glass to Smith. The latter examined the speck, and immediately seizing the spy-glass hurried to the window.

The engineer, sweeping the horizon with the glass, found the speck, and spoke one word. "A ship!"

In truth, a ship was in sight of Lincoln Island.

PART III

THE SECRET OF THE ISLAND

CHAPTER XLIII.

LOST OR SAVED?—AYRTON RECALLED—
IMPORTANT DISCUSSION—IT IS NOT THE DUNCAN—
SUSPICION AND PRECAUTION—APPROACH OF THE
SHIP—A CANNON SHOT—THE BRIG ANCHORS IN
SIGHT OF THE ISLAND—NIGHT FALL.

Two years and a half ago, the castaways had been thrown on Lincoln Island; and up to this time they had been cut off from their kind. Once the reporter had attempted to establish communication with the civilized world, by a letter tied to the neck of a bird; but this was an expedient on whose success they could place no reliance. Ayrton, indeed, under the circumstances which have been related, had joined the little colony. And now, on the 17th of October, other men had appeared within sight of the island, on that desert sea! There could be no doubt of it; there was a ship, but would she sail away into the offing, or put in shore? The question would soon be decided. Smith and Herbert hastened to call the others into the great hall of Granite House, and inform them of what had been observed. Pencroff seized the spy-glass and swept the horizon till his gaze fell upon the point indicated.

"No doubt of it, she's a ship!" said he in a tone of no great pleasure.

"Is she coming towards us?" asked Spilett.

"Impossible to say yet," replied Pencroff, "for only her sails are visible; her hull is below the horizon.

"What must we do?" said the boy.

"We must wait," said Smith.

And for a time which seemed interminable, the colonists remained in silence, moved alternately by fear and hope. They were not in the situation of castaways upon a desert island, constantly struggling with niggardly Nature for the barest means of living, and always longing to got back to their fellow-men. Pencroff and Neb, especially, would have quitted the island with great regret. They were made, in truth, for the new life which they were living in a region civilized by their own exertions! Still, this ship would bring them news of the Continent; perhaps it was an American vessel; assuredly it carried men of their own race, and their hearts beat high at the thought!

From time to time, Pencroff went to the window with the glass. From thence he examined the ship carefully. She was still twenty miles to the east, and they had no means of communication with her. Neither flag nor fire would have been seen; nor would the report of a gun be heard. Yet the island, with Mount Franklin towering high above it, must be visible to the lookout men on the ship. But why should the vessel land there? Was it not mere chance which brought it into that part of the Pacific, out of the usual track, and when Tabor Island was the only land indicated on the maps? But here a suggestion came from Herbert.

"May it not be the Duncan?" cried he.

The Duncan, as our readers will remember, was Lord Glenarvan's yacht, which had abandoned Ayrton on the islet, and was one day to come back for him. Now the islet was not so far from Lincoln Island but that a ship steering for one might pass within sight of the other. They were only 150 miles distant in longitude, and 75 in latitude.

"We must warn Ayrton," said Spilett, "and tell him to come at once. Only he can tell us whether she is the Duncan."

This was every one's opinion, and the reporter, going to the telegraph apparatus, which communicated with the corral, telegraphed. "Come at once." Soon the wire clicked, "I am coming." Then the colonists turned again to watch the ship.

"If it is the Duncan," said Herbert, "Ayrton will readily recognize her, since he was aboard her so long."

"It will make him feel pretty queer!" said Pencroff.

"Yes," replied Smith, "but Ayrton is now worthy to go on board again, and may Heaven grant it to be indeed the Duncan! These are dangerous seas for Malay pirates."

"We will fight for our island," said Herbert.

"Yes, my boy," answered the engineer, smiling, "but it will be better not to have to fight for her."

"Let me say one thing," said Spilett. "Our island is unknown to navigators, and it is not down in the most recent maps. Now, is not that a good reason for a ship which unexpectedly sighted it to try to run in shore?"

"Certainly," answered Pencroff.

"Yes," said the engineer, "it would even be the duty of the captain to report the discovery of any island not on the maps, and to do this he must pay it a visit."

"Well," said Pencroff, "suppose this ship casts anchor within a few cables' length of our island, what shall we do?"

This downright question for a while remained unanswered. Then Smith, after reflection, said in his usual calm tone:—

"What we must do, my friends, is this. We will open communication with the ship, take passage on board of her, and leave our island, after having taken possession of it in the name of the United States of America.

Afterwards we will return with a band of permanent colonists, and endow our Republic with a useful station on the Pacific!"

"Good!" said Pencroff, "that will be a pretty big present to our country! We have really colonized it already. We have named every part of the island; there is a natural port, a supply of fresh water, roads, a line of telegraph, a wood yard, a foundry; we need only put the island on the maps!"

"But suppose some one else should occupy it while we are gone?" said Spilett.

"I would sooner stay here alone to guard it," cried the sailor, "and, believe me, they would not steal it from me, like a watch from a gaby's pocket!"

For the next hour, it was impossible to say whether or not the vessel was making for the island. She had drawn nearer, but Pencroff could not make out her course. Nevertheless, as the wind blew from the northeast, it seemed probable that she was on the starboard tack. Besides, the breeze blew straight for the landing, and the sea was so calm that she would not hesitate to steer for the island, though the soundings were not laid down in the charts.

About 4 o'clock, an hour after he had been telegraphed for, Ayrton arrived. He entered the great hall, saying, "Here I am, gentlemen."

Smith shook hands with him, and drawing him to the window, "Ayrton," said he, "we sent for you for a weighty reason. A ship is within sight of the island."

For a moment Ayrton looked pale, and his eyes were troubled. Then he stooped down and gazed around the horizon.

"Take this spy-glass," said Spilett, "and look well, Ayrton, for it may be the Duncan come to take you home."

"The Duncan!" murmured Ayrton. "Already!"

The last word escaped him involuntarily and he buried his face in his hands. Did not twelve years' abandonment on a desert island seem to him a sufficient expiation?

"No," said he, "no, it cannot be the Duncan."

"Look, Ayrton," said the engineer, "for we must know beforehand with whom we have to deal."

Ayrton took the glass and levelled it in the direction indicated. For some minutes he observed the horizon in silence. Then he said:—

"Yes, it is a ship, but I do not think it is the Duncan.

"Why not?" asked Spilett.

"Because the Duncan is a steam-yacht, and I see no trace of smoke about this vessel."

"Perhaps she is only under sail," observed Pencroff. "The wind is behind her, and she may want to save her coal, being go far from land."

"You may be right, Mr. Pencroff," said Ayrton. "But, let her come in shore, and we shall soon know what to make of her."

So saying, he sat down in a corner and remained silent, taking no part in the noisy discussion about the unknown ship. No more work was done. Spilett and Pencroff were extremely nervous; they walked up and down, changing place every minute. Herbert's feeling was one of curiosity. Neb alone remained calm; his master was his country. The engineer was absorbed in his thoughts, and was inclined to believe the ship rather an enemy than a friend. By the help of the glass they could make out that she was a brig, and not one of those Malay proas, used by the pirates of the Pacific. Pencroff, after a careful look, affirmed that the ship was square-rigged, and was running obliquely to the coast, on the starboard tack, under mainsail, topsail, and top-gallant sail set.

Just then the ship changed her tack, and drove straight towards the island. She was a good sailer, and rapidly neared the coast. Ayrton took the glass to try to ascertain whether or not she was the Duncan. The Scotch yacht, too, was square-rigged. The question therefore was whether a smokestack could be seen between the two masts of the approaching vessel. She was now only ten miles off, and the horizon was clear. Ayrton looked for a moment, and then dropped his glass.

"It is not the Duncan," said he.

Pencroff sighted the brig again, and made out that she was from 300 to 400 tons burden, and admirably built for sailing. To what nation she belonged no one could tell.

"And yet," added the sailor, "there's a flag floating at her peak, but I can't make out her colors."

"In half an hour we will know for certain," answered the reporter. "Besides, it is evident that their captain means to run in shore, and to-day, or to-morrow at latest, we shall make her acquaintance."

"No matter, "said Pencroff, "we ought to know with whom we have to deal, and I shall be glad to make out those colors."

And he kept the glass steadily at his eye. The daylight began to fail, and the sea-wind dropped with it. The brig's flag wrapped itself around the tackle, and could hardly be seen.

"It is not the American flag," said Pencroff, at intervals, "nor the English, whose red would be very conspicuous, nor the French, nor German colors, nor the white flag of Russia, nor the yellow flag of Spain. It seems to be of one solid color. Let us see; what would most likely be found in these waters? The Chilian—no, that flag is tri-colored; the Brazilian is green; the Japanese is black and yellow; while this—"

Just then a breeze struck the flag. Ayrton took the glass and raised it to his eyes.

"Black!" cried he, in a hollow voice.

They had suspected the vessel with good reason. The piratical ensign was fluttering at the peak!

A dozen ideas rushed across the minds of the colonists; but there was no doubt as to the meaning of the flag. It was the ensign of the spoilers of the sea; the ensign which the Duncan would have carried, if the convicts had succeeded in their criminal design. There was no time to be lost in discussion.

"My friends," said Smith, "this vessel, perhaps, is only taking observations of the coast of our island, and will send no boats on shore. We must do all we can to hide our presence here. The mill on Prospect Plateau is too conspicuous. Let Ayrton and Neb go at once and take down its fans. "We must cover, the windows of Granite House under thicker branches. Let the fires be put out, and nothing be left to betray the existence of man!"

"And our sloop?" said Herbert.

"Oh," said Pencroff, "she is safe in port in Balloon Harbor, and I defy the rascals to find her there!"

The engineer's orders were instantly carried out. Neb and Ayrton went up to the plateau and concealed every trace of human habitation. Meanwhile their companions went to Jacamar Woods and brought back a great quantity of branches and climbing plants, which could not, from a distance, be distinguished from a natural foliation, and would hide well enough the windows in the rock. At the same time their arms and munitions were piled ready at hand, in case of a sudden attack. When all these precautions had been taken Smith turned to his comrades—

"My friends," said he, in a voice full of emotion, "if these wretches try to get possession of the island we will defend it, will we not?"

"Yes, Cyrus," answered the reporter, "and, if need be, we will die in its defense."

And they shook hands upon it. Ayrton alone remained seated in his corner. Perhaps he who had been a convict himself once, still deemed himself unworthy! Smith understood what was passing in his mind, and, stepping towards him, asked

"And what will you do, Ayrton?"

"My duty," replied Ayrton. Then he went to the window, and his eager gaze sought to penetrate the foliage. It was then half-past 7 o'clock. The sun had set behind Granite House twenty minutes before, and the eastern horizon was darkening. The brig was nearing Union Bay. She was now about eight miles away, and just abreast of Prospect Plateau, for having tacked off Claw Cape, she had been carried in by the rising tide. In fact she was already in the bay, for a straight line drawn from Claw Cape to Mandible Cape would have passed to the other side of her.

Was the brig going to run into the bay? And if so, would she anchor there? Perhaps they would be satisfied with taking an observation. They could do nothing but wait. Smith was profoundly anxious. Had the pirates been on the island before, since they hoisted their colors on approaching it? Might they not have effected a descent once before, and might not some accomplice be now concealed in the unexplored part of the island. They were determined to resist to the last extremity. All depended on the arms and the number of the pirates.

Night had come. The new moon had set a few moments after the sun. Profound darkness enveloped land and sea. Thick masses of clouds were spread over the sky. The wind had entirely died away. Nothing could be seen of the vessel, for all her lights were hidden—they could tell nothing of her whereabouts.

"Who knows?" said Pencroff. "Perhaps the confounded ship will be off by morning."

His speech was answered by a brilliant flash from the offing, and the sound of a gun. The ship was there, and she had artillery. Six seconds had elapsed between the flash and the report; the brig, therefore, was about a mile and a-quarter from the shore. Just then, they heard the noise of chain-cables grinding across the hawse-holes. The vessel was coming to anchor in sight of Granite House!

CHAPTER XLIV.

DISCUSSIONS—PRESENTIMENTS—
AYRTON'S PROPOSAL—IT IS ACCEPTED—
AYRTON AND PENCROFF ON SAFETY ISLET—
NORFOLK CONVICTS—THEIR PROJECTS—
HEROIC ATTEMPT OF AYRTON—HIS RETURN—
SIX AGAINST FIFTY.

There was no longer room for doubt as to the pirate's intentions. They had cast anchor at a short distance from the island, and evidently intended to land on the morrow.

Brave as they were, the colonists felt the necessity of prudence. Perhaps their presence could yet be concealed in case the pirates were contented with landing on the coast without going up into the interior. The latter, in fact, might have nothing else in view than a supply of fresh water, and the bridge, a mile and a half up stream, might well escape their eye.

The colonists knew now that the pirate ship carried heavy artillery, against which they had nothing but a few shot-guns.

"Still," said Smith, "our situation is impregnable. The enemy cannot discover the opening in the weir, so thickly is it covered with reeds and grass, and consequently cannot penetrate into Granite House."

"But our plantations, our poultry-yard, our corral,—in short everything," cried Pencroff, stamping his foot. "They can destroy everything in a few hours."

"Everything, Pencroff!" answered Smith, "and we have no means of preventing them?"

"Are there many of them?" said the reporter. "That's the question. If there are only a dozen, we can stop them, but forty, or fifty, or more—"

"Mr. Smith," said Ayrton, coming up to the engineer, "will you grant me one request!"

"What, my friend?"

"To go to the ship, and ascertain how strongly she is manned."

"But, Ayrton," said the engineer, hesitating, "your life will be in danger."

"And why not, sir?"

"That is more than your duty."

"I must do more than my duty," replied Ayrton.

"You mean to go to the ship in the canoe?" asked Spilett.

"No, sir. I will swim to her. A man can slip in where a boat could not pass."

"Do you know that the brig is a mile and a half from the coast?" said Herbert."

"I am a good swimmer, sir."

"I repeat to you that you are risking your life," resumed the engineer.

"No matter," answered Ayrton—"Mr. Smith, I ask it as a favor. It may raise me in my own estimation."

"Go, Ayrton," said the engineer, who knew how deeply a refusal would affect the ex-convict, now become an honest man.

"I will go with you," said Pencroff.

"You distrust me!" said Ayrton, quickly. Then, he added, more humbly, "and it is just."

"No, no!" cried Smith, eagerly, "Pencroff has no such feeling. You have misunderstood him."

"Just so," answered the sailor; "I am proposing to Ayrton to accompany him only as far as the islet. One of these rascals may possibly have gone on shore there, and if so, it will take two men to prevent him from giving the alarm. I will wait for Ayrton on the islet."

Everything thus arranged, Ayrton got ready for departure. His project was bold but not impracticable, thanks to the dark night. Once having reached the ship, Ayrton, by clinging to the chains of the shrouds, might ascertain the number and perhaps the designs of the convicts. They walked down upon the beach. Ayrton stripped himself and rubbed himself with grease, the better to endure the chill of the water; for he might have to be in it several hours. Meanwhile Pencroff and Neb had gone after the canoe, fastened on the bank of the Mercy some hundreds of paces further up. When they came back, Ayrton was ready to start.

They threw a wrap over his shoulders, and shook hands with him all round. Then he got into the boat with Pencroff, and pushed off into the darkness. It was now half-past 10, and their companions went back to wait for them at the Chimneys.

The channel was crossed without difficulty, and the canoe reached the opposite bank of the islet. They moved cautiously, lest pirates should have landed there. But the island was deserted. The two walked rapidly over it, frightening the birds from their nests in the rocks. Having reached the further side, Ayrton cast himself unhesitatingly into the sea, and swam noiselessly towards the ship's lights, which now were streaming across the water. Pencroff hid himself among the rocks, to await his companion's return.

Meanwhile, Ayrton swam strongly towards the ship, slipping through the water. His head only appeared above the surface; his eyes were fixed on the dark hull of the brig, whose lights were reflected in the water. He thought only of his errand, and nothing of the danger he encountered, not only from the pirates but from the sharks which infested these waters. The current was in his favor, and the shore was soon far behind.

Half an hour afterwards, Ayrton, without having been perceived by any one, dived under the ship, and clung with one hand to the bowsprit. Then he drew breath, and, raising himself by the chains, climbed to the end of the cut-water. There some sailors' clothes hung drying. He found an easy position, and listened.

They were not asleep on board of the brig. They were talking, singing, and laughing. These words, intermingled with oaths, came to Ayrton's ears;—

"What a famous find our brig was!"

"The Speedy is a fast sailor. She deserves her name."

"All the Norfolk shipping may do their best to take her."

"Hurrah for her commander. Hurrah for Bob Harvey!"

Our readers will understand what emotion was excited in Ayrton by this name, when they learn that Bob Harvey was one of his old companions in Australia, who had followed out his criminal projects by getting possession, off Norfolk Island, of this brig, charged with arms, ammunition, utensils, and tools of all kinds, destined for one of the Sandwich Islands. All his band had gotten on board, and, adding piracy to their other crimes, the wretches scoured the Pacific, destroying ships and massacring their crews. They were drinking deep and talking loudly over their exploits, and Ayrton gathered the following facts:—

The crew were composed entirely of English convicts, escaped from Norfolk Island. In 29° 2' south latitude, and 165° 42' east longitude, to the east of Australia, is a little island about six leagues in circumference, with Mount Pitt rising in the midst, 1,100 feet above the level of the sea. It is Norfolk Island, the seat of an establishment where are crowded together the most dangerous of the transported English convicts. There are 500 of them; they undergo a rigid discipline, with severe punishment for disobedience, and are guarded by 150 soldiers and 150 civil servants, under the authority of a Governor. A worse set of villains cannot be imagined. Sometimes, though rarely, in spite of the extreme precautions of their jailors, some of them contrive to escape by seizing a ship, and become the pest of the Polynesian archipelagos. Thus had done Harvey and his companions. Thus had Ayrton formerly wished to do. Harvey had seized the Speedy, which was anchored within sight of Norfolk Island, had massacred the crew, and for a year had made the brig the terror of the Pacific.

The convicts were most of them gathered on the poop, in the after part of the ship; but a few were lying on deck, talking in loud voices. The conversation went on amid noise and drunkenness. Ayrton gathered that chance only had brought them within sight of Lincoln Island. Harvey had never set foot there; but, as Smith had foreseen, coming upon an island not in the maps, he had determined to go on shore, and, if the land suited him, to make it the Speedy's headquarters. The black flag and the cannon-shot were a mere freak of the pirates, to imitate a ship-of-war running up her colors.

The colonists were in very serious danger. The island, with its easy water supply, its little harbor, its varied resources so well turned to account by the colonists, its secret recesses of Granite House—all these would be just what the convicts wanted. In their hands the island would become an excellent place of refuge, and the fact of its being unknown would add to their security. Of course the colonists would instantly be put to death. They could not even escape to the interior, for the convicts would make the island their headquarters, and if they went on an expedition would leave some of the crew behind. It would be a struggle for life and death with these wretches, every one of whom must be destroyed before the colonists would be safe. Those were Ayrton's thoughts, and he knew that Smith would agree with him. But was a successful resistance possible? Everything depended on the calibre of the brig's guns and the number of her men. These were facts which Ayrton must know at any cost.

An hour after he had reached the brig the noise began to subside, and most of the convicts lay plunged in a drunken sleep. Ayrton determined to risk himself on the ship's deck, which the extinguished lanterns left in profound darkness. He got in the chains by the cut-water, and by means of the bowsprit climbed to the brig's forecastle. Creeping quietly through the sleeping crew, who lay stretched here and there on the deck, he walked completely around the vessel and ascertained that the Speedy carried four guns, from eight to ten-pounders. He discovered also that the guns were breech-loading, of modern make, easily worked, and capable of doing great damage.

There were about ten men lying on deck, but it might be that others were asleep in the hold. Moreover, Ayrton had gathered from the conversation that there were some fifty on board; rather an overmatch for the six colonists. But, at least, the latter would not be surprised; thanks to Ayrton's devotion, they would know their adversaries force, and would make their dispositions accordingly. Nothing remained for Ayrton but to go back to his comrades with the information he had gathered, and he began walking towards the forecastle to let himself down into the sea.

And now to this man, who wished to do more than his duty, there came a heroic thought, the thought of sacrificing his life for the safety of his comrades. Smith could not of course resist fifty well-armed marauders, who would either overcome him or starve him out. Ayrton pictured to himself his preservers who had made a man of him, and an honest man, to whom he owed everything, pitilessly murdered, their labors brought to nothing, their island changed to a den of pirates. He said to himself that he, Ayrton, was the first cause of these disasters, since his old companion, Harvey, had only carried out Ayrton's projects; and a feeling of horror came over him. Then came the irresistible desire to blow up the brig, with all on board. He would perish in the explosion, but he would have done his duty.

He did not hesitate! It was easy to reach the powder magazine, which is always in the after part of the ship. Powder must be plenty on board such a vessel, and a spark would bring destruction.

Ayrton lowered himself carefully between-decks, where he found many of the pirates lying about, overcome rather by drunkenness than sleep. A ship's lantern, was lighted at the foot of the mainmast, from which hung a rack full of all sorts of firearms. Ayrton took from the rack a revolver, and made sure that it was loaded and capped. It was all that he needed to accomplish the work of destruction. Then he glided back to the poop, where the powder magazine would be.

Between decks it was dark, and he could hardly step without knocking against some half-asleep convict, and meeting with an oath or a blow. More than once he had to stop short, but at length he reached the partition separating the after-compartment, and found the door of the magazine. This he had to force, and it was a difficult matter to accomplish without noise, as he had to break a padlock. But at last, under his vigorous hand, the padlock fell apart and the door opened.

Just then a hand was laid upon his shoulder.

"What are you doing there?" said a harsh voice, and a tall form rose from the shadow and turned the light of a lantern fall on Ayrton's face.

Ayrton turned around sharply. By a quick flash from the lantern, he saw his old accomplice, Harvey; but the latter, believing Ayrton, as he did, to be dead, failed to recognize him.

"What are you doing there?" said Harvey, seizing Ayrton by the strap of his trousers. Ayrton made no answer but a vigorous push, and sprang forward to the magazine. One shot into those tons of powder, and all would have been over!

"Help, lads!" cried Harvey.

Two or three pirates, roused by his voice, threw themselves upon Ayrton, and strove to drag him to the ground. He rid himself of them with two shots from his revolver; but received in so doing, a wound from a knife in the fleshy part of the shoulder. He saw in a moment that his project was no longer feasible. Harvey had shut the door of the magazine, and a dozen pirates were half-awake. He most save himself for the sake of his comrades.

Four barrels were left. He discharged two of them right and left, one at Harvey, though without effect; and then, profiting by his enemies' momentary recoil, rushed towards the ladder which led to the deck of the brig. As he passed the lantern he knocked it down with a blow from the butt-end of his pistol, and left everything in darkness.

Two or three pirates, awakened by the noise, were coming down the ladder at that moment. A fifth shot stretched one at the foot of the steps, and the others got out of the way, not understanding what was going on. In two bounds Ayrton was on the brig's deck, and three seconds afterwards, after discharging his last shot at a pirate who tried to seize him by the neck, he made his way down the netting and leaped into the sea. He had not swam six fathoms before the bullets began to whistle around him like hail.

What were the feelings of Pencroff, hidden behind a rock on the islet, and of his comrades in the Chimneys, when they heard these shots from the brig! They rushed out upon the shore, and, with their guns at their shoulders, stood ready to meet any attack. For them no doubt remained. They believed that Ayrton had been killed, and the pirates were about to make a descent on the island. Thus half an hour passed away. They suffered torments of anxiety. They could not go to the assistance of Ayrton or Pencroff, for the boat had been taken, and the high tide forbade them crossing the channel.

Finally, at half-past 12, a boat with two men came along shore. It was Ayrton, with a slight wound in his shoulder, and Pencroff. Their friends received them with open arms.

Then all took refuge at the Chimneys. There Ayrton told them all that happened, including his plan to blow up the brig.

Every one grasped the man's hand, but the situation was desperate. The pirates knew that Lincoln Island was inhabited, and would come down upon it in force. They would respect nothing. If the colonists fell into their hands they had no mercy to hope for!

"We can die like men," said the reporter.

"Let us go in and keep watch," said the engineer.

"Do you think there is any chance, Mr. Smith?" said the sailor.

"Yes, Pencroff."

"How! Six against fifty!"

"Yes, six—and one other—"

"Who?" asked Pencroff.

Smith did not answer, but he looked upwards

CHAPTER XLV.

THE MIST RISES—THE ENGINEER'S DISPOSITION OF
FORCES—THREE POSTS—AYRTON AND PENCROFF—
THE FIRST ATTACK—TWO OTHER BOAT LOADS—
ON THE ISLET—SIX CONVICTS ON SHORE—
THE BRIG WEIGHS ANCHOR—THE SPEEDY'S
PROJECTILES—DESPERATE SITUATION—
UNEXPECTED DENOUEMENT.

The night passed without incident. The colonists were still at the Chimneys, keeping a constant lookout. The pirates made no attempt at landing. Since the last shots fired at Ayrton, not a sound betrayed the presence of the brig in the bay. They might have supposed she had weighed anchor and gone off in the night.

But it was not so, and when daylight began to appear the colonists could see her dark hulk dim through the morning mists.

"Listen, my friends," then said the engineer. "These are the dispositions it seems to me best to make before the mist dispels, which conceals us from view. We must make these convicts believe that the inhabitants of the island are numerous and well able to resist them. Let us divide ourselves into three groups, one posted at the Chimneys, one at the mouth of the Mercy, and the third upon the islet, to hinder, or at least, retard, every attempt to land. We have two carbines and four guns, so that each of us will be armed; and as we have plenty of powder and ball, we will not spare our shots. We have nothing to fear from the guns, nor even from the cannon of the brig. What can they effect against these rocks? And as we shall not shoot from the windows of Granite House, the pirates will never think of turning their guns upon it. What we have to fear is a hand-to-hand fight with an enemy greatly superior in numbers. We must try to prevent their landing without showing ourselves. So don't spare your ammunition. Shoot fast, and shoot straight. Each of us has eight or ten enemies to kill, and must kill them."

Smith had precisely defined the situation, in a voice as quiet as if he were directing some ordinary work. His companions acted upon his proposal without a word. Each hastened to take his place before the mist should be entirely dissipated.

Neb and Pencroff went back to Granite House and brought back thence abundance of ammunition. Spilett and Ayrton, both excellent shots, were armed with the two carbines, which would carry nearly a mile. The four shot-guns were divided between Smith, Neb, Pencroff, and Herbert. The posts were thus filled:—Smith and Herbert remained in ambush at the Chimneys, commanding a large radius of the shore in front of Granite House. Spilett and Neb hid themselves among the rocks at the mouth of the Mercy (the bridge and causeways over which had been removed), so as to oppose the passage of any boat or even any landing on the opposite side. As to Ayrton and Pencroff, they pushed the canoe into the water, and got ready to push across the channel, to occupy two different points on the islet, so that the firing, coming from four different points, might convince the pirates that the island was both well manned and vigorously defended.

In case a landing should be effected in spite of their opposition, or should they be in danger of being cut off by a boat from the brig, Pencroff and Ayrton could return with the canoe to the shore of the island, and hasten to the threatened point.

Before going to their posts, the colonists shook hands all round. Pencroff concealed his emotion as he embraced "his boy" Herbert, and they parted. A few minutes afterwards each was at his post. None of them could have been seen, for the brig itself was barely visible through the mist. It was half-past 6 in the morning. Soon the mist rose gradually; the ocean was covered with ripples, and, a breeze rising, the sky was soon clear. The Speedy appeared, anchored by two cables, her head to the north, and her larboard quarter to the island. As Smith had calculated, she was not more than a mile and a quarter from the shore. The ominous black flag floated at the peak. The engineer could see with his glass that the four guns of the ship had been trained on the island, ready to be fired at the first signal; but so far there was no sound. Full thirty pirates could be seen coming and going on the deck. Some were on the poop; two on the transoms of the main topmast were examining the island with spy-glasses. In fact, Harvey and his crew must have been exceedingly puzzled by the adventure of the night, and especially by Ayrton's attempt upon the powder magazine. But they could not doubt that the island before them was inhabited by a colony ready to defend it. Yet no one could be seen either on the shore or the high ground.

For an hour and a half there was no sign of attack from the brig. Evidently Harvey was hesitating. But about 8 o'clock there was a movement on board. They were hauling at the tackle, and a boat was being let down into the sea. Seven men jumped into it, their guns in their hands. One was at the tiller, four at the oars, and the two others squatting in the bow, ready to shoot, examined the island. No doubt their intention was to make a reconnoissance, and not to land, or they would have come in greater number.

The pirates, perched on the rigging of the topmast, had evidently perceived that an islet concealed the shore, lying about half a mile away. The boat was apparently not running for the channel, but was making for the islet, as the most prudent beginning of the reconnoissance. Pencroff and Ayrton, lying hidden among the rocks, saw it coming down upon them, and even waiting for it to get within good reach.

It came on with extreme caution. The oars fell at considerable intervals. One of the convicts seated in front had a sounding-line in his hand, with which he was feeling for the increased depth of water caused by the current of the Mercy. This indicated Harvey's intention of bringing his brig as near shore as possible. About thirty pirates were scattered among the shrouds watching the boat and noting certain sea-marks which would enable them to land without danger. The boat was but two cables' length from the islet when it stopped. The helmsman, standing erect, was trying to find the best place to land. In a moment burst forth a double flash and report. The helmsman and the man with the line fell over into the boat. Ayrton and Pencroff had done their work. Almost at once came a puff of smoke from the brig, and a cannon ball struck the rock, at whose foot the two lay sheltered, making it fly into shivers; but the marksmen remained unhurt.

With horrible imprecations the boat resumed its course. The helmsman was replaced by one of his comrades, and the crew bent to their oars, eager to get beyond reach of bullets. Instead of turning back, they pulled for the southern extremity of the islet, evidently with the intention of coming up on the other side and putting Pencroff and Ayrton between two fires. A quarter of an hour passed thus without a sound. The defenders of the islet, though they understood the object of the flanking movement, did not leave their post. They feared the cannon of the Speedy, and counted upon their comrades in ambush.

Twenty minutes after the first shots, the boat was less than two cables' length off the Mercy. The tide was running up stream with its customary swiftness, due to the narrowness of the river, and the convicts had to row hard to keep themselves in the middle of the channel. But as they were passing within easy range of the river's mouth, two reports were heard, and two of the crew fell back into the boat. Neb and Spilett had not missed their shot. The brig opened fire upon their hiding place, which was indicated by the puff of smoke; but with no result beyond shivering a few rocks.

The boat now contained only three men fit for action. Getting into the current, it shot up the channel like an arrow, passed Smith and Herbert, who feared to waste a shot upon it, and turned the northern point of the islet, whence the two remaining oarsmen pulled across to the brig.

So far the colonists could not complain. Their adversaries had lost the first point in the game. Four pirates had been grievously wounded, perhaps killed, while they were without a scratch. Moreover, from the skilful disposition of their little force, it had no doubt given the impression of a much greater number.

A half hour elapsed before the boat, which was rowing against the current, could reach the Speedy. The wounded were lifted on deck, amid howls of rage. A dozen furious convicts manned the boat; another was lowered into the sea, and eight more jumped into it; and while the former rowed straight for the islet, the latter steered around its southern point, heading for the Mercy.

Pencroff and Ayrton were in a perilous situation. They waited till the first boat was within easy range, sent two balls into her, to the great discomfort of the crew; then they took to their heels, running the gauntlet of a dozen shots, reached their canoe on the other side of the islet, crossed the channel just as the second boat load of pirates rounded the southern point, and hastened to hide themselves at the Chimneys. They had hardly rejoined Smith and Herbert, when the islet was surrounded and thoroughly searched by the pirates.

Almost at the same moment shots were heard from the mouth of the Mercy. As the second boat approached them, Spilett and Neb disposed of two of the crew; and the boat itself was irresistibly hurried upon the rocks at the mouth of the river. The six survivors, holding their guns above their heads to keep them from contact with the water, succeeded in getting on shore on the right bank of the river; and, finding themselves exposed to the fire of a hidden enemy, made off towards Jetsam Point, and were soon out of range.

On the islet, therefore, there were twelve convicts, of whom some no doubt were wounded, but who had a boat at their service. Six more had landed on the island itself, but Granite House was safe from them, for they could rot get across the river, the bridges over which were raised.

"What do you think of the situation, Mr. Smith?" said Pencroff.

"I think," said the engineer, "that unless these rascals are very stupid, the battle will soon take a new form."

"They will never get across the channel," said Pencroff. "Ayrton and Mr. Spilett have guns that will carry a mile!"

"No doubt," said Herbert, "but of what avail are two carbines against the brig's cannon?"

"The brig is not in the channel yet," replied Pencroff.

"And suppose she comes there?" said Smith.

"She will risk foundering and utter destruction."

"Still it is possible," said Ayrton. "The convicts may profit by the high tide to run into the channel, taking the risk of running aground; and then, under their heavy guns, our position will become untenable."

"By Jove!" said the sailor, "the beggars are weighing anchor."

It was but too true. The Speedy began to heave her anchor, and showed her intention of approaching the islet.

Meanwhile, the pirates on the islet had collected on the brink of the channel. They knew that the colonists were out of reach of their shot-guns, but forgot that their enemies, might carry weapons of longer range. Suddenly, the carbines of Ayrton and Spilett rang out together, carrying news to the convicts, which must have been very disagreeable, for two of them fell flat on their faces. There was a general scamper. The other ten, leaving their wounded or dying comrades, rushed to the other side of the islet, sprang into the boat which had brought them over, and rowed rapidly off.

"Eight off!" cried Pencroff, exultingly.

But a more serious danger was at hand. The Speedy had raised her anchor, and was steadily nearing the shore. From their two posts at the Mercy and the Chimneys, the colonists watched her movements without stirring a finger, but not without lively apprehension. Their situation would be most critical, exposed as they would be at short range to the brig's cannon, without power to reply by an effective fire. How then could they prevent the pirates from landing?

Smith felt that in a few minutes he must make up his mind what to do. Should they shut themselves up in Granite House, and stand a siege there? But their enemies would thus become masters of the island, and starve them out at leisure. One chance was still left; perhaps Harvey would not risk his ship in the channel. If he kept outside his shots would be fired from a distance of half a mile, and would do little execution.

"Bob Harvey is too good a sailor," repeated Pencroff, "to risk his ship in the channel. He knows that he would certainly lose her if the sea turned rough! And what would become of him without his ship?"

But the brig came nearer and nearer, and was evidently heading for the lower extremity of the islet. The breeze was faint, the current slack, and Harvey could manœuvre in safety. The route followed by the boats had enabled him to ascertain where the mouth of the river was, and he was making for it with the greatest audacity. He intended to bring his broadside to bear on the Chimneys, and to riddle them with shell and cannon balls. The Speedy soon reached the extremity of the islet, easily turning it, and, with a favoring wind, was soon off the Mercy.

"The villains are here!" cried Pencroff. As he spoke, Neb and Spilett rejoined their comrades. They could do nothing against the ship, and it was better that the colonists should be together when the decisive action was about to take place. Neither of the two were injured, though a shower of balls had been poured upon them as they ran from rock to rock.

"You are not wounded, lad?" said the engineer.

"No, only a few contusions from the ricochet of a ball. But that cursed brig is in the channel!"

"We must take refuge in Granite House," said Smith, "while we have time, and before the convicts can see us. Once inside, we can act as the occasion demands."

"Let us start at once, then," said the reporter.

There was not a moment to lose. Two or three detonations, and the thud of balls on the rocks apprised them that the Speedy was near at hand.

To jump into the elevator, to hoist themselves to the door of Granite House, where Top and Jup had been shut up since the day before, and to rush into the great hall, was the work of a moment. Through the leaves they saw the Speedy, environed with smoke, moving up the channel. They had not left a moment too soon, for balls were crashing everywhere through the hiding places they had quitted. The rocks were splintered to pieces.

Still they hoped that Granite House would escape notice behind its leafy covering, when suddenly a ball passed through the doorway and penetrated into the corridor.

"The devil! we are discovered!" cried Pencroff.

But perhaps the colonists had not been seen, and Harvey had only suspected that something lay behind the leafy screen of the rock. And soon another ball, tearing apart the foliage, exposed the opening in the granite.

The situation of the colonists was now desperate. They could make no answer to the fire, under which the rock was crashing around them. Nothing remained but to take refuge in the upper corridor of Granite House, giving up their abode to devastation, when a hollow sound was heard, followed by dreadful shrieks!

Smith and his comrades rushed to the window.

The brig, lifted on the summit of a sort of waterspout, had just split in half; and in less than ten seconds she went to the bottom with her wicked crew!!

CHAPTER XLVI.

THE COLONISTS ON THE BEACH—AYRTON AND
PENCROFF AS SALVORS—TALK AT BREAKFAST—
PENCROFF'S REASONING—EXPLORATION OF
THE BRIG'S HULL IN DETAIL—THE MAGAZINE
UNINJURED—NEW RICHES—A DISCOVERY—
A PIECE OF A BROKEN CYLINDER.

"They have blown up!" cried Herbert.

"Yes, blown up as if Ayrton had fired the magazine," answered
Pencroff, jumping into the elevator with Neb and the boy,

"But what has happened?" said Spilett, still stupefied at the unexpected
issue.

"Ah, this time we shall find out—" said the engineer,

"What shall we find out?"

"All in time; the chief thing is that the pirates have been disposed
of."

And they rejoined the rest of the party on beach. Not a sign of the
brig could be seen, not even the masts. After having been upheaved by
the water-spout, it had fallen back upon its side, and had sunk in this
position, doubtless owing to some enormous leak.' As the channel here
was only twenty feet deep, the masts of the brig would certainly reappear
at low tide.

Some waifs were floating on the surface of the sea. There was a whole
float, made up of masts and spare yards, chicken coops with the fowls still

living, casks and barrels, which little by little rose to the surface, having escaped by the traps; but no debris was adrift, no flooring of the deck, no plankage of the hull; and the sudden sinking of the Speedy seemed still more inexplicable.

However, the two masts, which had been broken some feet above the "partner," after having snapped their stays and shrouds, soon rose to the surface of the channel, with their sails attached, some of them furled and some unfurled. But they could not wait for low tide to carry away all their riches, and Ayrton and Pencroff jumped into the canoe, for the purpose of lashing these waifs either to the shore of the island or of the islet. But just as they were about to start, they were stopped by a word from Spilett.

"And the six convicts who landed on the right bank of the Mercy," said he.

In fact, it was as well to remember the six men who had landed at Jetsam Point, when their boat was wrecked off the rocks. They looked in that direction, but the fugitives were not to be seen. Very likely, when they saw the brig go down, they had taken flight into the interior of the island.

"We will see after them later," said Smith. "They may still be dangerous, for they are armed; but with six to six, we have an even chance. Now we have more urgent work on hand."

Ayrton and Pencroff jumped into the canoe and pulled vigorously out to the wreck. The sea was quiet now and very high, for the moon was only two days old. It would be a full hour before the hull of the brig would appear above the water of the channel.

Ayrton and Pencroff had time enough to lash together the masts and spars by means of ropes, whose other end was carried along the shore to Granite House, where the united efforts of the colonists succeeded in hauling them in. Then the canoe picked up the chicken coops, barrels, and casks which were floating in the water, and brought them to the Chimneys.

A few dead bodies were also floating on the surface. Among them Ayrton recognized that of Bob Harvey, and pointed it out to his companion, saying with emotion:—

"That's what I was, Pencroff."

"But what you are no longer, my worthy fellow," replied the sailor.

It was a curious thing that so few bodies could be seen floating on the surface. They could count only five or six, which the current was already carrying out to sea. Very likely the convicts, taken by surprise, had not had time to escape, and the ship having sunk on its side, the greater part of the crew were left entangled under the nettings. So the ebb which was carrying the bodies of these wretches out to sea would spare the colonists the unpleasant task of burying them on the island.

For two hours Smith and his companions were wholly occupied with hauling the spars up on the sands, and in unfurling the sails, which were entirely uninjured, and spreading them out to dry. The work was so absorbing that they talked but little; but they had time for thought. What a fortune was the possession of the brig, or rather of the brig's contents! A ship is a miniature world, and the colonists could add to their stock a host of useful articles. It was a repetition, on a large scale, of the chest found on Jetsam Point.

"Moreover," thought Pencroff, "why should it be impossible to get this brig afloat? If she has only one leak, a leak can be stopped up, and a ship of 300 or 400 tons is a real ship compared to our Good Luck! We would go where we pleased in her. We must look into this matter. It is well worth the trouble."

In fact, if the brig could be repaired, their chance of getting home again would be very much greater. But in order to decide this important question, they must wait until the tide was at its lowest, so that the brig's hull could be examined in every part.

After their prizes had been secured upon the beach, Smith and his companions, who were nearly famished, allowed themselves a few minutes for breakfast. Fortunately the kitchen was not far off, and Neb could cook them a good breakfast in a jiffy. They took this meal at the Chimneys, and one can well suppose that they talked of nothing during the repast but the miraculous deliverance of the colony.

"Miraculous is the word," repeated Pencroff, "for we must own that these blackguards were blown up just in time! Granite House was becoming rather uncomfortable."

"Can you imagine, Pencroff, how it happened that the brig blew up?" asked the reporter.

"Certainly, Mr. Spilett; nothing is more simple," replied Pencroff. "A pirate is not under the same discipline as a ship-of-war. Convicts don't make sailors. The brig's magazine must have been open, since she cannonaded us incessantly, and one awkward fellow might have blown up the ship."

"Mr. Smith," said Herbert, "what astonishes me is that this explosion did not produce more effect. The detonation was not loud, and the ship is very little broken up. She seems rather to have sunk than to have blown up."

"That astonishes you, does it, my boy?" asked the engineer.

"Yes, sir."

"And it astonishes me too, Herbert," replied the engineer; "but when we examine the hull of the brig, we shall find some explanation of this mystery."

"Why, Mr. Smith," said Pencroff, "you don't mean to say that the Speedy has just sunk like a ship which strikes upon a rock?"

"Why not," asked Neb, "if there are rocks in the channel?"

"Good, Neb," said Pencroff. "You did not look at the right minute. An instant before she went down I saw the brig rise on an enormous wave, and fall back over to larboard. Now, if she had struck a rock, she'd have gone straight to the bottom like an honest ship."

"And that's just what she is not," said Neb.

"Well, we'll soon find out, Pencroff," said the engineer.

416

"We will find out," added the sailor, "but I'll bet my head there are no rocks in the channel. But do you really think, Mr. Smith, that there is anything wonderful in this event?"

Smith did not answer.

"At all events," said Spilett, "whether shock or explosion, you must own, Pencroff, that it came in good time."

"Yes! yes!" replied the sailor, "but that is not the question. I ask Mr. Smith if he sees anything supernatural in this affair?"

"I give no opinion, Pencroff," said the engineer; a reply which was not satisfactory to Pencroff, who believed in the explosion theory, and was reluctant to give it up. He refused to believe that in the channel which he had crossed so often at low tide, and whose bottom was covered with sand as fine as that of the beach, there existed an unknown reef.

At about half-past 1, the colonists got into the canoe, and pulled out to the stranded brig. It was a pity that her two boats had not been saved; but one, they knew, had gone to pieces at the mouth of the Mercy, and was absolutely useless, and the other had gone down with the brig, and had never reappeared.

Just then the hull of the Speedy began to show itself above the water. The brig had turned almost upside down, for after having broken its masts under the weight of its ballast, displaced by the fall, it lay with its keel in the air. The colonists rowed all around the hull, and as the tide fell, they perceived, if not the cause of the catastrophe, at least the effect produced. In the fore part of the brig, on both sides of the hull, seven or eight feet before the beginning of the stem, the sides were fearfully shattered for at least twenty feet. There yawned two large leaks which it would have been impossible to stop. Not only had the copper sheathing and the planking disappeared, no doubt ground to powder, but there was not a trace of the timbers, the iron bolts, and the treenails which fastened them. The false-keel had been torn off with surprising violence, and the keel itself, torn from the carlines in several places, was broken its whole length.

"The deuce!" cried Pencroff, "here's a ship which will be hard to set afloat."

"Hard! It will be impossible," said Ayrton.

"At all events," said Spilett, "the explosion, if there has been an explosion, has produced the most remarkable effects. It has smashed the lower part of the hull, instead of blowing up the deck and the topsides. These great leaks seem rather to have been made by striking a reef than by the explosion of a magazine."

"There's not a reef in the channel," answered the sailor. "I will admit anything but striking a reef."

"Let us try to get into the hold," said the engineer. "Perhaps that will help us to discover the cause of the disaster."

This was the best course to take, and would moreover enable them to make an inventory of the treasures contained in the brig, and to get them ready for transportation to the island. Access to the hold was now easy; the tide continued to fall, and the lower deck, which, as the brig lay, was now uppermost, could easily be reached. The ballast, composed of heavy pigs of cast iron, had staved it in several places. They heard the roaring of the sea, as it rushed through the fissures of the hull.

Smith and his companions, axe in hand, walked along the shattered deck. All kinds of chests encumbered it, and as they had not been long under water, perhaps their contents had not been damaged.

They set to work at once to put this cargo in safety. The tide would not return for some hours, and these hours were utilized to the utmost at the opening into the hull. Ayrton and Pencroff had seized upon tackle which served to hoist the barrels and chests. The canoe received them, and took them ashore at once. They took everything indiscriminately, and left the sorting of their prizes to the future.

In any case, the colonists, to their extreme satisfaction, had made sure that the brig possessed a varied cargo, an assortment of all kinds of articles, utensils, manufactured products, and tools, such as ships are loaded with for the coasting trade of Polynesia. They would probably find there a little of everything, which was precisely what they needed on Lincoln Island.

Nevertheless, Smith noticed, in silent astonishment, that not only the hull of the brig had suffered frightfully from whatever shock it was which caused the catastrophe, but the machinery was destroyed, especially in the fore part. Partitions and stanchions were torn down as if some enormous shell had burst inside of the brig. The colonists, by piling on one side the boxes which littered their path, could easily go from stem to stern. They were not heavy bales which would have been difficult to handle, but mere packages thrown about in utter confusion.

The colonists soon reached that part of the stern where the poop formerly stood. It was here Ayrton told them they must search for the powder magazine. Smith, believing that this had not exploded, thought they might save some barrels, and that the powder, which is usually in metal cases, had not been damaged by the water. In fact, this was just what had happened. They found, among a quantity of projectiles, at least twenty barrels, which were lined with copper, and which they pulled out with great care. Pencroff was now convinced by his own eyes that the destruction of the Speedy could not have been caused by an explosion. The part of the hull in which the powder magazine was situated was precisely the part which had suffered the least.

"It may be so," replied the obstinate sailor, "but as to a rock, there is not one in the channel." Then he added:—"I know nothing about it, even Mr. Smith does not know. No one knows, or ever will."

Several hours passed in these researches, and the tide was beginning to rise. They had to stop their work of salvage, but there was no fear that the wreck would be washed out to sea, for it was as solidly imbedded as if it had been anchored to the bottom. They could wait with impunity for the turn of the tide to commence operations. As to the ship itself, it was of no use; but they must hasten to save the debris of the hull, which would not take long to disappear in the shifting sands of the channel.

It was 5 o'clock in the afternoon. The day had been a hard one, and they sat down to their dinner with great appetite; but afterwards, notwithstanding their fatigue, they could not resist the desire of examining some of the chests. Most of them contained ready-made clothes, which, as may be imagined, were very welcome. There was enough to clothe a whole colony, linen of every description, boots of all sizes.

"Now we are too rich," cried Pencroff. "What shall we do with all these things?"

Every moment the sailor uttered exclamations of joy, as he came upon barrels of molasses and rum, hogsheads of tobacco, muskets and side-arms, bales of cotton, agricultural implements, carpenters' and smiths' tools, and packages of seeds of every kind, uninjured by their short sojourn in the water. Two years before, how these things would have come in season! But even now that the industrious colonists were so well supplied, these riches would be put to use.

There was plenty of storage room in Granite House, but time failed them now to put everything in safety. They must not forget that six survivors of the Speedy's crew were now on the island, scoundrels of the deepest dye, against whom they must be on their guard.

Although the bridge over the Mercy and the culverts had been raised, the convicts would make little account of a river or a brook; and, urged by despair, these rascals would be formidable. Later, the colonists could decide what course to take with regard to them; in the meantime, the chests and packages piled up near the Chimneys must be watched over, and to this they devoted themselves during the night.

The night passed, however, without any attack from the convicts. Master Jup and Top, of the Granite House guard, would have been quick to give notice.

The three days which followed, the 19th, 20th, and 21st of October, were employed in carrying on shore everything of value either in the cargo or in the rigging. At low tide they cleaned out the hold, and at high tide, stowed away their prizes. A great part of the copper sheathing could be wrenched from the hull, which every day sank deeper; but before the sands had swallowed up the heavy articles which had sunk to the bottom, Ayrton and Pencroff dived and brought up the chains and anchors of the brig, the iron ballast, and as many as four cannon, which could be eased along upon empty barrels and brought to land; so that the arsenal of the colony gained as much from the wreck as the kitchens and store-rooms. Pencroff, always enthusiastic in his projects, talked already about constructing a battery which should command the channel and the mouth of the river. With four cannon, he would guarantee to prevent any fleet, however powerful, from coming within gunshot of the island.

Meanwhile, after nothing of the brig had been left but a useless shell, the bad weather came to finish its destruction. Smith had intended to blow it up, so as to collect the debris on shore, but a strong northeast wind and a high sea saved his powder for him. On the night of the 23d, the hull was thoroughly broken up, and part of the wreck stranded on the beach. As to the ship's papers, it is needless to say, although they carefully rummaged the closet in the poop, Smith found no trace of them. The pirates had evidently destroyed all that concerned either the captain or the owner of the Speedy, and as the name of its port was not painted on the stern, there was nothing to betray its nationality. However, from the shape of the bow, Ayrton and Pencroff believed the brig to be of English construction.

A week after the ship went down, not a trace of her was to be seen even at low tide. The wreck had gone to pieces, and Granite House had been enriched with almost all its contents. But the mystery of its strange destruction would never have been cleared up, if Neb, rambling along the beach, had not come upon a piece of a thick iron cylinder, which bore traces of an explosion. It was twisted and torn at the edge, as if it had been submitted to the action of an explosive substance. Neb took it to his master, who was busy with his companions in the workshop at the Chimneys. Smith examined it carefully, and then turned to Pencroff.

"Do you still maintain, my friend," said he, "that the Speedy did not perish by a collision?"

"Yes, Mr. Smith," replied the sailor, "you know as well as I that there are no rocks in the channel."

"But suppose it struck against this piece of iron?" said the engineer, showing the broken cylinder.

"What, that pipe stem!" said Pencroff, incredulously.

"Do you remember, my friends," continued Smith, "that before foundering the brig was lifted up by a sort of waterspout?"

"Yes, Mr. Smith," said Herbert.

"Well, this was the cause of the waterspout," said Smith, holding up the broken tube.

"That?" answered Pencroff.

"Yes; this cylinder is all that is left of a torpedo!"

"A torpedo!" cried they all.

"And who put a torpedo there?" asked Pencroff, unwilling to give up.

"That I cannot tell you," said Smith, "but there it was, and you witnessed its tremendous effects!"

CHAPTER XLVII.

THE ENGINEER'S THEORY—
PENCROFF'S MAGNIFICENT SUPPOSITIONS—
A BATTERY IN THE AIR—FOUR PROJECTILES—
THE SURVIVING CONVICTS—AYRTON HESITATES—
SMITH'S GENEROSITY AND
PENCROFF'S DISSATISFACTION.

Thus, then, everything was explained by the submarine action of this torpedo. Smith had had some experience during the civil war of these terrible engines of destruction, and was not likely to be mistaken. This cylinder, charged with nitro-glycerine, had been the cause of the column of water rising in the air, of the sinking of the brig, and of the shattered condition of her hull. Everything was accounted for, except the presence of this torpedo in the waters of the channel!

"My friends," resumed Smith, "we can no longer doubt the existence of some mysterious being, perhaps a castaway like ourselves, inhabiting our island. I say this that Ayrton may be informed of all the strange events which have happened for two years. Who our unknown benefactor may be, I cannot say, nor why he should hide himself after rendering us so many services; but his services are not the less real, and such as only a man could render who wielded some prodigious power. Ayrton is his debtor as well; as he saved me from drowning after the fall of the balloon, so he wrote the document, set the bottle afloat in the channel, and gave us information of our comrade's condition. He stranded on Jetsam

Point that chest, full of all that we needed; he lighted that fire on the heights of the island which showed you where to land; he fired that ball which we found in the body of the peccary; he immersed in the channel that torpedo which destroyed the brig; in short, he has done all those inexplicable things of which we could find no explanation. Whatever he is, then, whether a castaway or an exile, we should be ungrateful not to feel how much we owe him. Some day, I hope, we shall discharge our debt."

"We may add," replied Spilett, "that this unknown friend has a way of doing things which seems supernatural. If he did all these wonderful things, he possesses a power which makes him master of the elements."

"Yes," said Smith, "there is a mystery here, but if we discover the man we shall discover the mystery also. The question is this:—Shall we respect the incognito of this generous being, or should we try to find him? What do you think?"

"Master," said Neb, "I have an idea that we may hunt for him as long as we please, but that we shall only find him when he chooses to make himself known."

"There's something in that, Neb," said Pencroff.

"I agree with you, Neb," said Spilett; "but that is no reason for not making the attempt. Whether we find this mysterious being or not, we shall have fulfilled our duty towards him."

"And what is your opinion, my boy?" said the engineer, turning to Herbert.

"Ah," cried Herbert, his eye brightening; "I want to thank him, the man who saved you first and now has saved us all."

"It wouldn't be unpleasant for any of us, my boy," returned Pencroff. "I am not curious, but I would give one of my eyes to see him face to face."

"And you, Ayrton?" asked the engineer.

"Mr. Smith," replied Ayrton, "I can give no advice. Whatever you do will be right, and whenever you want my help in your search, I am ready."

"Thanks, Ayrton," said Smith, "but I want a more direct answer. You are our comrade, who has offered his life more than once to save ours, and we will take no important step without consulting you."

"I think, Mr. Smith," replied Ayrton, "that we ought to do everything to discover our unknown benefactor. He may be sick or suffering. I owe him a debt of gratitude which I can never forget, for he brought you to save me. I will never forget him!"

"It is settled," said Smith. "We will begin our search as soon as possible. We will leave no part of the island unexplored. We will pry into its most secret recesses, and may our unknown friend pardon our zeal!"

For several days the colonists were actively at work haymaking and harvesting. Before starting upon their exploring tour, they wanted to finish all their important labors. Now, too, was the time for gathering the vegetable products of Tabor Island. Everything had to be stored; and, happily, there was plenty of room in Granite House for all the riches of the island. There all was ranged in order, safe from man or beast. No dampness was to be feared in the midst of this solid mass of granite. Many of the natural excavations in the upper corridor were enlarged by the pick, or blown out by mining, and Granite House thus became a receptacle for all the goods of the colony.

The brig's guns were pretty pieces of cast-steel, which, at Pencroff's instance, were hoisted, by means of tackle and cranes, to the very entrance of Granite House; embrasures were constructed between the windows, and soon they could be seen stretching their shining nozzles through the granite wall. From this height these fire-breathing gentry had the range of all Union Bay. It was a little Gibraltar, to whose fire every ship off the islet would inevitably be exposed.

"Mr. Smith," said Pencroff one day—it was the 8th of November—"now that we have mounted our guns, we ought to try their range."

"For what purpose?"

"Well, we ought to know how far we can send a ball."

"Try, then, Pencroff," answered the engineer; "but don't use our powder, whose stock I do not want to diminish; use pyroxyline, whose supply will never fail."

"Can these cannon support the explosive force of pyroxyline?" asked the reporter, who was as eager as Pencroff to try their new artillery.

"I think so. Besides," added the engineer, "we will be careful."

Smith had good reason to think that these cannon were well made. They were of cast steel, and breech-loaders, they could evidently bear a heavy charge, and consequently would have a long range, on account of the tremendous initial velocity.

"Now," said Smith, "the initial velocity being a question of the amount of powder in the charge, everything depends upon the resisting power of the metal; and steel is undeniably the best metal in this respect; so that I have great hope of our battery."

The four cannon were in perfect condition. Ever since they had been taken out of the water, Pencroff had made it his business to give them a polish. How many hours had been spent in rubbing them, oiling them, and cleaning the separate parts! By this time they shone as if they had been on board of a United States frigate.

That very day, in the presence of all the colony, including Jup and Top, the new guns were successively tried. They were charged with pyroxyline, which, as we have said, has an explosive force fourfold that of gunpowder; the projectile was cylindro-conical in shape. Pencroff, holding the fuse, stood ready to touch them off.

Upon a word from Smith, the shot was fired. The ball, directed seaward, passed over the islet and was lost in the offing, at a distance which could not be computed.

The second cannon was trained upon the rocks terminating Jetsam Point, and the projectile, striking a sharp boulder nearly three miles from Granite House, made it fly into shivers. Herbert had aimed and fired the shot, and was quite proud of his success. But Pencroff was prouder of it even than he. Such a feather in his boy's cap!

The third projectile, aimed at the downs which formed the upper coast of Union Bay, struck the sand about four miles away, then ricocheted into the water. The fourth piece was charged heavily to test its extreme range, and every one got out of the way for fear it would burst; then the fuse was touched off by means of a long string. There was a deafening report, but the gun stood the charge, and the colonists, rushing to the windows, could see the projectile graze the rocks of Mandible Cape, nearly five miles from Granite House, and disappear in Shark Gulf.

"Well, Mr. Smith," said Pencroff, who had cheered at every shot, "what do you say to our battery? I should like to see a pirate land now!"

"Better have them stay away, Pencroff," answered the engineer.

"Speaking of that," said the sailor, "what are we going to do with the six rascals who are prowling about the island? Shall we let them roam about unmolested? They are wild beasts, and I think we should treat them as such. What do you think about it, Ayrton?" added Pencroff, turning towards his companion.

Ayrton hesitated for a moment, while Smith regretted the abrupt question, and was sincerely touched when Ayrton answered humbly:—

"I was one of these wild beasts once, Mr. Pencroff, and I am not worthy to give counsel."

And, with bent head, he walked slowly away. Pencroff understood him.

"Stupid ass that I am!" cried he. "Poor Ayrton! and yet he has as good a right to speak as any of us. I would rather have bitten off my tongue than have given him pain! But, to go back to the subject, I think these wretches have no claim to mercy, and that we should rid the island of them."

"And before we hunt them down, Pencroff, shall we not wait for some fresh act of hostility?"

"Haven't they done enough already?" said the sailor, who could not understand these refinements.

"They may repent," said Smith.

"They repent!" cried the sailor, shrugging his shoulders.

"Think of Ayrton, Pencroff!" said Herbert, taking his hand. "He has become an honest man."

Pencroff looked at his companions In stupefaction. He could not admit the possibility of making terms with the accomplices of Harvey, the murderers of the Speedy's crew.

"Be it so!" he said. "You want to be magnanimous to these rascals. May we never repent of it!"

"What danger do we run if we are on our guard?" said Herbert.

"H'm!" said the reporter, doubtfully. "There are six of them, well armed. If each of them sighted one of us from behind a tree—"

"Why haven't they tried it already?" said Herbert. "Evidently it was not their cue."

"Very well, then," said the sailor, who was stubborn in his opinion, "we will let these worthy fellows attend to their innocent occupations without troubling our heads about them."

"Pencroff," said the engineer, "you have often shown respect for my opinions. Will you trust me once again?"

"I will do whatever you say, Mr. Smith," said the sailor, nowise convinced.

"Well, let us wait, and not be the first to attack."

This was the final decision, with Pencroff in the minority. They would give the pirates a chance, which their own interest might induce them to seize upon, to come to terms. So much, humanity required of them. But they would have to be constantly on their guard, and the situation was a very serious one. They had silenced Pencroff, but, perhaps, after all, his advice would prove sound.

CHAPTER XLVIII.

THE PROJECTED EXPEDITION—AYRTON AT THE
CORRAL—VISIT TO PORT BALLOON—
PENCROFF'S REMARKS—DESPATCH SENT TO THE
CORRAL—NO ANSWER FROM AYRTON—SETTING
OUT NEXT DAY—WHY THE WIRE DID NOT ACT—
A DETONATION.

Meanwhile the thing uppermost in the colonists' thought was to achieve the complete exploration of the island which had been decided upon, an exploration which now would have two objects:—First, to discover the mysterious being whose existence was no longer a matter of doubt; and, at the same time to find out what had become of the pirates, what hiding place they had chosen, what sort of life they were leading, and what was to be feared from them.

Smith would have set off at once, but as the expedition would take several days, it seemed better to load the wagon with all the necessaries for camping out. Now at this time one of the onagers, wounded in the leg, could not bear harness; it must have several days' rest, and they thought it would make little difference if they delayed the departure a week, that is, till November 20. November in this latitude corresponds to the May of the Northern Hemisphere, and the weather was fine. They were now at the longest days in the year, so that everything was favorable to the projected expedition, which, if it did not attain its principal object, might be fruitful in discoveries, especially of the products of the soil; for Smith intended to explore those thick forests of the Far West, which stretched to the end of Serpentine Peninsula.

During the nine days which would precede their setting out, it was agreed that they should finish work on Prospect Plateau. But Ayrton had to go back to the corral to take care of their domesticated animals. It was settled that he should stay there two days, and leave the beasts with plenty of fodder. Just as he was setting out, Smith asked him if he would like to have one of them with him, as the island was no longer secure. Ayrton replied that it would be useless, as he could do everything by himself, and that there was no danger to fear. If anything happened at or near the corral, he would instantly acquaint the colonists of it by a telegram sent to Granite House.

So Ayrton drove off in the twilight, about 9 o'clock, behind one onager, and two hours afterwards the electric wire gave notice that he had found everything in order at the corral.

During these two days Smith was busy at a project which would finally secure Granite House from a surprise. The point was to hide completely the upper orifice of the former weir, which had been already blocked up with stones, and half hidden under grass and plants, at the southern angle of Lake Grant. Nothing could be easier, since by raising the level of the lake two or three feet, the hole would be entirely under water.

Now to raise the level, they had only to make a dam across the two trenches by which Glycerine Creek and Waterfall Creek were fed. The colonists were incited to the task, and the two dams, which were only seven or eight feet long, by three feet high, were rapidly erected of closely cemented stones. When the work had been done, no one could have suspected the existence of the subterranean conduit. The little stream which served to feed the reservoir at Granite House, and to work the elevator, had been suffered to flow in its channel, so that water might never be wanting. The elevator once raised, they might defy attack.

This work had been quickly finished, and Pencroff, Spilett, and Herbert found time for an expedition to Port Balloon. The sailor was anxious to know whether the little inlet up which the Good Luck was moored had been visited by the convicts.

"These gentry got to land on the southern shore," he observed, "and if they followed the line of the coast they may have discovered the little harbor, in which case I wouldn't give half a dollar for our Good Luck."

So off the three went in the afternoon of November 10. They were well armed, and as Pencroff slipped two bullets into each barrel of his gun, he had a look which presaged no good to whoever came too near, "beast or man," as he said. Neb went with them to the elbow of the Mercy, and lifted the bridge after them. It was agreed that they should give notice of their return by firing a shot, when Neb would come back to put down the bridge.

The little band walked straight for the south coast. The distance was only three miles and a half, but they took two hours to walk it. They searched on both sides of the way, both the forest and Tadorn's Fens; but they found no trace of the fugitives. Arriving at Port Balloon, they saw with great satisfaction that the Good Luck was quietly moored in the narrow inlet, which was so well hidden by the rocks that it could be seen neither from sea nor shore, but only from directly above or below.

"After all," said Pencroff, "the rascals haven't been here. The vipers like tall grass better, and we shall find them in the Far-West."

"And it's a fortunate thing," added Herbert, "for if they had found the Good Luck, they would have made use of her in getting away, and we could never have gone back to Tabor Island."

"Yes," replied the reporter, "it will be important to put a paper there stating the situation of Lincoln Island, Ayrton's new residence, in case the Scotch yacht should come after him."

"Well, here is our Good Luck, Mr. Spilett," said the sailor, "ready to start with her crew at the first signal!"

Talking thus, they got on board and walked about the deck. On a sudden the sailor, after examining the bit around which the cable of the anchor was wound, cried,

"Hallo! this is a bad business!"

"What's the matter, Pencroff?" asked the reporter.

"The matter is that that knot was never tied by me—"

And Pencroff pointed to a rope which made the cable fast to the bit, so as to prevent its tripping.

"How, never tied by you?" asked Spilett.

"No, I can swear to it. I never tie a knot like that."

"You are mistaken, Pencroff."

"No, I'm not mistaken," insisted the sailor. "That knot of mine is second nature with me."

"Then have the convicts been on board?" asked Herbert.

"I don't know," said Pencroff, "but somebody has certainly raised and dropped this anchor!"

The sailor was so positive that neither Spilett nor Herbert could contest his assertion. It was evident that the beat had shifted place more or less since Pencroff had brought it back to Balloon Harbor. As for the sailor, he had no doubt that the anchor had been pulled up and cast again. Now, why had these manœuvres taken place unless the boat had been used on some expedition?

"Then why did we not see the Good Luck pass the offing?" said the reporter, who wanted to raise every possible objection.

"But, Mr. Spilett," answered the sailor, "they could have set out in the night with a good wind, and in two hours have been out of sight of the island."

"Agreed," said Spilett, but I still ask with what object the convicts used the Good Luck, and why, after using her, they brought her back to port?"

"Well, Mr. Spilett," said the sailor, "we will have to include that among our mysterious incidents, and think no more of it. One thing is certain, the Good Luck was there, and is here! If the convicts take it a second time, it may never find its way back again."

"Then, Pencroff," said Herbert, "perhaps we had better take the Good Luck back and anchor her in front of Granite House."

"I can hardly say," answered the sailor, "but I think not. The mouth of the Mercy is a bad place for a ship; the sea is very heavy there."

"But by hauling it over the sand to the foot of the Chimneys—"

"Well, perhaps," answered Pencroff. "In any case, as we have to leave Granite House for a long expedition, I believe the Good Luck will be safer here during oar absence, and he will do well to leave her here until the island is rid of these rascals."

"That is my opinion, too," said the reporter. At least in case of bad weather, she will not be exposed as she would be at the mouth of the Mercy."

"But if the convicts should pay her another visit?" said Herbert.

"Well, my boy," said Pencroff, "if they do not find the boat here they will search until they do find her; and in our absence there is nothing to prevent their carrying her off from the front of Granite House. I agree with Mr. Spilett that we had better leave her at Balloon Harbor; but if we have not rid the island of these wretches by the time we come back it will be more prudent to take our ship back to Granite House, until we have nothing more to fear from our enemies."

"All right," said Spilett. "Let us go back now."

When they returned to Granite House, they told Smith what had happened, and the latter approved their present and future plans. He even promised Pencroff he would examine that part of the channel situated between the island and the coast, so as to see if it would be possible to make an artificial harbor by means of a dam. In this way the Good Luck would be always within reach, in sight of the colonists, and locked up if necessary.

On the same evening they sent a telegram to Ayrton, asking him to bring back from the corral a couple of goats, which Neb wished to acclimatize on the plateau. Strange to say, Ayrton did not acknowledge the receipt of this despatch, as was his custom to do. This surprised the engineer, but he concluded that Ayrton was not at the corral at the moment, and perhaps had started on his way back to Granite House. In fact, two days had elapsed since his departure; and it had been agreed that on the evening of the 10th or the morning of the 11th, at latest, he would return.

The colonists were now waiting to see Ayrton on Prospect Plateau. Neb and Herbert both looked after the approach by way of the bridge, so as to let it down when their companion should appear, but when 6 o'clock in the evening came, and there was no sign of Ayrton, they agreed to send another despatch, asking for an immediate answer.

The wire at Granite House remained silent.

The uneasiness of the colonists was now extreme. What had happened? "Was Ayrton not at the corral? or, if there, had he not power over his own movements? Ought they to go in search of him on this dark night?

They discussed the point. Some were for going, and others for waiting.

"But," said Herbert, "perhaps some accident has happened to the wires which prevents their working."

"That may be," said the reporter.

"Let us wait until to-morrow," said Smith. "It is just possible that either Ayrton has not received our despatch, or we have missed his."

They waited, as may be imagined, with much anxiety. At daylight on the 11th of November, Smith sent a message across the wires, but received no answer. Again, with the same result.

"Let us set off at once for the corral," said he.

"Aid will armed," added Pencroff.

It was agreed that Granite House must not be deserted, so Neb was left behind to take charge. After accompanying his companions to Glycerine Creek, he put up the bridge again, and hid behind a tree, to wait either for their return or for that of Ayrton. In case the pirates should appear, and should attempt to force the passage, he would try to defend it with his gun; and in the last resort he would take refuge in Granite House, where, the elevator once drawn up, he would be in perfect safety. The others were to go direct to the corral, and failing to find Ayrton there, were to scour the neighboring woods.

At 6 o'clock in the morning the engineer and his three companions had crossed Glycerine Creek, and Neb posted himself behind a low cliff, crowned by some large dragon trees on the left side of the brook. The colonists, after leaving Prospect Plateau, took the direct route to the corral. They carried their guns on their shoulders, ready to fire at the first sign of hostility. The two rifles and the two guns had been carefully loaded.

On either side of the path was a dense thicket, which might easily hide enemies, who, as they were armed, would be indeed formidable. The colonists walked on rapidly without a word. Top preceded them, sometimes keeping to the path, and sometimes making a detour into the wood, but not appearing to suspect anything unusual; and they might depend upon it that the faithful dog would not be taken by surprise, and would bark at the slightest appearance of danger.

Along this same path Smith and his companions followed the telegraphic wires which connected the corral with Granite House. For the first two miles they did not notice any solution of continuity. The posts were in good condition, the insulators uninjured, and the wire evenly stretched. From this point the engineer noticed that the tension was less complete, and at last, arriving at post No. 74, Herbert, who was ahead of the others, cried, "The wire is broken!"

His companions hastened forward and arrived at the spot where the boy had stopped. There the overturned post was lying across the path. They had discovered the break, and it was evident that the dispatches from Granite House could not have been received at the corral.

"It can't be the wind that has overturned this post," said Pencroff.

"No," answered the reporter, "there are marks of footsteps on the ground; it has been uprooted by the hand of man."

"Besides, the wire is broken," added Herbert, showing the two ends of the wire which had been violently torn asunder.

"Is the break a fresh one?" asked Smith.

"Yes," said Herbert, "it was certainly made a very short time ago."

"To the corral! to the corral!" cried the sailor.

The colonists were then midway between Granite House and the corral, and had still two miles and a half to go. They started on a run.

In fact, they might well fear that something had happened at the corral. Ayrton doubtless might have sent a telegram which had not arrived. It was not this which alarmed his companions, but a circumstance more remarkable. Ayrton, who had promised to come back the evening before, had not reappeared! The communication, between Granite House and the corral had been out with a sinister design.

They hurried on, their hearts beating quick with fear for their comrade, to whom they were sincerely attached; Were they to find him struck down by the hand of those he had formerly led?

Soon they reached the place where the road lay along by the little brook flowing from Red Creek, which watered the meadows of the corral. They had moderated their pace, so as not to be out of breath at the moment when a deadly struggle might occur. Their guns were uncocked, but loaded. Each of them watched one side of the woods. Top kept up an ill-omened growling.

At last the fenced enclosure appeared behind the trees. They saw no signs of devastation. The door was closed as usual; a profound silence reigned at the corral. Neither the accustomed bleatings of the sheep nor the voice of Ayrton was to be heard.

"Let us go in," said Smith, and the engineer advanced, while his companions, keeping guard twenty feet in the rear, stood ready to fire.

Smith raised the inner latch, and began to push back the door, when Top barked loudly. There was a report from behind the fence, followed by a cry of pain, and Herbert, pierced by a bullet, fell to the ground!

CHAPTER XLIX.

THE REPORTER AND PENCROFF IN THE CORRAL—
MOVING HERBERT—DESPAIR OF THE SAILOR—
CONSULTATION OF THE ENGINEER AND THE
REPORTER—MODE OF TREATMENT—A GLIMMER
OF HOPE—HOW TO WARN NEB—A FAITHFUL
MESSENGER—NEB'S REPLY.

At Herbert's cry, Pencroff, dropping his gun, sprang towards him.

"They have killed him!" cried he. "My boy—they have killed him."

Smith and Spilett rushed forward. The reporter put his ear to the boy's heart to see if it were still beating.

"He's alive," said he, "but he must be taken—"

"To Granite House? Impossible!" said the engineer.

"To the corral, then," cried Pencroff.

"One moment," said Smith, and he rushed to the left around the fence. There he found himself face to face with a convict, who fired at him and sent a ball through his cap. An instant later, before he had time to fire again, he fell, struck to the heart by Smith's poniard, a surer weapon even than his gun.

While this was going on, the reporter and Pencroff hoisted themselves up to the angle of the fence, strode over the top, jumped into the enclosure, made their way into the empty house, and laid Herbert gently down on Ayrton's bed.

A few minutes afterwards Smith was at his side. At the sight of Herbert, pale and unconscious, the grief of the sailor was intense. He sobbed and cried bitterly; neither the engineer nor the reporter could calm him. Themselves over whelmed with emotion, they could hardly speak.

They did all in their power to save the poor boy's life. Spilett, in his life of varied experience, had acquired some knowledge of medicine. He knew a little of everything; and had had several opportunities of learning the surgery of gunshot wounds. With Smith's assistance, he hastened to apply the remedies which Herbert's condition demanded.

The boy lay in a complete stupor, caused either by the hemorrhage or by concussion of the brain. He was very pale, and his pulse beat only at long intervals, as if every moment about to stop. This, taken in conjunction with his utter loss of consciousness, was a grave symptom. They stripped his chest, and, staunching the blood by means of handkerchiefs, kept bathing the wounds in cold water.

The ball had entered between the third and fourth rib, and there they found the wound. Smith and Spilett turned the poor boy over. At this he uttered a moan so faint that they feared it was his last breath. There was another wound on his back, for the bullet had gone clean through.

"Thank Heaven!" said the reporter, "the ball is not in his body; we shall not have to extract it."

"But the heart?" asked Smith.

"The heart has not been touched, or he would be dead."

"Dead!" cried Pencroff, with a groan. He had only heard the reporter's last word.

"No, Pencroff," answered Smith. "No he is not dead; his pulse still beats; he has even uttered a groan. For his sake, now, you must be calm. We have need of all our self-possession; you must not be the means of our losing it, my friend."

Pencroff was silent, but large tears rolled down his cheeks.

Meanwhile, Spilett tried to recall to memory the proper treatment of the case before him. There seemed no doubt that the ball had entered in front and gone out by the back; but what injuries had it done by the way? Had it reached any vital spot? This was a question which even a professional surgeon could not have answered at once.

There was something, however, which Spilett knew must be done, and that was to keep down the inflammation, and to fight against the fever which ensues upon a wound. The wound must be dressed without delay. It was not necessary to bring on a fresh flow of blood by the use of tepid water and compresses, for Herbert was already too weak. The wounds, therefore, were bathed with cold water.

Herbert was placed upon his left side and held in that position.

"He must not be moved," said Spilett; "he is in the position most favorable to an easy suppuration, and absolute repose is necessary."

"Cannot we take him to Granite House?" asked Pencroff.

"No, Pencroff," said the reporter.

Spilett was examining the boy's wounds again with close attention. Herbert was so frightfully pale that he became alarmed.

"Cyrus," said he, "I am no doctor. I am in a terrible strait; you must help me with your advice and assistance."

"Calm yourself, my friend," answered the engineer, pressing his hand. "Try to judge coolly. Think only of saving Herbert."

Spilett's self-possession, which in a moment of discouragement his keen sense of responsibility had caused him to lose, returned again at these words. He seated himself upon the bed; Smith remained standing, Pencroff had torn up his shirt and began mechanically to make lint.

Spilett explained that the first thing to do was to check the hemorrhage, but not to close the wounds or bring on immediate cicatrization—for there had been internal perforation, and they must not let the suppurated matter collect within. It was decided therefore to dress the two wounds, but not to press them together. The colonists possessed a most powerful agent for quelling inflamation, and one which nature supplies in the greatest abundance; to-wit, cold water, which is now used by all doctors. It has, moreover, the advantage of allowing the wound perfect rest, and dispensing with the frequent dressing, which by exposing the wound to the air in the early stages, is so often attended with lamentable results.

Thus did Smith and Spilett reason, with clear, native good sense, and acted as the best surgeon would have done. The wounds were bandaged with linen and constantly soaked with fresh water. The sailor had lighted a fire in the chimney, and the house fortunately contained all the necessaries of life. They had maple-sugar and the medicinal plants which the boy had gathered on the shores of Lake Grant. From these they made a refreshing drink for the sick boy. His fever was very high, and he lay all that day and night without a sign of consciousness. His life was hanging on a thread.

On the next day, November 12, they began to have some hopes of his recovery. His consciousness returned, he opened his eyes and recognized them all. He even said two or three words, and wanted to know what had happened. Spilett told him, and begged him to keep perfectly quiet; that his life was not in danger, and his wounds would heal in a few days. Herbert suffered very little, for the inflammation was successfully kept down by the plentiful use of cold water. A regular suppuration had set in, the fever did not increase, and they began to hope that this terrible accident would not end in a worse catastrophe.

Pencroff took heart again; he was the best of nurses, like a Sister of Charity, or a tender mother watching over her child. Herbert had fallen into another stupor, but this time the sleep appeared more natural.

"Tell me again that you have hope, Mr. Spilett," said Pencroff; "tell me again that you will save my boy!"

"We shall save him," said the reporter. "The wound is a serious one, and perhaps the ball has touched the lung; but a wound in that organ is not mortal."

"May God grant it!" answered the sailor.

As may be imagined, the care of Herbert had occupied all their time and thoughts for the first twenty-four hours at the corral. They had not considered the urgent danger of a return of the convicts, nor taken any precautions for the future. But on this day while Pencroff was watching over the invalid, Smith and the reporter took counsel together as to their plans.

They first searched the corral. There was no trace of Ayrton, and it seemed probable that he had resisted his former companions, and fallen by their hands. The corral had not been pillaged, and as its gates had remained shut, the domestic animals had not been able to wander away into the woods. They could see no traces of the pirates either in the dwelling or the palisade. The only thing gone was the stock of ammunition.

"The poor fellow was taken by surprise," said Smith, "and as he was a man to show fight, no doubt they made an end of him."

"Yes," replied the reporter, "and then, no doubt, they took possession here, where they found everything in great plenty, and took to flight only when they saw us coming."

"We must beat the woods," said the engineer, and rid the island of these wretches. But we will have to wait some time in the corral, till the day comes when we can safely carry Herbert to Granite House."

"But Neb?" asked the reporter.

"Neb's safe enough."

"Suppose he becomes anxious and risks coming here?"

"He must not come," said Smith sharply. "He would be murdered on the way!"

"It's very likely he will try."

"Ah! if the telegraph was only in working order, we could warn him! But now it's impossible. We can't leave Pencroff and Herbert here alone. Well, I'll go by myself to Granite House!"

"No, no, Cyrus," said the reporter, "you must not expose yourself. These wretches are watching the corral from their ambush, and there would be two mishaps instead of one!"

"But Neb has been without news of us for twenty-four hours," repeated the engineer. "He will want to come."

While he reflected, his gaze fell upon Top, who, by running to and fro, seemed to say, "Have you forgotten me?"

"Top!" cried Smith.

The dog sprang up at this master's call.

"Yes, Top shall go!" cried the reporter, who understood in a flash. Top will make his way where we could not pass, will take our message and bring us back an answer."

"Quick!" said Smith, "quick!"

Spilett tore out a page of his note-book and wrote these lines:—

"Herbert wounded. We are at the corral. Be on your guard. Do not leave Granite House. Have the convicts shown themselves near you? Answer by Top!"

This laconic note was folded and tied in a conspicuous way to Top's collar.

"Top, my dog," said the engineer, caressing the animal, "Neb, Top, Neb! Away! away!"

Top sprang high at the words. He understood what was wanted, and the road was familiar to him. The engineer went to the door of the corral and opened one of the leaves.

"Neb, Top, Neb!" he cried again, pointing towards Granite House.

Top rushed out and disappeared almost instantly.

"He'll get there!" said the reporter.

"Yes, and come back, the faithful brute!"

"What time is it?" asked Spilett.

"Ten o'clock."

"In an hour he may be here. We will watch for him.

The door of the corral was closed again. The engineer and the reporter re-entered the house. Herbert lay in a profound sleep. Pencroff kept his compresses constantly wet with cold water. Spilett, seeing that just then there was nothing else to do, set to work to prepare some food, all the time keeping his eye on that part of the inclosure which backed up against the spur, from which an attack might be made.

The colonists awaited Top's return with much anxiety. A little before 11 o'clock Smith andSpilett stood with their carbines behind the door, ready to open it at the dog's first bark. They knew that if Top got safely to Granite House, Neb would send him back at once.

They had waited about ten minutes, when they heard a loud report, followed instantly by continuous barking. The engineer opened the door, and, seeing smoke still curling up among the trees a hundred paces off, he fired in that direction. Just then Top bounded into the corral, whose door was quickly shut.

"Top, Top!" cried the engineer, caressing the dog's large, noble head. A note was fastened to his collar, containing these words in Neb's sprawling handwriting:—

"No pirates near Granite House. I will not stir. Poor Mr. Herbert!"

CHAPTER L.

THE CONVICTS IN THE NEIGHBORHOOD OF
THE CORRAL—PROVISIONAL OCCUPATION—
CONTINUATION OF HERBERT'S TREATMENT—
PENCROFF'S JUBILATION—REVIEW OF THE PAST—
FUTURE PROSPECTS—SMITH'S IDEAS.

So, then, the convicts were close by, watching the corral, and waiting to kill the colonists one after another. They must be attacked like wild beasts, but with the greatest precaution, for the wretches had the advantage of position, seeing and not being seen, able to make a sudden attack, yet not themselves to be surprised.

So Smith made his arrangements to live at the corral, which was fully provisioned. Ayrton's house was furnished with all the necessaries of life, and the convicts, frightened away by the colonists' arrival, had not had time to pillage. It was most likely, as Spilett suggested, that the course of events had been this:—The convicts had followed the southern coast, and after getting over into Serpentine Peninsula, and being in no humor to risk themselves in the woods of the Far West, they had reached the month of Fall River. Then, walking up the right bank of the stream, they had come to the spur of Mount Franklin; here was their most natural place of refuge. And they had soon discovered the corral. They had probably installed themselves there, had been surprised by Ayrton, had overcome the unfortunate man, and—the rest was easily divined!

Meanwhile the convicts, reduced to five, but well armed, were prowling in the woods, and to pursue them was to be exposed to their fire without the power either of avoiding or of anticipating them.

"There is nothing else to do but wait," repeated Smith. "When Herbert is well again, we will beat the island, and have a shot at these rascals; while at the same time—"

"We search for our mysterious protector," added Spilett, finishing the sentence. "Ah! we must confess, dear Cyrus, that, for once, his protection has failed us."

"We don't know about that," answered the engineer.

"What do you mean?" asked the reporter.

"We are not at the end of our troubles, my dear Spilett, and his powerful interference may still be exercised. But now we must think of Herbert."

Several days passed, and the poor boy's condition was happily no worse; and to gain time was a great thing. The cold water, always kept at the proper temperature, had absolutely prevented the inflammation of the wounds. Nay, it seemed to the reporter that this water, which contained a little sulphur, due to the neighborhood of the volcano, had a direct tendency towards cicatrization. The suppuration was much less copious, and, thanks to excellent nursing, Herbert had returned to consciousness, and his fever had abated. He was, moreover, strictly dieted, and, of course, was very weak; but he had plenty of broths and gruels, and absolute rest was doing him great good.

Smith, Spilett, and Pencroff had become very skilful in tending him. All the linen in the house had been sacrificed. The wounded parts, covered with lint and compresses, were subjected to just enough pressure to cicatrize them without bringing on a reaction of inflammation. The reporter dressed the wounds with the greatest care, repeating to his companions the medical axiom that good dressing is as rare as a good operation.

At the end of ten days, by the 22d of November, Herbert was decidedly better. He had begun to take some nourishment. The color came back to his cheeks, and he smiled at his nurse. He talked a little, in spite of Pencroff, who chattered away all the time to keep the boy from saying a word, and told the most remarkable stories. Herbert inquired about Ayrton, and was surprised not to see him at the bedside; but the sailor, who would not distress his patient, answered merely that Ayrton had gone to be with Neb at Granite House in case the convicts attacked it. "Nice fellows they are," said he. "To think that Mr. Smith wanted to appeal to their feelings! I'll send them my compliments in a good heavy bullet!"

"And nobody has seen them?" asked Herbert.

"No, my boy," answered the sailor, "but we will find them, and when you are well we shall see whether these cowards, who strike from behind, will dare to meet us face to face."

"I am still very weak, dear Pencroff."

"Oh! your strength will come back little by little. What's a ball through the chest? Nothing to speak of. I have seen several of them, and feel no worse for it."

In fine, things were growing better, and it no unlucky complication occurred, Herbert's cure might be regarded as certain. But what would have been the colonists' situation if the ball had remained in his body, if his arm or leg had had to be amputated? They could not think of it without a shudder.

It seemed to Smith that he and his companions, until now so fortunate, had entered upon an ill-omened time. For the two and a half years which had elapsed since their escape from Richmond they had succeeded in everything. But now luck seemed to be turning against them. Ayrton, doubtless, was dead, and Herbert severely wounded; and that strange but powerful intervention, which had done them such mighty services, seemed now to be withdrawn. Had the mysterious being abandoned the island, or himself been overcome?

446

They could give no answer to these questions; but though they talked together about them, they were not men to despair. They looked the situation in the face; they analyzed the chances; they prepared themselves for every contingency; they stood firm and undaunted before the future; and if adversity should continue to oppress them, she would find them men prepared to do their utmost.

CHAPTER LI.

NO NEWS OF NEB—A PROPOSAL FROM PENCROFF
AND SPILETT—THE REPORTER'S SORTIES—
A FRAGMENT OF CLOTH—A MESSAGE—HURRIED
DEPARTURE—ARRIVAL AT PROSPECT PLATEAU.

Herbert's convalescence progressed steadily. Only one thing was left to wish for, to wit, that he would get well enough to be taken to Granite House. However well arranged and provisioned might be the dwelling in the corral, there was nothing like the solid comfort of their abode in the rock. Besides, they were not safe here, and, in spite of their watchfulness, they were always in dread of a shot from the woods. Whereas there in the midst of that unassailable and inaccessible mass of rock there would be nothing to fear. They waited, therefore, with impatience for the moment when Herbert could be carried, without danger to his wound, across the difficult route through Jacamar Woods.

Though without news of Neb, they had no fear for him. The brave negro, occupying a position of such strength, would not let himself be surprised. Top had not been sent back to him, for it seemed useless to expose the faithful dog to some shot which might deprive the colonists of their most useful helper. The engineer regretted to see his forces divided, and thus to play into the hands of the pirates. Since Ayrton's disappearance, they were only four against five, for Herbert could not be counted. The poor boy knew and lamented the danger of which he was the cause.

One day, November 29, when he was asleep, they discussed their plans of action against the convicts.

"My friends," said the reporter, after they had talked over the impossibility of communicating with Neb, "I agree with you that to risk ourselves on the path leading from the corral would be a useless exposure. But why should we not beat the woods for these wretches?"

"That's what I was thinking," replied Pencroff. "We're not afraid of a bullet, and for my part, if Mr. Smith approves, I am ready to take to the woods. Surely one man is as good as another!"

"But is he as good as five?" asked the engineer.

"I will go with Pencroff,' answered the reporter, "and the two of us, well armed, and Top with us—"

"My dear Spilett, and you, Pencroff, let us discuss the matter coolly. If the convicts were in hiding in some place known to us, from which we could drive them by an attack, it would be a different affair. But have we not every reason to fear that they will get the first shot?"

"Well, sir," cried Pencroff, "a bullet doesn't always hit its mark!"

"That which pierced Herbert did not go astray," answered the engineer. "Besides, remember that if you both leave the corral, I shall be left alone to defend it. Can you answer that the convicts will not see you go off, that they will not wait till you are deep in the woods, and then make their attack in your absence upon a man and a sick boy?"

There was nothing to say in answer to this reasoning, which went home to the minds of all.

"If only Ayrton was yet one of the party!" said Spilett. "Poor fellow! his return to a life with his kind was not for long!"

"If he is dead!" added Pencroff, in a peculiar tone.

"Have you any hope that those rascals have spared him, Pencroff?" asked Spilett.

"Yes, if their interest led them to do so."

"What! do you suppose that Ayrton, among his former companions in guilt, would forget all he owed to us—"

"Nobody can tell," answered the sailor, with some hesitation.

"Pencroff," said Smith, laying his hand on the sailor's arm, "that was an unworthy thought. I will guarantee Ayrton's fidelity!"

"And I too," added the reporter, decidedly.

"Yes, yes, Mr. Smith, I am wrong," answered Pencroff. "But really I am a little out of my mind. This imprisonment in the corral is driving me to distraction."

"Be patient, Pencroff," answered the engineer. "How soon, my dear Spilett, do you suppose Herbert can be carried to Granite House?"

"That is hard to say, Cyrus," answered the reporter, "for a little imprudence might be fatal. But if he goes on as well as he is doing now for another week, why then we will see."

At that season the spring was two months advanced. The weather was good, and the heat began to be oppressive. The woods were in fall leaf, and it was almost time to reap the accustomed harvest. It can easily be understood how this siege in the corral upset the plans of the colonists.

Once or twice the reporter risked himself outside, and walked around the palisade. Top was with him, and his carbine was loaded.

He met no one and saw nothing suspicious. Top would have warned him of any danger, and so long as the dog did not bark, there was nothing to fear.

But on his second sortie, on the 27th of November, Spilett, who had ventured into the woods for a quarter of a mile to the south of the mountain, noticed that Top smelt something. The dog's motions were no longer careless; he ran to and fro, ferreting about in the grass and thistles, as if his keen nose had put him on the track of an enemy.

Spilett followed the dog, encouraging and exciting him by his voice; his eye on the alert, his carbine on his shoulder, and availing himself of the shelter of the trees. It was not likely that Top had recognized the presence of a man, for in that case he would have announced it by a half-stifled but angry bark. Since not even a growl was to be heard, the danger was evidently neither near nor approaching.

About five minutes had passed in this way, Top ferreting about and the reporter cautiously following him, when the dog suddenly rushed towards a thicket and tore from it a strip of cloth. It was a piece from a garment, dirty and torn. Spilett went back with it to the corral. There the colonists examined it and recognized it as a piece of Ayrton's waistcoat, which was made of the felt prepared only in the workshop at Granite House.

"You see, Pencroff," observed Smith, "Ayrton resisted manfully, and the convicts dragged him off in spite of his efforts. Do you still doubt his good faith?"

"No, Mr. Smith," replied the sailor; "I have long ago given up that momentary suspicion. But I think we may draw one conclusion from this fact."

"What is that?"

"That Ayrton was not killed at the corral. They must have dragged him out alive, and perhaps he is still alive."

"It may be so," said the engineer, thoughtfully.

The most impatient of them all to get back to Granite House was Herbert. He knew how necessary it was for them all to be there, and felt that it was he who was keeping them at the corral. The one thought which had taken possession of his mind was to leave the corral, and to leave it as soon as possible. He believed that he could bear the journey to Granite House. He was sure that his strength would come back to him sooner in his own room, with the sight and the smell of the sea.

It was now November 29. The colonists were talking together in Herbert's room, about 7 o'clock in the morning, when they heard Top barking loudly. They seized their guns, always loaded and cocked, and went out of the house.

Top ran to the bottom of the palisade, jumping and barking with joy.

"Some one is coming!"

"Yes."

"And not an enemy."

"Neb, perhaps?"

"Or Ayrton?"

These words had scarcely been exchanged between the engineer and his comrade, when something leaped the palisade and fell on the ground inside. It was Jup. Master Jup himself, who was frantically welcomed by Top.

"Neb has sent him!" said the reporter.

"Then he must have some note on him," said the engineer.

Pencroff rushed to the orang. Neb could not have chosen a better messenger, who could get through obstacles which none of the others could have surmounted. Smith was right. Around Jup's neck was hung a little bag, and in it was a note in Neb's handwriting. The dismay of the colonists may be imagined when they read these words:—

"FRIDAY, 6 A. M."—The convicts are on the plateau. NEB."

They looked at each other without saying a word, then walked back to the house. What was there to do? The convicts on Prospect Plateau meant disaster, devastation and ruin! Herbert knew at once from their faces that the situation had become grave, and when he saw Jup, he had no more doubt that misfortune was threatening Granite House.

"Mr. Smith," said he, "I want to go. I can bear the journey. I want to start."

Spilett came up to Herbert and looked at him intently.

"Let us start then," said he.

The question of Herbert's transportation was quickly decided. A litter would be the most comfortable way of travelling, but it would necessitate two porters; that is, two guns would be subtracted from their means of defense. On the other hand, by placing the mattresses on which Herbert lay in the wagon, so as to deaden the motion, and by walking carefully they could escape jolting him, and would leave their arms free.

The wagon was brought out and the onagga harnessed to it; Smith and the reporter lifted the mattresses with Herbert on them, and laid them in the bottom of the wagon between the rails. The weather was fine, and the sun shone brightly between the trees.

"Are the arms ready?" asked Smith.

They were. The engineer and Pencroff, each armed with a double-barrelled gun, and Spilett with his carbine, stood ready to set out.

"How do you feel, Herbert?" asked the engineer.

"Don't be troubled, Mr. Smith," answered the boy, "I shall not die on the way."

They could see that the poor fellow was making a tremendous effort. The engineer felt a grievous pang. He hesitated to give the signal for departure. But to stay would have thrown Herbert into despair.

"Let us start," said Smith.

The corral door was opened. Jup and Top, who knew how to be quiet on emergency, rushed on ahead. The wagon went out, the gate was shut, and the onagga, under Pencroff's guidance, walked on with a slow pace.

It was necessary, on account of the wagon, to keep to the direct road from the corral to Granite House, although it was known to the convicts. Smith and Spilett walked on either side of the chariot, ready to meet any attack. Still it was not likely that the convicts had yet abandoned Prospect Plateau. Neb's note had evidently been sent as soon as they made their appearance. Now this note was dated at 6 o'clock in the morning, and the active orang, who was accustomed to the way, would have got over the five miles from Granite House in three-quarters of an hour. Probably they would have no danger to fear till they approached Granite House.

But they kept on the alert. Top and Jup, the latter armed with his stick, sometimes in front, and sometimes beating the woods on either side, gave no signal of approaching danger. The wagon moved on slowly, and an hour after leaving the corral, they had passed over four of the five miles without any incident.

They drew near the plateau another mile, and they saw the causeway over Glycerine Creek. At last, through an opening in the wood, they saw the horizon of the sea. But the wagon went on slowly, and none of its defenders could leave it for a moment. Just then Pencroff stopped the wagon and cried, fiercely,

"Ah, the wretches!"

And he pointed to a thick smoke which curled up from the mill, the stables, and the buildings of the poultry-yard. In the midst of this smoke a man was running about. It was Neb.

His companions uttered a cry. He heard them and rushed to meet them.

The convicts had abandoned the plateau half an hour before, after having done all the mischief they could.

"And Mr. Herbert?" cried Neb.

Spilett went back to the wagon. Herbert had fainted.

CHAPTER LII.

HERBERT CARRIED TO GRANITE HOUSE—
NEB RELATES WHAT HAD HAPPENED—VISIT OF
SMITH TO THE PLATEAU—RUIN AND DEVASTATION—
THE COLONISTS HELPLESS—WILLOW BARK—
A MORTAL FEVER—TOP BARKS AGAIN.

The convicts, the dangers threatening Granite House, the ruin on the plateau, none of these were thought of, in the present condition of Herbert. It was impossible to say whether the transportation had occasioned some internal rupture, but his companions were almost hopeless.

The wagon had been taken to the bend of the river, and there the mattress, on which lay the unconscious lad, was placed on a litter of branches, and within a few minutes Herbert was lying on his bed in Granite House. He smiled for a moment on finding himself again in his chamber, and a few words escaped feebly from his lips. Spilett looked at his wounds, fearing that they might have opened, but the cicatrices were unbroken. What, then, was the cause of this prostration, or why had his condition grown worse?

Soon the lad fell into a feverish sleep, and the reporter and Pencroff watched beside him.

Meantime, Smith told Neb of all that had happened at the corral, and Neb told his master of what had passed at the plateau.

It was not until the previous night that the convicts had shown themselves beyond the edge of the forest, near Glycerine Creek. Neb, keeping watch near the poultry-yard, had not hesitated to fire at one of them who was crossing the bridge; but he could not say with what result. At least, it did not disperse the band, and Neb had but just time to climb up into Granite House, where he, at least, would be safe.

But what was the next thing to do? How prevent the threatened devastation to the plateau? How could he inform his master? And, moreover, in what situation were the occupants of the corral?

Smith and his companions had gone away on the 11th inst., and here it was the 29th. In that time all the information that Neb had received was the disastrous news brought by Top. Ayrton gone, Herbert badly wounded, the engineer, the reporter, and the sailor imprisoned in the corral.

The poor negro asked himself what was to be done. Personally, he had nothing to fear, as the convicts could not get into Granite House. But the works, the fields, all the improvements, were at the mercy of the pirates. Was it not best to let Smith know of the threatened danger?

Then Neb thought of employing Jup on this errand. He knew the intelligence of the orang. Jup knew the word "corral." It was not yet daylight. The agile brute could slip through the woods unperceived. So the negro wrote a note, which he fastened round Jup's neck, and taking the monkey to the door and unrolling a long cord, he repeated the words:—

"Jup! Jup! To the corral! the corral!"

The animal understood him, and, seizing the cord, slid down to the ground, and disappeared in the darkness.

"You did well, Neb, although In not forewarning us perhaps you would have done better!" said Smith, thinking of Herbert, and how the carrying him back had been attended with such serious results.

Neb finished his recital. The convicts had not shown themselves upon the beach, doubtless fearing the inhabitants of Granite House, whose number they did not know. But the plateau was open and unprotected by Granite House. Here, therefore, they gave loose reins to their instinct of depredation and destruction, and they had left but half-an-hour before the colonists returned.

Neb had rushed from his retreat, and at the risk of being shot, he had climbed to the plateau and had tried to put out the fire which was destroying the inclosure to the poultry-yard. Ho was engaged in this work when the others returned.

Thus the presence of the convicts was a constant menace to the colonists, heretofore so happy, and they might expect the most disastrous results from them.

Smith, accompanied by Neb, went to see for himself, the extent of the injury done. He walked along by the Mercy and up the left bank without seeing any trace of the convicts. It was likely that the latter had either witnessed the return of the colonists, and had gone back to the corral, now undefended, or that they had gone back to their camp to await an occasion to renew the attack.

At present, however, all attempts to rid the island of these pests were subject to the condition of Herbert.

The engineer and Neb reached the place. It was a scene of desolation. Fields trampled; the harvest scattered; the stables and other buildings burned; the frightened animals roaming at large over the plateau. The fowls, which had sought refuge on the lake, were returning to their accustomed place on its banks. Everything here would have to be done over again.

The succeeding days were the saddest which the colonists had passed on the island. Herbert became more and more feeble. He was in a sort of stupor, and symptoms of delirium began to manifest themselves. Cooling draughts were all the remedies at the disposition of the colonists. Meantime, the fever became intermittent, and it was necessary to check, it before it developed greater strength.

"To do this," said Spilett, "we must have a febrifuge."

"And we have neither cinchonia nor quinine," answered the engineer.

"No, but we can make a substitute from the bark of the willow trees at the lake."

"Let us try it immediately," replied Smith.

Indeed, willow bark has been partly considered succedaneous to cinchonia, but since they had no means of extracting the salicin, the bark must be used in its natural state.

Smith, therefore, cut some pieces of bark from a species of black willow, and, reducing them to powder, this powder was given to Herbert the same evening.

The night passed without incident. Herbert was somewhat delirious, but the fever did not manifest itself. Pencroff became more hopeful, but Spilett, who knew that the fever was intermittent, looked forward to the next day with anxiety.

They noticed that during the apyrexy, Herbert seemed completely prostrated, his head heavy, and subject to dizziness. Another alarming symptom was a congestion of the liver, and soon a more marked delirium manifested itself.

Spilett was overwhelmed by this new complication. He drew the engineer aside and said to him:—

"It is a pernicious fever!"

"A pernicious fever!" cried Smith. "You must be mistaken, Spilett. A pernicious fever never declares itself spontaneously; it must have a germ."

"I am not mistaken," replied the reporter. "Herbert may have caught the germ in the marshes. He has already had one attack; if another follows, and we cannot prevent a third—he is lost!"

"But the willow bark?—"

"Is insufficient. And a third attack of pernicious fever, when one cannot break it by means of quinine, is always mortal!"

Happily Pencroff had not heard this conversation. It would have driven him wild.

Towards noon of the 7th, the second attack manifested itself. The crisis was terrible. Herbert felt that he was lost! He stretched out his arms towards Smith, towards Spilett, towards Pencroff! He did not want to die! The scene was heartrending, and it became necessary to take Pencroff away.

The attack lasted five hours. It was plain that the lad could not support a third. The night was full of torture. In his delirium, Herbert wrestled with the convicts; he called Ayrton; he supplicated that mysterious being, that protector, who had disappeared but whose image haunted him— then he fell into a profound prostration, and Spilett, more than once, thought the poor boy was dead!

The next day passed with only a continuation of the lad's feebleness. His emaciated hands clutched the bed clothing. They continued giving him doses of the willow powder, but the reporter anticipated no result from it.

"If," said he, "before to-morrow morning we cannot give him a more powerful febrifuge than this, Herbert will die!"

The night came—doubtless the last night for this brave lad, so good, so clever, whom all loved as their own child! The sole remedy against this pernicious fever, the sole specific which could vanquish it, was not to be found on Lincoln Island!

During the night Herbert became frightfully delirious. He recognized no one. It was not even probable that he would live till morning. His strength was exhausted. Towards 3 o'clock he uttered a frightful cry. He was seized by a terrible convulsion. Neb, who was beside him, rushed, frightened, into the adjoining chamber, where his companions were watching.

At the same moment Top gave one of his strange barks.

All returned to the chamber and gathered round the dying lad, who struggled to throw himself from the bed. Spilett, who held his arms, felt his pulse slowly rising.

Five o'clock came. The sun's rays shone into the chambers of Granite House. A beautiful day, the last on earth for poor Herbert, dawned over Lincoln Island.

A sunbeam crept on to the table beside the bed.

Suddenly Pencroff, uttering an exclamation, pointed to something on that table.

It was a small oblong box, bearing these words:—
Sulphate of quinine.

CHAPTER LIII.

AN INEXPLICABLE MYSTERY—HERBERT'S
CONVALESCENCE—THE UNEXPLORED PARTS OF
THE ISLAND—PREPARATIONS FOR DEPARTURE—
THE FIRST DAY—NIGHT—SECOND DAY—
THE KAURIS—CASSOWARIES—FOOTPRINTS IN THE
SAND—ARRIVAL AT REPTILE END.

Spilett took the box and opened it. It contained a white powder, which he tasted. Its extreme bitterness was unmistakable. It was indeed that precious alkaloid, the true anti-periodic.

It was necessary to administer it to Herbert without delay. How it came there could be discussed later.

Spilett called for some coffee, and Neb brought a lukewarm infusion, in which the reporter placed eighteen grains of quinine and gave the mixture to Herbert to drink.

There was still time, as the third attack of the fever had not yet manifested itself. And, indeed, it did not return. Moreover, every one became hopeful. The mysterious influence was again about them, and that too in a moment when they had despaired of its aid.

After a few hours, Herbert rested more quietly, and the colonists could talk of the incident. The intervention of this unknown being was more evident than ever, but how had he succeeded in getting in to Granite House during the night? It was perfectly inexplicable, and, indeed, the movements of this "genius of the island" were as mysterious as the genius himself.

The quinine was administered to Herbert every three hours, and the next day the lad was certainly better. It is true he was not out of danger, since these fevers are often followed by dangerous relapses; but, then, here was the specific, and, doubtless, not far off, the one who had brought it. In two days more Herbert became convalescent. He was still feeble, but there had been no relapse, and he cheerfully submitted to the rigorous diet imposed upon, him. He was so anxious to get well.

Pencroff was beside himself with joy. After the critical period had been safely passed he seized the reporter in his arms, and called him nothing but Doctor Spilett.

But the true physician was still to be found.

""We will find him!" said the sailor.

The year 1867, during which the colonists had been so hardly beset, came to an end, and the new year began with superb weather. A fine warmth, a tropical temperature, moderated by the sea breeze. Herbert's bed was drawn close to the window, where he could inhale long draughts of the salt, salubrious air. His appetite began to return, and what tempting savory morsels Neb prepared for him!

"It made one wish to be ill," said Pencroff.

During this time the convicts had not shown themselves, neither was there any news of Ayrton. The engineer and Herbert still hoped to get him back, but the others thought that the unhappy man had succumbed. In a month's time, when the lad should have regained his strength, the important search would be undertaken, and all these questions set at rest.

During January the work on the plateau consisted simply in collecting the grain and vegetables undestroyed in the work of devastation, and planting some for a late crop during the next season. Smith preferred to wait till the island was rid of the convicts before he repaired the damage to the mill, poultry-yard, and stable.

In the latter part of the month Herbert began to take some exercise. He was eighteen years old, his constitution was splendid, and from this moment the improvement in his condition was visible daily.

By the end of the month he walked on the shore and over the plateau, and strengthened himself with sea-baths. Smith felt that the day for the exploration could be set, and the 15th of February was chosen. The nights at this season were very clear, and would, therefore, be advantageous to the search.

The necessary preparations were begun. These were important, as the colonists had determined not to return to Granite House until their double end had been obtained—to destroy the convicts and find Ayrton, if he was still alive; and to discover the being who presided so efficiently over the destinies of the colony.

The colonists were familiar with all the eastern coast of the island between Claw Cape and the Mandibles; with Tadorn's Fens; the neighborhood of Lake Grant; the portion of Jacamar Wood lying between the road to the corral and the Mercy; the courses of the Mercy and Red Creek, and those spurs of Mount Franklin where the corral was located.

They had partially explored the long sweep of Washington Bay from Claw Cape to Reptile End; the wooded and marshy shore of the west coast, and the interminable downs which extended to the half-open mouth of Shark Gulf.

But they were unacquainted with the vast woods of Serpentine Peninsula; all the right bank of the Mercy; the left bank of Fall River, and the confused mass of ravines and ridges which covered three-fourths of the base of Mount Franklin on the west, north, and east, and where, doubtless, there existed deep recesses. Therefore, many thousands of acres had not yet been explored.

It was decided that the expedition should cross the Forest of the Far West, in such a manner as to go over all that part situated on the right of the Mercy. Perhaps it would have been better to have gone at once to the corral, where it was probable the convicts had either pillaged the place or installed themselves there. But either the pillage was a work accomplished or the convicts had purposed to entrench themselves there, and it would always be time to dislodge them.

So the first plan was decided upon, and it was resolved to cut a road through these woods, placing Granite House in communication with the end of the peninsula, a distance of sixteen or seventeen miles.

The wagon was in perfect order. The onagers, well rested, were in excellent condition for a long pull. Victuals, camp utensils, and the portable stove, were loaded into the wagon, together with a careful selection of arms and ammunition.

No one was left in Granite House; even Top and Jup took part in the expedition. The inaccessible dwelling could take care of itself.

Sunday, the day before the departure, was observed as a day of rest and prayer, and on the morning of the 15th Smith took the measures necessary to defend Granite House from invasion. The ladders were carried to the Chimneys and buried there, the basket of the elevator was removed, and nothing left of the apparatus. Pencroff, who remained behind in Granite House, saw to this latter, and then slid down to the ground by means of a double cord which, dropped to the ground, severed the last connection between the entrance and the shore.

The weather was superb.

"It is going to be a warm day," said the reporter, joyfully.

"But, Doctor Spilett," said Pencroff, "our road is under the trees, and we will never see the sun!"

"Forward!" said the engineer.

The wagon was ready on the bank. The reporter insisted on Herbert taking a seat in it, at least for the first few hours. Neb walked by the onagers. Smith, the reporter, and the sailor went on ahead. Top bounded off into the grass; Jup took a seat beside Herbert, and the little party started.

The wagon went up the left bank of the Mercy, across the bridge, and there, leaving the route to Balloon Harbor to the left, the explorers began to make a way through the forest.

For the first two miles, the trees grew sufficiently apart to permit the wagon to proceed easily, without any other obstacle than here and there a stump or some bushes to arrest their progress. The thick foliage made a cool shadow over the ground. Birds and beasts were plenty, and reminded the colonists of their early excursions on the island.

"Nevertheless," remarked Smith, "I notice that the animals are more timid than formerly. These woods have been recently traversed by the convicts, and we shall certainly find their traces."

And, indeed, in many places, they saw where a party of men had passed, or built a fire, but in no one place was there a definite camp.

The engineer had charged his companions to abstain from hunting, so as not to make the convicts aware of their presence by the sound of firearms.

In the afternoon, some six miles from Granite House, the advance became very difficult, and they had to pass certain thickets, into which Top and Jup were sent as skirmishers.

The halt for the night was made, nine miles from Granite House, on the bank of a small affluent to the Mercy, of whose existence they had been unaware. They had good appetites, and all made a hearty supper, after which the camp was carefully organized, in order to guard against a surprise from the convicts. Two of the colonists kept guard together in watches of two hours, but Herbert, in spite of his wishes, was not allowed to do duty.

The night passed without incident. The silence was unbroken save by the growling of jaguars and the chattering of monkeys, which seemed particularly to annoy Jup.

The next day, they were unable to accomplish more than six miles. Like true "frontiersmen," the colonists avoided the large trees and cut down only the smaller ones, so that their road was a winding one.

During the day Herbert discovered some specimens of the tree ferns, with vase-shaped leaves, and the algarobabeau (St. John's bread), which the onagers eat greedily. Splendid kauris, disposed in groups, rose to a height of two hundred feet, their cylindrical trunks surmounted by a crown of verdure.

As to fauna, they discovered no new specimens, but they saw, without being able to approach them, a couple of large birds, such as are common in Australia, a sort of cassowary, called emus, which were five feet high, of brown plumage, and belonged to the order of runners. Top tried his best to catch them, but they outran him easily, so great was their speed.

The colonists again found traces of the convicts. Near a recently-extinguished fire they found footprints, which they examined with great attention. By measuring these tracks they were able to determine the presence of five men. The five convicts had evidently camped here; but—and they made minute search—they could not discover a sixth track, which would have been that of Ayrton.

"Ayrton is not with them!" said Herbert.

"No," replied Pencroff, "the wretches have shot him." But they must have a den, to which we can track them."

"No," replied the reporter. "It is more likely that they intend to camp about in places, after this manner, until they become masters of the island."

"Masters of the island!" cried the sailor. "Masters of the island, indeed" he repeated in a horrified voice. Then he added:—

"The ball in my gun is the one which wounded Herbert and it will do its errand!"

But this just reprisal would not restore Ayrton to life, and the only conclusion to be drawn, from the footprints was that they would never see him again!

That evening the camp was made fourteen miles front Granite House, and Smith estimated that it was still five miles to Reptile End.

The next day this point was reached, and the full length of the forest had been traversed; but nothing indicated the retreat of the convicts, nor the asylum of the mysterious unknown.

CHAPTER LIV.

EXPLORATION OF REPTILE END—CAMP AT
THE MOUTH OF FALL RIVER—BY THE CORRAL—
THE RECONNOISSANCE—THE RETURN—FORWARD—
AN OPEN DOOR—A LIGHT IN THE WINDOW—
BY MOONLIGHT.

The next day, the 18th, was devoted to an exploration of the wooded shore lying between Reptile End and Fall River. The colonists were searching through the heart of the forest, whose width, bounded by the shores of the promontory, was from three to four miles. The trees, by their size and foliage, bore witness to the richness of the soil, more productive here than in any other portion of the island. It seemed as if a portion of the virgin forests of America or Central Africa had been transported here. It seemed, also, as if these superb trees found beneath the soil, moist on its surface, but heated below by volcanic fires, a warmth not belonging to a temperate climate. The principal trees, both in number and size, were the kauris and eucalypti.

But the object of the colonists was not to admire these magnificent vegetables. They knew already that, in this respect, their island merited a first place in the Canaries, called, formerly, the Fortunate Isles. But, alas! their island no longer belonged to them alone; others had taken possession, wretches whom it was necessary to destroy to the last man.

On the west coast they found no further traces of any kind.

"This does not astonish me," said Smith. "The convicts landed near Jetsam Point, and, after having crossed Tadorn's Fens, they buried themselves in the forests of the Far West. They took nearly the same route which we have followed. That explains the traces we have seen in the woods. Arrived upon the shore, the convicts saw very clearly that it offered no convenient shelter, and it was then, on going towards the north, that they discovered the corral—"

"Where they may have returned," said Pencroff.

"I do not think so," answered the engineer, "as they would judge that our searches would be in that direction. The corral is only a provisional and not a permanent retreat for them."

"I think so, too," said the reporter, "and, further, that they have sought a hiding place among the spurs of Mount Franklin."

"Then let us push on to the corral!" cried Pencroff. "An end must be put to this thing, and we are only losing time here."

"No, my friend," replied the engineer.

"You forget that we are interested in determining whether the forests of the Far West do not shelter some habitation. Our exploration has a double end, Pencroff; to punish crime and to make a discovery."

"That is all very well, sir," replied the sailor, "but I have an idea that we will not discover our friend unless he chooses!"

Pencroff had expressed the opinion of the others as well as his own. It was, indeed, probable that the retreat of the unknown being was no less mysterious than his personality.

This evening the wagon halted at the mouth of Fall River. The encampment was made in the usual way, with the customary precautions. Herbert had recovered his former strength by this march in the fresh salt air, and his place was no longer on the wagon, but at the head of the line.

On the 19th, the colonists left the shore and followed up the left bank of Fall River. The route was already partially cleared, owing to the previous excursions made from the corral to the west coast. They reached a place six miles from Mount Franklin.

The engineer's project was to observe with great care all the valley through which flowed the river, and to work cautiously up to the corral. If they should find it occupied, they were to secure it by main force, but if it should be empty, it was to be used as the point from which the explorations of Mount Franklin would be made.

The road was through a narrow valley, separating two of the most prominent spurs of Mount Franklin. The trees grew closely together on the banks of the river, but were more scattered on the upper slopes. The ground was very much broken, affording excellent opportunities for an ambush, so that it was necessary to advance with great caution. Top and Jup went ahead, exploring the thickets on either hand, but nothing indicated either the presence or nearness of the convicts, or that these banks had been recently visited.

About 5 o'clock the wagon halted 600 paces from the enclosure, hidden by a curtain of tall trees.

It was necessary to reconnoitre the place, in order to find out whether it was occupied, but to do this in the day-time was to run the risk of being shot; nevertheless Spilett wanted to make the experiment at once, and Pencroff, out of all patience, wanted to go with him. But Smith would not permit it.

"No, my friends," said he, "wait until nightfall. I will not allow one of you to expose yourselves in the daylight."

"But, sir,"—urged the sailor, but little disposed to obey.

"Pray do not go, Pencroff," said the engineer.

"All right," said the sailor. But he gave vent to his anger by calling the convicts everything bad that he could think of.

The colonists remained about the wagon, keeping a sharp lookout in the adjoining parts of the forest.

Three hours passed in this manner. The wind fell, and absolute silence reigned over everything. The slightest sound—the snapping of a twig, a step on the dry leaves—could easily have been heard. But all was quiet. Top rested with his head between his paws, giving no sign of inquietude.

By 8 o'clock the evening was far enough advanced for the reconnoissance to be undertaken, and Spilett and Pencroff set off alone. Top and Jup remained behind with the others, as it was necessary that no bark or cry should give the alarm.

"Do not do anything imprudently," urged Smith. "Remember, you are not to take possession of the corral, but only to find out whether it is occupied or not."

"All right," answered Pencroff.

The two set out, advancing with the greatest caution. Under the trees, the darkness was such as to render objects, thirty or forty paces distant, invisible. Five minutes after having left the wagon they reached the edge of the opening, at the end of which rose the fence of the enclosure. Here they halted. Some little light still illuminated the glade. Thirty paces distant was the gate of the corral, which seemed to be closed. These thirty paces which it was necessary to cross constituted, to use a ballistic expression, the dangerous zone, as a shot from the palisade would certainly have killed any one venturing himself within this space,

Spilett and the sailor were not men to shirk danger, but they knew that any imprudence of theirs would injure their companions as well as themselves. If they were killed what would become of the others?

Nevertheless, Pencroff was so excited in finding himself again close to the corral that he would have hurried forward had not the strong hand of Spilett detained him. "In a few minutes it will be dark," whispered the reporter.

Pencroff grasped his gun nervously, and waited unwillingly.

Very soon the last rays of light disappeared. Mount Franklin loomed darkly against the western sky, and the night fell with the rapidity peculiar to these low latitudes. Now was the time.

470

The reporter and Pencroff, ever since their arrival on the edge of the wood, had watched the corral. It seemed to be completely deserted. The upper edge of the palisade was in somewhat stronger relief than the surrounding shades, and nothing broke its outlines. Nevertheless, if the convicts were there, they must have posted one of their number as a guard.

Spilett took the hand of his companion, and crept cautiously forward to the gate of the corral. Pencroff tried to push it open, but it was, as they had supposed, fastened. But the sailor discovered that the outer bars were not in place. They, therefore, concluded that the convicts were within, and had fastened the gate so that it could only be broken open.

They listened. No sound broke the silence. The animals were doubtless sleeping in their sheds. Should they scale the fence? It was contrary to Smith's instructions. They might be successful or they might fail. And, if there was now a chance of surprising the convicts, should they risk that chance in this way?

The reporter thought not. He decided that it would be better to wait until they were all together before making the attempt. Two things were certain, that they could reach the fence unseen, and that the place seemed unguarded.

Pencroff, probably, agreed to this, for he returned with the reporter to the wood, and a few minutes later Smith was informed of the situation.

"Well," said he after reflecting for a moment, "I don't think that the convicts are here."

"We will find out when we have climbed in." cried Pencroff.

"To the corral, my friends."

"Shall we leave the wagon in the wood?" cried Neb.

"No," said Smith, "it may serve as a defense in case of need."

The wagon issued from the wood and rolled noiselessly over the ground. The darkness and the silence were profound. The colonists kept their guns in readiness to fire. Jup kept behind, at Pencroff's order, and Neb held Top.

Soon the dangerous zone was crossed, and the wagon was drawn up beside the fence. Neb stood at the head of the onagers to keep them quiet, and the others went to the gate to determine if it was barricaded on the inside.

One of its doors was open!

"What did you tell us?" exclaimed the engineer, turning to the sailor and Spilett.

They were stupefied with amazement.

"Upon my soul," cried the sailor, "It was shut a minute ago!"

The colonists hesitated. The convicts must have been in the corral when Pencroff and the reporter had made their reconnoissance; for the gate could only have been opened by them. Were they still there?

At this moment, Herbert, who had ventured some steps within the inclosure, rushed back and seized Smith's hand.

"What have you seen?" asked the engineer.

"A light!"

"In the house?"

"Yes, sir."

All went forward and saw a feeble ray of light trembling through the windows of the building.

Smith determined what to do at once.

"It is a fortunate chance, finding the convicts shut up in this house not expecting anything! They are ours! Come on!"

The wagon was left under charge of Top and Jup, and the colonists glided into the enclosure. In a few moments they were before the closed door of the house.

Smith, making a sign to his companions not to move, approached the window. He looked into the one room which formed the lower story of the building. On the table was a lighted lantern, Near by was Ayrton's bed. On it was the body of a man.

Suddenly, Smith uttered a stiffled exclamation.

"Ayrton!" he cried.

And, at once, the door was rather forced than opened, and all rushed into the chamber.

Ayrton seemed to be sleeping. His face showed marks of long and cruel suffering. His wrists and ankles were much bruised.

Smith leaned over him.

"Ayrton!" cried the engineer, seizing in his arms this man found so unexpectedly.

Ayrton opened his eyes, and looked first at Smith, then at the others.

"You! Is it you?" he cried.

"Ayrton! Ayrton!" repeated the engineer.

"Where am I?"

"In the corral."

"Am I alone?"

"Yes."

"Then they will come here!" cried Ayrton. "Look out for yourselves! Defend yourselves!" and he fell back, fainting.

"Spilett," said the engineer, "We may be attacked at any minute. Bring the wagon inside the enclosure, and bar the gate, and then come back here."

Pencroff, Neb, and the reporter hastened to execute the orders of the engineer. There was not an instant to be lost. Perhaps the wagon was already in the hands of the convicts!

In a moment the reporter and his companions had gained the gate of the enclosure, behind which they heard Top growling.

The engineer, leaving Ayrton for a moment, left the house, and held his gun in readiness to fire. Herbert was beside him. Both scrutinized the outline of the mountain spur overlooking the corral. If the convicts were hidden in that place they could pick off the colonists one after the other.

Just then the moon appeared in the east above the black curtain of the forest, throwing a flood of light over the interior of the corral, and bringing into relief the trees, the little water-course, and the grassy carpet.

Towards the mountain, the house and a part of the palisade shone white; opposite it, towards the gate, the fence was in shadow.

A black mass soon showed itself. It was the wagon entering within the circle of light, and Smith could hear the sound of the gate closing and being solidly barricaded by his companions.

But at that moment Top, by a violent effort, broke his fastening, and, barking furiously, rushed to the extremity of the corral to the right of the house.

"Look out, my friends, be ready!" cried Smith.

The colonists waited, with their guns at the shoulder. Top continued to bark, and Jup, running towards the dog, uttered sharp cries.

The colonists, following him, came to the border of the little brook, overshadowed by large trees.

And there, in the full moonlight, what did they see?

Five corpses lay extended upon the bank!

They were the bodies of the convicts, who, four months before, had landed upon Lincoln Island.

CHAPTER LV.

AYRTON'S RECITAL—PLANS OF HIS OLD COMRADES—
TAKING POSSESSION OF THE CORRAL—
THE RULES OF THE ISLAND—THE GOOD LUCK—
RESEARCHES ABOUT MOUNT FRANKLIN—
THE UPPER VALLEYS—SUBTERRANEAN RUMBLINGS—
PENCROFF'S ANSWER—AT THE BOTTOM OF
THE CRATER-THE RETURN.

How had it happened? Who had killed the convicts? Ayrton? No, since the moment before he had feared their return!

But Ayrton was now in a slumber from which it was impossible to arouse him. After he had spoken these few words, he had fallen back upon his bed, seized by a sudden torpor.

The colonists, terribly excited, preyed upon by a thousand confused thoughts, remained all night in the house. The next morning Ayrton awoke from his sleep, and his companions demonstrated to him their joy at finding him safe and sound after all these months of separation.

Then Ayrton related in a few words all that had happened.

The day after his return to the corral, the 10th of November, just at nightfall, he had been surprised by the convicts, who had climbed over the fence. He was tied and gagged and taken to a dark cavern at the foot of Mount Franklin, where the convicts had a retreat.

His death had been resolved upon, and he was to be killed the following day, when one of the convicts recognized him and called him by the name he had borne in Australia. These wretches, who would have massacred Ayrton, respected Ben Joyce.

From this moment Ayrton was subjected to the importunities of his old comrades. They wished to gain him over to them, and they counted upon him to take Granite House, to enter that inaccessible dwelling, and to become masters of the island, after having killed the colonists.

Ayrton resisted. The former convict, repentant and pardoned, would rather die than betray his companions.

For four months, fastened, gagged, watched, he had remained in this cavern.

Meanwhile the convicts lived upon the stock in the corral, but did not inhabit the place.

On the 11th of November, two of these bandits, inopportunely surprised by the arrival of the colonists, fired on Herbert, and one of them returned boasting of having killed one of the inhabitants. His companion, as we know, had fallen at Smith's hand.

One can judge of Ayrton's despair, when he heard of Herbert's death! It left but four of the colonists, almost at the mercy of the convicts!

Following this event, and during all the time that the colonists, detained by Herbert's illness, remained at the corral, the pirates did not leave their cave; indeed, after having pillaged Prospect Plateau, they did not deem it prudent to leave it.

The bad treatment of Ayrton was redoubled. His hands and feet still bore the red marks of the lines with which he remained bound, day and night. Each moment he expected to be killed.

This was the third week in February. The convicts, awaiting a favorable opportunity, rarely left their retreat, and then only to a point in the interior or on the west coast. Ayrton had no news of his friends, and no hopes of seeing them again.

Finally, the poor unfortunate, enfeebled by bad treatment, fell in a profound prostration in which he neither saw nor heard anything. From this moment, he could not say what had happened.

"But, Mr. Smith," he added, "since I was imprisoned in this cavern, how is it that I am here?"

"How is that the convicts are lying there, dead, in the middle of the corral?" answered the engineer.

"Dead!" cried Ayrton, half rising, notwithstanding his feebleness. His companions assisted him to get up, and all went to the little brook.

It was broad daylight. There on the shore, in the position in which they had met their deaths, lay the five convicts.

Ayrton was astounded. The others looked on without speaking. Then, at a sign from Smith, Neb and Pencroff examined the bodies. Not a wound was visible upon them. Only after minute search, Pencroff perceived on the forehead of one, on the breast of another, on this one's back, and on the shoulder of a fourth, a small red mark, a hardly visible bruise, made by some unknown instrument.

"There is where they have been hit!" said Smith.

"But with what sort of a weapon?" cried the reporter.

"A destructive weapon enough, though unknown to us!"

"And who has destroyed them?" asked Pencroff.

"The ruler of the island," answered Smith, "he who has brought you here, Ayrton, whose influence is again manifesting itself, who does for us what we are unable to do for ourselves, and who then hides from us."

"Let us search for him!" cried Pencroff.

"Yes, we will search," replied Smith; "but the being who accomplishes such prodigies will not be found until it pleases him to call us to him!"

This invisible protection, which nullified their own actions, both annoyed and affected the engineer. The relative inferiority in which it placed him wounded his pride. A generosity which so studiously eluded all mark of recognition denoted a sort of disdain for those benefited, which, in a measure, detracted from the value of the gift.

"Let us search," he repeated, "and Heaven grant that some day we be permitted to prove to this haughty protector that he is not dealing with ingrates! What would I not give to be able, in our turn, to repay him, and to render him, even at the risk of our lives, some signal service!"

From this time, this search was the single endeavor of the inhabitants of Lincoln Island. All tried to discover the answer to this enigma, an answer which involved the name of a man endowed with an inexplicable, an almost superhuman power.

In a short time, the colonists entered the house again, and their efforts soon restored Ayrton to himself. Neb and Pencroff carried away the bodies of the convicts and buried them in the wood. Then, Ayrton was informed by the engineer of all that had happened during his imprisonment.

"And now," said Smith, finishing his recital, "we have one thing more to do. Half of our task is accomplished; but if the convicts are no longer to be feared, we did not restore ourselves to the mastership of the island!"

"Very well," replied Spilett, "let us search all the mazes of Mount Franklin. Let us leave no cavity, no hole unexplored! Ah! if ever a reporter found himself in the presence of an exciting mystery. I am in that position!"

"And we will not return to Granite House," said Herbert, "until we have found our benefactor."

"Yes," said Smith, "we will do everything that is possible for human beings to do—but, I repeat it, we will not find him till he wills it."

"Shall we stay here at the corral?" asked Pencroff.

"Yes," replied the engineer, "let us remain here. Provisions are abundant, and we are in the centre of our circle of investigation, and, moreover, if it is necessary, the wagon can go quickly to Granite House."

"All right," said Pencroff. "Only one thing."

"What is that?"

"Why, the fine weather is here, and we must not forget that we have a voyage to make."

"A voyage?" asked Spilett.

"Yes, to Tabor Island. We most put up a notice, indicating our island, in case the Scotch yacht returns. Who knows that it is not already too late?"

"But, Pencroff," asked Ayrton, "how do you propose to make this voyage?"

"Why, on the Good Luck!"

"The Good Luck!" cried Ayrton. "It's gone!"

"Gone!" shouted Pencroff, springing to his feet.

"Yes. The convicts discovered where the sloop lay, and, a week ago, they put out to sea in her, and—"

"And?" said Pencroff, his heart trembling.

"And, not having Harvey to manage her, they ran her upon the rocks, and she broke all to pieces!"

"Oh! the wretches! the pirates! the devils!" exclaimed the sailor.

"Pencroff," said Herbert, taking his hand, "we will build another, a larger Good Luck. We have all the iron, all the rigging of the brig at our disposal!"

"But, do you realize," answered Pencroff, "that it will take at least five or six months to build a vessel of thirty or forty tons."

"We will take our time," replied the reporter, "and we will give up our voyage to Tabor Island for this year."

"We must make the best of it, Pencroff," said the engineer, "and I hope that this delay will not be prejudicial to us."

"My poor Good Luck! my poor boat!" exclaimed the sailor, half broken-hearted at the loss of what was so dear to him.

The destruction of the sloop was a thing much to be regretted, and it was agreed that this loss must be repaired as soon as the search was ended.

This search was begun the same day, the 19th of February, and lasted throughout the week. The base of the mountain was composed of a perfect labyrinth of ravines and gorges, and it was here that the explorations must be made. No other part of the island was so well suited to hide an inhabitant who wished to remain concealed. But so great was the intricacy of these places that Smith explored them by a settled system.

In the first place, the colonists visited the valley opening to the south of the volcano, in which Fall River rose. Here was where Ayrton showed them the cavern of the convicts. This place was in exactly the same condition as Ayrton had left it. They found here a quantity of food and ammunition left there as a reserve by the convicts.

All this beautiful wooded valley was explored with great care, and then, the south-western spur having been turned, the colonists searched a narrow gorge where the trees were less numerous. Here the stones took the place of grass, and the wild goats and moufflons bounded among the rocks. The arid part of the island began at this part. They saw already that, of the numerous valleys ramifying from the base of Mount Franklin, three only, bounded on the west by Fall River and on the east by Red Creek, were as rich and fertile as the valley of the corral. These two brooks, which developed into rivers as they progressed, received the whole of the mountain's southern water-shed and fertilized that portion of it. As to the Mercy it was more directly fed by abundant springs, hidden in Jacamar Wood.

Now any one of these three valleys would have answered for the retreat of some recluse, who would have found there all the necessaries of life. But the colonists had explored each of them without detecting the presence of man. Was it then at the bottom of these arid gorges, in the midst of heaps of rocks, in the rugged ravines to the north, between the streams of lava, that they would find this retreat and its occupant?

The northern part of Mount Franklin had at its base two large, arid valleys strewn with lava, sown with huge rocks, sprinkled with pieces of obsidian and labradorite. This part required long and difficult exploration. Here were a thousand cavities, not very comfortable, perhaps, but completely hidden and difficult of access. The colonists visited sombre tunnels, made in the plutonic epoch, still blackened by the fires of other

480

days, which plunged into the heart of the mountain. They searched these dark galleries by the light of torches, peering into their least excavations and sounding their lowest depths. But everywhere was silence, obscurity. It did not seem as if any human being had ever trodden these antique corridors or an arm displaced one of these stones.

Nevertheless, if these places were absolutely deserted, if the obscurity was complete, Smith was forced to notice that absolute silence did not reign there.

Having arrived at the bottom of one of those sombre cavities, which extended several hundred feet into the interior of the mountain, he was surprised to hear deep muttering sounds which were intensified by the sonority of the rocks.

Spilett, who was with him, also heard these distant murmurs, which indicated an awakening of the subterranean fires.

Several times they listened, and they came to the conclusion that some chemical reaction was going on in the bowels of the earth.

"The volcano is not entirely extinct," said the reporter.

"It is possible that, since our exploration of the crater, something has happened in its lower regions. All volcanoes, even those which are said to be extinct, can, evidently, become active again."

"But if Mount Franklin is preparing for another eruption, is not Lincoln Island in danger?"

"I don't think so," answered the engineer, "The crater, that is to say, the safety-valve, exists, and the overflow of vapors and lavas will escape, as heretofore, by its accustomed outlet."

"Unless the lavas make a new passage towards the fertile parts of the island."

"Why, my dear Spilett, should they not follow their natural course?"

"Well, volcanoes are capricious."

"Notice," said Smith, "that all the slope of the mountain favors the flow of eruptive matter towards the valleys which we are traversing at present. It would take an earthquake to so change the centre of gravity of the mountain as to modify this slope."

"But an earthquake is always possible under these conditions."

"True," replied the engineer, "especially when the subterranean forces are awakening, and the bowels of the earth, after a long repose, chance to be obstructed. You are right, my dear Spilett, an eruption would be a serious thing for us, and it would be better if this volcano has not the desire to wake up; but we can do nothing. Nevertheless, in any case, I do not think Prospect Plateau could be seriously menaced. Between it and the lake there is quite a depression in the land, and even if the lavas took the road to the lake, they would be distributed over the downs and the parts adjoining Shark Gulf."

"We have not yet seen any smoke from the summit, indicating a near eruption," said Spilett.

"No," answered the engineer, "not the least vapor has escaped from the crater. It was but yesterday that I observed its upper part. But it is possible that rocks, cinders, and hardened lavas have accumulated in the lower part of its chimney, and, for the moment, this safety-valve is overloaded. But, at the first serious effort, all obstacles will disappear, and you may be sure, my dear Spilett, that neither the island, which is the boiler, nor the volcano, which is the valve, will burst under the pressure. Nevertheless, I repeat, it is better to wish for no eruption."

"And yet we are not mistaken," replied the reporter. "We plainly hear ominous rumblings in the depths of the volcano!"

"No," replied the engineer, after listening again with the utmost attention, "that is not to be mistaken. Something is going on there the importance of which cannot be estimated nor what the result will be."

Smith and Spilett, on rejoining their companions, told them of these things.

"All right!" cried Pencroff. "This volcano wants to take care of us! But let it try! It will find its master!"

"Who's that?" asked the negro.

"Our genius, Neb, our good genius, who will put a gag in the mouth of the crater if it attempts to open it."

The confidence of the sailor in the guardian of the island was absolute, and, indeed, the occult power which had so far been manifested seemed limitless; but, thus far this being had escaped all the efforts the colonists had made to discover him.

From the 19th to the 25th of February, the investigations were conducted in the western portion of Lincoln Island, where the most secret recesses were searched. They even sounded each rocky wall, as one knocks against the walls of a suspected house. The engineer went so far as to take the exact measure of the mountain, and he pushed his search to the last strata sustaining it. It was explored to the summit of the truncated cone which rose above the first rocky level, and from there to the upper edge of the enormous cap at the bottom of which opened the crater.

They did more; they visited the gulf, still extinct, but in whose depths the rumblings were distinctly heard. Nevertheless, not a smoke, not a vapor, no heat in the wall, indicated a near eruption. But neither there, nor in any other part of Mount Franklin, did the colonists find the traces of him whom they sought.

Their investigations were then directed over all the tract of downs. They carefully examined the high lava walls of Shark Gulf from base to summit, although it was very difficult to reach the water level. No one! Nothing!

These two words summed up in brief the result of all the useless fatigues Smith and his companions had been at, and they were a trifle annoyed at their ill success.

But it was necessary now to think of returning, as these researches could not be pursued indefinitely. The colonists were convinced that this mysterious being did not reside upon the surface of the island, and strange thoughts floated through their over-excited imaginations; Neb and Pencroff, particularly, went beyond the strange into the region of the supernatural. The 25th of February, the colonists returned to Granite House, and by means of the double cord, shot by an arrow to the door-landing, communication was established with their domain.

One month later, they celebrated the third anniversary of their arrival on Lincoln Island.

CHAPTER LVI.

AFTER THREE YEARS—THE QUESTION OF A NEW
SHIP—ITS DETERMINATION—PROSPERITY OF THE
COLONY—THE SHIPYARD—THE COLD WEATHER—
PENCROFF RESIGNED—WASHING—
MOUNT FRANKLIN.

Three years had passed since the prisoners had fled from Richmond, and in all that time their conversation and their thoughts had been of the fatherland.

They had no doubt that the war was ended, and that the North had triumphed. But how? At what cost? What friends had fallen in the struggle? They often talked of these things, although they had no knowledge when they would be able to see that country again. To return, if only for a few days; to renew their intercourse with civilization; to establish a communication between their island and the mother country, and then to spend the greater part of their lives in this colony which they had founded and which would then be raised to a metropolis, was this a dream which could not be realized?

There were but two ways of realizing it: either a ship would some day show itself in the neighborhood of Lincoln Island, or the colonists must themselves build a vessel staunch enough to carry them to the nearest land.

"Unless our genius furnishes us with the means of returning home," said Pencroff.

And, indeed, if Neb and Pencroff had been told that a 300-ton ship was waiting for them in Shark Gulf or Balloon Harbor, they would not have manifested any surprise. In their present condition they expected every thing.

But Smith, less confident, urged them to keep to realities, and to build the vessel, whose need was urgent, since a paper should be placed on Tabor Island as soon as possible, in order to indicate the new abode of Ayrton.

The Good Luck was gone. It would take at least six mouths to build another vessel, and, as winter was approaching, the voyage could not be made before the next spring.

"We have time to prepare ourself for the fine weather," said the engineer, talking of these things with Pencroff. "I think, therefore, since we have to build our own ship, it will be better to make her dimensions greater than before. The arrival of the Scotch yacht is uncertain. It may even have happened that it has come and gone. What do you think? Would it not be better to build a vessel, that, in case of need, could carry us to the archipelagoes or New Zealand?"

"I think, sir, that you are as able to build a large vessel as a small one. Neither wood nor tools are wanting. It is only a question of time."

"And how long would it take to build a ship of 250 or 300 tons?"

"Seven or eight months at least. But we must not forget that winter is at hand, and that the timber will be difficult to work during the severe cold. So, allowing for some weeks' delay, you can be happy if you have your ship by next November."

"Very well, that will be just the season to undertake a voyage of some length, be it to Tabor Island of further."

"All right, Mr. Smith, make your plans. The workmen are ready, and I guess that Ayrton will lend a helping hand."

The engineer's project met the approval of the colonists, and indeed it was the best thing to do. It is true that it was a great undertaking, but they had that confidence in themselves, which is one of the elements of success.

While Smith was busy preparing the plans of the vessel, the others occupied themselves in felling the trees and preparing the timber. The forests of the Far West furnished the best oak and elm, which were carried over the new road through the forest to the Chimneys, where the ship-yard was established.

It was important that the timber should be cut soon, as it was necessary to have it seasoning for some time. Therefore the workmen worked vigorously during April, which was not an inclement month, save for some violent wind storms. Jup helped them by his adroitness, either in climbing to the top of a tree to fasten a rope, or by carrying loads on his strong shoulders.

The timber was piled under a huge shed to await its use; and, meanwhile, the work in the fields was pushed forward, so that soon all traces of the devastation caused by the pirates had disappeared. The mill was rebuilt, and a new inclosure for the poultry yard. This had to be much larger than the former, as the number of its occupants had increased largely. The stables contained five onagas, four of them well broken, and one little colt. A plough had been added to the stock of the colony, and the onagas were employed in tillage as if they were Yorkshire or Kentucky cattle. All the colonists did their share, and there were no idle hands. And thus, with good health and spirits, they formed a thousand projects for the future.

Ayrton, of course, partook of the common existence, and spoke no longer of returning to the corral. Nevertheless, he was always quiet and uncommunicative, and shared more in the work than the pleasure of his companions. He was a strong workman, vigorous, adroit, intelligent, and he could not fail to see that he was esteemed and loved by the others. But the corral was not abandoned. Every other day some one went there and brought back the supply of milk for the colony, and these occasions were also hunting excursions. So that, Herbert and Spilett, with Top in advance, oftenest made the journey, and all kinds of game abounded in the kitchen of Granite House. The products of the warren and the oyster-bed, some turtles, a haul of excellent salmon, the vegetables from the plateau, the natural fruits of the forest, were riches upon riches, and Neb, the chief cook, found it difficult to store them all away.

The telegraph had been repaired, and was used whenever one of the party remained over night at the corral. But the island was secure now from any aggression—at least from men.

Nevertheless, what had happened once might happen again, and a descent of pirates was always to be feared. And it was possible that accomplices of Harvey, still in Norfolk, might be privy to his projects and seek to imitate them. Every day the colonists searched the horizon visible from Granite House with the glass, and whenever they were at the corral they examined the west coast. Nothing appeared, but they were always on the alert.

One evening the engineer told his companions of a project to fortify the corral. It seemed prudent to heighten the palisade, and to flank it with a sort of block house, in which the colonists could defend themselves against a host of enemies. Granite House, owing to its position, was impregnable, and the corral would always be the objective point of pirates.

About the 15th of May the keel of the new vessel was laid, and the stem and stern posts raised. This keel was of oak, 110 feet long, and the breadth of beam was 25 feet. But, with the exception of putting up a couple of the frame pieces, this was all that could be done before the bad weather and the cold set in.

During the latter part of the month the weather was very inclement. Pencroff and Ayrton worked as long as they were able, but severely cold weather following the rain made the wood impossible to handle, and by the 10th of June the work was given up entirely, and the colonists were often obliged to keep in-doors.

This confinement was hard for all of them, but especially so for Spilett.

"I'll tell you what, Neb," he said, "I will give you everything I own if you will get me a newspaper! All that I want to make me happy is to know what is going on in the world!"

Neb laughed.

"Faith!" said he, "I am busy enough with my daily work."

And, indeed, occupation was not wanting. The colony was at the summit of prosperity. The accident to the brig had been a new source of riches. Without counting a complete outfit of sails, which would answer for the new ship, utensils and tools of all sorts, ammunition, clothing, and instruments filled the store-rooms of Granite House. There was no longer a necessity to manufacture cloth in the felting mill. Linen, also, was plenty, and they took great care of it. From the chloride of sodium Smith had easily extracted soda and chlorine. The soda was easily transformed into carbonate of soda, and the chlorine was employed for various domestic purposes, but especially for cleaning the linen. Moreover, they made but four washings a year, as was the custom in old times, and Pencroff and Spilett, while waiting for the postman to bring the paper, made famous washermen!

Thus passed June, July, and August; very rigorous months, in which the thermometer measured but 8° Fahrenheit. But a good fire burned in the chimney of Granite House, and the superfluity of wood from the ship-yard enabled them to economize the coal, which required a longer carriage.

All, men and beasts, enjoyed good health. Jup, it is true, shivered a little with the cold, and they had to make him a good wadded wrapper. What servant he was! Adroit, zealous, indefatigable, not indiscreet, not talkative. He was, indeed, a model for his biped brethren in the New and the Old World!

"But, after all," said Pencroff "when one has four hands, they cannot help doing their work well!"

During the seven months that had passed since the exploration of the mountain nothing had been seen or heard of the genius of the island.

Although, it is true, that nothing had happened to the colonists requiring his assistance.

Smith noticed, too, that the growling of the dog and the anxiety of the orang had ceased during this time. These two friends no longer ran to the orifice of the well nor acted in that strange way which had attracted the attention of the engineer. But did this prove that everything had happened that was going to happen? That they were never to find an answer to the enigma? Could it be affirmed that no new conjunction of circumstances would make this mysterious personage appear again? Who knows what the future may bring forth?

On the 7th of September, Smith, looking towards Mount Franklin, saw a smoke rising and curling above the crater.

CHAPTER LVII.

THE AWAKENING OF THE VOLCANO—
THE FINE WEATHER—RESUMPTION OF WORK—
THE EVENING OF THE 15TH OF OCTOBER—
A TELEGRAPH—A DEMAND—AN ANSWER—
DEPARTURE FOR THE CORRAL—THE NOTICE—
THE EXTRA WIRE—THE BASALT WALL—
AT HIGH TIDE—AT LOW TIDE—THE CAVERN—
A DAZZLING LIGHT.

The colonists, called by Smith, had left their work, and gazed in silence at the summit of Mount Franklin.

The volcano had certainly awakened, and its vapors had penetrated the mineral matter of the crater, but no one could say whether the subterranean fires would bring on a violent eruption.

But, even supposing an eruption, it was not likely that Lincoln Island would suffer in every part. The discharges of volcanic matter are not always disastrous. That the island had already been subjected to an eruption was evident from the currents of lava spread over the western slope of the mountain. Moreover, the shape of the crater was such as to vomit matter in the direction away from the fertile parts of the island.

Nevertheless, what had been was no proof of what would be. Often the old craters of volcanoes close and new ones open. An earthquake phenomenon, often accompanying volcanic action, may do this by changing the interior arrangement of the mountain and opening new passages for the incandescent lavas.

Smith explained these things to his companions, and without exaggerating the situation, showed them just what might happen.

After all, they could do nothing. Granite House did not seem to be menaced, unless by a severe earthquake. But all feared for the corral, if any new crater opened in the mountain.

From this time the vapor poured from the cone without cessation, and, indeed, increased in density and volume, although no flame penetrated its thick folds. The phenomenon was confined, as yet, to the lower part of the central chimney.

Meanwhile, with good weather, the work out of doors had been resumed. They hastened the construction of the ship, and Smith established a saw-mill at the waterfall, which cut the timber much more rapidly.

Towards the end of September the frame of the ship, which was to be schooner-rigged, was so far completed that its shape could be recognized. The schooner, sheer forward and wide aft, was well adapted for a long voyage, in case of necessity, but the planking, lining, and decking still demanded a long time before they could be finished. Fortunately, the iron-work of the brig had been saved after the explosion, and Pencroff and Ayrton had obtained a great quantity of copper nails from the broken timber, which economized the labor for the smiths; nevertheless the carpenters had much to accomplish.

Often, however, after the day's work was ended, the colonists sat late into the night, conversing together of the future and what might happen in a voyage in the schooner to the nearest land. But in discussing these projects they always planned to return to Lincoln Island. Never would they abandon this colony, established with so much difficulty, but so successfully, and which would receive a new development through communication with America.

Pencroff and Neb, indeed, hoped to end their days here.

"Herbert," asked the sailor, "you would never abandon Lincoln Island?"

"Never, Pencroff, especially if you made up your mind to remain."

"Then, it's agreed, my boy. I shall expect you! You will bring your wife and children here, and I will make a jolly playmate for the babies!"

"Agreed," answered Herbert, laughing and blushing at the same time.

"And you, Mr. Smith," continued the sailor, enthusiastically, "you will always remain governor of the island! And, by the way, how many inhabitants can the island support? Ten thousand, at the very least!"

They chatted in this way, letting Pencroff indulge in his whims, and one thing leading to another, the reporter finished by founding the *New Lincoln Herald!*

Thus it is with the spirit of man. The need of doing something permanent, something which will survive him, is the sign of his superiority over everything here below. It is that which has established and justifies his domination over the whole world.

After all, who knows if Jup and Top had not their dream of the future?

Ayrton, silent, said to himself that he wanted to see Lord Glenarvan, and show him the change in himself.

One evening, the 15th of October, the conversation was prolonged longer than usual. It was 9 o'clock, and already, long, ill-concealed yawns showed that it was bed-time. Pencroff was about starting in that direction, when, suddenly, the electric bell in the hall rang.

Every one was present, so none of their party could be at the corral. Smith rose. His companions looked as if they had not heard aright.

"What does he want?" cried Neb. "Is it the devil that's ringing?"

No one replied.

"It is stormy weather," said Herbert; "perhaps the electric influence—"

Herbert did not finish the sentence. The engineer, towards whom all were looking, shook his head.

"Wait a minute," said Spilett. "If it is a signal, it will be repeated."

"But what do you think it is?" asked Neb.

"Perhaps it—"

The sailor's words were interrupted by another ring.

Smith went to the apparatus, and, turning on the current, telegraphed to the corral:—

"What do you want?"

A few minutes later the needle, moving over the lettered card, gave this answer to the inmates of Granite House:—

"Come to the corral as quickly as possible."

"At last!" cried Smith.

Yes! At last! The mystery was about to be solved! Before the strong interest in what was at the corral, all fatigue and need of repose vanished. Without saying a word, in a few minutes they were out of Granite House and following the shore. Only Top and Jup remained behind.

The night was dark. The moon, new this day, had set with the sun. Heavy clouds obscured the stars, but now and then heat-lightning, the reflection of a distant storm, illuminated the horizon.

But, great as the darkness was, it could not hinder persons as familiar with the route as were the colonists. All were very much excited, and walked rapidly. There could be no doubt that they were going to find the answer to the engineer, the name of that mysterious being, who was so generous in his influence, so powerful to accomplish! It could not be doubted that this unknown had been familiar with the least detail of their daily lives, that he overheard all that was said in Granite House.

Each one, lost in his reflections, hurried onward. The darkness under the trees was such that the route was invisible. There was no sound in the forest. Not a breath of wind moved the leaves.

This silence during the first quarter of an hour was uninterrupted, save by Pencroff, who said:—

"We should have brought a lantern."

And by the engineer's answer:—

"We will find one at the corral."

Smith and his companions had left Granite House at twelve minutes past 9. In thirty-five minutes they had traversed three of the five miles between the mouth of the Mercy and the corral.

Just then, brilliant flashes of lightning threw the foliage into strong relief. The storm was evidently about to burst upon them. The flashes became more frequent and intense. Heavy thunder rolled through the heavens. The air was stifling.

The colonists rushed on, as if impelled by some irresistible force.

At a quarter past 9, a sudden flash showed them the outline of the palisade; and scarcely had they passed the gateway when there came a terrible clap of thunder. In a moment the corral was crossed, and Smith stood before the house. It was possible that the unknown being was here, since it was from this place that the telegraph had come. Nevertheless, there was no light in the window.

The engineer knocked at the door, but without response.

He opened it, and the colonists entered the room, which was in utter darkness.

A light was struck by Neb, and in a moment the lantern was lit, and its light directed into every corner of the chamber.

No one was there, and everything remained undisturbed.

"Are we victims to a delusion?" murmured Smith.

No! that was impossible! The telegraph had certainly said:—

"Come to the corral quickly as possible."

He went to the table on which the apparatus was arranged. Everything was in place and in order.

"Who was here last?" asked the engineer.

"I, sir," answered Ayrton.

"And that was—"

"Four days ago."

"Ah! here is something!" exclaimed Herbert, pointing to a paper lying on the table.

On the paper were these words, written in English:—

"Follow the new wire."

"Come on!" cried Smith, who comprehended in a moment that the dispatch had not been sent from the corral, but from the mysterious abode which the new wire united directly with Granite House.

Neb took the lantern and all left the corral.

Then the storm broke forth with extreme violence. Flashes of lightning and peals of thunder followed in rapid succession. The island was the centre of the storm. By the flashes of lightning they could see the summit of Mount Franklin enshrouded in smoke.

There were no telegraph poles inside the corral, but the engineer, having passed the gate, ran to the nearest post, and saw there a new wire fastened to the insulator, and reaching to the ground.

"Here it is!" he cried.

The wire lay along the ground, and was covered with some insulating substance, like the submarine cables. By its direction it seemed as if it went towards the west, across the woods, and the southern spurs of the mountain.

"Let us follow it," said Smith.

And sometimes by the light of the lantern, sometimes by the illumination of the heavens, the colonists followed the way indicated by the thread.

They crossed in the first place, the spur of the mountain between the valley of the corral and that of Fall River, which stream was crossed in its narrowest part. The wire, sometimes hanging on the lower branches of the trees, sometimes trailing along the ground, was a sure guide.

The engineer had thought that, perhaps, the wire would end at the bottom of the valley, and that the unknown retreat was there.

But not so. It extended over the southwestern spur and descended to the arid plateau which ended that fantastic wall of basalt. Every now and

496

then one or other of the party stooped and took the direction of the wire. There could be no doubt that it ran directly to the sea. There, doubtless, in some profound chasm in the igneous rocks, was the dwelling so vainly sought for until now.

At a few minutes before 10, the colonists arrived upon the high coast overhanging the ocean. Here the wire wound among the rocks, following a steep slope down a narrow ravine.

The colonists followed it, at the risk of bringing down upon themselves a shower of rocks or of being precipitated into the sea. The descent was extremely perilous, but they thought not of the danger; they were attracted to this mysterious place as the needle is drawn to the magnet.

At length, the wire making a sudden turn, touched the shore rocks, which were beaten by the sea. The colonists had reached the base of the granite wall.

Here there was a narrow projection running parallel and horizontal to the sea. The thread led along this point, and the colonists followed. They had not proceeded more than a hundred paces, when this projection, by a south inclination, sloped down into the water.

The engineer seized the wire and saw that it led down into the sea.

His companions stood, stupefied, beside him.

Then a cry of disappointment, almost of despair, escaped them! Must they throw themselves into the water and search some submarine cavern? In their present state of excitement, they would not have hesitated to have done it.

An observation made by the engineer stopped them. He led his companions to the shelter of a pile of rocks and said:—

"Let as wait here. The tide is up. At low water the road will be open."

"But how do you think—" began Pencroff.

"He would not have called us, unless the means of reaching him had been provided."

Smith had spoken with an air of conviction, and, moreover, his observation was logical. It was, indeed, quite possible that an opening existed at low water which was covered at present.

It was necessary to wait some hours. The colonists rested in silence under their shelter. The rain began to fall in torrents. The echoes repeated the roaring of the thunder in sonorous reverberations.

At midnight the engineer took the lantern and went down to the water's edge. It was still two hours before low tide.

Smith had not been mistaken. The entrance to a vast excavation began to be visible, and the wire, turning at a right angle, entered this yawning mouth.

Smith returned to his companions and said:—

"In an hour the opening will be accessible."

"Then there is one," said Pencroff.

"Do you doubt it?" replied Smith.

"But it will be half full of water," said Herbert.

"Either it will be perfectly dry," answered the engineer, "in which case we will walk, or it will not be dry, and some means of transport will be furnished us."

An hour passed. All went down through the rain to the sea. In these hours the tide had fallen fifteen feet. The top of the mouth of the opening rose eight feet above the water, like the arch of a bridge.

Looking in, the engineer saw a black object floating on the surface. He drew it toward him. It was a canoe made of sheet-iron bolted together. It was tied to a projecting rock inside the cavern wall. A pair of oars were under the seats.

"Get in," said Smith.

The colonists entered the boat, Neb and Ayrton took the oars, Pencroff the tiller, and Smith, in the bows holding the lantern, lit the way.

The vault, at first very low, rose suddenly; but the darkness was too great for them to recognize the size of this cavern, its heighth and depth.

An imposing silence reigned throughout this granite chamber. No sound, not even the pealing of the thunder penetrated its massive walls.

In certain parts of the world there are immense caves, a sort of natural crypts which date back to the geologic epoch. Some are invaded by the sea; others contain large lakes within their walls. Such is Fingal's Cave, in the Island of Staffa; such are the caves of Morgat on the Bay of Douarnenez in Brittany; the caves of Bonifacio, in Corsica; those of Lyse-Fjord, in Norway; such is that immense cavern, the Mammoth Cave of Kentucky, which is 500 feet high and more than twenty miles long!

As to this cavern which the colonists were exploring, did it not reach to the very centre of the island? For a quarter of an hour the canoe advanced under the directions of the engineer. At a certain moment he said:—

"Go over to the right."

The canoe, taking this direction, brought up beside the wall. The engineer wished to observe whether the wire continued along this side.

It was there fastened to the rock.

"Forward!" said Smith.

The canoe kept on a quarter of an hour longer, and it must have been half a mile from the entrance, when Smith's voice was heard again.

"Halt!" he exclaimed.

The canoe stopped, and the colonists saw a brilliant light illuminating the enormous crypt, so profoundly hidden in the bowels of the earth.

They were now enabled to examine this cavern of whose existence they had had no suspicion.

A vault, supported on basaltic shafts, which might all have been cast in the same mould, rose to a height of 100 feet. Fantastic arches sprung at irregular intervals from these columns, which Nature had placed here by thousands. They rose to a height of forty or fifty feet, and the water, in despite of the tumult without, quietly lapped their base. The light noticed by the engineer seized upon each prismatic point and tipped it with fire;

penetrated, so to speak, the walls as if they had been diaphanous, and changed into sparkling jewels the least projections of the cavern.

Following a phenomenon of reflection, the water reproduced these different lights upon its surface, so that the canoe seemed to float between two sparkling zones.

They had not yet thought of the nature of irradiation projected by the luminous centre whose rays, straight and clear, were broken on all the angles and mouldings of the crypt. The white color of this light betrayed its origin. It was electric. It was the sun of this cavern.

On a sign from Smith, the oars fell again into the water, and the canoe proceeded towards the luminous fire, which was half a cable's length distant.

In this place, the sheet of water measured some 300 feet across, and an enormous basaltic wall, closing all that side, was visible beyond the luminous centre. The cavern had become much enlarged, and the sea here formed a little lake. But the vault, the side walls, and those of the apsis, all the prisms, cylinders, cones, were bathed in the electric fluid.

In the centre of the lake a long fusiform object floated on the surface of the water, silent, motionless. The light escaped from its sides as from two ovens heated to a white heat. This machine, looking like the body of an enormous cetacea, was 250 feet long, and rose ten to twelve feet above the water.

The canoe approached softly. In the bows stood Smith. He was greatly excited. Suddenly he seized the arm of the reporter.

"It is he! It can be no other than he." he cried. "He!—"

Then he fell back upon the seat murmuring a name which Spilett alone heard.

Doubtless the reporter knew this name, for it affected him strangely, and he answered in a hoarse voice:—

"He! a man outlawed!"

"The same!" said Smith.

500

Under the engineer's direction the canoe approached this singular floating machine, and came up to it on its left side, from which escaped a gleam of light through a thick glass.

Smith and his companions stepped on to the platform. An open hatchway was there, down which all descended.

At the bottom of the ladder appeared the waist of the vessel lit up by electric light. At the end of the waist was a door, which Smith pushed open.

A richly ornamented library, flooded with light, was rapidly crossed by the colonists. Beyond, a large door, also closed, was pushed open by the engineer.

A vast saloon, a sort of museum, in which were arranged all the treasures of the mineral world, works of art, marvels of industry, appeared before the eyes of the colonists, who seemed to be transported to the land of dreams.

Extended upon a rich divan they saw a man, who seemed unaware of their presence.

Then Smith raised his voice, and, to the extreme surprise of his companions, pronounced these words:—

"Captain Nemo, you have called us. Here we are.'

CHAPTER LVIII.

CAPTAIN NEMO—HIS FIRST WORDS—HISTORY OF
A HERO OF LIBERTY—HATRED OF THE INVADERS—
HIS COMPANIONS—THE LIFE UNDER WATER—
ALONE—THE LAST REFUGE OF THE NAUTILUS—
THE MYSTERIOUS GENIUS OF THE ISLAND.

At these words the man arose, and the light shone full upon his face: a magnificent head, with abundance of hair thrown back from a high forehead, a white beard, and an expression of haughtiness.

This man stood, resting one hand upon the divan, from which he had risen. One could see that a slow disease had broken him down, but his voice was still powerful, when he said in English, and in a tone of extreme surprise:—

"I have no name, sir!"

"I know you!" answered Smith.

Captain Nemo looked at the engineer as if he would have annihilated him. Then, falling back upon the cushions, he murmured:—

"After all, what does it matter; I am dying!"

Smith approached Captain Nemo, and Spilett took his hand, which was hot with fever. The others stood respectfully in a corner of the superb saloon, which was flooded with light.

Captain Nemo withdrew his hand, and signed to Smith and the reporter to be seated.

All looked at him with lively emotion. Here was the being whom they had called the "genius of the island," the being whose intervention had been so efficacious, the benefactor to whom they owed so much. Before their eyes, here where Pencroff and Neb had expected to find some godlike creature, was only a man-a dying man!

But how did Smith know Captain Nemo? Why had the latter sprung up on hearing that name pronounced?

The Captain had taken his seat upon the divan, and, leaning upon his arm, he regarded the engineer, who was seated near him.

"You know the name I bore?" he asked.

"I know it as well as I know the name of this admirable submarine apparatus."

"The Nautilus," said the Captain, with a half smile.

"The Nautilus."

"But do you know-do you know, who I am?"

"I do."

"For thirty years I have had no communication with the inhabited world, for thirty years have I lived in the depths of the sea, the only place where I have found freedom! Who, now, has betrayed my secret?"

"A man who never pledged you his word, Captain Nemo, one who, therefore, cannot be accused of betraying you."

"The Frenchman whom chance threw in my way?"

"The same."

"Then this man and his companions did not perish in the maelstrom into which the Nautilus had been drawn?"

"They did not, and there has appeared under the title of *Twenty Thousand Leagues Under the Sea*, a work which contains your history."

"The history of but a few months of my life, sir," answered the Captain, quickly.

"True," replied Smith, "but a few months of that strange life sufficed to make you known—"

"As a great criminal, doubtless," said Captain Nemo, smiling disdainfully. "Yes, a revolutionist, a scourge to humanity."

The engineer did not answer.

"Well, sir?"

"I am unable to judge Captain Nemo," said Smith, "at least in what concerns his past life. I, like the world at large, am ignorant of the motives for this strange existence, and I am unable to judge of the effects without knowing the causes, but what I do know is that a beneficent hand has been constantly extended to us since our arrival here, that we owe everything to a being good, generous, and powerful, and that this being, powerful, generous, and good, is you, Captain Nemo!"

"It is I," answered the captain, quietly.

The engineer and the reporter had risen, the others had drawn near, and the gratitude which swelled their hearts would have sought expression in words and gesture, when Captain Nemo signed to them to be silent, and in a voice more moved, doubtless, than he wished:—

"When you have heard me," he said. And then, in a few short, clear sentences, he told them the history of his life.

The history was brief. Nevertheless, it took all his remaining strength to finish it. It was evident that he struggled against an extreme feebleness. Many times Smith urged him to take some rest, but he shook his head, like one who knew that for him there would be no to-morrow, and when the reporter offered his services—

"They are useless," he answered, "my hours are numbered."

Captain Nemo was an Indian prince, the Prince Dakkar, the son of the rajah of the then independent territory of Bundelkund, and nephew of the hero of India, Tippo Saib. His father sent him, when ten years old, to Europe, where he received a complete education; and it was the secret intention of the rajah to have his son able some day to engage in equal combat with those whom he considered as the oppressors of his country.

From ten years of age until he was thirty, the Prince Dakkar, with superior endowments, of high heart and courage, instructed himself in everything; pushing his investigations in science, literature, and art to the uttermost limits.

He travelled over all Europe. His birth and fortune made his company much sought after, but the seductions of the world possessed no charm for him. Young and handsome, he remained serious, gloomy, with an insatiable thirst for knowledge, with implacable anger fixed in his heart.

He hated. He hated the only country where he had never wished to set foot, the only nation whose advances he had refused: he hated England more and more as he admired her. This Indian summed up in his own person all the fierce hatred of the vanquished against the victor. The invader is always unable to find grace with the invaded. The son of one of those sovereigns whose submission to the United Kingdom was only nominal, the prince of the family of Tippo-Saib, educated in ideas of reclamation and vengeance, with a deep-seated love for his poetic country weighed down with the chains of England, wished never to place his foot on that land, to him accursed, that land to which India owed her subjection.

The Prince Dakkar became an artist, with a lively appreciation of the marvels of art; a savant familiar with the sciences; a statesman educated in European courts. In the eyes of a superficial observer, he passed, perhaps, for one of those cosmopolites, curious after knowledge, but disdaining to use it; for one of those opulent travellers, high-spirited and platonic, who go all over the world and are of no one country.

It was not so. This artist, this savant, this man was Indian to the heart, Indian in his desire for vengeance, Indian in the hope which he cherished of being able some day to re-establish the rights of his country, of driving on the stranger, of making it independent.

He returned to Bundelkund in the year 1849. He married a noble Indian woman whose heart bled as his did at the woes of their country. He had two children whom he loved. But domestic happiness could not make him forget the servitude of India. He waited for an opportunity. At length it came.

The English yoke was pressed, perhaps, too heavily upon the Indian people. The Prince Dakkar became the mouthpiece of the malcontents. He instilled into their spirits all the hatred he felt against the strangers. He went over not only the independent portions of the Indian peninsula, but into those regions directly submitted to the English control. He recalled to them the grand days of Tippo-Saib, who died heroically at Seringapatam for the defense of his country.

In 1857 the Sepoy mutiny broke forth. Prince Dakkar was its soul. He organized that immense uprising. He placed his talents and his wealth at the service of that cause. He gave himself; he fought in the first rank; he risked his life as the humblest of those heroes who had risen to free their country; he was wounded ten times in twenty battles, and was unable to find death when the last soldiers of independence fell before the English guns.

Never had British rule in India been in such danger; and, had the Sepoys received the assistance from without which they had hoped for, Asia would not to-day, perhaps, be under the dominion of the United Kingdom.

At that time the name of Prince Dakkar was there illustrious. He never hid himself, and he fought openly. A price was put upon his head, and although he was not delivered up by any traitor, his father, mother, wife, and children suffered for him before he knew of the dangers which they ran on his account.

Once again right fell before might. Civilization never goes backwards, and her laws are like those of necessity. The Sepoys were vanquished, and the country of the ancient rajahs fell again under the strict rule of England.

Prince Dakkar, unable to die, returned again to his mountains in Bundelkund. There, thenceforward alone, he conceived an immense disgust against all who bore the name of man—a hatred and a horror of the civilized world—and wishing to fly from it, he collected the wreck of his fortune, gathered together twenty of his most faithful companions, and one day disappeared.

Where did Prince Dakkar seek for that independence which was refused him upon the inhabited earth? Under the waters, in the depths of the seas, where no one could follow him.

From a man of war he became a man of science. On a desert island of the Pacific he established his workshops, and there he constructed a submarine ship after plans of his own. By means which will some day be known, he utilized electricity, that incommensurable force, for all the necessities of his apparatus as a motor, for lighting and for heat. The sea, with its infinite treasures, its myriads of fishes, its harvests of varech and sargassum, its enormous mammifers, and not only all that nature held, but all that man had lost, amply sufficed for the needs of the Prince and his equipage;—and thus he accomplished his heart's desire, to have no further communication with the earth. He named his submarine ship the Nautilus, he called himself Captain Nemo, and he disappeared under the seas.

During many years, the Captain visited all the oceans, from one pole to the other. Pariah of the earth, he reaped the treasures of the unknown worlds. The millions lost in Vigo Bay, in 1702, by the Spanish galleons, furnished him with an inexhaustible mine of wealth, which he gave, anonymously, to people fighting for their independence.

For years he had had no communication with his kindred, when, during the night of the 6th of November, 1866, three men were thrown upon his deck. They were a French professor, his servant, and a Canadian fisherman. These men had been thrown overboard by the shock of the collision between the Nautilus and the United States frigate Abraham Lincoln, which had given it chase.

Captain Nemo learned from the Professor that the Nautilus, sometimes taken for a gigantic mammifer of the cetacean family, sometimes for a submarine apparatus containing a gang of pirates, was hunted in every sea.

Captain Nemo could have thrown these three men, whom chance had thrown across his mysterious life, into the ocean. He did not do it, he kept them prisoners, and, during seven months, they were able to perceive all the marvels of a voyage of 20,000 leagues under the sea.

One day, the 22nd of June, 1867, these three men, who knew nothing of Captain Nemo's past life, seized the boat belonging to the Nautilus and attempted to escape. But just then the Nautilus was upon the coast of Norway in the eddy of the Maelstrom, and the Captain believed that the fugitives, caught in its terrible vortex, had been swallowed up in the gulf. He was unaware that the Frenchman and his companions had been miraculously thrown upon the coast, that the fishermen of the Loffodin Islands had rescued them, and that the Professor, on his return to France, had published a book in which seven months of this strange and adventurous navigation was narrated.

For a long time Captain Nemo continued this mode of life, traversing the sea. One by one his companions died and found their rest in the coral cemetery at the bottom of the Pacific, and in time Captain Nemo was the last survivor of those who had sought refuge in the depths of the oceans.

He was then sixty years old. As he was alone, it was necessary to take his Nautilus to one of those submarine ports which served him in former days as a harbor.

One of these ports was under Lincoln Island, and was the present asylum of the Nautilus. For six years the Captain had remained there awaiting that death which would reunite him with his companions, when chance made him witness to the fall of the balloon which carried the prisoners. Clothed in his impermeable jacket, he was walking under the water, some cables' lengths from the shore of the islet, when the engineer was thrown into the sea. A good impulse moved Captain Nemo—and he saved Cyrus Smith.

On the arrival of these five castaways he wished to go from them, but his port of refuge was closed. Some volcanic action had raised up the basalt so that the Nautilus could not cross the entrance to the crypt, although there was still sufficient water for a boat of light draught.

Captain Nemo, therefore, remained and watched these men, thrown without resources upon a desert island, but he did not wish to be seen. Little by little, as he saw their honest, energetic lives, how they were bound together in fraternal amity, he interested himself in their efforts. In spite of himself, he found out all the secrets of their existence. Clothed in his impermeable jacket, he could easily reach the bottom of the well in Granite House, and climbing by the projections of the rock to its mouth, he heard the colonists talk of their past and discuss their present and future. He learned from them of the struggle of America against itself, for the abolition of slavery. Yes! these men were worthy to reconcile Captain Nemo with that humanity which they represented so honestly on the island.

Captain Nemo had saved Smith. It was he who had led the dog to the Chimneys, who threw Top out of the water, who stranded the box of useful articles on Jetsam Point, who brought the canoe down the Mercy, who threw the cord from Granite House, when it was attacked by the monkeys, who made known the presence of Ayrton on Tabor Island by means of the paper inclosed in the bottle, who blew up the brig by means of a torpedo, who saved Herbert from certain death by bringing the quinine, who, finally, killed the convicts by those electric balls which he employed in his submarine hunting excursions. Thus was explained all those seemingly supernatural incidents, which, all of them, attested the generosity and the power of the Captain.

Nevertheless, this intense misanthrope thirsted to do good. He had some useful advice to give to his proteges, and moreover, feeling the approach of death, he had summoned, as we have seen, the colonists from Granite House, by means of the wire which reached from the corral to the Nautilus. Perhaps he would not have done it, had he thought that Smith knew enough of his history to call him by his name of Nemo.

The Captain finished the recital of his life, and then Smith spoke. He recalled all the instances of the salutary influences exercised over the colonists, and then, in the name of his companions, and in his own, he thanked this generous being for all that he had done.

But Captain Nemo had never dreamed of asking any return for his services. One last thought agitated his spirit, and, before taking the hand which the engineer held out to him, he said:—

"Now, sir, you know my life, judge of it!"

In speaking thus, the Captain evidently alluded to an incident of a serious nature which had been witnessed by the three strangers on the Nautilus—an incident which the French professor had necessarily recounted in his book, an incident whose very recital was terrible.

In brief, some days before the flight of the professor and his companions, the Nautilus, pursued by a frigate in the North Atlantic, had rushed upon her like a battering-ram, and sunk her without mercy.

Smith, understanding this allusion, made no answer.

"It was an English frigate, sir!" cried Captain Nemo, becoming for the moment Prince Dakkar, "an English frigate, you understand! She attacked me! I was shut in, in a narrow and shallow bay; I had to pass out, and—I passed!"

Then, speaking with more calmness:—

"I had right and justice on my side," he added. "I did good when I could, and evil when I must. All justice is not in forgiveness."

Some moments of silence followed this response, and Captain Nemo asked again:—

"What do you think of me?"

Smith took the hand of the Captain, and answered him in a grave voice:—

"Captain, your mistake has been in believing that you could bring back the old order of things, and you have struggled against necessary progress.

It was one of those errors which some of us admire, others blame, but of which God alone can judge, and which the human mind exonerates. We can disagree with one who misleads himself in an intention which he believes laudable, and at the same time esteem him. Your error is of a kind which does not preclude admiration, and your name has nothing to fear from the judgment of history. She loves heroic follies, though she condemns the results which follow."

The breast of Captain Nemo heaved; he raised his hand towards heaven.

"Was I wrong, or was I right?" he murmured.

Smith continued:—

"All great actions return to God, from whom they came! Captain Nemo, the worthy men here, whom you have succored, will always weep for you!"

Herbert approached him. He knelt down and took the hand of the captain, and kissed it.

A tear glistened in the eye of the dying man.

"My child," he said, "bless you!"

CHAPTER LIX.

THE LAST HOURS OF CAPTAIN NEMO—HIS DYING
WISHES—A SOUVENIR FOR HIS FRIENDS—
HIS TOMB—SOME COUNSEL TO THE COLONISTS—
THE SUPREME MOMENT—AT THE BOTTOM OF
THE SEA.

It was morning, though no ray of daylight penetrated the vault. The sea, at this moment high, covered the outlet. But the artificial light escaping in long rays from the sides of the Nautilus, had not diminished, and the sheet of water around the vessel glowed resplendent.

Captain Nemo, overcome by an extreme fatigue, fell back upon the divan. They did not dream of transporting him to Granite House, as he had shown a wish to remain among the priceless treasures of the Nautilus, awaiting that death which could not be long in coming.

Smith and Spilett observed with great attention his prostration. They saw that he was slowly sinking. His strength, formerly so great, was almost gone, and his body was but a frail envelope for the spirit about escaping. All life was concentrated at the heart and brain.

The engineer and the reporter consulted together in low tones. Could they do anything for the dying man? Could they, if not save him, at least prolong his life for a few days? He himself had said that there was no remedy, and he awaited death calmly and without fear.

"We can do nothing," said Spilett.

"What is he dying of?" asked Pencroff.

"Of exhaustion," answered the reporter.

"Supposing we take him out into the open air, into the sunlight, perhaps he would revive?"

"No, Pencroff," responded the engineer, "there is nothing to do. Moreover, Captain Nemo would not be willing to leave here. He has lived on the Nautilus for thirty years, and on the Nautilus he wishes to die."

Doubtless Captain Nemo heard Smith's words, for, raising himself up a little, and speaking in a feeble but intelligible voice, he said:—

"You are right. I wish to die here. And I have a request to make."

Smith and his companions had gathered round the divan, and they arranged the cushions so that the dying man was more comfortably placed.

They saw that his gaze was fixed upon the marvels of the saloon, lit up by the rays of electric light sifting through the arabesques of the luminous ceiling. He looked upon the pictures, those *chefs d'œuvre* of Italian, Flemish, French, and Spanish masters, which hung on the tapestried walls, upon the marbles and bronzes, upon the magnificent organ at the opposite end of the saloon, upon the glasses arranged around a central vase in which were disposed the rarest products of the seas, marine plants, zoophytes, chaplets of pearls of an inappreciable value, and at length his attention was fixed upon this device, the device of the Nautilus inscribed upon the front of this museum:—

MOBILIS IN MOBILI.

It seemed as if he wished to caress with his regard, one last time, those *chefs d'oeuvre* of art and nature which had been ever visible to him in the years of his sojourn in the depths of the sea!

Smith respected Captain Nemo's silence. He waited for him to speak.

After some moments, during which passed before him, doubtless, his whole life, Cap-Nemo turned to the colonists and said:—

"You wish to do me a favor?"

"Captain, we would give our lives to prolong yours!"

"Well, then, promise me that you will execute my last wishes, and I will be repaid for all that I have done for you."

"We promise," answered Smith, speaking for his companions and himself.

"To-morrow," said the Captain, "to-morrow I will be dead."

He made a sign to Herbert, who was about to protest.

"To-morrow I will be dead, and I wish for no other tomb than the Nautilus. It is my coffin! All my friends rest at the bottom of the sea, and I wish to rest there also."

A profound silence followed the words of Captain Nemo.

"Attend to what I say," he continued. "The Nautilus is imprisoned in this grotto. But if she cannot leave this prison, she can at least sink herself in the abyss, which will cover her and guard my mortal remains."

The colonists listened religiously to the words of the dying man.

"To-morrow, after I am dead, Mr. Smith," continued the Captain, "you and your companions will leave the Nautilus, all of whose riches are to disappear with me. One single remembrance of Prince Dakkar, whose history you now know, will remain to you. That coffer, there, encloses diamonds worth many millions, most of them souvenirs of the time when, a husband and father, I almost believed in happiness, and a collection of pearls gathered by my friends and myself from the bottom of the sea. With this treasure, you will be able, some time, to accomplish good. In your hands and those of your companions, Mr. Smith, wealth will not be dangerous. I shall be ever present with you in your works."

After some moments of rest, necessitated by his extreme feebleness, Captain Nemo continued as follows:—

"To-morrow, you will take this coffer, you will leave this saloon, and close the door; then you will ascend to the platform of the Nautilus and you will bolt down the hatchway."

"We will do it, sir," replied Smith.

"Very well. You will then embark in the boat which brought you here. But, before abandoning the Nautilus, go to the stern, and there, open two large cocks which you will find at the water-line. The water will penetrate and the Nautilus will sink beneath the waves and rest upon the bottom of the abyss."

Then, upon a gesture from Smith, the Captain added:—

"Fear nothing! you will only be burying the dead!"

Neither Smith nor his companions could say a word to Captain Nemo. These were his last wishes, and they had nothing else to do but obey them.

"I have your promise?" asked Captain Nemo.

"You have it, sir," answered the engineer.

The Captain made a sign thanking them, and then motioned to be left alone for a few hours. Spilett insisted on remaining with him, in case of an emergency, but the other refused, saying:—

"I will live till morning, sir."

All left the salon, passing through the library, the dining-room, and reached the forward part of the vessel, where the electric apparatus, furnishing heat, light, and motive power to the Nautilus was placed.

The Nautilus was a *chef-d'oeuvre* containing *chefs-d'oeuvre*, which filled the engineer with amazement.

The colonists mounted the platform, which rose seven or eight feet above the water. Then they saw a thick lenticular glass closing up a sort of bull's-eye, through which penetrated a ray of light. Behind this bull's-eye was the wheel-house, where the steersman stood when directing the Nautilus under the sea, by means of the electric light.

Smith and his companions stood here in silence, impressed by what they saw, and what they had heard, and their hearts bled to think that he, their protector, whose arm had been so often raised to aid them, would soon be counted among the dead.

Whatever would be the judgment of posterity upon this, so to say, extra-human existence, Prince Dakkar would always remain one of those strange characters who cannot be forgotten.

"What a man!" said Pencroff. "Is it credible that he has lived so at the bottom of the ocean! And to think that he has not found rest even there!"

"The Nautilus," observed Ayrton, "would, perhaps, have served us to leave Lincoln Island and gain some inhabited country."

"A thousand devils!" cried Pencroff. "You couldn't get me to steer such a craft. To sail over the seas is all very well, but under the seas,—no, sir!"

"I think, Pencroff," said the reporter, "that it would be easy to manage a submarine apparatus like the Nautilus, and that we would soon get accustomed to it. No storms, no boarding to fear. At some little distance under the waves the waters are as calm as those of a lake."

"That's likely enough," answered the sailor, "but give me a stiff breeze and a well rigged ship. A ship is made to go on the water and not under it."

"My friends," said the engineer, "it is useless, at least as far as the Nautilus is concerned, to discuss this question of submarine vessels. The Nautilus is not ours, and we have no right to dispose of it. It could not, moreover, serve us under any circumstances. Aside from the fact that it cannot get out of this cavern, Captain Nemo wishes it to be engulfed with him after his death. His wish is law, and we will obey it."

Smith and his companions, after talking for a while longer, descended into the interior of the Nautilus. There they ate some food and returned to the salon.

Captain Nemo had recovered from his prostration, and his eyes had regained their brilliancy. They saw a smile upon his lips.

The colonists approached him. "Sirs," said the Captain, "you are brave men, and good and honest. You have given yourselves up to the common cause. I have often watched you. I have loved you. I do love you!—Give me your hand, Mr. Smith."

Smith gave his hand to the Captain, who pressed it affectionately.

"That is well!" he murmured. Then he added:—

"But I have said enough about myself. I wish to speak of yourselves and of Lincoln Island, on which you have found refuge. You want to leave it?".

"To come back again!" said Pencroff eagerly.

"To return?—Oh! yes, Pencroff," answered the Captain, smiling, "I know how much you love this island. It has been improved by your care, and it is, indeed, yours."

"Our project, Captain," added Smith, "would be to make it over to the United States, and to establish a station, which would be well situated here in this part of the Pacific."

"You think of your country," replied the Captain. "You work for her prosperity, for her glory. You are right. The Fatherland! It is there we wish to return! It is there we wish to die! And I, I die far from everything that I have loved!"

"Have you no last wish to have executed," asked the engineer earnestly, "no souvenir to send to those friends you left in the mountains of India?"

"No, Mr. Smith, I have no friends! I am the last of my race—and I die long after those whom I have known.—But to return to yourselves. Solitude, isolation are sorrowful things, beyond human endurance. I die from having believed that man could live alone!—You wish to leave Lincoln Island and to return to your country. I know that these wretches have destroyed your boat-"

"We are building a ship," said Spilett, "a ship large enough to take us to the nearest country; but if sooner or later we leave the island, we will come back again. Too many associations attach us to the place, for us ever to forget it."

"Here we met Captain Nemo," said Smith.

"Here only will we find the perfect remembrance of you!" added Herbert."

"It is here that I will rest in an eternal sleep, if—" answered the Captain.

He hesitated, and, instead of finishing his sentence, said:—

"Mr. Smith, I wish to speak with you,—with you alone."

The companions of the engineer retired, and Smith remained for some time alone with Captain Nemo. He soon called back his friends, but said nothing to them of the secrets which the dying prince had confided to him.

Spilett observed the Captain with extreme attention. He was evidently living by the strength of his will, which could not long hold out against his physical weakness.

The day ended without any change manifesting itself. The colonists did not leave the Nautilus. Night came, although unseen in this crypt.

Captain Nemo did not suffer pain, but sunk slowly. His noble face, pale by the approach of death, was perfectly calm. Now and then he spoke, incoherently, of events in his strange existence.—All saw that life was retreating. His feet and hands were already cold.

Once or twice, he spoke a word to the colonists who were about him, and he looked upon them with that smile which remained when he was no more.

At last, just after midnight, Captain Nemo made a supreme effort, and crossed his arms upon his breast, as if he wished to die in that attitude.

Towards 1 o'clock all the life that was left was concentrated in his expression. One last spark burned in that eye which had formerly flashed fire! Then, murmuring these words, "God and Fatherland," he expired quietly.

Smith, stooping down, closed the eyes of him who had been Prince Dakkar, who was no more even Captain Nemo.

Herbert and Pencroff wept. Ayrton wiped away a furtive tear. Neb was on his knees near the reporter, who was immobile as a statue.

Smith raising his hand above the head of the dead man:—

"May God receive his soul!" he said, and then, turning towards his friends, he added:—

"Let us pray for him whom we have lost!"

* * * * *

Some hours later, the colonists, in fulfillment of their promise, carried out the last wishes of the dead.

They left the Nautilus, taking with them the sole souvenir of their benefactor, the coffer containing a hundred fortunes.

The marvellous salon, still flooded with light, was carefully closed. The cover to the hatchway was bolted down in such a manner that not a drop of water could penetrate to the inner chambers of the Nautilus. Then the colonists entered the boat, which was moored beside the submarine ship.

The boat was taken to the stern. There, at the water-line, they opened the two large cocks which communicated with the reservoirs designed to immerse the apparatus.

The cocks were opened, the reservoirs filled, and the Nautilus, sinking slowly, disappeared beneath the sea.

But the colonists were able still to follow her coarse through the lower depths. Her strong light lit up the transparent waters, as the crypt became darkened. Then at length the vast effusion of electric effulgence was effaced, and the Nautilus, the tomb of Captain Nemo, rested upon the bottom of the sea.

CHAPTER LX.

THE REFLECTIONS OF THE COLONISTS—RENEWAL
OF WORK—THE 1ST OF JANUARY, 1869—A SMOKE
FROM THE VOLCANO—SYMPTOMS OF AN
ERUPTION AYRTON AND SMITH AT THE CORRAL—
EXPLORATION OF THE CRYPT DAKKAR—
WHAT CAPTAIN NEMO HAD SAID TO THE ENGINEER.

In the early morning the colonists reached the entrance of the cavern, which they called Crypt Dakkar, in remembrance of Captain Nemo. The tide was low, and they easily passed under the archway, whose piers were washed by the waves.

The iron boat could remain in this place without danger from the sea; but as additional precaution they drew it up on a little beach on one side of the crypt.

The storm had ceased during the night. The last mutterings of the thunder were dying away in the west. It was not raining, although the sky was still clouded. In short, this month of October, the beginning of the southern spring, did not come in good fashion, and the wind had a tendency to shift from one point of the compass to another, so that it was impossible to say what the weather would be.

Smith and his companions, on leaving Crypt Dakkar, went towards the corral. On the way Neb and Herbert took care to take up the wire which had been stretched by Captain Nemo, as it might be useful in the future.

While walking the colonists spoke but little. The incidents of this night had made a vivid impression upon them. This unknown, whose influence had protected them so well, this man whom they imagined a genii, Captain Nemo, was no more. His Nautilus and himself were buried in the depths of the abyss. It seemed to each one of them that they were more isolated than before. They were, so to speak, accustomed to count upon this powerful intervention which to-day was wanting, and Spilett, and even Smith, did not escape this feeling. So, without speaking, they followed the road to the corral.

By 9 o'clock the colonists were in Granite House again.

It had been agreed that the construction of the ship should be pushed forward as rapidly as possible, and Smith gave the work more of his time and care than ever before. They did not know what the future might bring forth, and it would be a guarantee of safety for them to have a strong vessel, able to stand rough weather, and large enough to carry them, if need be, a long distance. If, when it was finished, the colonists decided not to leave the island they could at least make the voyage to Tabor Island and leave a notice there. This was an indispensable precaution in case the Scotch yacht returned to these seas, and it must on no account be neglected.

The work was undertaken at once. All worked at it without ceasing, except to prosecute other necessary work. It was important to have the new ship finished in five months, if they wished to make the voyage to Tabor Island before the equinoxial storms would render it impracticable. All the sails of the Speedy had been saved, so that they need not trouble themselves about making rigging.

The year ended in the midst of this work. At the end of two months and a half the ribs bad been put in place and the planking began, so that they were able to see that Smith's plans were excellent. Pencroff worked with ardor, and always grumbled when any of the others left off work to go hunting. It was, nevertheless, necessary to lay in a stock of provisions for the approaching winter. But that made no difference. The honest sailor was unhappy unless every one was at work in the ship-yard. At these times he grumbled and did—he was so put out—the work of half a dozen men.

All this summer season was bad. The heat was overpowering, and the atmosphere, charged with electricity, discharged itself in violent storms. It was seldom that the distant muttering of the thunder was unheard. It was like a dull, but permanent murmur, such as is produced in the equatorial regions of the globe.

On the 1st of January, 1869, a terrific storm burst over the island, and the lightning struck in many places. Tall trees were shattered, and among them was one of the enormous micocouliers which shaded the poultry-yard. Had this meteoric storm any relation to the phenomena which were occurring In the bowels of the earth? Was there a sort of connection between the disturbances in the air and those in the interior of the globe. Smith believed it to be so, since the development of these storms was marked by a recrudescence of the volcanic symptoms.

On the 3d of January, Herbert, who had gone at daybreak to Prospect Plateau to saddle one of the onagers, saw an immense black cloud rolling out from the summit of the volcano.

Herbert hastened to inform the others, who came at once to look at the mountain.

"Ah!" said Pencroff, "it is not vapor this time! It seems to me that the giant is not content to breathe, he must smoke!"

The image employed by the sailor expressed with exactness the change which had taken place at the mouth of the volcano. For three months the crater had been emitting vapors more or less intense, but there bad been no ebullition of mineral matters. This time, instead of vapors, a thick column of smoke rose, like an immense mushroom, above the summit of the mountain.

"The chimney is on fire!" said Spilett.

"And we cannot put it out!" answered Herbert.

"It would be well to sweep the volcanoes," said Neb, in good earnest.

"All right, Neb," said Pencroff, laughing. "Will you undertake the job?"

Smith looked attentively at the thick smoke, and at the same time he listened as if he expected to detect some distant rumbling. Then, turning towards his companions, who were at some little distance, he said:—

"In truth, my friends, it cannot be denied that an important change has taken place. The volcanic matters are not only in a state of ebullition, they have taken fire, and, without doubt, we are threatened with an eruption!"

"Very well, sir; we will witness this eruption," cried Pencroff, "and we will applaud it if it is a success! I don't think that anything over there need worry us!"

"No, Pencroff," answered Smith, "for the old course of the lava is open, and, thanks to its position, the crater has heretofore discharged towards the north. Nevertheless—"

"Nevertheless, since there is nothing to be gained by an eruption, it would be better not to have it," said the reporter.

"Who knows?" replied the sailor. "There may be some useful and precious matter in the volcano, which it will be good enough to throw up, which will be advantageous for us!"

Smith shook his head, as a man who anticipated nothing good from this phenomenon. He did not think so lightly of the consequences of an eruption. If the lava, on account of the position of the crater, did not menace the wooded and cultivated portions of the island, other complications might arise. Eruptions are often accompanied by earthquakes, and an island formed, like Lincoln Island, of such different materials: basalt on one side, granite on another, lavas to the north, a mixed soil inland, material which, therefore, could not be solidly bound together, ran the risk of being torn asunder. If, therefore, the outpouring of volcanic substances did not threaten serious results, any movement in the framework upholding the island might be followed by the gravest consequences.

"It seems to me," said Ayrton, who was kneeling down, with his ear to the ground, "it seems to me that I hear a noise, like the rattling of a wagon, loaded with iron bars."

The colonists listened carefully, and were convinced that Ayrton was not mistaken. With the rumbling mingled subterranean roaring, making a sort of "rinfordzando," which died away slowly, as if from some violent cleavage in the interior of the globe. But no detonation was heard, and it was fair to conclude that the smoke and vapor found a free passage through the central chimney, and, if the escape-pipe was sufficiently large, no explosion need be feared.

"Come," said Pencroff at length, "shall we not go back to work? Let Mount Franklin smoke, brawl, moan, and vomit fire and flames as much as it chooses, but that is no excuse for us to quit work! Come, Ayrton, Neb, all of you, we want all hands to-day! I want our new Good Luck— we will keep the name, will we not?—to be moored in Balloon Harbor before two months are passed! So there is not an hour to be lost!"

All the colonists went down to the shipyard and worked steadily all day without giving too much thought to the volcano, which could not be seen from the beach before Granite House. But once or twice heavy shadows obscured the sunlight, and, as the was day perfectly clear, it was evident that thick clouds of smoke were passing between the sun's disc and the island. Smith and Spilett noticed these sombre voyagers, and talked of the progress that the volcanic phenomenon was making, but they did not cease work. It was, moreover, of great importance, in every sense, that the ship should be finished with as little delay as possible. In the presence of events which might happen, the security of the colonists would be better assured. Who could say but that this ship might not, some day, be their sole refuge?

That evening, after supper, Smith, Spilett, and Herbert climbed to the plateau. It was already dark, and they would be able to distinguish whether flames or incandescent matter was mingled with the smoke and vapor of the volcano.

"The crater is on fire!" cried Herbert, who, more active than his companions, had reached the plateau the first.

Mount Franklin, six miles distant, appeared like a gigantic torch, with fuliginous flames twisting about its summit. So much smoke, such quantities of scoriæ and cinders, perhaps, were mingled with the flames, that their light did not glare upon the shades of night. But a sort of dull yellow glow spread over the island, making dimly visible the higher masses of forest. Enormous clouds obscured the heavens, between which glittered a few stars.

"The progress is rapid," said the engineer.

"It is not astonishing," answered the reporter. "The volcano has been awake for some time already. You remember, Cyrus, that the first vapors appeared about the time we were searching the mountain for the retreat of Captain Nemo. That was, if I am not mistaken, about the 15th of October.

"Yes" replied Herbert, "two months and a half ago."

"The subterranean fires have been brooding for ten weeks," continued Spilett, "and it is not astonishing that they develop now with this violence."

"Do not you feel certain vibrations in the ground?" asked Smith.

"I think so," replied Spilett, "but an earthquake—"

"I did not say that we were menaced by an earthquake," said Smith, "and Heaven preserve us from one! No. These vibrations are due to the effervesence of the central fire. The crust of the earth is nothing more than the covering of a boiler, and you know how the covering of a boiler, under pressure, vibrates like a sonorous plate. That is what is happening at this moment."

"What magnificent flames!" cried Herbert, as a sheaf of fire shot up, unobscured by the vapors, from the crater. From its midst luminous fragments and bright scintillations were thrown in every direction. Some of them pierced the dome of smoke, leaving behind them a perfect cloud of incandescent dust. This outpouring was accompanied by rapid detonations like the discharge of a battery of mitrailleuses.

Smith, the reporter, and the lad, after having passed an hour on Prospect Plateau, returned to Granite House. The engineer was pensive, and so much preoccupied that Spilett asked him if he anticipated any near danger.

"Yes and no," responded Smith.

"But the worst that could happen," said the reporter, "would be an earthquake, which would overthrow the island. And I don't think that is to be feared, since the vapors and lava have a free passage of escape."

"I do not fear an earthquake," answered Smith, "of the ordinary kind, such as are brought about by the expansion of subterranean vapors. But other causes may bring about great disaster."

"For example?"

"I do not know exactly—I must see—I must visit the mountain. In a few days I shall have made up my mind."

Spilett asked no further questions, and soon, notwithstanding the increased violence of the volcano, the inhabitants of Granite House slept soundly.

Three days passed, the 4th 5th, and 6th of January, during which they worked on the ship, and, without explaining himself further, the engineer hastened the work as much as possible. Mount Franklin was covered with a sinister cloud, and with the flames vomited forth incandescent rocks, some of which fell back into the crater. This made Pencroff, who wished to look upon the phenomenon from an amusing side, say—

"Look! The giant plays at cup and ball! He is a juggler."

And, indeed, the matters vomited forth fell back into the abyss, and it seemed as if the lavas, swollen by the interior pressure, had not yet risen to the mouth of the crater. At least, the fracture on the northeast, which was partly visible, did not pour forth any torrent on the western side of the mountain.

Meanwhile, however pressing the ship-building, other cares required the attention of the colonists in different parts of the island. First of all, they must go to the corral, where the moufflons and goats were enclosed, and renew the provisions for these animals. It was, therefore, agreed that Ayrton should go there the next day, and, as it was customary for but one to do this work, the others were surprised to hear the engineer say to Ayrton:—

"As you are going to the corral to-morrow, I will go with you."

"Oh! Mr. Smith!" cried the sailor, "our time is very limited, and, if you go off in this way, we lose just that much help!"

"We will return the next day," answered Smith, "but I must go to the corral—I wish to see about this eruption."

"Eruption! Eruption!" answered Pencroff, with a dissatisfied air. "What is there important about this eruption? It don't bother me!"

Notwithstanding the sailor's protest, the exploration was decided upon for the next day. Herbert wanted to go with Smith, but he did not wish to annoy Pencroff by absenting himself. So, early the next morning, Smith and Ayrton started off with the wagon and onagers.

Over the forest hung huge clouds constantly supplied from Mount Franklin with fuliginous matter. They were evidently composed of heterogeneous substances. It was not altogether the smoke from the volcano that made them so heavy and opaque. Scoriæ in a state of powder, pulverized puzzolan and grey cinder as fine as the finest fecula, were held in suspension in their thick folds. These cinders remain in air, sometimes, for months at a time. After the eruption of 1783, in Iceland, for more than a year the atmosphere was so charged with volcanic powder that the sun's rays were scarcely visible.

Usually, however, these pulverized matters fall to the earth at once, and it was so in this instance. Smith and Ayrton had hardly reached the corral, when a sort of black cloud, like fine gunpowder, fell, and instantly modified the whole aspect of the ground. Trees, fields, everything was covered with a coating several fingers deep. But, most fortunately, the wind was from the northeast, and the greater part of the cloud was carried off to sea.

"That is very curious," said Ayrton.

"It is very serious," answered Smith. This puzzolan, this pulverized pumice stone, all this mineral dust in short, shows how deep-seated is the commotion in the volcano.

"But there is nothing to be done."

"Nothing, but to observe the progress of the phenomenon. Employ yourself, Ayrton, at the corral, and meanwhile I will go up to the sources of Red Creek and examine the state of the mountain on its western side. Then—"

"Then, sir?"

"Then we will make a visit to Crypt Dakkar—I wish to see—Well, I will come back for you in a couple of hours."

Ayrton went into the corral, and while waiting for the return of the engineer occupied himself with the moufflons and goats, which showed a certain uneasiness before these first symptoms of an eruption.

Meantime Smith had ventured to climb the eastern spurs of the mountain, and he arrived at the place where his companions had discovered the sulphur spring on their first exploration.

How everything was changed! Instead of a single column of smoke, he counted thirteen escaping from the ground as if thrust upward by a piston. It was evident that the crust of earth was subjected in this place to a frightful pressure. The atmosphere was saturated with gases and aqueous vapors. Smith felt the volcanic tufa, the pulverulent cinders hardened by time, trembling beneath him, but he did not yet see any traces of fresh lava.

It was the same with the western slope of the mountain. Smoke and flames escaped from the crater; a hail of scoriæ fell upon the soil; but no lava flowed from the gullet of the crater, which was another proof that the volcanic matter had not attained the upper orifice of the central chimney.

"And I would be better satisfied if they had!" said Smith to himself. "At least I would be certain that the lavas had taken their accustomed route. Who knows if they may not burst forth from some new mouth? But that is not the danger! Captain Nemo has well foreseen it! No! the danger is not there!"

Smith went forward as far as the enormous causeway, whose prolongation enframed Shark Gulf. Here he was able to examine the ancient lava marks. There could be no doubt that the last eruption had been at a far distant epoch.

Then he returned, listening to the subterranean rumblings, which sounded like continuous thunder, and by 9 o'clock he was at the corral.

Ayrton was waiting for him.

"The animals are attended to, sir," said he.

"All right, Ayrton."

"They seem to be restless, Mr. Smith."

"Yes, it is their instinct, which does not mislead them."

"When you are ready—"

"Take a lantern and tinder, Ayrton, and let us go."

Ayrton did as he was told. The onagers had been unharnessed and placed in the corral, and Smith, leading, took the route to the coast.

They walked over a soil covered with the pulverulent matter which had fallen from the clouds. No animal appeared. Even the birds had flown away. Sometimes a breeze passed laden with cinders, and the two colonists, caught in the cloud, were unable to see. They had to place handkerchiefs over their eyes and nostrils or they would have been blinded and suffocated.

Under these circumstances they could not march rapidly. The air was heavy, as if all the oxygen had been burned out of it, making it unfit to breathe. Every now and then they had to stop, and it was after 10 o'clock when the engineer and his companion reached the summit of the enormous heap of basaltic and porphyritic rocks which formed the northwest coast of the island.

They began to go down this abrupt descent, following the detestable road, which, during that stormy night had led them to Crypt Dakkar. By daylight this descent was less perilous, and, moreover, the covering of cinders gave a firmer foothold to the slippery rocks.

The projection was soon attained, and, as the tide was low, Smith and Ayrton found the opening to the crypt without any difficulty.

"Is the boat there?" asked the engineer.

"Yes, sir," answered Ayrton, drawing the boat towards him.

"Let us get in, then, Ayrton," said the engineer.

The two embarked in the boat. Ayrton lit the lantern, and, placing it in the bow of the boat, took the oars, and Smith, taking the tiller, steered into the darkness.

The Nautilus was no longer here to illuminate this sombre cavern. Perhaps the electric irradiation still shone under the waters, but no light came from the abyss where Captain Nemo reposed.

The light of the lantern was barely sufficient to permit the engineer to advance, following the right hand wall of the crypt. A sepulchral silence reigned in this portion of the vault, but soon Smith heard distinctly the mutterings which came from the interior of the earth.

"It is the volcano," he said.

Soon, with this noise, the chemical combinations betrayed themselves by a strong odor, and sulphurous vapors choked the engineer and his companion.

"It is as Captain Nemo feared," murmured Smith, growing pale. "We must go on to the end."

Twenty-five minutes after having left the opening the two reached the terminal wall and stopped.

Smith standing on the seat, moved the lantern about over this wall, which separated the crypt from the central chimney of the volcano. How thick was it? Whether 100 feet or but 10 could not be determined. But the subterranean noises were too plainly heard for it to be very thick.

The engineer, after having explored the wall along a horizontal line, fixed the lantern to the end of an oar and went over it again at a greater height.

There, through scarcely visible cracks, came a pungent smoke, which infected the air of the cavern. The wall was striped with these fractures, and some of the larger ones came to within a few feet of the water.

At first, Smith rested thoughtful. Then he murmured these words:—

"Yes! Captain Nemo was right! There is the danger, and it is terrible!"

Ayrton said nothing, but, on a sign from the engineer, he took up the oars, and, a half hour later, he and Smith came out of Crypt Dakkar.

CHAPTER LXI.

SMITH'S RECITAL—HASTENING THE WORK—A LAST
VISIT TO THE CORRAL—THE COMBAT BETWEEN
THE FIRE AND THE WATER—THE ASPECT OF THE
ISLAND—THEY DECIDE TO LAUNCH THE SHIP—
THE NIGHT OF THE 8TH OF MARCH.

The next morning, the 8th of January, after a day and night passed at the corral, Smith and Ayrton returned to Granite House.

Then the engineer assembled his companions, and told them that Lincoln Island was in fearful danger—a danger which no human power could prevent.

"My friends," said he,—and his voice betrayed great emotion,— "Lincoln Island is doomed to destruction sooner or later; the cause is in itself and there is no means of removing it!"

The colonists looked at each other. They did not understand him.

"Explain yourself, Cyrus," said Spilett.

"I will, or rather I will give you the explanation which Captain Nemo gave me, when I was alone with him."

"Captain Nemo!" cried the colonists.

"Yes; it was the last service he rendered us before he died."

"The last service!" cried Pencroff. "The last service! You think, because he is dead, that he will help us no more!"

"What did he say?" asked the reporter.

"This, my friends," answered the engineer. "Lincoln Island is not like the other islands of the Pacific, and a particular event, made known to me by Captain Nemo, will cause, sooner or later, the destruction of its submarine framework."

"Destruction of Lincoln Island! What an idea!" cried Pencroff, who, in spite of his respect for Smith, could not help shrugging his shoulders.

"Listen to me, Pencroff," continued the engineer. "This is what Captain Nemo ascertained and what I verified yesterday In Crypt Dakkar. The crypt extends under the island as far as the volcano, and is only separated from the central chimney by the wall. Now this wall is seamed with fractures and cracks, through which the sulphurous gas is already escaping."

"Well?" asked Pencroff, wrinkling his forehead.

"Well, I have ascertained that these fractures are widening under the pressure from within, that the basalt wall la gradually bursting open, and that, sooner or later, it will give a passage to the waters of the sea."

"That's all right!" exclaimed Pencroff, trying still to make light of the subject. "That's all right! The sea will put out the volcano, and that will be the end of it."

"Yes, that will be the end of it!" answered Smith. "On the day that the sea rushes through the wall and penetrates by the central chimney to the bowels of the island, where the eruptive matter is boiling, on that day, Pencroff, Lincoln Island will go up, as Sicily would go up, if the Mediterranean was emptied into Aetna!"

The colonists made no reply. They understood the threatened danger.

It was no longer doubtful that the island was menaced by a frightful explosion. That it would last only as long as the wall to Crypt Dakkar remained intact. This was not a question of months, nor of weeks, bat of days, of hours, perhaps!

The first sensation the colonists experienced was one of profound sorrow. They did not think of the peril which menaced them directly, but of the destruction of that land which had given them asylum, of that island which they had cultivated, which they loved, which they wished to render so prosperous some day! All their labor uselessly employed, all their work lost!

Pencroff did not attempt to hide the tears which rolled down his cheeks.

They talked for some little time longer. The chances which they might count upon were discussed; but, in conclusion, they realized that not an hour was to be lost; that the ship must be completed as soon as possible, as, now, it was the only chance of safety left, to the inhabitants of Lincoln Island!

All hands were required. Where was the use, now, of sowing, or harvesting, of hunting or increasing the reserve at Granite House? The present contents of the magazine were sufficient to provision the ship for as long a voyage as she could make! What was necessary was that these should be at the disposal of the colonists before the accomplishment of the inevitable catastrophe.

The work was undertaken with feverish eagerness. By the 23d of January the ship was half planked. Up to this time there had been no change in the volcano. It was always the vapors, the smoke mixed with flames and pierced by incandescent stones, which escaped from the crater. But during the night of the 23d the upper cone, which formed the cap of the volcano, was lifted off by the pressure of the lava, which had reached the level of the lower cone. A terrible noise was heard. The colonists, believing that the island was going to pieces, rushed out of Granite House.

It was 2 o'clock in the morning. The heavens were on fire. The upper cone—a mass a thousand feet high, and weighing thousands of millions of pounds—had been thrown upon the island, making the earth tremble. Happily, this cone leaned to the north, and it fell upon the plain of sand and tufa which lay between the volcano and the sea. The crater, by this means greatly widened, threw towards the sky a light so intense, that, by the simple effect of reverberation, the atmosphere seemed to be incandescent. At the same time a torrent of lava swelled up over this new summit, falling in long streams, like water escaping from an overflowing vase, and a thousand fiery serpents writhed upon the talus of the volcano.

"The corral! The corral!" cried Ayrton.

It was, indeed, towards the corral that the lava took their way, following the slope of the new crater, and, consequently, the fertile parts of the island. The sources of Red Creek, and Jacamar Wood were threatened with immediate destruction.

At the cry of Ayrton, the colonists had rushed towards the stable of the onagers, and harnessed the animals. All had but one thought. To fly to the corral and let loose the beasts confined there.

Before 3 o'clock they were there. Frightful cries indicated the terror of the moufflons and goats. Already a torrent of incandescent matter, of liquified minerals, fell over the mountain spur upon the plain, destroying that side of the palisade. The gate was hastily opened by Ayrton, and the animals, wild with terror, escaped in every direction.

An hour later the boiling lava filled the corral, volatilizing the water of the little brook which traversed it, firing the house, which burned like a bit of stubble, devouring to the last stake the surrounding palisade. Nothing was left of the corral.

The colonists wanted to struggle against this invasion; they had tried it, but foolishly and uselessly: man is helpless before these grand cataclysms.

The morning of the 24th arrived. Smith and his companions, before returning to Granite House, wished to observe the definite direction which this inundation of lava would take. The general slope of the ground from Mount Franklin was towards the east coast, and it was to be feared that, notwithstanding the thick Jacamar Woods, the torrent would extend to Prospect Plateau.

"The lake will protect us," said Spilett.

"I hope so," answered Smith. But that was all he said.

The colonists would have liked to have advanced as far as the place on which the upper cone of Mount Franklin abutted, but their passage was barred by the lavas, which followed, on the one hand, the valley of Red Creek, and, on the other, the course of Fall River, vaporizing these two streams in their passage. There was no possible way of crossing this stream; it was necessary, on the contrary, to fly before it. The flattened volcano was no longer recognizable. A sort of smooth slab terminated it, replacing the old crater. Two outlets, broken in the south and east sides, poured forth unceasing streams of lava, which formed two distinct currents. Above the new crater, a cloud of smoke and cinders mixed with the vapors of the sky, and hung over the island. Peals of thunder mingled with the rumbling of the mountain. Burning rocks were thrown up thousands of feet, bursting in the sky and scattering like grape-shot. The heavens answered with lightning-flashes the eruption of the volcano.

By 7 o'clock the colonists were no longer able to keep their position on the edge of Jacamar Wood. Not only did the projectiles begin to fall about them, but the lavas, overflowing the bed of Red Creek, threatened to cut off the road from the corral. The first ranks of trees took fire, and their sap, vaporized, made them explode like fire-crackers; while others, less humid, remained intact in the midst of the inundation.

The colonists started back. The torrent, owing to the slope of the land, gained eastward rapidly, and as the lower layers of lava hardened, others, boiling, covered them.

Meantime the principal current in the Red Creek Valley became more and more threatening. All that part of the forest was surrounded, and enormous clouds of smoke rolled above the trees, whose roots were already in the lava.

The colonists stopped at the lake shore, half a mile from the mouth of Red Creek. A question of life or death was about to be decided for them. Smith, accustomed to think and reason in the presence of danger, and aware that he was speaking to men who could face the truth, whatever it might be, said to them:—

"Either the lake will arrest this current, and a part of the island will be preserved from complete devastation, or the current will invade the forests of the Far West, and not a tree, not a plant will be left upon the face of the ground. We will have, upon these rocks stripped of life, the prospect of a death which the explosion of the island may anticipate!

"Then," cried Pencroff, crossing his arms and stamping his foot on the ground, "it is useless to work on the ship! Isn't that so?"

"Pencroff," answered Smith, "it is necessary to do one's duty to the end."

At this moment, the flood of lava, after having eaten its way through the splendid trees of the forest, neared the lake. There was a certain depression in the ground, which, if it had been larger, might, perhaps, suffice to hold the torrent.

"Let us try!" cried Smith.

The idea of the engineer was instantly understood by all. It was necessary to dam, so to speak, this torrent and force it into the lake.

The colonists ran to the shipyard and brought back from there shovels, picks, and hatchets, and by means of earthworks and hewn trees they succeeded, in a few hours, in raising a barrier three feet high and some hundreds of feet long. It seemed to them, when they had finished, that they had not worked more than a few minutes!

It was time. The liquified matter already reached the extremity of the barrier. The flood spread like a swollen river seeking to overflow its banks and threatening to break down the only obstacle which could prevent its devastating all the Far West. But the barrier was sufficient to withstand it, and, after one terrible moment of hesitation, it precipitated itself into Lake Grant by a fall twenty feet high.

The colonists, breathless, without a word, without a gesture, looked upon this struggle of the elements.

What a sight was this, the combat between fire and water! What pen can describe this scene of marvellous horror; what pencil can portray it? The water hissed and steamed at the contact of the boiling lavas. The steam was thrown, whirling, to an immeasurable height in the air, as if the valves of an immense boiler had been suddenly opened. But, great as was the mass of water contained in the lake, it must, finally, be absorbed, since it was not renewed, while the torrent, fed from an inexhaustible source, was ceaselessly pouring in fresh floods of incandescent matter.

The first lavas which fell into the lake solidified at once, and accumulated in such a manner as soon to emerge above the surface. Over these slid other lavas, which in their turn became stone, forming a breakwater, which threatened to fill up the lake, which could not overflow, as its surplus water was carried off in steam. Hissings and shrivellings filled the air with a stunning noise, and the steam, carried off by the wind, fell to the ground in rain. The jetty spread, and where formerly had been peaceable waters appeared an enormous heap of smoking rocks, as if some upheaval of the ground had raised these thousands of reefs. If one can imagine these waters tossed about by a storm, and then suddenly solidified by cold, he will have the appearance of the lake three hours after the irresistible torrent had poured into it.

This time the water had been overcome by the fire.

Nevertheless, it was a fortunate thing for the colonists that the lavas had been turned into the lake. It gave them some days' respite. Prospect Plateau, Granite House, and the ship-yard were safe for the moment. In these few days they must plank and caulk the vessel, launch it, and take refuge upon it, rigging it after it was on the sea. With the fear of the explosion menacing the destruction of the island, it was no longer safe to remain on land. Granite House, so safe a retreat up to this time, might, at any moment, fall!

During the next six days, the colonists worked on the ship with all their might. Sleeping but little, the light of the flames from the volcano permitted them to work by night as well as by day. The eruption

538

continued without cessation, but, perhaps, less abundantly. A fortunate circumstance, since Lake Grant was nearly full; and if fresh lavas had slid over the surface of the former layers, they would inevitably have spread over Prospect Plateau and from there to the shore.

But while this part of the island was partially protected it was otherwise with the west coast.

The second current of lava, following the valley of Fall River, met with no obstacle. The ground on either side of the bank was low, and the incandescent liquid was spread through the forest of the Far West. At this season of the year the trees were dried by the warmth of the summer and took fire instantly, and the high interlacing branches hastened the progress of the conflagration. It seemed as if the current of flame traversed the surface of the forest more swiftly than the current of lavas its depths.

The beasts and birds of the woods sought refuge on the shore of the Mercy and in the marshes of Tadorn's Fens. But the colonists were too busy to pay any attention to these animals. They had, moreover, abandoned Granite House; they had not even sought refuge in the Chimneys, but they camped in a tent near the mouth of the Mercy.

Every day Smith and Spilett climbed up to Prospect Plateau. Sometimes Herbert went with them, but Pencroff never. The sailor did not wish to look upon the island in its present condition of devastation.

It was, indeed, a desolate spectacle. All its wooded part was now denuded. One single group of green trees remained on the extremity of Serpentine Peninsula. Here and there appeared some blackened stumps. The site of the forests was more desolate than Tadorn's Fens. The invasion of the lavas had been complete. Where formerly had been a pleasant verdure, was now nothing but a waste covered with volcanic tufa. The valleys of Fall River and Red Creek contained no water, and if Lake Grant had been completely filled up, the colonists would have had no means to slack their thirst. But fortunately its southern extremity had been spared, and formed a sort of pool, which held all the fresh water remaining on the island. To the northwest the spurs of the mountain, in jagged outline, looked like a gigantic claw grasping the ground. What a doleful spectacle! What a frightful aspect! How grevious for the colonists, who, from a domain, fertile, wooded,

traversed by water-courses, enriched by harvests, found themselves, in an instant, reduced to a devastated rock, upon which, without their stores, they would not have had the means of living.

"It is heart-breaking!" said the reporter.

"Yes, Spilett," answered the engineer. And pray heaven that we are given time to finish the ship, which is now our sole refuge!"

"Does it not seem to you, Cyrus, that the volcano is subsiding? It still vomits lava, but, I think, less freely!"

"It matters little," answered Smith. "The fire is still fierce in the bowels of the mountain, and the sea may rush in there at any moment. We are like persons on a ship devoured by a fire which they cannot control, who know that sooner or later the flames will reach the powder magazine. Come, Spilett, come, we have not an hour to lose!"

For eight days longer, that is to say until the 8th of February, the lavas continued to flow, but the eruption confined itself to the limits described. Smith feared more than anything else an overflow of the lavas on to the beach, in which case the ship-yard would be destroyed. But about this time the colonists felt vibrations in the ground which gave them the greatest uneasiness.

The 20th of February arrived. A month longer was necessary to fit the ship for sea. Would the island last that long? It was Smith's intention to launch her as soon as her hull should be sufficiently caulked. The deck, lining, arranging the interior, and the rigging could be done afterwards, but the important thing was to secure a refuge off the island. Perhaps it would be better to take the vessel round to Balloon Harbor, the point farthest from the eruptive centre, as, at the mouth of the Mercy, between the islet and the granite wall, she ran the risk of being crushed, in case of a breaking up of the island. Therefore, all the efforts of the workmen were directed to completing the hull.

On the 3d of March they were able to calculate that the ship could be launched in twelve days.

Hope returned to the hearts of these colonists, who had been so sorely tried during this fourth year of their sojourn on Lincoln Island! Even Pencroff was roused from the taciturnity into which he had been plunged by the ruin and devastation of his domain. He thought of nothing else but the ship, on which he concentrated all his hopes.

"We will finish her!" he said to the engineer, "we will finish her, Mr. Smith, and it is high time, for you see how far advanced the season is, and it will soon be the equinox. Well, if it is necessary, we will winter at Tabor Island! But Tabor Island after Lincoln Island! Alas! how unlucky I am! To think that I should live to see such a thing as this!"

"Let us make haste!" was the invariable answer of the engineer.

And every one worked unceasingly.

"Master," asked Neb, some days later, "if Captain Nemo had been alive, do you think this would have happened?"

"Yes, Neb," answered the engineer.

"I don't think so!" whispered Pencroff to the negro.

"Nor I!" replied Neb.

During the first week in March Mount Franklin became again threatening. Thousands of threads of glass, made by the fluid lavas, fell like rain to the ground. The crater gave forth fresh torrents of lava that flowed down every side of the volcano. These torrents flowed over the surface of hardened lava, and destroyed the last vestiges of the trees which had survived the first eruption. The current, this time following the southwest shore of Lake Grant, flowed along Glycerine Creek and invaded Prospect Plateau. This last calamity was a terrible blow to the colonists; of the mill, the poultry-yard, the stables, nothing remained. The frightened inhabitants of these places fled in every direction. Top and Jup gave signs of the utmost terror, and their instinct warned them of an impending disaster. A large number of animals had perished in the first eruption, and those which survived had found their only refuge in Tadorn's Fens, and on Prospect Plateau. But this last retreat was now closed from them, and the torrent of lava having reached the edge of the granite wall, began to fall over on to the shore in cataracts of fire. The sublime horror of this spectacle passes all description. At night it looked like a Niagara of molten matter, with its incandescent spray rising on high and its boiling masses below!

The colonists were driven to their last refuge, and, although the upper seams were uncaulked, they resolved to launch their ship into the sea!

Pencroff and Ayrton made the preparations for this event, which was to take place on the morning of the next day, the 9th of March.

But, during that night, an enormous column of steam escaped from the crater, rising in the midst of terrific detonations to a height of more than 3,000 feet. The wall of Crypt Dakkar had given way under the pressure of the gas, and the sea, pouring through the central chimney into the burning gulf, was turned into steam!

The crater was not a sufficient vent for this vapor!

An explosion, which could have been heard a hundred miles away, shook the very heavens! Fragments of the mountain fell into the Pacific, and, in a few minutes, the ocean covered the place where Lincoln Island had been!

CHAPTER LXII.

AN ISOLATED ROCK IN THE PACIFIC—THE LAST REFUGE OF THE COLONISTS—THE PROSPECT OF DEATH—UNEXPECTED SUCCOR—HOW AND WHY IT CAME—THE LAST GOOD ACTION—AN ISLAND ON TERRA FIRMA-THE TOMB OF CAPTAIN NEMO.

An isolated rock, thirty feet long, fifteen feet wide, rising ten feet above the surface of the water, this was the sole solid point which had not vanished beneath the waves of the Pacific.

It was all that remained of Granite House! The wall had been thrown over, then broken to pieces, and some of the rocks of the great hall had been so heaped together as to form this culminating point. All else had disappeared in the surrounding abyss: the lower cone of Mount Franklin, torn to pieces by the explosion; the lava jaws of Shark Gulf; Prospect Plateau, Safety Islet, the granite of Balloon Harbor; the basalt of Crypt Dakkar; Serpentine Peninsula—had been precipitated into the eruptive centre! All that remained of Lincoln Island was this rock, the refuge of the six colonists and their dog Top.

All the animals had perished in the catastrophe. The birds as well as the beasts, all were crashed or drowned, and poor Jup, alas! had been swallowed up in some crevasse in the ground!

Smith, Spilett, Herbert, Pencroff, Neb, and Ayrton had survived, because, being gathered together in their tent, they had been thrown into the sea, at the moment when the debris of the island rained down upon the water.

When they came again to the surface they saw nothing but this rock, half a cable length away, to which they swam.

They had been here nine days! Some provisions, brought from the magazine of Granite House before the catastrophe, a little soft water left by the rain in the crevice of the rock—this was all that the unfortunates possessed. Their last hope, their ship, had been broken to pieces. They had no means of leaving this reef. No fire, nor anything with which to make it. They were doomed to perish!

This day, the 18th of March, there remained a supply of food, which, with the strictest care, could last but forty-eight hours longer. All their knowledge, all their skill, could avail them nothing now. They were entirely at God's mercy.

Smith was calm, Spilett somewhat nervous, and Pencroff, ready to throw himself into the sea. Herbert never left the engineer; and gazed upon him, as if demanding the succor which he could not give. Neb and Ayrton were resigned after their manner.

"Oh, misery! misery!" repeated Pencroff. "If we had but a walnut-shell to take us to Tabor Island! But nothing; not a thing!"

"And Captain Nemo is dead!" said Neb.

During the five days which followed, Smith and his companions ate just enough of the supply of food to keep them from famishing. Their feebleness was extreme. Herbert and Neb began to show signs of delirium.

In this situation had they a shadow of hope? No! What was their sole chance? That a ship would pass in sight of the rock? They knew, by experience, that ships never visited this part of the Pacific. Could they count, then, by a coincidence which would be truly providential, upon the Scotch yacht coming just at this time to search for Ayrton at Tabor Island? It was not probable. And, moreover, supposing that it came, since the colonists had placed no notice there indicating the place where

Ayrton was to be found, the captain of the yacht, after a fruitless search of the island, would proceed at once to regain the lower latitudes.

No! they could entertain no hope of being saved, and a horrible death, a death by hunger and thirst, awaited them upon this rock!

Already they lay stretched out, inanimate, unconscious of what was going on around them. Only, Ayrton, by a supreme effort, raised his head, and cast a despairing look over this desert sea!

But, behold! on this morning of the 24th of March, Ayrton extended his arms towards some point in space; he rose up, first to his knees, then stood upright; he waved his hand—

A ship was in sight of the island! This ship did not sail these seas at hap-hazard. The reef was the point towards which she directed her course, crowding on all steam, and the unfortunates would have seen her many hours before, had they had the strength to scan the horizon!

"The Duncan!" murmured Ayrton, and then he fell senseless upon the rock.

* * * * *

When Smith and his companions regained consciousness, thanks to the care lavished upon them, they found themselves in the cabin of a steamer, unaware of the manner in which they had escaped death.

A word from Ayrton was sufficient to enlighten them.

"It is the Duncan," he murmured.

"The Duncan!" answered Smith. And then, raising his arms to heaven, he exclaimed:—

"Oh, all powerful Providence! thou hast wished that we should be saved!"

It was, indeed, the Duncan, Lord Glenarvan's yacht, at this time commanded by Robert, the son of Captain Grant, who had been sent to Tabor Island to search for Ayrton and bring him home after twelve years of expatriation!

The colonists were saved, they were already on the homeward route!

"Captain Robert," asked Smith, "what suggested to you the idea, after leaving Tabor Island, where you were unable to find Ayrton, to come in this direction?"

"It was to search, not only for Ayrton, Mr. Smith, but for you and your companions!"

"My companions and myself?"

"Doubtless! On Lincoln Island!"

"Lincoln Island!" cried the others, greatly astonished.

"How did you know of Lincoln Island?" asked Smith. "It is not on the maps."

"I knew of it by the notice which you left on Tabor Island," answered Grant.

"The notice?" cried Spilett.

"Certainly, and here it is," replied the other, handing him a paper indicating the exact position of the Lincoln Island, "the actual residence of Ayrton and of five American colonists."

"Captain Nemo!" said Smith, after having read the notice, and recognized that it was in the same handwriting as the paper found at the corral.

"Ah!" said Pencroff, "it was he who took our Good Luck, he who ventured alone to Tabor Island!"

"To place this notice there!" answered Herbert.

"Then I was right when I said," cried the sailor, "that he would do us a last service even after his death!"

"My friends," said Smith, in a voice moved by emotion, "may the God of sinners receive the soul of Captain Nemo; he was our savior!"

The colonists, uncovering as Smith spake thus, murmured the name of the captain.

Then Ayrton, approaching the engineer, said to him, simply:—

"What shall be done with the coffer?"

Ayrton had saved this coffer at the risk of his life, at the moment when the island was engulfed. He now faithfully returned it to the engineer.

"Ayrton! Ayrton!" exclaimed Smith, greatly affected.

Then addressing Grant:—

"Captain," he said, "where you left a criminal, you have found a man whom expiation has made honest, and to whom I am proud to give my hand!"

Thereupon Grant was informed of all the strange history of Captain Nemo and the colonists of Lincoln Island. And then, the bearings of this remaining reef having been taken, Captain Grant gave the order to go about.

Fifteen days later the colonists landed in America, which they found at peace after the terrible war which had ended in the triumph of justice and right. Of the wealth contained in the coffer, the greater part was employed in the purchase of a vast tract of land in Iowa. One single pearl, the most beautiful of all, was taken from the treasure and sent to Lady Glenarvan in the name of the castaways, who had been rescued by the Duncan.

To this domain the colonists invited to labor—that is, to fortune and to happiness—all those whom they had counted on receiving at Lincoln Island. Here they founded a great colony, to which they gave the name of the island which had disappeared in the depths of the Pacific. They found here a river which they called the Mercy, a mountain to which they gave the name of Franklin, a little lake which they called Lake Grant, and forests which became the forests of the Far West. It was like an island on terra-firma.

Here, under the skillful hand of the engineer and his companions, everything prospered. Not one of the former colonists was missing, for they had agreed always to live together, Neb wherever his master was, Ayrton always ready to sacrifice himself, Pencroff a better farmer than he had been a sailor, Herbert who finished his studies under Smith's direction, Spilett who founded the New Lincoln *Herald*, which was the best edited journal in the whole world.

Here Smith and his companions often received visits from Lord and Lady Glenarvan, from Captain John Mangles and his wife, sister to Robert Grant, from Robert Grant himself, from Major MacNabbs, from all those who had been mixed up in the double history of Captain Grant and Captain Nemo.

Here, finally, all were happy, united in the present as they had been in the past; but never did they forget that island upon which they had arrived poor and naked, that island which, for four years, had sufficed for all their needs, and of which all that remained was a morsel of granite, beaten by the waves of the Pacific, the tomb of him who was Captain Nemo!

THE END.

GLOSSARY.

AGOUTI. A genus of rodent animals, the size of a rabbit, but more like the squirrel in appearance, with the exception of the tail, which is a short, bare stump. When at rest, they sit upon their haunches, holding their food between their fore-paws.

ALBATROSS. A genus of large, web-footed, acquatic birds, possessing prodigious powers of flight. Its wings, when extended, sometimes measure 15 feet.

ALGAROBA BEANS. The seeds of the algaroba or carob tree. These seeds were formerly used by jewellers as weights, and the sweetish honey in the seed-pod is supposed by some to be the wild honey upon which St. John lived in the wilderness. Animals, especially horses, are fond of the bean.

AI. The three-toed sloth. The only animal which can neither walk nor stand. It is herbivorous, and lives in trees, moving suspended from a branch by its long and powerful arms.

ANTHROPOMORPHI. Animals resembling human beings in form.

APYREXY. The intermission of a fever.

ARADS. An order of plants of which dragon-root, or jack-in-the-pulpit is a familiar example. Portland sago is made from the corms of some of these plants.

ARGALL. A species of moufflon or wild sheep.

AZOTH. The old name for nitrogen.

BALEEN. The substance called whale-bone.

BALLISTIC. Relating to engines for throwing missiles; such as the ancient ballista.

BANKSIA. A genus of plants remarkable for the beauty of their flowers and their evergreen foliage. They are sometimes called honey-suckle trees.

BUSTARD. A kind of wild turkey inhabiting the open plains of Europe, Asia and Africa.

CABIAI. The largest known rodent. *Hystricidæ.* from its aquatic habits it is sometimes called a water-hog.

CARAPACE. A thick, solid shell covering some reptiles, as the turtle.

CASAURINÆ. Tropical plants, so named on account of the resemblance their leaves bear to the drooping feathers of the cassowary. For this reason they are sometimes called cassowary trees.

CASSOWARY. A large, long-legged bird of the ostrich family, famous for its speed in running.

CATACLYSM. An inundation or deluge.

CELLULOSE. Called also celluline. A substance which constitutes the cellular tissue of all plants.

CEMENTATION. The process of changing the properties of bodies by heating them in contact with the powder of other substances.

CETACEA. The name of the genus of marine animals which includes whales, dolphins, etc.

CINCHONIA. A vegetable alkali found in the cinchona,—a genus of trees found in Peru,—the bark of which is much used as a febrifugal, and is known as Peruvian Bark. Cinchonia is not much used in medicine.

COCKATOO. A genus of birds of the parrot family, distinguished from all other parrots by a crest of feathers on the head, which the bird can raise or depress at pleasure.

CONIFERS. *Coniferæ.* An order of cone-bearing plants, including fir-trees, pines, cedars, junipers, etc.

CO-ORDINATES. A system of lines and angles by which the position of any point may be determined with reference to a fixed point.

CORM. The solid, underground stem of a plant, like the bulb of a tulip; differing, however, from a bulb in being solid.

COUROUCOUS. Birds of the warbler family, which, excepting the humming bird family, contains the smallest birds in the world. The Nightingale, Wood wren and Golden-crests are familiar examples.

CURASSOW. A gallinaceous bird, about the size of turkeys, and capable of domestication.

CYCAS. A genus of trees intermediate between the palms and the ferns, cultivated in China, and valued for its pith, which furnishes a kind of sago.

DEODAR. The Himalayan cedar. A genus of trees belonging to the order *Pinaccæ*; the same order as the cedars of Lebanon, celebrated for its beauty, its longevity, its magnitude, and the durability of its timber.

DUGONG. An herbivorous mammal having an elongated body, with flippers near the head, and terminated by a crescent-shaped tail. It drags itself along the shore and browses on the herbage that grows along the banks of the rivers which it frequents.

ECHIDNA. A genus of ovoviparous mammals, which have the general form of the ant-eater, but the body is covered with spines like a porcupine; hence they are sometimes called porcupine ant-eaters.

EMUE. A species of cassowary found principally in Australia, and sometimes called Australian cassowary.

EUCALYPTUS. A genus of plants of the myrtle family, which grow to a prodigious height. Its leaves exude a substance resembling manna, which falls to the ground in pieces as large as nuts. The trees are sometimes called gum trees.

FEBRIFUGE. A medicine to drive away or allay fever.

FECULA. A term applied to the substance obtained from plants; also called starch or farina.

FULGURITE. A vitrified sand-tube made by the action of lightning.

FULIGINOUS. Resembling smoke; smokey.

FUSIFORM. Spindle-shaped.

GARGOYLE. A projecting water-spout, often grotesquely carved, attached to old gothic buildings.

HYDROGRAPHY. As opposed to orography; the water system of a country.

IZARD. The chamois of the Pyrenees.

JACAMAR. A genus of climbing birds, closely allied to the kingfishers, that live in forests, feed on insects, and build in low bushes. Their plumage has a carious metallic lustre.

JETSAM. Goods coming to land which have been thrown overboard from a ship in distress.

KAOLINE. The Chinese name for a kind of porcelain clay.

GLOSSARY.

KOULAS. See Ai.

LARDIZABALACEÆ. An order of twining shrubs, some of which furnish our greenhouses with pretty evergreen climbers.

LENTICULAR. Having the form of a double convex lens.

LIANA. A name used to designate the climbing, twining plants which abound in tropical forests, often growing to an immense size, and forming a perfect network of branches, impenetrable without the aid of a hatchet. They are comparatively rare in our climate, but honeysuckles may be mentioned as familiar examples.

LILIACKÆ. Plants of the order of amaryllids, growing to an enormous size. They are commonly known as the giant Lily. The stem is leafy, 15 or 20 feet high, and bears at the top a cluster of superb large crimson blossoms.

LITHODOMI. Molluscous animals which form holes in the solid rocks, in which they lodge themselves. One species (*Lithodomus Lithophagus*) is esteemed as an article of food, and is known by the name of the *sea-date shell*.

LORIES. Birds belonging to the parrot family, remarkable for their soft beaks.

MACAUCO. A genus of four-handed animals, resembling the monkey tribe.

MACRODACTYLS. Long-toed wading birds.

MAGOT. A small species of ape, sometimes called the Barbary ape.

MALACOLOGIST. One who treats of mollusks.

MANNIFERS. A name synonymous with mammals; meaning animals which suckle their young.

MANATEE. A marine animal closely related to the dugong. It Is sometimes called lamantine or sea-cow.

MARGARINE. A fatty solid matter obtained from oil.

MOUFFLON. *Caprovis Mussimon.* Resembling the mountain sheep of Arizona. It is the size of a deer; covered with hair which assumes a woolly character in winter.

OLEINE. The fluid portion of fats and oils.

ONAGER. Another name for the wild ass.

OROGRAPHY. As opposed to hydrography; the description of the mountain system of a country.

PALMIPEDS. Web-footed fowl.

PECCARY. An animal resembling a hog, sometimes called Mexican hog, or *tajacu.*

PELLICAN. A largo aquatic bird, having a long, straight and very strong bill. It lives upon fish, which It carries for some time in a pouch or bag attached to the lover mandible.

PIROGUE. A canoe, usually formed of a hollowed tree.

POLYPORUS. A genus of fungi, allied to mushrooms, toad-stools, sap-balls, etc.; used in Germany to make the tinder called Amadon.

PTEROPODA. A class of mollusks which live In the open sea, and have a pair of flippers or wings, by which they pass rapidly through the water.

PULP. The common name for marine animals of the genus octopus, such as the cuttle-fish. They have eight feet or arms around the head, with which they swim, creep, and seize their prey. It is the *Pieuvre* of Victor Hugo.

PUZZOLAN. Fine volcanic ashes, which harden under water, forming a kind of cement.

PYROXYLINE. Called also gun-cotton. It burns In the open air with a flash, though without smoke or report; but It is violently explosive when fired in a confined space.

QUADRUMANA. Animals having four hands, as apes, baboons, etc.

QUININE. The most important of the vegetable alkaloids found In the cinchona (see CINCHONIA). It is one of the most valuable antiperiodics and febrifuges known.

RECRUDESENCE. The state of becoming sore again.

RINFORDZANDO. A musical sign denoting an Increase of sound. Usually expressed by the abbreviation *rf.*

RUMINANT. An animal that chews the cud.

SAGOIN. A species of sapajo. The squirrel monkey; so called on account of its hairy tail.

SALICIN. A white and very bitter substance, obtained from the bark of the willow and other trees.

SAPAJOS. The proper name for tailed monkeys, as distinguishing them from apes, baboons and gorillas, which are tailless.

SEXTANT. An Instrument for measuring angles by reflection.

SPHENISCUS. Penguins; a sub-family of auks. Oceanic birds remarkable for their short legs, very short wings—which are useful only In swimming; and their upright position when at rest.

STEARINE. The most abundant of the solid constituents of fats and oils. Also a popular name for stearic acid, used in candles.

SUCCEDANEOUS. Supplying the place of something else.

TALUS. A sloping heap of fragments accumulated at the foot of a steep rock, from the face of which they have been broken off by the action of the weather.

TETRA. *Tetraonieda*, or grouse. The bird here described resembles the pinated grouse, or prairie-chicken.

TINAMONS. A family of birds belonging to the order *gallinæ*. They are about the size of quail.

TOURACO-LORIES. Climbing birds of the parrot family.

TRAGOPANS. A large species of pheasant.

TUFA. A name given to volcanic dust, cemented by the Infiltration of water into a porous rock.

END OF TRANSLATION OF THE MYSTERIOUS ISLAND

LaVergne, TN USA
02 December 2009

165765LV00003B/3/P